JASON BEECH

City of Forts

(City of Forts #1)

Second edition

ISBN: 9781980438786

This book was professionally typeset on Reedsy.
Find out more at reedsy.com

For Neeta & Sorrel

Contents

Acknowledgments

A massive thank you to Keith Nixon, Aidan Thorn, Robert Cowan, and Shervin Jamali for nitpicking the manuscript and making it so much better.

Praise for the Author

"A stunning tale of crime, corruption, friendship, and betrayal."

"Readers looking for a deep, multilayered thriller that neither pulls its punches nor shies away from the more emotional aspects of its protagonist will not be disappointed by *City of Forts*."

"Helluva storyteller ... He can take you to a dark place one page and then have you laughing out loud on another."

"Jason Beech has an amazing way with words and characters. His evocative turn of phrase, and his ability to guide us through this story from Ricky's point of view is breathtaking in its simplicity and execution. You can sense the impending doom from the very first chapter, and this feeling never goes away even in the novel's quieter moments."

"City of Forts is beautifully paced throughout, and every character is given their moment to shine. By the time the book comes to a close, each of their lives have changed, not always for the better."

"City of Forts is a compelling coming-of-age story that

crosses over into crime fiction, with teenage characters that are likeable and frustrating, just as they should be."

"Never Go Back is a fun, exciting read filled with twists you'll love and characters you'll love to hate."

"The line between good and evil blurs in this fast-paced thriller."

"Brit crime fiction at its very best."

"The story ends with a neck-snapping twist that is both surprising and darkly satisfying."

"This anthology is well-written, creative, thrilling, and bloody enthralling."

"... his tales have wonderfully unexpected twists, a disturbing sense of wry humour and characters that jump right off the page."

"Jason Beech has a pleasingly gritty writing style, chiseled, polished, a touch literary which I enjoy, instantly engaging and perfect for the hardboiled pulp and noir genres."

"What makes this book a joy to read is the fact that you can't guess what the ending of each story will be."

"But if you also (even secretly, without ever wanting to be a social worker or a psychologist) like thinking about motivation, about what people really want, about how people end up doing terrible things, then you might like this book even more."

"I think the reader's reaction is so profound because Beech has such a deft hand as he paints snapshots of the lives of hitmen, the utterly selfish, or cops twisted by murders they can't forget. He creates these vignettes through great descriptions, clever action, but above all, the relationships between characters."

"A great collection of shorts from an author with a stellar writing style."

"A writer to watch."

"The title says it all, this read was one of a kind. I loved everything about it."

"This is a gritty based story alive with character. Jason Beech is a master of description and it is compelling reading."

"This book has some serious grip."

"His writing is truly one of a kind and every story he writes has an epic feeling to it."

"There are edges in every sentence. They keep the reader attentive and slightly off balance, alarmed maybe by what could jump out from the next page."

"... all are of the hard-boiled noir type of tales that are right up my alley."

"4.5 rounded up because I could not put some stories down until the end and they are still on my mind."

"Vividly Written."

"... gritty coming-of-age tale from a master of description. Compelling reading."

"I haven't read a book like this in years... I so enjoyed it"

"a cracking good read and highly recommended."

"A gritty, compelling noir trilogy."

"At last, book #3 in the City of Forts series and it starts off with a flash/bang."

1

icky Nardilo sat at the breakfast table across from his six-year-old brother, Brett, and swung his feet, kicking the legs of the kid's chair at every repetition. Ricky stared at the boy as he might an insect caught in a web. Brett pretended he didn't notice and invested himself in the coloring book he thought Santa had brought him the Christmas before last.

"Remember when I showed you the real Santa?"

Ricky jolted the chair harder. Brett made the occasional glance towards ma, but she stared out the window for pa – who hadn't answered her hopes for months now. She pulled herself out of whatever fantasy she brooded on, and blurred into action. Ricky checked the clock. Ten-to-eight AM.

Ricky kicked like he meant it. Brett's chair wobbled. His red pen smudged an unwanted line across the Superman image he'd not finished.

Brett finally faced him. "Rickyyy. Why you doing that? Stop it."

Ma remained a smudge in Ricky's vision. He waited, as he always did in this situation, for her to come into focus and tell him off for teasing the munchkin. She didn't, as she never did. He jumped up, enjoyed his little brother's cringe, and ruffled the kid's hair. Brett ducked and weaved, but Ricky caught him. Didn't know why he resisted – his mop waved like a sea storm, anyway.

"What do you want for breakfast, brother?"

Brett's happy smile sparked Ricky.

"Same."

"As always? You got no taste buds?"

"No. Same, please."

"Positive? Sure, if you want to be a thumbnail all your life."

Ricky poured the milk, emptied the rest of the cereal after, and nudged it in front of his brother. Mum mumbled spells, or insults, about dad, as she shoved things out of harm's way.

"Make sure you eat a second bowl." Her voice softened for Brett. Ricky listened to her stroke his cheek before she charged into mental action again. She sprung to different points in the house as she remembered one thing, thought about another and forgot the last, and retraced her steps for the former. Their home was dark beneath the trees and he blinked through the blinds into the bright sunshine beyond.

"Why do you have to go to work, ma?" Brett pushed his chest into the tabletop out of frustration. Every frickin' morning. Brett answered for her. "Do you want to live in a cardboard box?"

She machine-gunned kisses on Brett's cheek. "You got it." Ricky pulled a face at his mock-protests. He stiffened at the clack of her shoes on the linoleum and tried to smile at the light touch on his upper arm.

"Don't let anyone in. I'll be back around seven. Food is in the fridge."

"Where else?"

Ricky didn't hear her sigh, but he felt it reach out to him. He picked a point on her old Datsun where the sun sparkled. She shimmered out of focus in the heat. Not that he paid enough attention to pinpoint any of her details. He stood by the sink until the car's asthmatic wheeze dipped from his senses.

"Can we go somewhere, Ricky?"

"Errr, I'm thirteen. Do you see my car?"

"Ahhh, you know what I mean. I want to hang around with you."

Ricky rummaged through the kitchen and down the back of the sofa and armchair in the living room. Checked the top of the TV behind the last photo they ever took as a whole family, with pa's eyes already looking west. He glared at the picture and planted it face down as he spotted the comb. He dragged it across Brett's hair until he tamed the waves and nudged him to finish the cereal.

Once he'd done all that, he grabbed the old wooden ruler and slapped it over his palm to gain Brett's attention. Brett had one eye half-shut, the other open wide.

"I know all this, Ricky. C'mon, every day?"

"I don't care. We must remember every detail. Your six-year-old brain needs a refresher."

He snapped the ruler against the microwave. "Don't touch it."

He pinged it off the toaster. "Don't touch it. And don't put any knife inside it, either."

"I never do."

He tap-tapped the oven and rattled the ruler on every knob. "Don't even look at this. Right?"

Brett swung his feet and pretended the coloring book still held his attention.

"Right?"

Brett locked rigid from the snap and nodded his head like a mechanical toy.

"Good." Ricky forced himself into the tied sneakers, opened the fridge to display all his brother's food options, and patted the boy's head.

"Look at me, bro. Never, ever leave the house. Okay?"

Brett's tears pooled at the edge of his lids as he craned his neck to his older brother. Ricky's right eyebrow expressed his disapproval. He shook his head and squeezed his sibling's shoulder.

Brett clasped the hand. "Don't go, Ricky. I'm sad here on my own all day."

"You'll be fine. You should be used to it. Keep away from the windows. I'll lock the door. Be good."

Ricky grabbed an old plastic bottle, filled it with water, and left his little brother to it.

2

Ricky dawdled through Town. Kept his head low past boarded houses for fear he'd gain someone's or something's attention. Number 93 down this side-road always opened a door for one man or other, most of them slouched and interested in their shoes. A woman with hair you could use to grease a squeaky wheel caught how Ricky showed interest. She stared until Ricky averted his eyes to fields out on the town's edge. He paced down alleys, beyond the ancient SUV where an old woman lived, turned a corner to avoid the Ghost Boys who pounded the streets to torment locals, their faces hidden deep inside hoods.

He reached Town's outskirts, linked his fingers and thrust his palms into the air to stretch. Blew away his tension. Town stunk of old sweat and iron. Out here, in the fields full of long grass and weeds, it smelled of freedom. He turned and half-expected his sad-faced brother on his trail. Fondled the prepaid phone in his pocket and rolled his tongue along the back of his teeth. Nah, he'd only left a half hour ago. The kid could handle himself.

Ricky thrust himself into the fields, almost a plunge into a refreshing sea. Ran with his hands out to palm the wild flowers and grass. Chased a butterfly with red dots on black wings, like laser dots he must paw. Dodged and ducked at some bee behind and above. A man and his son sat in a boat on the river. Ricky ran by. Checked his shoulder once, twice, and shut them out.

The factory pierced the sky. If God existed, he'd sit at the top of its tower while he guided them all, not in the spare space the strip mall owners let ma's church have for their Sunday worship. *This* is a church, a perfect spot to manage a preacher's numbing of the soul.

Ricky stepped over the chain-link fence, bent to the ground by the years. Hopped in the gaps between scattered bricks until he stood before the massive blue-painted iron gates at the factory's front.

"Are you here, Grandad?"

He smiled at how his voice hit off the walls and bounced around the fields.

"Grandad, are you here?"

"Yes, I'm here."

Ricky shot from his spot. He pressed at his heart and spun. "You idiot. I nearly –"

"Shit your pants, Ricky Nardilo?"

"No, Liz Panowich. Had a heart attack."

She wore long pants and sandals with a sleeveless top, and it all flapped on her bones as her hips navigated her to his side. She snatched a quick kiss and ran through the small opening within the larger gate. He ran after her, but her copper hair already merged with the rust in the girders and walkways criss-crossing this spaceship building.

"Your grandad's dead. Why you calling after him?"

He ducked and weaved through supporting pillars, jumped two steps at a time up stairs which wobbled and swayed.

"Because …"

"Because what?"

"Because you never know."

There. Her hair burned in that shaft of sunlight. He ran faster while trying to dampen his steps.

"Maybe you should try looking under the roller which squished him."

She'd gone by the time he reached where he'd pinpointed her voice. He doubled back on himself, climbed a ladder, and listened for her feet's pitter-patter. Peered over the walkway's iron bannister into the chasm. He'd reached the high platforms near the roof. A long strip of sunshine revealed the factory floor as if a giant welder fired the concrete.

His skin prickled at her quiet approach from behind. Kept his eyes on the vista. Her arm became a vine as she wrapped it around his. He locked his fingers in hers.

"You make me laugh, Liz Panowich."

"That's why I like you, Ricky Nardilo."

* * *

They pelted across the fields. Jumped streams and troughs. Laughed and pawed at each other. The house tilted right, half-sunk amongst the sea of grass. They'd pulled boards from the windows weeks ago to give their lair light. It allowed the elements inside, but they didn't mind that at this time of year. The glass-free holes gave the house a skull-like appearance they'd leave behind as the sun hit the horizon. Liz turned in the doorway, scoured the fields and other abandoned houses curving in a crescent.

"Look what I got …" She buried a hand in her pocket and

produced a little silver packet, the type he'd seen astronauts eat from on TV, except much smaller. She waved it about and searched him for recognition.

Ricky scratched behind an ear and put a fist in his pocket. "Looks ... a bit tasteless."

"We're not eating it." She ripped the top of the packet and pulled it out.

"Ah. That a –?"

"Yep."

"Here? Where?"

"The sofa, where else?"

"Liz, we dragged that up from the basement. I don't know how old it is. It covered us in dust, remember. We'll probably die in our twenties from that shit."

She smirked. Rolled the condom down two fingers. "Are you passing on me?"

He now had both hands in his pockets. Thumbed the phone. "Nah, Liz. It's just ... I wouldn't know what to do."

"Well, I can show you."

His heart pinched. "You know what to do?"

She angled a hip to the side. "No, Ricky. I don't. But I can guess." Her eyes urged him inside the house. "Well?"

"Where'd you get the rubber?"

"From my dad's drawer."

"Your dad?"

"Right? Who'd have thought he ... but here I am, so he did – obviously." She ironed away the quick frown crossing her forehead.

She grabbed his wrist, and how she'd planned all this made his feet follow her into the living room. The bay window let in the sun and the warm breeze. She'd thrown a blanket over the sofa, holding its position on the slanted floor. The floorboards creaked in protest at their weight. His excitement built at the same time as a stone sat in his belly. He stirred in his pants and independent thought seemed to evaporate. Liz pulled off her shirt, spun, and sprung backwards into the sofa. That smile. That bra. The bounce in her boobs. He laughed and moved towards her.

His step seemed to trigger an earthquake. The floor trembled and creaked. Liz's face melted.

She disappeared through the floor.

3

Liz didn't scare easy, but her voice erupted through the floor's new hole and burned his ears. Ricky made powder-steps to the edge and wafted a hand to help clear the air. Liz lay in the same position in the basement as she did in the living room. Her hands shot out, fingers splayed out.

"Ricky ..."

A jump down the hole might break his legs, so he swung open the basement door and skipped most of the steps down. Specks of dust danced like bugs in the shaft of sunlight.

"Ricky ... Ricky."

He couldn't get his head around the whine. Liz never moaned in that voice. Her complaints always wore an edge, a battle flag raised in a call to action. The fall must have hurt. Snapped her spine. He froze. Pushing her wheelchair seemed too much work for him.

"Liz ... You okay?"

Her words came out in lumps. Lots of Ms and Ns. She scared him into a rush towards her. He knelt by her knees. Forgot her half-naked status. She grasped his hands and dug nails into his flesh. He gritted his teeth against the pain.

"Liz, I'll call an ambulance."

She didn't see him. Stared past him into the room's cor-ner. Ricky swiveled to see. Shuddered at what imagination conjured behind his back. He adjusted to the dark and pierced the gloom. A man sat upright against the wall, chin resting against his breast. Ricky waited for the head to lift. Expected red eyes and bloody teeth.

Stillness.

Only the wind swishing through the upstairs floor made a sound. The man didn't snore, his chest didn't expand as he breathed – he didn't breathe at all.

Ricky tapped Liz's knee. "Do you think I should poke him?"

"I reckon it's your duty."

She leapt off the sofa and froze at the furniture's creak. Padded around the basement to the back wall as Ricky scoured the side wall. He became a statue at the crunch underfoot. Side-eyed the man and expected him to thrust into attack. Ricky crouched to pick up the bamboo cane he'd splintered and stayed low as he approached.

Liz covered her mouth with a hand. Ricky waved her towards the stairs for an easy escape if this didn't work out. He took his next step once she made the bottom of the staircase. Bent his knees and leaned forwards. Fought the shakes and extended his arm. Poked the man in his stomach.

No reaction.

He tried the ribs.

The man remained mute.

He jabbed at an ear and struggled to lift his chin.

Liz stood by his side. "He's dead."

Ricky straightened and let his heels rest on the floor. "I think so."

"I know so."

"What we going to do?"

She swiped her hair behind an ear. "Get out of here, I reckon."

She backed away, as did Ricky. Feared the supernatural if they turned their backs on the man. Liz grabbed her shirt from the sofa and scrunched it against her chest at noise from upstairs. They eyeballed each other. Worked on a mutual plan without words. Hammer-feet battered the floorboards until they stilled above the hole. Ricky's heart cocked slow and hammered hard, eyeballs hurting at how they failed to blink. Steps shuffled closer to the rim. A mop of black hair swung over the crest and hooded his face.

"What you two doing? Get out of here. Quick." Their friend, Bixby. He lingered on Liz and her bare shoulders. Finger-combed hair away and badgered them with his eyebrows. "The Ghost Boys are here. With fire."

"Shit." Ricky reached for Liz' hand, but she had already vaulted for the stairs.

He sprinted in her slipstream until he got to the front door. All three bunched together to peek around the wall. The house at the end shimmered in flames riding its walls.

Bixby scratched his scalp. Liz edged out and kept tight to the siding. Dragged the shirt down over her head. Bixby followed her on his belly. They made it to the back of the building and urged Ricky to make tracks. Ricky scanned the other way where hooded figures scythed the grass with sticks. The sun glinted off something metal, a machete or some other type of knife. The gang beat a path to the next abandoned house, the one Bixby liked best. Laughed and spat, and one pissed up a wall. Another clinked glass in a crate. He raised a bottle high, and they all cheered and cackled, faces obscured within deep hoods like a gathering of grim reapers. Some chunkier than others, but you couldn't distinguish them in a line-up. One of the shorter ones hunched over an object in his hand and the other lowered the bottle towards it. When he lifted it again, Ricky couldn't mistake the flame, even beneath the glare of early evening sun. Every one chanted and roared, and the Ghost Boy launched the bottle through the doorway.

Fire grabbed at bare wooden floors and bone-dry walls. The breeze fanned it up the walls to the roof and wood splintered. Ricky's bladder filled, and he wondered if he could get away with a piss. Checked his shoulder. Liz and Bixby scampered almost out of sight, past the last two houses towards the factory. Ricky stuck his head back in the house and bit his lower lip. He could run out the back door, like the other two should've. Hesitation trapped him, and the predators swung around to appraise their prey.

A beam crashed to the ground in the first dwelling and triggered his reaction. He jumped the steps and worked his arms so hard they must rip from his joints. He headed away from the factory and arced back towards Town, but once he got there, where then? Mustn't lead them back to his home. Brett's sad eyes pulled him that way, but he resisted. Instinct tempted a check of the shoulder, but he feared it would slow him down. He heard heavy breathing and their feet brushing the grass. Expected yelling and whooping, but their silence froze his blood and slowed him down.

He chanced a look back. Yelped at how close one of them reached. Cried louder as his feet disappeared beneath him. He rolled and tumbled down the bank. Settled on the ancient asphalt, softened by weeds in its cracks. Ricky jumped up, only to scuff along the ground again as one of the Ghost Boys tackled him, sucking the wind from his lungs. Fists found the gaps between his protective arms and hammered every rib. He wriggled and swung the occasional punch, but hit blind and never made contact. More joined in, a pack of wolves in a feeding frenzy.

A scream from somewhere deep in the earth tore the air. A thud struck flesh, though not his. The punches and kicks and stick-hits stopped. His attackers straightened and turned to the sound's source. Ricky blinked away tears until the fire's blur settled. The flame flickered, a dragon's snout at the end of a stick – held by Liz. She swayed it left and right at this pit of snakes.

"You boys have had your fun. Time to fuck off." She made the F extend until it lassoed their intention and held it tight.

Ricky made it to his feet. Coughed at the pain and sleeved away tears. Sneered at the one on the ground, head in his hands. A flash of sandy hair escaped his hood. Liz had smacked him across the skull, he guessed. Ricky shouldered his way through their bodies. Counted ten. Squinted to see details. They wore black face masks beneath their hoods, and boot polish on exposed flesh round their eyes.

A couple pulled their fallen comrade upright. Their silence communicated it all. Two lifted their hoodies to reveal guns in waistbands. The one at the front walked away, brushing the grass stalks from his face. In turn, his followers fell in step behind him until distance and heat made them flicker into wraiths where the town ate them up.

"Are you okay, Ricky-boy?"

He didn't like it when she said his name that way. "I've got to get home."

4

Ricky snuck home through the back of the house. Experience told him ma would get back in the next ten minutes or so. He peered round the side first, just to make sure her car didn't already sit in the driveway. He unlocked the back door and prepared himself.

"Hiya, little fella." His cheery voice dripped with guilt, but he transferred that to ma. She ought to look after Brett. She's his ma, too.

"Brett, I'm home."

He arched his back as much as he could. Strings of pain plucked with almost every movement. He checked himself in the hall mirror. Lifted his shirt. His ribs stuck out like pens in a plastic bag, his red torso a lump of beef latched to a butcher's hook. At least they had aimed all their blows to his trunk, so ma wouldn't see evidence he'd been outside. His face remained untouched, except for the tan, though he feared the wince might become permanent.

"Brett, get here, will ya? We need a word before ma gets home."

He let his shirt veil his bruises again and poked around the cupboards for his brother. He sometimes curled himself beneath the sink, but not today. Ricky growled into the pantry to induce some excitable squeals from Brett. Not there.

"C'mon Brett, before we're both in trouble."

Ricky just wanted to sprawl on the sofa and switch on the TV, but Brett needed guidance. He pushed through his pain all the way to the top of the stairs and checked the bedrooms. Flicked the lights on. The sun never illuminated their rooms. Brett didn't hide beneath his bed, or under the covers, nor the closet or wash basket.

The bathroom was empty, though Brett had emptied half the toothpaste into the sink. Ricky mumbled a few cusses as he wiped it all up with toilet roll. Searched ma's room and ran back downstairs. Stared down the basement steps into the murk. Brett didn't like the dark. He needed a night light to go to bed. Ricky rushed to the front door and checked the lock. It remained untouched. He rubbed at his chest and dragged at his cheeks. Switched on the bare forty watt bulb that lit the basement. His steps downstairs took forever, each full of pain and tension.

"Brett? Bro, are you down here?"

The dingy light hardly reached the room's edges. His imagination conjured beasts in the dark depths, but after what he'd gone through today, he thrust onward the best his limp allowed. All corners remained Brett-free. His brother had left the house. Got himself abducted. Probably dead in the woods beneath a heap of rotten leaves. Ricky linked his hands together to stop the shakes. An old engine's growl and the crunch of gravel told him ma arrived. Dim light in the laundry room led him forward. The corpse in the abandoned basement filled his head. Would he find Brett in the same position?

The light shone from the dryer. From the door, Ricky could see one of his little brother's legs inside the big machine pa bought from a failing laundromat. Ricky shuffled forwards and sat on his haunches. Two glassy eyes locked onto his, clean paths cleared by tears down his cheeks.

"Brett ... what you doing in the dryer?"

"I'm just sad." It came out a murmur, but it hammered Ricky in the gut.

The front door opened and ma called out. Her voice traveled down the stairs and made him check his shoulder as if she stood above him.

"C'mon, bring yourself out of there. I'm here now. I'll play with you."

"You only want to play because ma's here ... you just don't want trouble for leaving me home all day." His lower lip trembled, but he spoke brave words now ma crossed the threshold.

Ricky's smile curved weak. "You know that's not true. You're my bro. I love you."

The kid reached out and wrapped his arms around Ricky's neck. Squeezed tight. The older brother winced and pulled the rest of him from the dryer. He patted the kid's back and made zombie-steps to the stairs. "Don't tell ma I was out all day. You understand I have important things to do out there. Don't ruin it, or they'll put us both in a home."

Brett tightened his grip and drew out a long "No."

"I always knew you were a good kid. Despite what others say."

Ricky thought Brett would strangle him if he gripped any harder. "I am a good kid. I am."

Ricky stroked his hair. "I know that. You're a brave kid, I'll give you that."

* * *

Ma talked over the phone while she made dinner. Ricky listened to the eggs sizzle in the frying pan to drown her words. She sounded all schoolgirl – more Tanais than Liz – with her over-cooked laughter. Ricky crossed his eyes at Brett and sucked his lips. Brett giggled and swung his legs. Those blue whirlpool eyes wanted to draw in approval. Ricky pretended to read the book school gave him for his summer read. He must have scanned the same paragraph a dozen times each day. He'd reached page four. Just another two-hundred to go. He flung it on the spare chair pa had not rested his butt on for months.

Ma had been on the phone ages and pa didn't once ask to speak with him. Ricky balled his fist and scraped his knuckle against the chair. Leaned across the table and scuffed Brett's cheek. "Why you looking at me like that? Why don't you just piss off out my life?"

Ricky couldn't see Brett's reaction for the blur filming his vision. He wiped at his tears and kicked his little brother's chair. Dad. The dead body. His beating. Liz' black bra. The fear that someone broke into their house and abducted Brett. All competed for his thoughts and overwhelmed him.

He pulled himself together and stared at the tabletop. Ma hadn't noticed a thing. A pop in one of the eggs towed her away from love-talk. She shook the pan, tested the whites, and plopped them on a plate. When she shoved the food in front of them, she stopped her constant jabber. Ricky followed her hand to Brett's hair and how she wiped it back from his forehead.

"I'll call you later. Let me just sort something out."

18

She held the phone tight, scared pa would disappear if she let it go. "Why are you crying, my baby?"

"I'm not." Brett's voice wobbled all over the place.

"Sweet baby, yes you are. What's wrong?"

Ricky picked at the flaw in the table, the little nobble pa never sanded away. Ma dropped to her knees beside her youngest. Ricky's skin prickled and added a few degrees as her attention turned to him. He caught how she lifted Brett's chin, whose eyes were all bubble and toil.

"Ricky, what did you do?"

"Nothing."

"Your eyes are as red as his. What did you do?"

"Nothing."

"You clearly did something. And you never have tears." She sighed, a tired exasperation. "Why don't you look at me anymore, Ricky?"

"I always do. What do you mean?"

"You're not looking now."

The pressure bubbled and raised his eyes. She rested a hand on his forearm. Felt like an electric shock. Forced out those tears he'd dammed for so long. "I went to the shop, ma."

"What?"

"Just for ten minutes. Just to get some milk."

"Did you get any?"

"No."

"Why not?"

"Because we don't have any money."

"Exactly. Don't you ever leave the house again, Ricky. What if you're seen? They'll take you. They'll take you both."

5

"I'll tell ma you left me alone again."

Ricky sighed and ruffled Brett's hair. "No you won't, kid, no you won't. Because they'll take me away from you forever. And then they'll take you away from ma forever, too."

"They?"

"Yes – they." Ricky ignored Brett's wide arms, glassy eyes, and the quiver in his lips. Closed his ears to the sniffles and locked the door behind him.

The sun turned his skin to pork rind already, at nine in the morning. Whenever he walked the town's streets, he kept his attention on the pavement and his tatty sneakers. The town had nothing to latch his eyes, anyway, just rust and cracked pavements, and iron bars in store windows that made you screw your eyes when window-shopping. He paused at the ancient toy store and rubbed the twitch in his lips away. Shoved the paper bag beneath an armpit and plugged his hands to the glass. Old-school toys shone through the dusty partition. A fire truck so red Ricky expected it to blow its horn and chase the nearest blaze. A wooden clown with its mouth curved like one of those swords from *Aladdin*, and eyes that would tumble Brett back into the dryer. Ricky jangled the few coins in his pocket and released them when he saw the prices. Who could afford to buy these things?

He bent low and plowed the fields. Dove at every snap, palms flat on the ground ready to launch at first sight of the Ghost Boys. Drew in huge gobfuls of air and rubbed at bruised ribs. The abandoned development, their City of Forts as Liz called It, shimmered, unsafe now. His place of escape spoiled. He froze at the digger, empty, but claws poised over the field, and trembled. Circled it a few times as though it might tell him its intentions. He rushed away, alarmed his green patch would soon match the rust blighting the rest of Town.

He spat on the first strip of asphalt and watched how the sun would make it sizzle. The heat didn't encourage patience, so he charged to the house he'd so nearly popped his cherry in the previous day. Swung glances left and right until he made the porch. Cleared his eyes of sweat as he peered from behind a pillar to check for enemies. Only tall grass and the tree in the distance moved – in rhythm with the oven breeze.

Ricky skimmed the paper bag across the floor. It shhhhed until it hit Bixby's foot. His friend parked himself against the wall, knees beneath his chin. Carved a sharp point on the stick he intended to bolster his weaponry, along with the hunter's knife he used to carve it.

"Thanks, man."

"Welcome."

Ricky stuck his head over the hole to see the sofa below. "Is he ...?"

"He's still there. Hasn't moved a muscle. Just what a dead person would do."

Ricky nodded in agreement at Bixby's wisdom. Bixby fished in the bag and turned the sandwich to inspect its ingredients.

Stared at it same as a heron would a fish before the swoop, and it seemed to Ricky that he shoved it all in his pie-hole in one bite. It would last him a few hours. Ricky hoped Liz would bring Bixby something more.

"Did you sleep here last night?"

Bixby wiped his lips free of mayo and A1 Sauce and nodded. "Can't go back to the other, can I?"

"Is it all ruined?"

"All black, soot everywhere, and ready to crumble. Them asses busted it real good."

"There's other houses." Five more.

Bixby shrugged.

Ricky bent over the hole again. He couldn't believe the man would stay still all this time. Even if dead. "You weren't? ... You know ..."

"I'm not scared of anything."

"You're scared of Miss Veronica."

He screwed up his nose to show the social worker had no effect on him, but Ricky caught how he gripped the shake in his hands. "If you can deal with my dad, you can deal with anything. I plopped myself next to the dead man last night and slept by his side."

"You what?"

"Yeah. He's just a lump of meat. What's he gunna do? I admit - I was a bit scared, but you have to do stuff like that to get over yourself, sometimes."

Ricky pondered whether he ought to introduce his little brother to Bixby. His pal would soon make Brett get over his loneliness.

"I only moved up here because the stink on him's begun. It's a weird smell. A sweet sick stench. Makes your eyes run.

We'll have to clear all the crap from one of the other houses so we can hang out there."

Ricky sniffed the hole. A slight tang reached his nostrils, and he pulled away to lean against the wall opposite Bixby. Bixby finished the water from the old bottle Ricky filled. "You still want to fool around out here? After yesterday?"

"Where else?"

Ricky searched Bixby's eyes. Pa used to call them Asian eyes – sometimes "slit eyes" – though Bixby's pa is as white as snow until he reddened under the sun. Bixby didn't like Ricky's dad.

They couldn't hang out in Town. Those pavements had cracked for obvious reasons. Menace lurked beneath the surface and burst out any time it damn-well pleased. Their City of Forts provided refuge from that hellhole and the ones stalking it.

Ricky nodded, firm. "Do you want me to bring anything else? Shampoo?" Bixby scratched his head once too many times. Made Ricky want to scratch, too.

"How'm I going to use shampoo?" He lifted the bottle.

Ricky flubbed his lower lip. "When it rains?"

"I wish it would. The heat is boiling my balls."

"We got to get rid of him, Bix. He's making me dance. I can't settle with him down there."

"You want your love nest back?"

"What?"

"I saw Liz with her boobs out."

"I ... Nah, she had a bra on."

"Don't know about that ... our brother downstairs made sure she kept it on, too. Maybe he should stay."

Ricky pushed off the wall. "You like Liz?"

"I didn't think much about her like that until I got an eyeful of all that flesh. Now I guess I do. Yes."

"Well, she likes me. I didn't push her into anything. It was all her."

"Yeah, but she's not seen a real man yet."

"You're fourteen."

"Yep. Her age. You can't go around granny-snatching. It ain't right."

"You're shitting me, aren't you? You grimy-haired bastard. C'mon, let's get the fella in a ditch, or somethin'."

Ricky grabbed the hand Bixby offered. Winced as he pulled him to his feet.

6

The hole in the ceiling turned the basement into a goldfish bowl. Ricky half-expected a giant hand to reach down and pass him morsels to last the day. Hunger pangs infected him soon after that slim breakfast ma plopped on the table this morning. The boys' intentions waned now they hovered over the corpse. Covered their mouths to prevent that sweet decay from hanging onto taste buds. Ricky waved away the idea its aroma would infect and turn them into zombies. Sometimes he wouldn't mind if his brain switched off. It'd cut the cord yanking his stomach in all directions.

Ricky toe-poked the man.

"He's dead, can't you see?"

"I can see – but wanna make sure."

Ricky pulled off his t-shirt, twisted it, and wrapped and tied it around his face. His sweat took on a pleasant tang compared to the corpse's stink. Bixby followed his example.

Ricky lowered his voice, scared to wake death. "Legs or armpits?"

Bixby puffed. His concave chest seemed unsuitable for anything weightier than a pillow. Maybe even the pillowcase. "I'll have the legs."

"Sure."

Ricky grabbed the man's arms and pulled him away from the wall. His back slurped from the plaster to reveal a red blotch. He jumped aside as if the man shot a few volts through his frame. The bile folded into a tidal wave and surged up his pipes. He swallowed it back down and held his stomach. Gasped at the burn.

"Jeez." Bixby pushed himself so far into the wall he could have merged with its gray plaster. "I thought he was just a bum who'd come here to die."

Ricky picked at his nails and lassoed at thoughts. Edged around the man. Red and black stained the back of the man's coat, but no blood pooled beneath him. Ricky didn't shift his eyes from the body, still suspicious it would surprise them yet. "Do you think something sucked all his blood out?"

"What do you mean – something?"

"Don't know. Just ... how can he have a big hole in him and there's not a ton of blood? Don't you get a ton of blood when you get holed like this?"

"I guess. You got me all nervous, Ricky. Not sure I should stay here anymore."

"And go back to your old man?"

He could see Bixby pop goosebumps at that idea. Swung his limbs – to generate some heat, or spirit, Ricky didn't know, but he'd welcome any warmth right now.

"Grab a leg."

Bixby let his arms dangle. "You going to grab him under the pits?"

"No way, I don't want his mess all over me."

They gripped a leg each and dragged. An object fell out of the man. Ricky nudged at it in the dim light until its form emerged from the murk. He raised his eyes to Bixby. His lips wobbled, but produced no words. Bixby dropped the leg and toed it. Ricky lifted it between finger and thumb in case it exploded.

"It's not so strange he has a gun. Everybody has guns. My dad had guns. Left them behind when he ran off out west. Ma got rid of them." Ricky held it by the handle, firm now, and aimed it at the dead man to envision how he might have died. Bixby shook his head, awed. Ricky inserted the weapon inside a spare tire propped against the wall.

The man had stiffened so much it seemed they dragged wood. Its skull knocked every step until it rested on the flat wooden floor upstairs. They swung the ache from their arms and continued to the back of the house. Bixby shouldered the door open to scan the area. The breeze, from hell or the Dragon Lands, tingled his skin. They bumped the body down the cracked porch steps, across split asphalt on the sidewalk behind the houses where weeds reached for the sun, and over the bare earth to the high grass bordering the river.

Bixby squeezed his eyes at the turkey vultures above. "Doesn't seem right to leave him out in the open."

Ricky wished he'd brought water for himself. A headache knocked around his skull. "I'm not burying him. Can you feel how hard the ground is?" He stamped the earth. Dust plumed, but not enough to bury the body as it resettled.

"If I ever die out here, I'd like to think a bunch of birds won't eat me. Have you seen those things peck at dead deer? Freaks me out." Bixby patted an eye, just to make sure the vultures knew he understood their game.

"You'll not die. I brought you a sandwich."

"Thanks, but I reckon we should bury him."

"With our bare hands?"

Bixby swiveled his head to the burnt house he'd slept in before the Ghost Boys torched it. "There was a shovel in there."

Ricky shuffled his feet. Let a pregnant silence expand. Hoped Bixby'd pick up the message that he didn't have the arms to dig anything. His ribs still pinched at movement.

"Just the one. I'll dig if your weak-ass arms can't handle it."

Ricky kicked earth and grass at him. "Go get it then, and we'll see how weak-ass I am."

He swatted flies away while Bixby marched to the pitted house. The factory seemed to breathe in the heat's flicker. He daydreamed about chasing Liz through its passageways, open stretches and rickety stairways. Flung his arms and scrambled from bugs which found their feast and swarmed around the man. Ricky watched, fascinated they might strip his flesh in seconds.

He protected his face with a forearm and patted at the man's pockets. Pulled out a wallet. It contained dollars – a bunch of tens and twenties, enough to make his eyes pop. Tightened his lips to let that deep breath out slow. Filleted the wallet for more treasure and found a driver's license. Benny Ciaro. Twenty-eight years old. From Town. He almost expected the man to come from the shining city over the river. Could hear the urban beast's rhythm over the bank beyond. The wallet held a few business cards and not much else. He shoved everything back into the leather and plunged it into his pocket.

"Shit."

It bulged out as if Liz teased him again. He tried it in the same pocket as his old phone, but that wouldn't fly, either.

28

Bixby headed his way, the shovel over his shoulder, like a warrior in rest after battle. Ricky unwound the t-shirt from his face and wrapped the wallet. No, they'd question why he carried his shirt in this manner. He kicked through the grass and found a large enough stone. Pillaged the wallet's cash, plunged it into his pocket, and shoved the leather beneath the stone. Prepared for Bixby's return.

"Where do you reckon?" Bixby stabbed the shovel into the ground. It wobbled and fell over.

"The swamp might be an idea. Somewhere soft." Ricky kicked more dust into the air, confused about why he pilfered the money and hid the wallet.

"We don't have a swamp round here. We're stumped."

"What about the Dragon Lands?" A dig created as much enthusiasm in Ricky as the body.

"How we going to lug him that far?" Bixby glanced beyond the woods to the top of the bald hill. "With a bag of bones … that's like crossing the Appalachians."

Ricky *pfffed* at how Bixby measured the distance. He tried to appear as casual as possible as he shifted from the hidden wallet. "How about here? This is pretty soft." He kicked at the grass-smothered earth. Not much dust there.

Bixby tested it. Nodded in the way you do when more arguments aren't worth the bother. "Well, you or me?"

Ricky flipped the spade in the air with a foot and caught it. "I'll start."

He made a few cuts. The surface resisted, but the deeper soil gave way a little easier. He heaved another clump to the side and almost lopped Bixby's head from his neck when a call came out.

"What you boys doin'?" Liz bounded over, all free hair and

nervous grin. "Look who tagged along."

She threw an eye over her shoulder and Tanais appeared above the lip of a mound of earth. Tanais pursed an embarrassed smile and Liz shrugged – *nothing to do with me.* The boys reacted too late to stand in front of the corpse. Tanais' tight mouth opened wide and unleashed horror. She pointed a finger, and they followed it as if they had no clue what stretched out behind them.

Bixby shot his hands up, surrender-style. "Tanais, we didn't do any of this."

She managed to shift her attention to the shovel in Ricky's grip and smothered another scream, as if its release would mean her end.

Ricky dropped the tool and held out a palm to the girl as he moved to comfort her. Ran for her as she backed away. Tanais would have jumped off a cliff rather than take his support. She slipped down the mound and out of sight. The three of them bolted after. Ricky no longer had her solace in mind - she mustn't make it back to Town. But she sped and zigzagged and nobody could get a grip on her. She screamed to leave her alone. "I won't tell anybody."

Bixby fell by the wayside first. The fuel from the small sandwich Ricky brought for him burned out and he made teapot handles of his arms. The girl slipped away as Liz tried to hold onto Tanais' tight shirt. Liz bent over, hands on thighs. Sucked air as best she could.

Ricky avoided twisted ankles from broken bricks and stones, and bone-deep cuts from rusted barbed wire snaking from the grass. Tanais' check of the shoulder slowed her enough for Ricky to launch. He flew into her midriff and she collapsed beneath his weight. She fought for air and smacked open palms against his cheeks and ears. One slap rang a crystal sing through his nerves and he almost let her slip from his grip. He worked to hold her body tight between his legs as he sat on her belly. Pinned her arms to the ground and concentrated on her mouth. It moved, but he still couldn't hear what she said. He lip-read a few f-bombs and the occasional c-word, but he must have imagined them all. Tanais didn't swear. A respectable girl if ever he saw one. That smack to the ear fucked him up good.

He could only make sense of her words once her body collapsed into a fit of sobs. "I don't want to die. I don't want to die. I don't want to die."

Liz knelt by her head, and Bixby peered over her shoulder. Tanais screwed her eyes at them all and the hot lamp of a sun.

Liz stroked her cheek. "Tanais, sweets, that man was already dead. I don't know what the boys were doing just now, but they didn't kill him." She cocked an eyebrow at Ricky. "What were you doing?"

Ricky loosened his grip on Tanais to calm her, but kept his position. "We can't keep a body in the house. It's where we hang out. I wanted to leave him in the field. Bixby wanted to bury him."

Bixby peered inside a paper bag and shrugged. "We can't leave him in the basement. He's already stinking. And we can't leave him in the open. We'll always know he's there. Don't want to see him rot bit-by-bit. Not a chance." He lifted a sandwich out of the bag and sniffed. "You brought me sandwiches?"

Tanais nodded and closed her mouth a moment from the silent scream. "I thought you might be hungry. And lonely."

"Peanut butter and jelly. Nice. But … I don't know … you

shouldn't hang out with us."

She made a little noise, squeezing out from the pits of her nightmares.

"Nah, not because we killed that man – and we didn't – but you're ..."

Liz patted her on the arm. "You're way too nice for us. We thought you might have got the message by now, but, jeez, you're persistent. Boys, she popped out of nowhere as I arrived here. I swear."

"I made the sandwiches myself. An offering."

They laughed at her. She blinked and aimed to find another focal point, something neutral, but her eyes drew to Ricky's.

"We found him dead in the basement. Will you help us bury him?"

Her lips pursed a wealth of fears. She squeaked out a "yes."

7

Ricky dug about two feet down until he couldn't dam the sweat ruining his vision. He scrubbed a heel into the dry earth and wiped his face with the t-shirt Tanais held for him. He threw it back on when he caught Liz' eyes on his bare skin. Yesterday, alone with her, brought on a fever only a repeat could cure.

"You can do the rest." He stabbed the shovel into the mud. It swayed to the ground, black from the fire in the house.

Tanais edged to the body twenty-or-so yards away. Swatted at the flies and ran back with her arms across her chest. "Who is he?"

Shoulders drooped and shrugged. Nobody had asked. Ricky didn't want to know, except he read his name on the license. Questions bred questions, and he might like none of the answers. Bixby stabbed hard at the ground and threw earth to compete with Ricky's strength. Ricky folded his arms and watched. Did Bixby try to impress Tanais, or Liz?

Liz yanked a stalk of grass and twined it around a finger. "I'm hearing things."

"What you picking up?" Bixby froze at half-dig and examined her through low lids.

"This man is a devil. A zombie. He is death himself."

Ricky snorted. "He is *dead*, himself, you mean."

"I'm serious. There's talk about a man gone missing. Descriptions match him. And his disappearance has caused some plates to shift."

"Plates?" Bixby screwed his brow.

"Tectonic plates. The earth has shifted and no good will come of it."

"Bullshit." Ricky spat.

"Because you know it all, Ricky, don't you? Have your ear to the ground and all that."

"I'm not saying I understand it all, unlike you, but I can sniff the shit dangling from a bull's ass." He wanted to snatch at something she withdrew from him.

Liz turned sideways to him. "I notice everything, because I'm around everything. I see it, hear it, smell it. And that body is bad news."

"Isn't any body bad news?" Tanais' perfect O eyes cast her second thoughts about joining this bunch. "Shouldn't we call the cops?"

"No." The corner of Ricky's mouth curled. "They're no good to anyone."

Bixby worked his shoulders into the shovel. "I don't want them anywhere near here. They'll cart me off to some family across the river, or some orphanage where I'd get nothing better than abuse."

Ricky uttered a quiet cuss as Bixby made easier work of digging.

"Why would they haul you off? They have no right."

"You sound like you live over there, Tanais." Bixby gestured to the City in the distance.

"I wish I did."

"They're a bunch of snobs. Look down on us is what they do. Why do you think they never fixed the bridge?" Liz circled the green stalk around her red ponytail. Ricky drew imaginary lines across her freckles.

"But it's a dead body. The police ..."

Liz threw the grass at Tanais. "This is my place. My escape from ... from it all. I don't need cops tramping all over it, spoiling our fun. They'll put barriers across everything. It feels like, already, something is changing. We're all changing, and ..."

Ricky could have patted Bixby on the back for continuing his dig. Gave him a focus he didn't want to spend on that outburst.

"Well, I feel the same as I ever did." Bixby threw the spade down. Checked the grave's dimensions. "How tall is this man?"

"Taller than that rabbit hole you dug." Ricky played with his phone and burned red. Liz hadn't made eyes at him as she did yesterday. Not once.

Three missed calls, all from ma. What did pa want last night? He said he'd come back with money when he left all that time ago. Useless adults. All of them. Would he grow up as stupid? Break every promise he ever made?

He walked away from the gang and called ma. It went straight to voicemail. He tried again. She answered on the fifth ring in a whisper. Must have her boss nearby, over her shoulder, his magnifying glass on every movement.

"Where you been, son? I hope not outdoors?"

The air stood still and hot. His ear suckered wet against the phone. "Nah. I'm in the kitchen. Mr Walters is on his porch smoking."

"He can't see you, right?"

"Nah. I'm watching him through the slit in the blinds."

"Good. Good." Her voice trailed away like it disappeared down a disused well.

He wondered if she'd hung up on him. He scanned for the stone which hid the wallet. How'd he get it back without the others' knowledge?

"How's Brett?"

He stammered, surprised she still held on to his call. "Fine. He's having a nap."

"You got the window open?"

"Ma, will you stop asking a million questions? It's stuffy in here. Let us please have some air in the house. God knows, we'd boil to death so we could save some money."

"Don't speak to me like that, son. You can see I'm working the Lord knows how many hours to put food on the table, which you waste too much of. If your daddy would send home some of the riches he's making out west, well, it'd help. So don't you be pointing your fingers at me …"

Did every adult break their promises?

She dragged air into those ashy lungs and let out her regret. "I'm sorry, Ricky. I don't mean to snap."

"I know you don't, ma, I know."

"Can you put Brett on the phone?"

"He's asleep. I told you."

"Of course, of course. I'm tired is all. I'm just so damn tired. Thank God I got you, is all I can say. Thank God I got you."

Ricky chewed on his lower lip to bite that guilt down. "How long 'til you get back? We're bored without you."

"Let me see. What time we got. It's 3.30 … So I'll be home in another two hours. Maybe I should sneak out now, I'm not sure. I think the boss likes me. He's always telling me I do good work, though God, how hard is it to scan prices on a supermarket shelf?"

Ricky's chest did well to contain his heart after it bounced around in there. "Don't risk it, we need the money. I'll see you in a couple of hours."

He stabbed the phone to end the conversation. Told the others he had to go.

"So soon?" Liz jogged to his side.

"Yes, so soon. Can you finish the grave? That man has got to go in. Before the devil comes for him."

"He is the devil." Liz scrunched her nose at the body, or the flies which buzzed around him. "No, I can't."

"We need your help." Bixby scanned everybody to gather allies.

"I gotta go. I left my brother alone in the house. Ma might come home any minute."

"You leave your brother alone in the house? What is he, four?"

"Six. Mature six." He tried to stare Liz's shock away, but she pinned her horror on him. Made him want to return quicker, as though her concern caused the kid an accident.

"You're an idiot. Your mom's at work? No babysitter?"

He shrugged. It is what it is. "How do we pay for a babysitter?"

Bixby smashed the shovel into the earth to send him a message. Ricky grabbed the man's ankles and dragged him to the hole. Turned his face from the flies and stench. Wiped sweat from his brow and eyed the grave. Tumbled the corpse inside. The body's feet stuck out for want of proper measurement. He pushed at the legs to bend them, but they had as much give as a pair of planks. The grave's lack of depth meant the site would form a hill once they covered him. It'd only take a stray dog and those turkey vultures to expose him to unwanted eyes.

"You live here." Ricky dragged the man from the pit. Rubbed at his sore ribs. He kicked a little dirt at Bixby. "Make this hole bigger. You have all day and all of the night. You've got to hide him, or this is all finished."

Tanais clasped the sandwiches she'd brought Bixby to her chest and gave Ricky the stink-eye. "You're not kind."

"And you're not invited."

She slipped her tongue in and out, and Ricky returned a sarcastic wave before he turned and headed home. Liz caught up with him.

"Be nice, Ricky. She's in this now. All she has to do is tell her mom, or her dad – whichever she lives with, and we're all in trouble."

"Do you think she will?"

"I think so, if we don't give her a pep-talk."

"Ah, you're full of it, Liz."

"What's that mean?"

"Yesterday, you ..." He couldn't pull the sentence from the dead-end he'd sent it down.

"Because I was all over you? And now I'm not? You want me to tear your clothes from you right this moment? In front of –"

"No."

"Well, then?"

"Well, then."

"Yesterday was something. I don't understand what's happening to me, but sometimes I have silly feelings – like I did. Today I have none of it. Tomorrow it might come back. I'm scared, Ricky. Things, everything, it's all changing. I'm different. You seem different. This summer might be the last we have like this. I have high school in September. You ... middle school. It ... I'm excited and I'm sad all at the same time."

"I want nothing to change. I want this summer to last forever. I'm sick of change."

"Then we have to make it the best ever."

She circled to walk backwards in front of him. Made him stop. Rested her nose on his and invited him into her green eyes. Raised his hand and let it rest on her breast. "One day."

She sprinted back to the houses, their forts, their city, her hair a beacon. He ran home, fired by the fizz in his senses.

8

The sun made slits of Ricky's eyes. He didn't believe in the digger's existence until he kicked its tires and poked a stick in its exhaust pipe. Stabbed at the front tires in the hope he'd burst them. The giant wheels reached taller than his slight frame and would crush his resistance in one revolution of its wheels. As if he had no substance on this Earth. Why did it sit in their fields? He dug a stone from the ground, weighed it. Whirled to check if its operator lurked nearby, and hurled the rock at the cabin. The smash sent a deer and its family from their dinner and Ricky into Town's claws.

The soft green fields and the relaxed hush and whispers of trees gave way to stifled roads and houses of brick straight out the oven. Hard edges. Chipped walls. Chain-link fences. He hit Town's asphalt and wondered if this is how entering prison would feel. The men on the streets must have had God press down on their shoulders as they slow-walked, aimless, to buy lottery tickets and weed, some slouching to shitty jobs. He half-wished one of his ma's tickets would take them on a one-way exit out of this town.

Ricky kicked a Coke can down a back alley to avoid them all, not far from home now. Jumped at the occasional dog scratching nails against a wooden fence it guarded, or shaking a chain-link. Everything rattled his bones.

"Shut your pie-hole."

By the alleyway's end, he scuttled away from the lanky man, who appeared as if from nowhere. Dogs relaunched at their fences.

"Not seen you in a while, Ricky. Where've you been hidin'?"

Ricky couldn't find words, because his thoughts whirled in a bingo tumbler. Only followed the man's blond hair, which hung in strands as though bell-bottomed gloops of grease ought to gather at their ends, ready to fall. A stained cap sat on his head, its peak low over his eyes. He wondered if the man ran around with the Ghost Boys. Everyone in this town hid their eyes. Maybe he oughta. It's an ugly town.

"Did someone rip that tongue from your mouth?"

"No. I got my tongue." Ricky stuck it out. Exaggerated it.

"That's not nice. I'm only being polite, is all."

"How'd you know my name? I don't know you."

"Though you see me around. I know you look at me from the corners of your eyes. You all do. Turn your bodies and think if you don't look directly, then I'll cease to exist. Like now."

Ricky strained to pull his eyes from a paper bag the wind blew down the alleyway, just to prove him wrong. The paper bag's dance in the air – it grabbed his attention more than the crust stood before him.

"Sir, I have nothing to say to you. You're in my way and I need to get somewhere."

"I'm sure. Your little brother must be feeling sorry for himself."

"Fuck you, mister."

Ricky feinted left and slipped to the right of this lug. He changed speed and burned down the carcass of a street. Pinched his nose to rid the damp cardboard smell of the man from his nostrils. Heat piled around his legs and arms until its weight brought his sprint to a crawl. He checked his shoulder before he entered his home stretch. Didn't clock the cardboard man. But you might not in a road like this, where junk made much of the yard furniture.

Relief that ma stayed at work didn't relax his tight stomach. His steps clapped their warning to Brett. *Here I am. Don't be messing me around.* The back door handle burned beneath direct sunlight. He stabbed the key into the lock and barged the door open. Expected everything out of place. A table upturned. A glass smashed on the carpet. A streak of blood a pathway to the basement. But it all remained straight and normal.

Muffled moans sledgehammered his conscience. A gag. A sock in his brother's mouth. His hands and feet hog-tied. Ricky checked the cupboard beneath the sink and the space under the kitchen island. Brett sat fetal, his arms around his belly, his eyes screwed tight shut.

"Brett ... Brett?"

"Go away."

"Come here." He reached in and attempted to pull the kid out into the open. Brett donkey-kicked and told him to get off.

Ricky straightened and gasped at the vodka bottle on the island's Formica top.

"You've gotta be kiddin' me, Brett? Jesus."

Ricky dove beneath the island and clamped Brett's arm. The boy thrashed and moaned, one moment strong and violent, another weak and limp. Ricky held him tight, dragged him

42

into the open, and shunted him over a shoulder. His bruises squealed and burned and pinched, but he bore it all the way upstairs. He helped the kid to his knees, head over the bathtub. Shoved his fingers down Brett's throat. Had to pull them out at the angry bites. Slapped him for the attempt. Tried again until the gush splattered the tub and stunk out the entire upper floor.

* * *

Ricky bathed the kid, dressed him in pajamas, and sat him at the kitchen table with a bowl of cereal. Demanded he eat. Brett swayed and played with the cornflakes, but it seemed his jaw couldn't move up and down.

"You alright, pal?"

"Don't leave me again, Ricky. I don't like it."

"I don't like it either, brother."

Ricky let that sigh balloon in his chest and remain inflated. No chance he'd stay in the house all day while ma worked. Neither would he take Brett to the Forts. What if the Ghost Boys showed up? He doubted they'd hold any sentiment towards either of them.

"Try not to shiver. Here ..." Ricky took the spoon from Brett's faint grip, scooped the cereal, and tapped his brother's teeth through his closed lips. The boy's eyes flickered and waned on repeat, but Ricky got that spoonful in. Milk dribbled out the corner of his lips until he poked beneath Brett's chin to close his mouth.

Good, there's the chew. Ricky repeated until the bowl emptied. He clattered the spoon as a sort of triumph. The day had beaten the kid. Ricky bit at the skin on his index finger, worried about ma. What if they needed to take Brett to a doctor? Doctors fleeced you even if they only poked a lollipop stick in the back of your mouth. He peeked through a gap in the kitchen blind for the freak who blocked his path earlier, but saw nobody out there.

"You listening?"

"Yes, Ricky."

"Did anybody knock today?"

"Yeah."

"Do you know who?"

"No. I didn't open any door, I promise."

"It's okay, Brett, it's okay. I'm not accusing you of anything. But ... you gotta be careful. Okay? ... Okay?"

"Yeah. I'm always careful."

Ricky ruffled his hair. "I know you are. You're a good kid. Always a good kid. But don't you touch that shit again. The drink, I mean." He tucked the bottle back into its spot. Not much had gone down the kid's pipe, he hoped.

"I was thirsty."

"Tap water. Nothing but tap water."

He listened to ma's engine and the tick-tock of her feet as she made her way to his doom.

"You should get in bed. You had a busy day playing with your action figures and trucks. I chased you up and down the stairs and we played hide and seek. Right? ... Right?"

Ma's key clinked in the lock, and the jam in the door made her shoulder it open.

Brett's forehead formed trenches deep enough to bury Ciaro, but he whispered his agreement. There'd be a day when the kid's eyes didn't well-up, and he'd turn. On him.

"Hi, kids." Ma slouched like she'd spent hours down the

Dragon Land mines. She'd cook dinner, quick, and then scoot off to her second job.

He eyed her the same way Brett did to him.

9

"What did you two do? He's never burned out at this time of day." Ma rested hands on her hips. She closed the bedroom door on her youngest and sparked a cigarette as she descended the stairs. Ricky slid by her and slumped on the sofa to watch TV. The thing buzzed from old age before settling into normality. He flicked through basic cable, past ancient sitcoms where the picture blurred behind blotches and grain. He settled on some PBS show about sharks.

Felt ma's examination as she leaned on the wall beneath the arch. He furrowed his brow in mock-concentration. Watched the shark Elvis its hips through the oceans, but he didn't hear a word of the narrator's explanation. Only the blood in his ears. She suspected. Wanted him to confess before she lost her temper.

He scratched his face. Shuffled his ass this way and that. Reclined on the sofa. Sat back up. The dead man, Benny Ciaro, pointed at his conscience.

"He was sick? You were sick? I can smell the tang upstairs."

"He was sick."

"You ate his food, then? It's all gone, including food for tomorrow."

"Yes." He hid the wince which locked, ready to explode. Answered too quick. He prepared too cutely for the accusation.

Her puffs on the cigarette grated. The exaggerated blows of smoke even more.

"He didn't finish, so I ate the rest. You know what he's like. And he was sick." Better the little lie …

"I do. He's an eater. More than you ever were. Gunna be a big boy. Unlike you, skinny ass. Which is why I don't believe you. He wouldn't leave it and you wouldn't eat it."

"I ate it, ma. He wasn't feeling too good. I told you that already."

"You exhausted him so much you drove him sick? That's not like you."

He flicked the channel again and made the mental climb through the tunnel his vision dug. Listened to her tired steps into the kitchen, but didn't risk a glance. Couldn't stand for the truth to vomit out his mouth, though it hurt his stomach to hold it in. Bixby needed that food. What else would he eat? He'd no idea Tanais wanted to feed him, too.

The doorbell rang and saved him. He shot from his seat and peered through the peephole. Creaked open the door, nervous at an unfamiliar visit.

"Hey." He kept his hand on the handle.

"Hey. You coming out?"

He checked his shoulder. Ma eyed Liz with enough suspicion to make his blood simmer. She raised an eyebrow, a tick in the warning box.

"Sure. I keep you cooped in here all day long. Be back before sundown. Do you hear?"

"You not working?"

"You know it's my night off."

He'd already slammed the door and jumped off the porch steps.

* * *

They stared at their feet most of the way to Liz' house to avoid eye contact with broken men and women. As they got closer, she would say a cheerful "hi" to a few older folk. All had seen better times. The present brewed a whole lot of sadness in them. He had all this to look forward to?

She pointed at an old couple who swept their front yard, their tidiness a contrast to the neighbors' tardiness. "Their kids are everywhere. Florida, California, and I think their youngest is in London. All grown up."

Ricky could only imagine such places. Wondered if they bettered the City across the river.

She nodded to the old man standing by his post box. "His daughter died from a drug overdose. He used, himself. You can trace patterns all over his arms, if you wanted."

"What do you mean?"

"All the needle marks on his arm." Her eyes sparkled at him, confused if he joked or not.

"You talk to all these people?"

"Some of them, lover, not all of them." She started a playful skip, but dampened that spirit at the sight of a skinny man in baggy jeans and high-end sneakers. A skeleton of a man whose bones could stab if you bumped into him. Once they moved by him, she extended her stride and searched for Ricky's hand.

He held her, loose. "A man is watching our house when I'm out."

"Some cop? A junkie? Who's watching you?"

"Some bum. Skinny as that man we just passed."

"And?"

"He blocked me in a backstreet and said a load of weird shit. He knew I'd left my brother alone all day." Ricky enjoyed her hand in his, however brief her grip.

"Maybe he's your guardian angel. Maybe he's a pedophile."

"Jesus, don't talk like that."

"Sorry, lover. What you gunna do?"

"Keep an eye on him."

"The man or your brother?"

"Both."

She backpedaled in front of him, holding distance with his every step. "But you're right here. With me. How are you keeping an eye on them at all?"

"Liz, you give me nothing but pain."

"Right in the ass, yeah?"

He poked her ribs, and she ran off with a laugh.

They skirted Main Street and hurried past men in vests hanging out in their backyards, and kids who weighed the two of them up as they would meat at a butcher's. Ricky stared back, but she tugged at his arm and whispered through the side of her mouth to keep his eyes at a respectable level. No trouble. *We have enough.*

Ricky traced graffiti on rough surfaces with a finger and kicked at weeds pushing through cracks in the concrete. His brother's sad eyes bothered him. She grabbed at his sleeve and pulled him into the tiny gap between two houses. He eyed round both walls to see what scared her so much.

"There." She crouched real small, where the sun couldn't reach. He joined her and watched the boys walk like cocks around their hens. One scythed at weeds with a stick. In this heat and broad daylight, they still wore their oversized hoodies, the hoods over their heads and low across masked, boot-polished faces. None said a word. Ricky worried they communicated through telepathy. The Ghost Boys pounded and swished by. Ricky's heart jumped when one peered into the alley, but the shadows cloaked them from view. They lingered a few moments until the gang gained distance. Ricky darted out, grabbed a stone, and flung it their way. Liz grasped his wrist, and both hurried back to Main Street.

* * *

Ricky stood on the gate's bottom bar and swung in and out while he waited for Liz to leave her house. She'd been ages, and he wanted to eat. Promised him food. He'd settle for beef jerky right now. A rabbit ran through the overgrown grass in the front yard and he chased it around. Didn't expect to catch the bunny, but it sure passed the time.

Her face shone almost as red as her hair when she returned. "Dad allows you to come in."

"Does he?"

"As long as you don't touch his shit. He said."

"I won't touch his shit. Any of it."

"Good."

"Does he have a lot of shit?"

"Not as much as he used to, I guess."

She jerked her head to the house and invited him to follow. Linked fingers behind her back and swayed her hips. Ricky rushed to her side to avoid the distraction.

"In you go, my lover."

He wished she wouldn't say that, because most times she didn't mean it. He extended his head through the open doorway, like a cat sniffing at a box he wanted to explore, wary of a biting dog inside. Her pa hadn't opened the curtains. Indoors smelled of dust and bleach and he wondered how the stink never attached to Liz. She forced him forward and he almost stumbled across the rumpled carpet. Walked on the tips of his toes, nervous the floor would squelch at every step.

"This is my dad. Dad, this is Ricky. He's my friend."

A figure sat beneath a lampshade, a smudge in the darkness. He didn't move or acknowledge his daughter. Tempted Ricky to turn and run as he had from the bum with the greasy cap ...

"Is he your special friend?" Her pa's voice came out all gravel and broken glass.

"Yes he is." She shifted to the man's side and puffed the pillow behind him as if ... Liz' pa was paralyzed? No – the man crossed his legs and spread one arm over the sofa's back, the other around Liz' waist.

"You got any words in your mouth, son?"

Ricky thought of the bum-in-the-alley's comment. Wanted to throw a bit of sarcasm his way, but guessed it best to respect the old man. "I do, sir."

"Then spill. What you got to say for yourself?"

"I don't rightly know, sir. I mean, I'm friends with Liz. Your daughter."

"She is my daughter. You're damn right about that. You realize what I'd do to protect my girl?"

"I'm sure you'd lay down your life, sir."

"Goddamn, the kid is bright."

He squeezed Liz hard enough to unbalance her for a moment. She parked herself on the chair's arm and watched Ricky through innocent-girl eyes.

"Where'd you find this one, girl?"

"Out in the City of Forts ... you know, the old factory."

He saluted, yanked back the years. "That place produced something of value after all this time. Who'd have thought?"

The wood panels on the wall ought to conceal a secret compartment to somewhere more glamorous. Ricky anticipated what the man might say next. Head bobbed up and down as if in agreement. The man made wet sounds as he ran his tongue across his teeth. Ricky's leg shook, which infected Liz, who curled hair strands behind an ear and scratched phantom itches on her upper arm. Ricky adjusted to the gloom and the older man's eyes. Her pa didn't blink in the past minute, he swore. Caught Ricky like a fish on a hook. Ricky dipped his lower lip, and breathed through his mouth.

"I had a son like you once."

"You did?"

"Certainly did. Had the same attitude as you. Little sneaky bastard. Admired it in one so young. He'd talk to anybody. Soon have the measure of a person."

Ricky hadn't taken a seat. Neither father nor daughter invited him to do so, but he perched on the edge of the sofa beneath the blacked-out window. "You *did* have a son?"

"Straight to the point. I like it. I no longer have a son. His stupid ma took him to the bottom of the river down there – along with her stupid self, I might add. How I miss him."

Ricky followed the man's arm from wrist to exposed shoulder for those track marks Liz talked of. The near limb, his left, ran smooth as far as he could tell. The right arm remained cloaked by gloom and tattoos. Ricky offered Liz a sorrowful look.

"Still, I have my Liz. My girl. Always wanted her to be my boy. Don't know why – a daughter is as good as a son these days." He squeezed her in and puckered his lips. Liz leaned over and kissed him quick.

Ricky became conscious of how he nodded too much. The man loved his kid. Provided her a home, food on the table, and fishing trips. Ricky's pa remained out west, enough faces around him for his son's to melt into the mass, forgotten.

"You can watch my brother if you want."

Mr Panowich cocked his head sideways. "You want me to babysit?"

Liz pulled herself away from him and stiffened. Ricky shrugged off her annoyance. She couldn't have the man all to herself, even if he is her pa. He wanted Brett somewhere safe for the rest of the summer, without fear of the bum's eye on them both.

"Not babysit, sir. Just mold. Take him to do stuff. He needs a man's influence. Our pa – we have no idea where he is, or when he's coming back ... if he's ever coming back." Weird that ma never talked about her conversation with his old man. Had he even been on the end of the line? "I worry about my brother."

"Why don't you care for him? You're off school."

"I got a shitload to do, sir."

"A shitload, huh? You have a job? Damn, you're barely my girl's age and you have more employment than I do? Is it you that took my job?"

Ricky shook his head, vigorous. Wobbled a little that he offended Mr Panowich and lost an opportunity to lose Brett. He needed to rid himself of the guilty ache that infected his days.

"Course you didn't, son. That was the damn Chinese, the goddamn Latinos, and probably a bunch of Muslims, all working for peanuts to pay rent on a single room with one damn light bulb."

As the man shifted to perch on the edge of his chair, Ricky leaned into the sofa's folds. He straightened to keep the man's good opinion.

"Sir, I just think he could learn much from a man like you."

"You do, huh?" The man grinned as though he fed on his first compliment in years, even if from a boy. Stroked his scraggly black beard. "Damn, bring him here. I'll teach him things that'll make his old man redundant. I've got tools, fishing rods ... you name it."

A gust hit the window and almost sucked it out. Rain pinged off the glass, and some object hit the door. Everyone in the room jumped. Questioned each other at the size of that hail stone. The rap struck harder and with rhythm.

"That'll be Carrie. Liz, go answer will ya?" He patted her backside as she scurried to the entrance. Ricky had seen her nerves on show only once – when they crashed through the floorboards and came face-to-face with the body. They surfaced again.

He nodded at Mr Panowich as Liz talked to some woman at the doorstep. Their voices rumbled beneath clarity – sounded a little harsh here and there. Liz' pa didn't move. Could he stand? What would his brother do here all day with a man glued to the sofa?

Ah, there. The man jumped from his chair and muttered cusses until he reached the pair and burst into precision. "Goddammit, Liz, let the woman in, okay?"

Ricky stood and shoved hands into his pockets. He peered

round the door. A woman brushed past Liz and into the house, her scowl no match for Liz'. Ricky inched back a step at how her narrow eyes needled to mine any worth he might hold. He wrapped a hand around the corpse's cash in his pocket. She dismissed him with a hunched stomp across the floorboards, soaked body unable to dampen down the dust she'd unsettled.

Liz' pa hopped after her, a smile on his lips, followed by Liz herself, who heeled the door shut. Folded her arms.

"Ah, don't give me that look, kid. You should be grateful your old man has someone to comfort him." She shoved her coat at Mr Panowich.

"He has plenty of comfort from me. Thanks all the same." Liz swept her hair aside.

"Come now, my girl, there's comfort you can't provide. Be nice."

Ricky scratched an elbow at the *ewww* face curling Liz' lips into over-ripe orange peel.

This Carrie-woman straightened and wiped crow's feet bangs from her forehead. "This is business, too, Liz. Liz-Lizzy-Lou. Off you go."

Liz released the breath-stopper of a self-hug and clawed Ricky's arm. Ricky resisted the pull for a moment, but the anger in her second jerk forced him to follow upstairs. She shut the bedroom door behind them, reopened it, and peered through the slit. He gawked through, too, above her head. Carrie soothed the old man's protests about the way she talked to his offspring. Wet noises – puckered lips it sounded like – slapped up the staircase, and Carrie, in a fake low voice Ricky could tell she intended to funnel upstairs, told Liz's pa he spoiled his daughter and she would ruin his remaining years if he let her. Liz' pa mumbled and grumbled before the wet noise drowned out further dissent.

Liz slammed the door, swiveled, and kissed Ricky full on the lips.

He pulled himself from the suck and backed away. "That was weird."

She palm-pushed him in the chest. "You're weird, Ricky. You're fucking weird. Offering your brother to a man you don't know."

"He's your pa."

She bit her lip.

"He is your pa, right?"

She nipped him until he squirmed. "Of course he is."

Nervous giggles from the adults wriggled through the gap under the door. The grind of a lighter's flint wheel filled the dead air, and a groan wobbled the silence.

"God, Liz, what's the matter? What happened?"

Her face drained to milky-white. She pulled at his t-shirt and led the way downstairs. Rushed him outdoors so he could only glimpse the two adults on the sofa. Both had fallen asleep with their eyes open, bodies slumped. Ricky eyed Liz. *Are they dead?*

* * *

He kicked at stones and empty soda cans on his lonesome trek home. The rain had stopped, and the steam curled around his feet. Heat simmered the dusk and smeared a greasy sheen on his skin. Ma rung his cell until he answered on the fourth call. He bristled at her tone. *Where are you? Where've you been with that girl? Who is that girl?* As if he never mentioned her name. As if he'd not known her since elementary school.

56

The can hit the high brick wall that angled into a back alley, the border of an abandoned house's backyard, and rolled still. A groan escaped the alley. Ricky checked all the angles, his feet pinned to the ground. Rubbed his heart and palmed goosebumps from his forearm. Snooped around the wall into the alley's maw. A dull yellow light shone from above onto a man sprawled in the dirt, and another, with hair too big for his head, crouching over him with one hand on the prone man's shirt collar, his fist punch-ready.

The man beneath sobbed. Blood bubbled from his nose. The assailant above stared at Ricky. His eyes did a countdown, five-four-three-two ... Ricky pushed off his back foot and bolted from danger, the victim's groans a spur.

10

The next morning's heat drilled into the back of Ricky's neck, but it didn't needle as much as the cries and accusations thrown at him by his brother, who stood at the window with the curtains wide open. Brett banged the panes so hard his fists should have smashed through and scratched red streaks over his arms. Ricky squinted at the sun, a god he begged to help him at this moment. Summer would go as fast as a scratch of his nose and that'd see Liz slip from his life. High School would change her. Take her away.

"Ricky … Ricky …"

"Jesus, Brett."

He stormed back into the house before the boy piled through the window into a gory mess of limbs and smacked the kid over the head. Brett slumped into a fetal position and whimpered his apologies.

"I'm sorry, Ricky. I'm sorry. But … but … don't leave me, please. Don't leave me."

Ricky shut the front door and sat by his brother beneath the living room window. Combed Brett's hair with his fingers. "It's okay. I shouldn't have hit you like that. I'm sorry, bro. I'm sorry. This is the last day you'll be on your own, I promise. I promise you."

"You'll take me with you?"

Ricky inhaled irritation deep through his nose and exhaled it out of his mouth, filtered into calm. "Sort of."

* * *

"What's your pa's name? Do I just call him Mr Panowich?"

"That'd be the right thing to do, Ricky-lover."

He kicked at the scruff bordering the worn dirt path. It led to the back porch of the fort with the hole in the floor. "You won't call me that when you're off to high school and getting all high and mighty with boys and their fancy cars."

She laughed at him and joined his grass-kicks. "I don't think anyone will be too fancy. Not if they're like us. And I can control myself. I don't need any boy to make me high and mighty."

"You got your tits out for me."

She pinched him hard and twisted. He danced to escape and batted her away. "I didn't get them out all the way, and I didn't get them out for any old boy. I got them out for you. Who I've known since we were this high."

They tip-toed through the knee-high grass beyond the backyard's border. He ignored the burn she'd given him – through clenched teeth. Nothing compared to a snake's bite, he guessed. "Sorry, Liz. Sometimes I'm an ass."

"You're my ass. All mine."

They grabbed each other at the rustle in the grass' depths. Too big for a copperhead, and they lived too far north for an alligator to stalk them. They advanced in a crouch, shoulder to shoulder. Their heads bobbed up and down to glimpse what they might find ahead. Some sharp-toothed beast with an empty belly, the Ghost Boys, the phantom of the man they buried? Benny Ciaro himself, come back to life?

Ricky thrust a hand across Liz' abdomen and she gripped his wrist and dug in her fingers. Through the gap in the grass, they saw the man's foot stuck out of the earth. His other leg tried to free itself from the dirt – at least that's how it seemed from the shuffle.

"Benny Ciaro. His name is Benny Ciaro."

Ricky and Liz stumbled and flattened the pasture into their body shapes. Scrambled back on their palms until a girl peered at them, silhouetted by the sun over her shoulder.

"For God's sake, Tanais, you frightened us half to death." Liz shot to her feet and planted herself inches from her nose.

"His name is Benny Ciaro."

"How do you know that?"

Ricky pushed himself up, slow, his belly in a rumble. Worked on his face to iron out the embarrassment. Should have thrown the wallet into the river.

"I found his information."

"You dug the man up?"

"No, I discovered it under a stone."

The girls settled their attention on the foot sticking out of the ground. Flies buzzed. The smell suffocated.

"Let me look." Ricky stepped out onto the damp patch, his hand out.

Tanais opened the wallet and pulled out the driver's license. He snatched it from her reluctant fingers. Liz and Tanais gathered by him. The man's picture showed dead eyes and a pock-marked face his scruff couldn't hide. Creepy, but all adults had the same life-is-overrated expression on their license photos.

60

"I recognize him, I'm sure I do." Liz scratched at the photo to get through to Ciaro's identity.

"How do you know him?" The license slipped from Ricky's grip to the ground. He plucked it back. How could Liz know a man who'd died a horrible death in their fort?

"Not certain. I ... he just looks familiar."

They stood glum around the picture until rushes *shhhed* apart and Bixby approached. Eyed them all from the confidence of a successful hunt. A pair of dead squirrels hung from his left hand. "Anyone hungry?"

They all shook their heads, no, and clamped their teeth shut in case he snuck in a slither of meat between them.

He pointed at the card. "You know about Benny, then?"

"We do now." Liz poked a toe at the foot. "Did you bury him properly, Bixby? Or did he get out all by himself?" She barred her nose with a forearm.

"His leg got real stiff, and the hole I dug wasn't big enough. No way did I want to pull him out again and make the grave bigger. Not by myself." He flashed a glare at Ricky.

"Hey, I'm sorry." Ricky shrugged. "Distractions and stuff. Alright?. I forgot to bring you food this morning, too." He hoped Brett remained quiet behind the curtained window.

"I didn't forget, Bixby. I got you sandwiches." Tanais scrunched her face at the squirrels.

"I'm starting to like you." He strode to Tanais and gave her a playful smack on the arm, helping her to relax.

He seized the license from Ricky's grip, ignored the "hey," and frisbee'd the card into the field. "We could dig him out and let the turkey vultures have at him. I'd prefer him gone. This is our place. Our escape. What if people are looking for him? What if people shut all this off? What if the authorities find me? And send me away?"

Ricky jerked his neck back. Bixby didn't want vultures anywhere near him.

"He's somebody's son." Tanais reached for the paper bag she'd brought for Bixby and fiddled with the fold. "Might be somebody's dad. I'd wish someone told me – if it was my dad."

"Well, I wouldn't." Bixby swung the animals to keep the man's stench from them.

Liz had nothing to say about her pa, and Ricky could only imagine what his own might look like now. Would he have changed much from the photographs?

"It's time we got Tanais all initiated." Ricky grinned at the newbie. She bit her lip and squealed. Ricky hoped excitement would make them all forget Ciaro's name. Knowledge made them all complicit in the man's death.

11

The raft sat half-buried in the sand by the river's bank. Ricky said they hadn't used it since last summer. Liz claimed two summers. Tanais still worried for the man's family. Her nerves made them all flicker their necks like birds for unseen observers.

Ricky shifted her attention from their fears. "Don't you want to know what to do?"

"I'm unsure. I … yeah … but … what you gunna make me do?"

"We get the raft out the sand, first. Then we get in the river and paddle. Then … you'll have to wait for that bit."

"On the river?"

"You can swim, right?"

"I'm able to keep my head above water, but that's all."

Liz curled an arm around Tanais and squeezed her in. "We'll save you if you fall in."

"I'd like that."

Bixby squashed her from the other side to make a Tanais sandwich. "Who's going to provide me food if you float off into the ocean? Of course we'll save you."

"Hey, come on." Ricky hunched his shoulders and showed his palms. "I bring you all kinds of food."

"Not the same as Tanais. Hers has a bit of flavor. Yours - not much different to eating cardboard and mayo."

Tanais giggled and Ricky *pah'ed* his comments away.

They scraped sand aside and dragged the raft to the water's edge. A little wear loosened the planks tied to the bright blue barrels. It all shifted and slid, but held. Liz helped Ricky pull the frayed rope to secure everything a little tighter. Tanais huffed and puffed the boat into the shallows and clapped in surprise at the cold water lapping her ankles.

"This is fun."

"You don't get out a lot, do ya?" Liz arched an eyebrow.

Tanais pursed her lips. Shook her head. "My parents are getting better."

"Parents?" Ricky examined her. Tanais' open face showed how she trusted them all, though she knew none of them much. Two parents. He supposed he had two, too. But it seemed both of hers lived beneath the same roof.

"Yeah. Parents. What you saying?"

"Nothing." Ricky pushed and pulled the boat. Checked for holes in the barrels. The river didn't drop to any great depth, but in places it could gush over your head.

"The oars."

Bixby waded into the water with a couple of planks and his worn-out sneakers in the air. Liz clambered aboard and steadied the sway. Relieved Bixby of the timber, screwed up her nose at the footwear, and helped Tanais onboard as the boys pushed the boat out to deeper waters. Ricky grabbed her arm for purchase and pulled himself up. Bixby held onto the edge and kicked his feet to motor the raft. Liz and Ricky argued with Tanais about who should paddle.

Tanais gripped Liz' oar. "I'm new. Let me pull my weight."

"Then grab Ricky's. Why grab mine, sister?"

Tanais beamed at the moniker and urged Ricky to relent.

"What'll I do, then?"

Liz nodded at Bixby. "Join in with fish-boy down there. We'll get there quicker."

"Get where?" Tanais paddled the wrong way and slowed them down. Liz showed her how.

Ricky slipped off his shoes, warned the girls not to lose them, and jumped in with Bixby to paddle.

The bridge reached over the river, a broken limb dangling all useless in the middle. Didn't seem much from a distance, but as they approached, it hulked above them, rotten, its arches rusted orange. Liz rested the plank. Ricky and Bixby relaxed their legs and shuffled their sneakers into a less precarious position.

"Why's it like that, then?" Tanais scanned the bridge's shortened length. Ricky had often hopped along its potholed surface and tip-toed over the outcrop, anxious heavy steps would crumble the structure. The bridge ended halfway across the tributary, its jagged fingers reaching for the City opposite.

"It fell into the river years ago, ma said. A couple of cars went down with it." Liz kept her eyes on the ruin. " Been like that since."

"Those poor people. Did they die?" Tanais' mouth hung open in shock.

"I'm guessing, though it's not that deep."

Bixby lifted himself onto the raft. "Gets spooky out here knowing that. When the sun dips. When there's a bit of fog. Brrrr."

"Why'd they not rebuild it? How does anybody get across to the City?"

"You never been to the City, Tanais?" Liz shifted her eyes to their new friend.

"No. We only moved here a couple months ago."

"From where?"

"Ohio. Dad got a job here."

They laughed at her.

"Doing what, girl?" Liz nudged Tanais and grabbed her arm at how she almost toppled off the raft. "You leave to get a job, not the other way round."

Tanais connected her eyebrows. "My dad got one, though, didn't he? He's here to help folks who have … he said who have fallen off the map."

"Are we part of his project?" Bixby's hands tightened into a ball. He lifted them waist-high.

"No. Only adults. The ones who need guidance."

"Is that so?" Ricky laughed.

Tanais shuffled, wary of a push. "So … how long's it been like that? Why didn't they rebuild it?" Tanais raised her hand against the sun.

"Because we're the shit on their shoe." Ricky splashed out of the water and joined them on the raft's tight surface. He spat at the City rising from the opposite bank, two hundred or more yards away, the buildings jewels set in a crown they could only gaze at from afar. "Ma works over there, in a little convenience store."

"How's she get there?"

"Has to take a ton of roads round the back, onto the highway. Seems she has to sneak into the place so she doesn't offend anyone."

"It's not that bad, my Ricky-boy. You're such an exaggerator."

"Just sayin' what ma tells me."

"As if you listen to her stories."

"I listen enough."

"What's my initiation, you guys?" Tanais' smile smudged to one side. She sensed Bixby's irritation. Lifted a finger to touch the stretched end of his soaked t-shirt and flinched when he denied her the sentiment.

"You're climbing the girders of this bridge from here." Bixby glared at her. "Then up the arch right to the top. You get up there and you will stand straight. Once you get your bearings and balance, you jump into the river."

Tanais' eyes rolled across the stretch of water from raft to bridge, up the gnarled joists beneath the ramp, and high to the arch's summit. "Do I go feet first, or head first?"

"Belly flop if you like. See if I care."

"Hey, Bixby, that's more than I ..."

"Shut up, Ricky. She wants an initiation – there it is. You don't do it, Tanais, and this is your last day with us."

"Bixby, what the hell?" Liz threw her hands about in confusion. "Is it deep enough?"

"It's okay. I'll do it. I can do it. I can climb things. It can't be as hard as it looks. I just need to try, is all ..."

Ricky shuffled his feet and Liz joined in the nervous dance. A massive-sounding bee flew around somewhere and a motor ripped the quiet from a distance. "Well, you do what you have to do, Tanais. But I'll be your pal if you don't do it."

Liz, eyes still on the hulk ahead, reached a hand out to Ricky's wrist and squeezed.

Bixby caught the gesture and prodded Tanais. "I won't. Are you going, or what?"

Ricky and Liz paddled Tanais closer to the bridge – the

new girl's paddle speed would exhaust her long before she got to the structure. Tanais pulled her shorts higher as she maneuvered from the raft. Didn't matter – the water rose to her neck, and she still had to kick her feet so she didn't submerge. Deep enough, then. A few waves from a motor boat rolled in and bobbed Tanais. Ricky, Liz and Bixby bent their knees to keep balance on the surf. Tanais made it to the diagonal girder and edged her way up. Showed agility, sufficient to make Spider-Man nod in appreciation, as she grabbed the next criss-crossing the one she left behind. A few wobbles and a slip almost sent her back to the others with a splash, but she held on and wrapped an arm over the rim. A leg dangled out. Two legs. She tried to pull herself up. Not enough strength.

Bixby snorted, but sat on the edge with his feet in the river as she got a leg up and made it. Liz whooped. Ricky grinned. Tanais jumped up and down with her arms in the air in triumph. Lifted her chin to scan the arch closest to the bridge's end, hands on hips. Her chest heaved as she planted a foot in the ridge, palms on the edges.

Ricky squinted over at the motorboat, its engine now a low thrum. A man and some kid, his son, watched them. Enjoyed the show. Tanais made it halfway up the slope. At one point, her toes almost touched her hands as her body bent out. A slip could kill her. She squirmed past the loose barbed wire which previous climbers had snipped. Ricky rubbed his clammy hands together as he watched Tanais. Watched the dad and son watch them all. The man examined them through binoculars. Lowered them. *Ha.* Ricky expected the man had seen his sneer. The kid grabbed the lenses and observed them in a sweep, making Ricky fidget as if goggle-eyed tourists studied him behind zoo bars.

"I did it. I did it. Look. I did it."

"Stay cool up there. That's a height." Liz cracked knuckles and flickered her tongue.

Tanais made tiny steps to the edge of the arch and lowered her chin to scan the water. Put her arms wide so she looked like Jesus in the fancier churches. One of those ma didn't attend.

"I'm not into this." Liz tightened on Ricky's wrist. "It's too much. You've done some shit, Bixby, but I think this one is the worst."

Bixby didn't even care to face Tanais anymore. Ricky realized he gripped Liz' wrist too tight and relaxed his fingers a moment before he squeezed again.

Tanais screamed. They all froze.

"There's a bee or something up here. There's a bee. It's huge." Tanais arced her head to see where it came from.

Ricky cupped hands to his mouth to target his voice. "Stop moving about, you'll fall. Stand still and keep your eyes on the water. Or ahead. Ahead. Definitely ahead."

"Okay. I will. But I'm scared."

"No need. You climbed right up there. More than any of us have done, including him."

Bixby shrugged and reclined on the raft to stare at the late morning blue.

"But what if it stings?"

"It'll only sting if you attack it. Relax. The best way down now is to jump." He nudged Liz and whispered. "The water … it's deep enough, right?"

"Deep enough to drown, yeah."

The light breeze ruffling their hair seemed like a tornado in this tense moment, enough to thrust their new friend into the water's claws.

Tanais bent her knees and exploded from the bridge. She tumbled and spun. Ricky winced at how she must break her neck, or back, when she smashed into the river.

12

Tanais' cannonball splash reached the sun. She must have hit something at the bottom and become entangled in weeds, because she sure didn't surface like a plank of lifeless wood.

"Shit."

Ricky dove in, followed by Liz. He expected a third splash from Bixby but as he checked his shoulder on his fourth or fifth crawl, his old friend remained as still as the oars beside him.

Ricky climbed a lot of trees, but swimming's a different exercise. His breath shortened at the exertion. Liz reached him. Spurred him on, but his lungs burned. Liz's breathing started to hack and fill with phlegm. They paddled in one spot and called Tanais' name. Ricky plunged beneath the surface. Authorities cleaned the water about a decade ago, ma said. Used to flow yellow with chemical spill for years until regulators bucked up their ideas.

He saw pretty far down, deeper than he imagined this river could reach. Tanais didn't shimmer wrapped in reeds and metal shopping carts. He exploded to the surface before his lungs popped.

"You see her?" Liz swiveled this way and that.

"No. Just fish. It's dark at the bottom."

The water washed against the bridge's pillars and rolled Ricky and Liz up and down on waves. "There." Ricky pointed to the form about twenty-or-so yards away. "Jesus, I ... I think it's her. She looks ..."

"Don't say it, Ricky. If you say it, then it is."

He pulled a "what are you on about" face and pushed on. His arms ached and weakened, as though joined to his shoulder by loose thread.

"Tanais ..." He doggy-paddled around her. Liz stared from the other side. Tanais' eyes, open, reached out from their sockets to scour the clear blue above. "Are you okay?"

"I'm amazing. I'm absolutely in the best ... mood ... I've ever ... been in." A smile scorched across her calm expression. "I want to do it again."

Ricky splashed water on her face and laughed. "You're mad. I thought you could hardly swim?"

"This is not swimming. This is floating."

They floated toward the bridge, helped along by the wave from the motorboat which buzzed thier way. It gleamed unused white and wore the side of a man's face painted on the front, in silhouette, a feathered Roman helmet on its head.

"You kids alright?"

They squinted up at the man and his boy as they peered over the boat's rim, silhouetted by the sun.

"We sure are." Liz gave him two thumbs up, annoyed at the intrusion.

"We got a little concerned, didn't we, son?" His kid nodded, a lazy smile a substitute for a shrug. "You – up there like that. You're a proper daredevil, aren't you, girl?"

Tanais shifted to vertical and giggled. "I am, aren't I?"

The dad took shape through the glare. Sunglasses covered his eyes, and he had a smile exposing more lower teeth than the uppers. The boy twirled string around a finger and eyed them. Ricky expected him to throw them some bread.

"You need a lift to the bank? You all look exhausted." The man pushed the sunglasses up his businessman's hair.

"We're fine, mister. They're with me." Bixby's grin competed with the son's half-hearted version as he rowed towards them.

The man's smile shone as bright as the sun. Ricky had never seen such a sparkling set of teeth.

"No worries, son. Glad you could make it for your friends." He surveyed the kids in the water as they all worked their feet to stay afloat. "You're lucky. All of you. To have such a friend."

Bixby scowled.

Ricky enjoyed how the man's sarcasm hit. "Thank you anyway, sir. We all appreciate it. Right?"

Liz and Tanais nodded, enthusiastic. Bixby motioned them all to jump aboard and reached over to help pull Tanais from the river.

"You were great." Bixby patted her shoulder as she stood, legs all jelly. Her frown crackled against a smile, creating a confused spasm around her lips.

Liz helped Ricky onboard and they paddled away in silence, Ricky's attention on man and son as they motored into the distance. He spat in the water.

13

The heat sat beneath the skin of Ricky's neck, a parasite he rubbed until the friction hurt worse than the burn. They all helped Bixby shift stuff to the end-house, the nicest in the row, and heaped praise on Tanais, who absorbed it all and shone it back through xylophone teeth.

Bixby's grin broke lopsided. "Don't you forget to return, all."

Concrete set in Bixby's bones at the lack of response from anybody. They left him to his fort and trudged, weary, to their homes. Ricky and Liz walked Tanais close to her home. They stood and watched as she strolled the last stretch alone, alert lemmings on the prairie for any danger to her. She entered a cookie-cutter development full of houses the size of aircraft carriers. The girl could get lost in there. Ricky pictured his house fitting into the corner of of Tanais' garden, nothing more than a shed to keep their lawnmower out of the weather.

Ricky and Liz returned to the fields, batting bugs from ears and eyes, keeping to shade beneath the trees. Thoughtful silence enveloped both, each unsure how they ended behind the fort, in the rushes and the bare patch of earth, where a couple of turkey vultures patrolled close to the exposed foot. They raised their t-shirts to block the stink as they scavenged the ground. Brushed away prickly plants and avoided deer and goose shit until Liz lifted what they searched for between two fingers. Ricky shuffled to her side. Thumbed the dirt from the address on the driver's license. 129 Atlantic Drive. He'd scurried through this street's back alleys before, though he couldn't pinpoint the house.

Grass swished around the body behind them and they both dropped low. The afternoon sun's strength dissipated down by the cool earth and a chill nipped at Ricky's burnt neck. Bixby's mumbles filtered through the growth and hit them angry. Ricky shifted, but Liz steadied his position with a firm hand. Bixby had freaked them out a little with his treatment of Tanais, and Ricky obeyed his gut to keep away from him for now.

Bixby kicked the man's foot. "I'm glad you died, you fuck. Coming here, causing all kinds of shit. Fuck you. Glad you're dead."

He shoveled dirt over the limb until the sun couldn't shine on it anymore and threw the shovel at one of the turkey vultures. It hopped and flapped away, but the body wound the bird back in. It kept a wary eye on their friend.

They waited until his footsteps disappeared into the lap of the river and the chirp of birds. Ricky led Liz from the Forts. He scanned for the digger he'd smashed, but the ten-by-ten square patch of disturbed earth remained the only evidence it had stood there. Liz hunched until they reached the blacktop, brick, and the rust of the town, as if her hair would alert Bixby to their presence.

She shoved the license's flat surface into Ricky's belly. "Why would you take me back? Just to get this?"

"I take you back? What you on about? I thought we had

some connection up here," – he tapped his head – "which took us there."

"I followed you."

"You never asked why we crawled about like that. Just got on your knees and went for it. You're the one who found this." He slipped the license from her fingers.

"We should burn it. It's not good. It's just not good. I'm hearing things."

"So you said."

"Bad people are looking for this man. That's all I know. Maybe we should call the cops."

"No way. No. We ignore it and it'll go away."

"You sound like my dad."

"You sound like my ma."

She rubbed her arms. "What do we think about Bixby? Acting all strange and that."

"You reckon he killed the man?"

A laugh spurted from her lips and she backhanded his shoulder. "Are you mad, Ricky-boy? Bixby ... he's thin as a rake. Thinner than you. He can manage his squirrels" – she yucked – "but not somebody that size. No way."

She slipped an arm through one of his. "Burn that thing. And let's not hang around here for a while."

* * *

Ricky's heart burned a whole lot more than the back of his neck. He found a quiet slip behind an abandoned gas station full of dead air and called ma. She asked the usual questions. He palmed her off and headed home. The toy shop hauled him in. He fingered the cash in his pocket and pictured Brett in the dryer. Bit his lip and dropped into his shoulders. The old man at the counter watched him through thick glasses above an open laptop. His deep gray beard would fit in with the reeds and bushes wrapped around the City of Forts.

Ricky shuffled. The shop worked to make him feel out of place – beneath such a store. From outside, the interior appeared dingy, as he guessed a second-hand store would. God knows he'd been in enough of them with ma. It made Ricky's jaw slack now he stood inside at last. Wooden puppets stared at him with arch eyes. *What you doing in here? Did you take a wrong turn? Did you mean to slouch into Burger King to nibble on something from the dollar menu?*

Ricky's open mouth set firm. Caged resentful thoughts behind his teeth. Board games in wooden boxes. Toy soldiers – all hand-painted. A boat large enough to fill the bathtub at home, with detail inside where he imagined little people sat for dinner and danced on a wide dance floor framed by pillars. A little carved man peered from a tiny window. Ricky's heart jumped all over the place. What kid had this kind of toy? What kind of parent would care so much for their children to buy such a wonder? Spotlights shone bright on the toys from above, treasures in a moodily lit cave.

He scrunched the money in his pocket and listened to the whisper. Checked the price tag on the boat – one thousand dollars. A thousand? A thousand? What the fuck? Who could afford such a toy? He wanted to burn it, to smash it against an iceberg, like that stupid ship in that stupid movie ma simpered over so much.

He caught the man's attention. The owner's eyes filled his specs and Ricky knew a wrong move would see him pounce.

"Who can pay for all this, mister?"

The man's eyeballs seemed to balloon over the frames. "People with money, son."

Ricky bristled. *I'm not his son. Why'd he say that?*

"In this town? Who has cash?"

"You ever heard of the internet?"

"Yeah. Obviously."

"I sell most of this stuff there now."

Ricky nodded. They only had the Internet over ma's phone, and she never let him touch the thing. He finger-tipped the soldier in the white clothes. It wore a metal helmet which covered the face. Held a sword high above its head, ready to smash an imaginary skull.

"You buyin' it?"

"Maybe. Thinkin' about it."

"What's the tag tellin' ya?"

Ricky squinted in the low light. The owner lit the place with fake candles and dim wall lights. The price winded him. "Seventy-five dollars? For that?"

"It's handmade, here in America. Hand-painted, too. You're not my market, son."

Ricky had no idea what he meant, but it hit the same as a put-down. "I'll buy it."

"The soldier?"

"Yeah."

The owner rubbed at his bristles. Sounded like sandpaper on a stubborn table in this quiet. "I have key rings. Ten bucks a-piece, but you can have 'em for five."

Ricky snatched the toy from the glass cabinet and marched to the desk. "I want the soldier, sir. Here." He planted the figure on the counter, firm, and counted out the notes. Once he reached the right amount, he shoved the rest back in his pocket and glared at the man. The store owner didn't once examine the money. Left the cash there like it might infect him if he slid it into ownership.

"Take it." Ricky sniffed. "My money's as good as anybody's."

"Your money?"

"What, because I'm from round here, I can't have money? You're from this town, I'm guessin', and you have money."

"I'm not from here, son. Settled in this place a long time ago, but I'm not native. Will move across the river soon so I can open up my new shop and air it out without worry."

"My cash is good. My ma and pa work – and I want this soldier."

The man blinked. "You look a little old to play with soldiers."

"I'm young enough. Thirteen."

"Thirteen, huh? That's old. You're on the cusp of a whole bunch of stuff, son. Why you playing with toys at your ripe age?"

Ricky shuffled. What would Liz say if he carried this thing around? "Why you selling them?"

"Business. I enjoy others playing with them. I don't play with them myself. Stopped that when I was ten, eleven."

"I want it. There's my money. It has a price tag on it. You're peddling, right?"

The man leaned across the counter. Smelled of coffee, and donut crumbs decorated his mustache. "Tell you what. I'm out of here soon. I never sold this toy, though I've had it a while. You can have it – on me."

A bargain, but Ricky cooked a frown which rattled the old man.

"There's a reason I'm not taking your payment, son. I know what this town's become and I'm unsure what's real and what's not these days. Even if I take your word for it, and this is your money, I don't know its source. I'm driving a good deal with you, boy. I give you this toy, and you never grace my store again."

Ricky's frown boiled over the pan and he spat at the man. He stiffened, shocked at his action, and eyed the foam as it rolled down the man's glasses. Snatched the soldier and ran for the door, a wide eye over his shoulder as he spewed back into the street.

* * *

Ricky walked stiff and slump-shouldered, the toy loose in his hand. He shifted the toy tight to his leg, hidden from the cars passing by. Made detours, as always, when he saw people on the sidewalk.

The shock of footsteps behind had his bones all rattled. The gravel crunched and birds fluttered away. Buildings on either side of the secluded path loomed above as though interested in how this played out.

"You went to McGarry's toy store, then?"

Ricky picked up pace and glimpsed back. The man's yellow teeth buzzed radioactive through his sickly smile. His eyes, pinpricks, shone beneath the pulled-down cap. Needled into him.

"What's it to you?" Ricky had seen enough wildlife shows to know you don't run from a grizzly bear. He slowed to a casual rhythm and swung the toy to-and-fro to show he hadn't a care in the world. That the man didn't scare him.

"That place is real expensive. Real expensive. I've been in there."

"Why've you been in there? You got a kid?"

"I have nobody, Ricky. Nobody on this Earth to call my own."

Okay, weird. Time to hit the main streets. The end of this path stood about a hundred yards away. He had to pass long weeds, low branches from unkempt trees, and the empty-eyed windows in the rear of scraggy houses to get there. Stay calm. The man's a man, but his willow-branch arms and broken teeth made Ricky guess he could snap the creep's bones with little sweat.

"So you visit toy stores to hang around kids? Who does that?"

"No need to imply any of that, young fella. I'm out here to protect. This town ain't what it used to be."

Ricky laughed. "You're Batman?" He halted and almost caused the greaseball to flip over him and sprawl across the dirt.

"You leave your brother alone in that house, all day, and you have money to spend in that fancy store. There's not many in this town with deep enough pockets for such a place."

He snatched the toy from Ricky's relaxed hand and batted away his protest. The man had strength, after all. As Ricky pushed and grabbed, he brushed toned muscle beneath the man's long coat. The adult examined the soldier and thumbed its details as if he assessed it for sale. He extended the string and squinted at the tag.

"Seventy-five dollars. That's some money for a boy like you."

"I got it free. The owner gave it to me."

"McGarry is many things, but generous ain't one of them. How'd you steal it? The man can spot an amoeba through those jelly-jar glasses he wears."

Ricky snatched the soldier and shivered. The corpse in the hole. Bixby's strange behavior. Liz sending odd impulses through his body. This stranger. What the hell happened to his summer?

"Stay away from me and my brother." He vaulted a chain fence and didn't crane his neck back for fear it'd slow him down. Darted down Main Street, an alleyway, behind a grocery store, and across a litter-strewn stretch of wasteland until he reached his own road. He snuck over the fence behind his home and unlocked the door.

Trails of cereal led him to Brett, who slept on his bedroom floor, head on his arm. Ricky sat against the wall by him and scratched at mental itches. The kid seemed peaceful, glad of freedom from his older brother. Right? *He doesn't miss me – he misses ma.* Ma should look after him. Instead, she's all obsessed with her jobs. *Sure, they needed food and all, but how much can it cost that she needs to work all the hours?*

He closed his lids just to rest his eyes, but shadows from the sun had shifted across the room when he reopened them and Brett made sword noises as he swished McGarry's toy through the air.

"You got me this, Ricky?"

Ricky had been by that shop so many times. Pained him for years to pass it, unable to run his fingers over the goods. Intended to play with the soldier himself. He sank into the wall and smiled as Brett ran around and pretend-fought a bunch of enemies. One thwack sung off the walls and triggered Ricky to his feet. He jumped on Brett and caged him between his knees. The kid screamed and whooped as Ricky tickled him and brought an imaginary sword down on the kid's head.

"Get off me. Get off."

"I must destroy you."

Ricky laughed at his brother's joy and dug fingers into his ribs. Howls a wolf would own with pride set a neighborhood dog into a barking fit. The door swung wide and ma stood wild-eyed at them. Her stance suggested readiness to swing a disciplinary hand. She softened at their unconstrained giggles. Sat on the bed's edge and dropped a bunch of tears.

Too much. Ricky scrambled from the bed and questioned how much she cared for them.

"You're late."

14

The smell of stale cornflakes settled in Ricky's nostrils next morning as he reached the bottom of the stairs. He yawned until his eyes watered. His brother and ma blurred. He stood still, confused why they both stared at him, his ma's arms folded.

"You're up late. I have to go to work. Maybe you can explain this when I return?"

Her hand swept to the table, index pointed as sharp as the sword held by the soldier. Ricky squeezed his eyebrows. "I found it. In a dumpster. What's the problem?"

She sucked her teeth. "One – you went out without me. Two - you won't talk to me that way."

"You're late for work."

She so wanted to pound him, it made Ricky step back. Her eyes widened with his at the horror of her thoughts. She grabbed her purse and car keys. Brushed past him, mouth a tumble dryer of complaints at him and his father.

Ricky stood by the kitchen window and watched her drive away. Patches of grass withered beneath the sun already, beige and brittle. He scratched at the skin on his neck and inspected the peel. She must have noticed that and the tan. He turned to Brett as the boy mimicked how swords clashed in battle.

The funky, smelly man would visit again today. His brother bounced happy with the toy, busy in a fantasy land. Ricky caught the occasional moment of dread from the kid as he flickered wary eyes at him.

"Get your sneakers on, bro."

The kid's neck shifted backwards and his chin hit his chest. "What?"

"Wha? Wha? Who says 'what?' Put on your sneakers before I change my mind."

"I'm coming out with you?"

"Yeah, you're coming with me. Outside. I'll introduce you to someone."

"Who?"

"Slip your damn sneakers on and I'll tell you."

* * *

Brett jabbered through the streets and back alleys. Ricky diverted him with stories of people Liz told him about, whose kids had left for far-flung places.

"Like where ma works?"

"I think the world's a little bigger than that."

"How big is the world?"

Ricky sighed and plunged both hands into his pockets, despite the heat. "Shut up, Brett."

Ricky charged up splintered steps and banged on the door. Brett asked who lived in this place. Ricky elbowed him to lock his mouth. He knocked again, louder. Some noise made it through the walls, which made his brother shift into Ricky's leg for protection against some dragon's fire. Bolts clunked and a chain slid from its perch. The door creaked open a notch.

Ricky's smile, meant for Liz, dampened at the woman peering through.

"Yes?"

"Is Liz home?"

"No."

He shuffled his feet. Squeezed Brett's arm to reassure him. "Is Mr Panowich home?"

"Who wants him?"

Ricky scanned the street for a man she seemed to expect instead of him. "I do."

"And who's you? Who you with?"

"My brother, here." He pushed the boy into her sight-line and offered a smile he hoped could win a statue's heart.

"You know him?"

"Yeah, course I do. I was here the other night. When you were here. You're Carrie, right?"

"What? How do you know my name?"

"I just told you, I was in this house with Liz. The other night."

A haze smoked her eyes – obscuring whatever the hell sat in her brain. She chewed on memory to spit out anything she could recall beyond the last hour.

"Who is it?" The deep voice from inside rumbled and forced its way outside.

Ricky held Brett's shoulders firm to contain the kid's shakes. Heavy footsteps thudded to the entrance and a grizzled face with cracks round the eyes as encrusted as the town's dry earth stood exposed in the harsh light. He pulled the door wide and grinned. Ricky matched it.

"Well, if it ain't my little Lizzy's boyfriend. What brings you here?"

86

Ricky rattled the boy back and forth. "This, sir, is my brother."

"Sir? Nobody but you's called me that since I rolled steel back in the day. And what's your brother doing here?"

Ricky mooched his eyebrows and lost his grin. "You said you'd look after him?"

The man's laugh exploded all cannon fire and ended in an asthmatic dog's bark. "I can't remember no such thing. What you talkin' about?"

"You did say, Mr Panowich. You were loud and clear." Ricky recognized the whine in his own voice, though he moderated it as well as ma cut the cigarettes blackening her lungs.

Liz' pa scratched his chin and contemplated the sun-dazzled street. The Carrie woman slipped inside, a nudge to his shoulder on her way to encourage a decision. He grumbled and swatted a hand at her jabs and jibes.

"I don't remember any of it, kid. Not a thing –"

"Can you hurry so we can get back to it? Tell them to get lost."

The man rolled his eyes, all friendly, his orbs dancing more in those few seconds than the whole of their previous meeting. "Sure. Bring him inside. I'll show him life. If you can't."

"Oh, I'm able to show him life sir, it's just –"

"You don't have the hours and minutes, son ... I know, I know ... you said that last time." He waved a hand, winked, and retreated to the living room shadows.

Ricky pushed Brett forward. The kid's steps staggered as he dug his heels and toes into the porch's base. Ricky pinched the whine from him before it developed into a full blown protest. Angled his mouth to the side. "It'll be okay, brother. You'll like it. He'll take you fishing and stuff. Come on, try it out."

"I don't wanna. I don't wanna. I wanna go home."

"You don't. You're just ... you're always chicken-cooped inside our house, so you've forgotten what you want. It'll be same as having a dad."

"But we have pa."

"Do we, though? I don't see him around. You either spend the day here with this man, who's a good man, or you go back to the house and spend all day alone."

Brett tightened. Ricky sensed how his belly screwed to the size of a nut. The kid shook his head and restrained his lower lip to a pout. They entered together and opened their eyes wide to capture light. Ricky turned a little dizzy at first – from the aroma as much as transformation from bright to cave-dark. He brushed the feeling away and breathed through his mouth. Brett would enjoy it here. The man, though strange, had molded Liz. Carrie sat on the sofa's edge. Mr Panowich rummaged through a lot of metal in the back.

"Is Liz home?"

"Liz is not home." Carrie's voice shifted from dozy to sharp. "She's off with her boyfriend somewhere."

"I'm her boyfriend."

She snorted. "You're a scrawny little runt. Do you even have pubic hair? She's off with a boy with pubes up to his armpits."

Ricky's eyes rolled as much as a skew-shot bowling bowl. Breath hot in his mouth.

Mr Panowich showed himself, a hand in his mane, the other holding some ornament. He smiled toothy at Brett. "So, little man, you ever shoot a gun?"

15

Shoot a gun – that'd do Brett the world of good. That's what he needs, to fire some bullets. Ricky would love to blast some slugs – right up the ass of Liz's so-called boyfriend. He kicked stones down the street and peered into the toy shop. Still plenty of cash in his pocket and some of those toys tempted him. He'd not played with the soldier since he brought it home, and McGarry would not have forgotten the spit in his eye. So the moment passed, and he booted an empty coke can until it hit the ankle of an old woman, who shook over her walking cane. He'd had his eyes on the pavement for so long that this bit of life startled him. He mumbled "sorry" and ran.

Atlantic Drive, an area of Lego blocks a toddler must have slammed together. The district slumped into its neck to remain unnoticed by outsiders. Ricky stared at Benny Ciaro's home from behind a beat-up truck on the opposite side of the street. The house seemed normal. It stood alone, unlike most of the houses down this road, though you would have to slide sideways between the gap between his home and the next if you took the trip. Same rusted railing down its steps as much of this town, nostril-hair weeds in the cracks around its border. Nobody looked out the windows, and no car sat in the front.

He wristed sweat from his eyes and strained to hear any noise above the air conditioners in the house behind him. He checked his shoulder as if a fly bothered him and jumped at the woman in the window behind. Her face accused him of designs on the shitty truck which blocked, or maybe saved, her view. He read the cusses she mouthed, none diffused by dusty glass and the air conditioner. It all planted his attention on the pavement and he rushed away. Snuck a peek at the house again as he reached the street corner. Ciaro's front door opened and Ricky hopped behind the wall. Spied round the edge. The white man wore bushy hair which dangled in strands, tarantula legs ready to pounce. Even from this distance, the man's muscles popped in his tight Under Armour shirt, antennas looking for a hint of trouble.

Ricky grabbed the gasp before it cannoned out of his mouth and scurried from view. Recognized him. He'd beaten up that poor man down the alley. Ricky shuffled further down the wall. The man's feet clacked along the sidewalk, louder it seemed to Ricky than the couple of cars crackling by. The noise bounced off the houses until he couldn't tell which direction they headed. He sat low against the brick beneath the shade of a small tree, ten-or-so yards from the walkway, and clutched fistfuls of grass. If the man noticed him, he'd see only a young kid at play. The beast prowled down the pavement. Headed to that black BMW with the ultra-polished rims, parked up on the pavement. He glanced at Ricky, but moved on. Ricky, a clump of grass in his hand, pulled in relief. The rip from the soil made the man stand still, twist his neck, and coil towards him.

Shit.

Attention locked on Ricky. Purposeful steps toward him. Ricky scanned the fences and alleyways in search of crevices too big for the man to penetrate. He squinted up at him, the adult's head haloed by the sun, hair a tangle of tree branches. The scruff attempted to fire some warmth out of his eyes, but they pierced him cold.

"Not seen you round here before, kid."

"Nah. I'm passing through."

"Where you from?"

"Other end of town. Just passing through."

"You said." He leaned a hand on the wall above Ricky. Crowded him. His cologne caught Ricky's throat, so he had to clear it. "What you doing this side of town?"

"I just said, sir. I'm passing through."

"Passing through to where? Nobody passes through this place. People circumnavigate the hole."

"Sir, I don't mean no disrespect –"

"I feel some disrespect heading my way, anyway."

Ricky pushed against the wall and pulled his feet back. "In no sense, sir. But it's my business. I don't know you."

"And your ma told you never to talk to strangers, right?"

Ricky nodded, claustrophobic in this man's body-cave.

"You know anyone on this street?"

Ricky shook his head, the swivels emphatic. Sat on his hands to hide the shakes.

"Do you know Benny Ciaro?"

He hoped his negative response didn't look rehearsed. He should have thought about the name, bit his lip, eyed the sky for a moment, and then burned into his eyes, all sincere, and tell him no.

"Never heard of him."

"Is that right?"

Ricky primed himself to lunge for that fence over there. It had a gap big enough to squirm through. This man, though slim and packed, would have to smash his way to the other side. He'd suffer splinters from the effort. Slow him right down. It's what Ricky wanted to do, but here's the kind who would hunt him across all barriers. As awkward as he felt, he set his teeth together and endured.

"Because it seems to me, boy, that you were hiding behind this wall. Watching things. Weighing up events. A kid who passes through doesn't sit against no wall like this."

"I'm just resting, sir. I'm out exploring the town. That's all."

"No school?"

"It's summer, sir."

"Cut the sir shit, kid. You ain't got Benny's olive skin, so you ain't family. You work for somebody who wants to deal with Benny? I don't know. But you run ahead now, and watch yourself. Got it?"

"I never met a Benny, but I got it."

The man stepped back and Ricky turned from the sun's glare. Used the wall to push himself up. Straightened his t-shirt, plunged hands into his pockets, and walked. Casual as he could muster, despite the fire in his chest. His neck muscles twitched to turn and see if he followed his tracks, but he kept his eyes ahead to the empty hardware store and the man at the gas station.

* * *

Out by the strip mall, near Liz' home, Ricky shot to the

doorway of a vacant lot at some motorbike's growl. Tarantula Man put jumping beans into his bones and now Ricky peered round the doorway's alcove at the noise's source. The man on the bike seemed late-teens, early twenties. Wore a tight t-shirt to show off muscles. Strapped a Stars and Stripes bandana around his thick skull. Shades made a fly of his face. Another rev reverberated across the blacktop and rumbled through Ricky. A girl skipped out of the shop, in shorts and sleeveless t-shirt, red hair in a ponytail. Ricky's eyes narrowed to dagger-slits at how she hopped onto the back of his motorcycle and wrapped her arms around the biker's waist. Ricky rubbed at his palms and stared after them as the biker roared onto the road and beat the red light.

What the fuck?

* * *

Ricky climbed a white oak to rise above his frustrations. The bark scratched and branches bashed his head in his haste to get high as possible. He settled on a limb overlooking the City of Forts. The whitewashed homes and green boughs of trees calmed him somewhat, but sudden rushes of anger almost toppled him from his perch. How could she? She's fourteen. He's a man. What's she thinking?

Bixby bashed about the bushes in the distance with a stick he held like a rifle. Made machine gun noises and rattled his body as if he fired live rounds and the kickback shook him all up. Ricky snorted as Bixby crouched for cover and threw himself into the long grass as an imaginary grenade blew him to pieces. They'd play like this together sometimes – him, Liz, and Bixby. Seemed stupid from up here.

Ricky laughed and rat-a-tatted a few cusses. "Loser." He itched to join in with his friend, but Liz' comment about Bixby's possible role in Ciaro's death kept him still.

A steel gray car pulled up by the half-busted gate which blocked the old road to the abandoned houses. A woman, hair as red as Liz', stepped out business-like and scoured the area through binoculars. Could have been bird-watching. Some geeks enjoy that. Might have been hunting for a lost dog. The only dogs round here crossed these fields from bordering households, not from the overgrown entrance. Nobody, apart from those bastard Ghost Boys, set foot in this wasteland. It must remind people of past glories their present couldn't stomach.

Bile stirred in his belly. Another invader crossing the border to their sanctuary. What did this outsider want? She ducked through a gap in the metal gate and drew a red mist over Ricky. He lurched off the branch down to the next, and the next, until he recognized the woman as Miss Veronica. She swung her binoculars at the disturbance and saw him. She stared hard. Skinny frame, about the same size as Bixby, but less wiry than his friend. She turned and slithered back into her car. Ricky jumped to another branch to warn Bixby, lost his grip near the bottom in his hurry, and slipped. He hit his head on the last branch and fell on his shoulder. Passed out.

16

The pinch in Ricky's shoulder woke him. He blinked away the glue from his dried tears and circled his joints. Jerked himself to a seated position, but the rustle in the undergrowth sent him low again. He chewed the inside of his mouth at the sun's dip below the horizon. Brett. Mr Panowich. Ma.

Black hooded shapes outlined against the dark sky, mountains on the move, their feet hard across baked earth. They marched, as they did around Town, as an army unit on drill, in pairs and focused on their goal to intimidate. As soon as they passed, Ricky rolled over and jumped to his haunches. They'd see his white t-shirt if he didn't take precautions, even with bark from the white oak dimming the glare. He padded over to the next tree and dug his nails into it's bark, peeking from behind. He couldn't make out much detail, and he couldn't tell if they headed for the houses or the factory.

What did they want here, in his place of escape? Had they killed Ciaro and returned for the body? Come to beat Ricky into tomato soup? His instinct pushed him to backpedal. Ma would have the phone in her hand, fingers all over nine-one-one. Mr Panowich headed into a world of trouble. All because Ricky fucked up. Again.

But ...

Bixby's down there, unaware of the approaching danger. Might never find out. Ricky pivoted from backpedal to lunge, into the woods skirting the fields, growing like hair up the dragon's back of a hill. A light whooshed from a stick. Fire. He dashed from tree to tree, sweating as multiple torches sparked. Like one of those medieval movies where monks haunted damp corridors below crackling torches.

They wanted Ricky. Hadn't discovered where he lived, so here they tramped. But why this time of day? They must know he'd not come out here in the dark. Yet, here he ran, his eyes on them in the night. He crouched low and dug out the ancient phone. Cupped the light and checked time.

9.45pm? *Oh, God, save me from the hell I shall pay.* He muttered half-a-dozen apologies at the missed calls and voicemails from ma and Liz. Liz could do one, but his ma and Brett ...

He switched off the cell and ducked and weaved until he came out of the woods again on the river-side of the houses. Vaulted the steps from the backyard with light feet and opened the screen door slow enough to dampen the creak. It moaned – loud as the alarm of a bat in the night's still air. He dragged breath through his nose and slipped inside. Hands along the wall guided him through the rooms until he made it to the front where Bixby slept. A floorboard complained, and a flashlight drew towards the house.

"Don't move, shithead."

Ricky sucked his teeth at the sharp point pricking his neck. "It's me, shitbrain."

"What you doing here? Are you with those mothers?"

It hurt Ricky to work his jaw or shake his head. He grasped

Bixby's fingers and guided the weapon away from his throat. A flash of light came through the window. Exposed the threat for a second – a sharpened stick. Why not use the knife he'd carved it with? Another flicker lit up squirrels' heads and blood streaks on the table. He balked at the sick-sweet stink of death.

Bixby knuckled Ricky's chest. "Are you with them?"

"Why question me like that? I saw them headed this way and had to warn you. Let's sneak out, fast."

"I knew you couldn't be. Knew it. Come on, we need to get out of here."

"Well – yeah."

They edged out through the route Ricky had entered and froze at how a lighter sparked and lit a torch. The man in the hood, a black pit where his face should sit, shimmered behind the light. Another torch to his left kindled bright, and another and another until a row of six, seven, several others semi-circled the back yard and trapped them both. Bixby wrapped a hand around Ricky's skinny wrist and raced to the front door. They recoiled at the man in the opening, his flame outstretched ahead of his body as if he warded off a snake. He stamped a foot forward, and the boys tumbled over each other in fright.

"Never come back." The figure stood at the door's side for them to pass, like a supernatural guardian to some treasure they'd disturbed.

Both scrambled out and flailed for balance at the gunshots whizzing past their ears. Neither had an idea which direction they headed until the river's scent steadied their internal compasses. They rumbled over uneven ground and tangled themselves in reeds of grass.

The cell shook in Ricky's hands. Bixby slapped it free from his grip.

"No police. Alright?"

Ricky stared at him, at the moon eyes which must mirror his own. He nodded and rubbed at his neck. Made spider legs of his fingers until he found the phone and switched on the light. Shadows stretched bony fingers across the fields, deforming their imaginations, but the rotten foot sticking out the ground had nothing to do with tricks of the mind.

"Damn it." Bixby crawled and reburied the limb. Ricky couldn't understand how his friend didn't cover his nose at the smell. Lifted the t-shirt over his own nostrils. A shot thudded nearby. Its twin missed them by a few feet at most. They ran again. Bixby hissed at him to turn off the damn glare. Ricky organized his fingers and darkness enveloped them. Provided a lot more comfort than the violent shapes the phone's flashlight threw around. They smothered their breathing until the fire in their lungs dimmed to a pilot light.

"You alright?" Ricky nudged Bixby.

"You never have to worry about me. I can look after myself."

"I won't bring you any more sandwiches, then. Eat squirrels all day, every day if you want."

Bixby formed Tanais' name on his lips, but wiped her away with his forearm and shrugged. Ricky saw the struggle in his moonlit eyes.

They scooched low, their heads bobbing like buoys in the sea. Two Ghost Boys guarded, as far as they could see, the front door, while others carried a rectangular container down the path and into the house.

"Is that a coffin?" Bixby raised himself a little higher.

Ricky pulled at his arm to hide the target he'd become.

"Another body? Nah ..."

"Why not?"

"Because – that's why."

"Well-argued."

Ricky snorted. "Because they'd have killed us. They see us around. If they murdered a man, they'd have wiped us out, too."

"They killed the other one."

"Ciaro? We don't know that." The bullets rattled his core, if not his flesh, but how they missed convinced him they'd sent a warning. Tarantula Man – what did he want with Ciaro?

"We do know that. Who else, Ricky-boy?"

Ricky side-eyed him for how he mocked the lover-talk from Liz. He shrugged. "They don't belong here. This is our place. How do we get them out?"

"Maybe we kill them all? Who'd miss them?"

"You can gut a squirrel, Bixby, but no way can you handle these big boys."

"You'd help me. Slit their throats in the dark and bleed them out."

Ricky glared at him, the whites of his friend's eyes as cold as stars. The Ghost Boys' company took on sudden warmth. "Don't talk like that, freak."

Bixby shrugged. "They need to go, or I need a new bed tonight."

"Then come home with me. I'm sure ma will let you sleep on the couch."

"Can I use your shower?"

"I can ask. I just got to butter her up – I'm in deep shit."

17

Ricky rushed to Liz', halting a hundred yards from her house. Dim lights shone a jaundiced yellow across her and Brett, his brother ten-or-so steps ahead as if she had him on a lead. Ricky puffed out his chest and marched towards them. Liz would try to deflate him.

"Where've you been, Ricky? Jesus."

"I ... I'll tell you later. Let me get this one home."

"You better, before the cops come sniffing round my home. What were you thinking, leaving him with my dad?"

"Why, what's the problem?"

"Nothing – just don't do it again."

"You had a good day? Not seen you at all."

"Get your brother where he belongs."

"See you tomorrow?"

"Probably not."

He nodded, curt, and jerked his brother's arm to follow him. Brett shook him off and ran ahead, Ricky cursing and chasing until it all snipped his willpower. Checked his shoulder, but Liz turned her back to him, arms folded, mind on that dick on the motorbike.

"Wait up, Brett."

"I'm tired. I want to go to bed."

"You can't just charge through these streets, brother."

"Why not?"

"'Cause there are snakes in the grass."

Brett brushed his hand through clumps escaping cracks in the sidewalk. "There's no snakes here."

"It's a saying, Brett." He clamped the tut down. "You have a good time with Mr Panowich?"

He nodded. The smile broadened, genuine. "We went fishing. I know how to fire a gun."

"Fishing? Where'd you go fishing?" His moment with Tarantula Man and the Ghost Boys fuzzed into ancient memory.

"The river. We caught a beast, Mr Panowich said."

"And the gun?"

"Yeah. It was loud. Really loud. And hurt my shoulder."

"Right."

Ricky kicked at loose stones and litter. He'd missed out. Next time, he'd hang out with Liz' old man. Mr Panowich wouldn't mind.

"Can I go again tomorrow?"

"We'll see."

"Ahh, come on. It was fun."

"We'll see. Let me do the talking when we get home."

Brett battled his eyelids. Ricky crouched for him to jump on his back and they zig-zagged through alleys. Jumped out of his flesh at the odd tire screech and gunshot in the distance. Ma sat on the porch, back rod-straight, hands worrying each other. Ricky guessed fingernails made tracks in her thighs. She exploded to her feet once she saw them. Staggered down the steps, drunk with worry, and sprinted down the road to greet them. He'd never seen her run so fast. She never watched sport on TV and never hung colors from a mast. Except the old Stars and Stripes, which fluttered, all weary, in the breeze.

One hand darted to her mouth and the other to her younger boy. "What happened? Oh my God, what happened?"

"Nothing." Ricky squirmed Brett off his back into her arms. He'd fallen asleep. A soft snore escaped him. Ricky wound the ache from his shoulder and scratched the lump on his head.

"Nothing? You took him outside – all night. For what reason?"

Mr Walters stood silhouetted in his window to see the fuss. Ma ushered Ricky up the driveway and through the back door. He slumped at the table, exhausted. The bump drummed ma's words away. She backed into the door and rested against it, eyes all kinds of punctuations.

"I need more than nothing, son. I demand an explanation."

* * *

He propped his head on an arm and tapped the tabletop to every heavy footstep ma made upstairs. The smack of her lips on Brett's forehead forced him straight and the thud she created downstairs set him off to the fridge. He rummaged through cartons and jars and plastic boxes of curled salad to get to the week-old lasagna. Shoved what remained in the microwave. The buzz coincided with ma's first words. He screwed his face and mouthed a "wha-?" She marched to the microwave and opened it.

"Ma – I'm hungry."

"Where'd you go? Where'd you take him?"

"Just around. Nowhere special. Time got away from us, that's all." He pushed the microwave door shut again, but she slapped his hand from the handle.

"I've got this knot in my stomach which has twisted so hard I'm ready to vomit. I had no idea ..." She ignored the sneer on his face, or tried to. He'd never curled his lips at her this way. "You cannot leave the house when I'm gone. You can't."

"Why? I feel like a chicken in here, all day looking after him."

She laughed, the sound of a sticky finger across a balloon. "Take some responsibility. You're thirteen."

"Me? Take responsibility? What about you, ma?"

"I work my ass off for you. For you both. I'm ... I'm up to here with responsibility. And I'm exhausted."

Ricky turned from the tear that escaped her unwilling eye, as if it washed his argument away. "I'm sorry, ma. I just wanted to get outside. You keep us locked up here all day. I can't breathe."

"I asked him – "

"Asked who? Asked what?"

"Your brother. Who else?"

"Oh."

She wouldn't wipe the wet from her face. Saw its value against him. "I asked him where you both went." Folded her arms and watched for shifts and fidgets. Ricky attempted to heat his lasagna again. She shooed him away. "This is too old. It'll upset your stomach."

"I'm hungry." His stomach did hurt. He'd not eaten or drunk much all day.

"I'll make you mac'n'cheese ... Do you know what he said?"

"Said? Who said? Who said what?"

"Don't try cute with me. Your brother said nothing." She nodded at Ricky's surprise. "Yeah – not a thing. You understand the influence you have over that kid? He adores you. And with that comes a lot of responsibility."

"I'm not his daddy."

"No. You're a bunch better than his daddy. Because you're here doing all the looking-after. But you worry me."

"You don't need to worry."

"I have every need to worry. Such as – where did you get this thing from? Did you steal it?"

Damn. He'd forgotten the toy. It stood on ma's mystery novel – which she'd had on the go all his life. The soldier's broken arm dangled by a thread. Brett had ruined the thing already. Ungrateful little bastard. Ricky would have guarded the plaything with pa's guns if someone gave it to him. The toy's still good limb reached out for ma's attention. Why'd he bought the damn thing?

"I found it."

"Don't lie to me, Ricky. Don't. It has a price tag on it."

"I'm not lying. It was in the dumpster behind McGarry's toy shop. He must have thrown it out because it's bust."

"McGarry's? All the way downtown? When did you go down there?"

* * *

Ma dragged the curtain across the rail. He covered his ears at the screech and flipped his torso from the sun's glare, burying his face in the pillow. Dribbled some protest, his grunting having no effect on his ma.

"Get your scrawny ass outta bed, young man. We have work to do."

"Work?" He crowbarred an eye open despite sleep's best

effort to keep it glued shut.

"Yes. Work. I'm not having you turn into what most men in this town have become. Get up." She dragged the thin sheet to the floor. He clawed at it to cover himself, but he'd lost. "Get up." She backhanded his thigh. He shot up.

"Okay, okay. I'm up. What's the problem?"

"Out of bed. Now. Get your brother ready and eat some breakfast."

"What we doing?"

"I'll tell you in good time. You've five whole minutes to get by the front door."

He stared at the carpet until her last step downstairs. Made it to his feet, creaky enough to kindle pity from an arthritic old man. Stared out the window until he couldn't handle the day's bright welcome.

He small-stepped into Brett's room and yanked the kid's arm. Pulled until Brett edged to the bed's end, flailing at his brother. Mr Panowich would take both of them fishing tomorrow instead of today. Liz could join them if she fancied. Otherwise, she could fuck off with that perv on the bike.

"Ricky, whatyer doin'?"

"Time to rise and shine."

"Nooo. Too early."

"Get up. Ma wants us ready. Now."

"Is she taking us somewhere?"

Ricky shrugged. "Come and brush your teeth."

He stood guard behind Brett as he brushed. Watched him in the mirror. The kid worked his teeth way too hard. Had a funny tooth which stuck out. Other kids would bully him when he went back to school. Ricky bristled at the thought. Ran his fingers through Brett's hair to straighten the kinks.

"Ma knows you were out all night."

He nodded, enthusiastic. "Aha. She asked. With Mr Panwitch."

"Panowich, you jerk."

"Don't call me bad words. I'll tell on you."

"And you'll never see Mr Panowich again if you do." He bent to whisper in Brett's ear. "You tell ma you stayed with me all day. We just played around town. We climbed some trees. That's all we did. Got it?"

The kid spat his toothpaste and rinsed it down the plug hole. Scowled at Ricky through the mirror. "Yeah. Whatever you want."

"Don't say it in that tone. I'm protecting your interests."

"What's that mean?"

"I'm looking after you. That's all I do."

They ate in silence as ma wiped dishes and glared at the road. Brett poked the soldier and Ricky tapped the boy's shins with his toes in despair at how the kid ruined the toy already.

"Okay, stand up, both of you. Let me inspect."

They scraped the chairs and slouched to their feet. Ricky pulled at his white shirt collar. "Why we wearing our church clothes?"

"Because you've got some repenting to do."

* * *

Ricky rode shotgun and rode bumps as the beat-up old Datsun dropped in and out of potholes. Its suspension gave up a generation-or-so ago. Ma drove distracted and saw none of the road's hazards. Ricky fought the trembles at this meet-and-apology session with Mr McGarry.

"I sometimes wonder ... I ... I just sometimes wonder why I even bother. I might as well drive us all off the bridge into the river. Save everyone from this bullshit, day-in and day-out."

Ricky shuffled in his seat. Saw in every pothole a mouth ready to feed on them. Rubbed at the quiver in his stomach. Wanted to say something nice but couldn't form a word, never mind a sentence.

"If it's not you boys, it's your damn father. And Johnson, that son-of-a-bitch ..."

Ricky swiveled to check Brett. The boy had eyes on the sky. Ricky reckoned its blue transported his thoughts to the water and Mr Panowich, because contentment played on his lips. His own family? Why think of them when it conjured days imprisoned inside?

"Who's Johnson?"

"Some guy at work." She sighed. "A nobody."

Ma wore herself out the last couple of years. She wore her hair tight, almost so it stretched her wrinkles smooth, and the odd spot erupted where she worried her skin. He reached over and squeezed her hand. Let go, glad and embarrassed at the same time. He stared ahead but caught her confusion. She jerked the wheel to avoid a gash in the road, hit another, and swerved the next enough for him to grab the handle above the door as his ass slid over the seat.

"Sorry, boys. I'm sorry."

Ricky sensed the apology meant more than the crazy driving.

"No worries." He cleared his throat.

The car chugged and gabbled in protest at events until the engine cut and it rolled to a stop.

"Shit." Ma's eyes circled big in disbelief. She threw can-you-believe-it glances at Ricky and Brett, slammed the steering wheel, grabbed it tight, and rocked until the Datsun creaked like a sinking boat.

"Gas? Are you kiddin' me?" She slumped as if this defeat lost her the war. Cars honked and sidled by. Some drivers pinpointed an object in the distance to avoid eye contact with her. Some flipped the finger. Who'd want to stop here to help anyone? Ricky didn't know if he would. Houses with rusty chain fences ran down one side of the road, some abandoned to raccoons, dogs, and homeless people. On the other side, old factories sat silent and glum. You wouldn't get out of your car round here unless somebody forced you out at gunpoint.

He pulled the door handle, but ma's intake of breath made him pause. Her piercing eyes made him pay attention. "You stay here. In the car. I need to go find a gas station and buy a canister to get us by. Lock the doors and shut the windows."

"But it's hot. We'll toast in here."

Brett sandwiched his face between both hands. "Maaa."

"It's okay, son. There's one not far away. I shouldn't be too long."

She crept out as if snipers lay in wait for her, and marched down the street. Ricky wound all four windows down and rested an elbow in the gap. He watched an old man let his dog pee up a lamppost, and some girl hold a book to her chest as she strode along with some hope in her head. He snorted. Not in this part of the world, lady. Ricky knew little about other towns. He saw many a sign say "Welcome to this Town, Welcome to that Town," but they all slid into each other like rusted girders. Had no idea where one started and another began. The girl wore a short-sleeved white shirt with buttons. Fancy. Sort of thing Liz sometimes wore when she didn't want to get down and dirty with the boys. Always reminded him of her sex, because sometimes he forgot. Sometimes, did Liz forget? She draped herself in nicer stuff more and more these days. For that ass, no doubt.

Ma, whose hope had drained and diverted into people like this girl, trooped round the bend and out of sight. He couldn't remember any gas station on the journey here, but he had paid little attention. He snatched glances at parts of the neighborhood. The hopeful girl, the man made of string who walked the street same as a nervous bird, the pinched eyes of passing drivers. Ricky grabbed at objects in the car to hold against the coming doom.

"Fuck, ma. You're ..."

"Fuck." Brett laughed and Ricky spun to silence him. Brett opened his mouth and the small *o* expanded to uppercase. Traffic stretched long from the red light at the road's end and shifted as quick as a lazy dog's tail. A BMW pulled up beside them. The driver stared at the red in the distance, hands tight on the wheel as they'd been on the poor man down the alley. His hair dangled – twisted rope which could strangle him. Ricky slid down the seat. Mistake. It attracted his attention. Tarantula Man's glance turned into a stare, which crystallized into recognition, though it seemed he couldn't place Ricky. This day's heat competed with the furnace Ricky generated from the pit of his stomach. The light switched to green, the line advanced, and the man eyeballed him until a horn forced him forwards.

"Jesus." Ricky gulped at air and beat his chest to bring him back to life. Beat harder as Tarantula Man pulled in at the curb, twenty yards ahead. Ricky leaned across the driver's seat and wound up the windows. Couldn't quite tell from this distance, but he guessed the man watched him through his rearview.

Tarantula Man opened the door when traffic thinned, so slow it seemed an hour flew by before a foot emerged. The man hauled himself out, a gym rat's perfect exit. He shuffled around his car. Heeled his door shut and lounged against the vehicle. Flipped a carton and slid out a cigarette. Grabbed the stick from the packet with his lips, and lit. Lifted his chin as if he needed to slide fish down his neck as he took that long drag. Twisted his head to stare as he pumped smoke out of his nostrils.

Ricky scrambled to wind all the other windows shut.

"I'm hot, Ricky. Really hot."

"I know, bro. Tough it out a while, yeah?"

"But –"

"I'll make it up to you, I promise. Just hold out."

Ricky wanted his ma to charge back and intimidate the scary monster into his hole. He was always reluctant to seek her help, but panic set in now. He'd fought the Ghost Boys, but this man towered above them all. In a different league.

Tarantula Man's first step rippled the sidewalk slabs and rumbled until the buildings shook and the lampposts swayed. That, or his bones, quaked and his eyes wobbled. Ricky couldn't say if the man walked, or his spider hair carried him forwards. He saw only his body's upper half above the rim of the dashboard. Slid back up the seat to avoid foolishness. Ensured he'd locked the all doors. Picked out a scrawl of graffiti on the factory over the road to keep his eyes occupied. He couldn't make out what the scribble told the world, but the time to decipher had arrived. A rap on the pane, even though expected, jolted him into reality. The man crouched, hands on thighs, cigarette drooping from his lips.

"Who's that man?"

"I don't know, Brett, I don't know."

"Wind the window down." The man's hair swayed in the breeze. Could hypnotize Ricky if he stared long enough.

Brett shuffled. Ricky pretended he didn't understand what he said. Sweat soaked his hair, forehead, armpits and pants. Sat in a pool of panic and hoped his bladder wouldn't contribute to the swampy brew. He shrugged his shoulders and screwed his eyebrows.

The man made a winding motion and rapped the window again. Ricky shook his head and turned back to the graffiti. Deciphered a W and an N. That had to be an E. Couldn't tell because his stomach pulled in a ton of concrete and bile. Rumbled it all together. The man fisted the car's roof and made tortured violin strings of Brett's crying. Ricky faced the intruder and ensured his lips read easy. "I can't open the door to strangers. Sorry."

"You know me. I saw you yesterday. Who are you? What connects you to Benny Ciaro? How the fuck do you know him?"

"Rickkky ... where's ma?"

"She's coming. Stay cool, Brett, stay cool." Ricky fought the chatter in his teeth. Clamped his jaw tight to avoid contagion to his brother. The man slammed a palm on the roof and headed back to his car. He popped the trunk and rummaged. Ricky would start the car and drive if ma hadn't taken the keys. Ah – no gas. They sat on a slight incline, enough to roll the Datsun if he could push the stick into neutral. Ma always complained about this auto. If he smashed it through the man and his motor, she wouldn't mind too much.

Tarantula Man drew an iron bar out of the trunk and weighed it in a palm. Let it swing by his side as he pounded toward them. Ricky yelped, unbuckled his belt, and scrambled to the driver's side. He yanked at the stick to get it into neutral, but the damn thing didn't budge. Brett craned his neck and rocked the booster seat in the hope he could eject himself from the situation. The car swayed with the frantic movements of both children. Ricky's clammy hands slipped on the stick. His arms ran slick and failed to clear away the drench from his eyes. The man inserted the bar into the crack at the door's edge and wrenched. The door creaked and moaned, but didn't give. His exertions dripped from the tip of his nose. The sun bounced off the sheen on his forehead. He slapped the window and Ricky dodged backwards, despite the barrier. Brett entered scream mode. Eyes wide, face melted plastic. Cars drove on by. The odd driver bent a neck, others pretended events by the lights and beyond had more importance. Nobody stopped. Why would they? The man wore a vest, his tattoos the sleeves down his arms. Skulls, daggers, a rose ... a hooded ghost.

Tarantula Man had eyes Ricky feared would burn through the glass, enabling him to grab his shirt and drag him through the window. As much as those hateful pinpricks would chisel scars into Ricky's dreams, he couldn't help but stare into them. He became lost, hauled into the man's inner being in a swirl of violence and servitude. Until Tarantula Man twirled the bar and readied it to shatter the window, then dropped as if beneath the wheels of ma's car. The iron bar rung out as it hit the sidewalk and held its tone for hours – minutes at least. Another man appeared, bent outside his door, raised a fist, piston-like, and hammered it hard into whatever remained of Tarantula Man.

Brett's scream pivoted to a laugh, and he rocked to position himself for a better view. Ricky levered himself to his knees and angled himself so he didn't need to open the window.

17

Tarantula Man splattered against the sidewalk, on his front, face turned sideways to the factory wall. Out cold. This new man sat on the attacker's back, hands in the stiff's pockets. He pulled a wallet, checked a few cards, and shuffled the money. Hundreds and fifties. A couple of singles at the end. Slid the gun from the back of the man's pants. Threw it into the litter-strewn bushes. Ricky maneuvered to read the man's thoughts, his eyes half-hidden beneath the beak of his grungy cap and lank hair. Liz called this man Ricky's guardian angel when he told her about him. Ricky wound down the window, hot air hitting him fresh compared to the dead heat inside. Brett froze at the gap, scared Ricky opened a tiger's cage.

Ricky hung his hand out of the car and tap-tapped the car's side. "Where did you come from?"

"My name's Floyd. I'm everywhere. Have eyes in the back of my head and a nose on the bottom of my feet."

Brett mewled. "Ewwww."

He, Floyd, shoved the money into his long coat, stood, and dragged Tarantula Man to the rough patch by the sidewalk. Left him amongst gravel and litter. Floyd wiped his hands on his pants to add to the mix and pulled his cap lower.

"This gentleman is called Michael Trent – according to his driver's license. You should keep an eye out so I don't have to."

"Why do you have to? Why you watching me?"

"I'm watching you all. You're good kids, despite your occasional rudeness. There's sewage in this town, and I'd like to clean it up. Keep the good folks good." He tipped his cap and headed down the street towards the traffic light, Trent's crowbar in his hand. Drivers from a line of cars gawped at him the same as Ricky, some with camera phones aimed at him. Horns honked once the novelty wore off, and the boys stared at this Michael Trent, nervous he'd wake up to start their horror all over again. Ricky wiped his drenched hair back and scrambled backwards into the passenger seat as ma filled his view, as sudden as Floyd before her.

"Ma. Jeez."

"Maaaa."

She leaned forwards on her thighs, breathing hard from carrying the can, her eyes dots below exclamation mark eyebrows. "What the hell happened here?" Her ponytail had loosened. Candy floss strands lifted in the air.

"Ricky?" She ran a hand down the marks on the door. Turned her neck to the man in the rough. "Son?"

"Get in the car, ma. Come on ... before he wakes up."

18

Ma poured gas into the car, stowed the can in the trunk, glared between the man and her sons, and kicked the Datsun into a splutter. It complained as much as an old donkey carrying kids along the beach, but it found its rhythm. Ricky rolled his ass as they halted at the red light. Tarantula Man – Michael Trent – balanced on his knees, a hand on the back of his head. He checked his surroundings, rubbed his temple, and bobbed like a predator. Ricky slunk down in case this Michael Trent eyes used auto-target technology.

Ma made a slingshot out of the junction and round the bend once the light turned green. Ricky preferred her dark scowl over Tarantula Man's.

"Either of you gunna tell me what happened?"

Brett rocked in the back. "He was hitting our car, ma. He got this big metal stick and tried to get in. Ricky wouldn't wind the window down and the man turned all angry."

"What the hell? What did he want? Did he say?" Her voice sounded like tires screeching.

"He said he knew Ricky. And someone called Benny Cartio?"

Ricky almost corrected the last name, but stopped himself.

"Benny Cartio? Who is Benny Cartio?"

"Dunno, ma." Ricky frowned and pursed his lips to manufacture confusion. "He thought I was this Cartio."

"Nah, Ricky, he wanted to know how you knew him."

"No, Brett, he said I was him."

"No –"

"Yes."

Ricky's tone shut the boy down. He sensed how Brett bristled at the untruth, but the kid folded at his older brother's power.

"The man was mad. Crazy. Thought I was someone he wanted to kill. I'm scared, ma. Real scared."

She shot out a hand and held his tight. Let go and swung it backwards to squeeze Brett's outstretched hand, too. "It's okay, boys." Her free foot tapped. "How the hell did he end on the sidewalk, unconscious?"

"Some man, some stranger, caught him off guard. Knocked him out. It was sweet – you should have seen it. I didn't even see him coming. He came from nowhere, like some superhero. Ma, it was crazy. Scared me for real at first. Thought he was with the crazy one, but he slammed him over, sat on him, and punched his lights out."

Ma's mouth opened wide at the shock of it all. "This is why you stay indoors. Ricky, this isn't a town to wander. You understand?"

He nodded. "Yes, ma."

"I mean it. A whole bag of deadbeats and drug addicts. Which means it's full of bad folk who sell their junk. You're not safe out here."

"I can go out sometimes, right?"

She licked the edge of her upper teeth. Understood she had a tiger for a son who'd turn nuts if kept indoors. "Never again while I'm at work. And under my supervision or a friend's parents when I'm home ... Shit."

"What?"

"I'm late for work."

"You gunna lose your job?"

"No. I'm never late. Haven't been for months. I'll be okay. That asshole Johnson wouldn't dare ... I wanted you to say your apologies to Mr McGarry for stealing his goods."

Ricky's mind raced at how he'd get out of trouble when they met Toy Man McGarry.

"Did you really find the toy in his garbage?"

Ricky nodded, all persuasive.

"We should call the police about that man back there. Make some statement." She puffed her cheeks. "Though what's the point? They never did anything about your father ..."

Ricky grabbed her hand this time. She rubbed a thumb over his fingers. Weather-stained buildings and part-empty strip malls blurred by. He wound the window down to compensate for the faulty air conditioner. Town smelled of long-stored cardboard and fried food. The pitter-patter of relief tingled across his scalp when he noticed the familiar landmarks close to home. The Seven-11, the faded mosaic on an attractive brick building, the shutters on the closed pharmacy, and the fields in the distance where his City of Forts harbored an invasion force. Ma had forgiven him. Believed his story about the toy soldier and Michael Trent. Would she entertain Bixby in their home?

19

Ricky dropped Brett at Liz' for a happy Mr Panowich to entertain. Liz grunted on her way down the stairs. Had no intention of opening her eyes, never mind running around the City of Forts. He could have dragged Brett back into his company, but the kid jabbered to Liz' pa about the events to come and Ricky didn't crave drama. Didn't want to spend a day with Mr Panowich, after all. He smelled of damp basement.

Ricky ran the fields' perimeter, past the ruined houses and the factory until he reached the river beyond their usual haunt. The day already stuck its grease to him so he shook off his sneakers, pants and t-shirt, and paddled in the river. Blinked at the sun's glint off the water and released the knot tangling his insides. Ma should buy him a bike. He'd get around much quicker.

The morning sun primed to scorch the Earth again, so he waded deeper until water lapped at his neck. His teeth chattered from the cold, but he hoped to thaw, slow, throughout the day. The City of Forts sat peaceful, the green stains on the white sidings invisible from distance. He imagined it one of those ideal European villages framed on Grandma's wall that time he visited.

"You alright, son?"

Ricky splashed as if snakes wrapped his ankles. The boat had floated, silent, from the blind side. The man, a tree trunk, sat straight. A reeled-in fishing rod rested over his leg. His son lounged beside him, eyes half-closed from sleepiness and a signal for other people not to bother him. His rod leaned against the boat's rim, unused. He swiped at a phone. The duo who'd watched Tanais jump from the bridge.

"I'm good, sir. Thank you."

"I'm impressed with your manners, kid. I like your whole way of life. Out here in the river, in nature, keeping it real." His smile showed his lower teeth and wrapped his uppers. He cocked an eyebrow at the son, who recognized his pa's meaning, but swiped away anyway.

Ricky nodded. Had no more to tell the man. The boat said 'Leo I' in big black letters. "I love it round here ... Leo."

"Ha. My name is not Leo, son. I'm Mr Vale." He leaned over to stretch a hand. "Pleased to meet you. Again."

Ricky took his grip and gasped at the strength. Mr Vale kept Ricky in his grasp. "You should take my boy in hand – though I'm sure you're younger than Charlie-boy here. He's soft. Likes his video games too much. Needs toughening up."

"Dad."

"It's true, son. I don't see you doing stuff like this. Jeez, you're only on this boat with me because I threatened video game time."

Charlie plunged the phone into his pocket and reached out for Ricky, too. Mr Vale released Ricky for the son to have his turn. Video games must make powerful hands – Ricky guessed the kid could have lifted him into the boat.

"Well, I just wanted to see that you're okay, son. These

waters get choppy. Town can be a dangerous place. And these are dangerous times. You look after yourself."

Ricky rose and dipped with the waves Leo I left behind. Once the boat became a dot on the landscape he splashed to the thin slip of sand to stare at the world.

Too much change.

* * *

"Did your old man ever beat your ma?"

Liz scratched a heel on the tree bark and peered into the past, through leaves framing the City of Forts. She sat too casual, both legs straight, her skinny butt not enough to grip either side of the seat. One slip and she'd splat to the ground far below, hit every branch on the way. That'd make her ugly. Too ugly for biker boy.

She sniffed. "Not that I remember."

"You had to think about it."

"I recall the shouting, is all. She called him 'loser' a lot, which bugged the hell out of him. Still does when I call him that."

"Why's he a loser? Why'd you disrespect him?"

"Ah Ricky, you can have the old fart. You seem ready to test your brother with him."

"But ..."

"I love him. Don't get me wrong, lover, I love him. He's my dad. But that's hardly my fault, is it? I didn't choose him."

"But he is your pa. Brett loves him. He jabbered all the way to your house today about fishing. He will take him fishing, right?"

"Dad'll do what dad wants to do. You put too much on him."

"He's only looking after Brett. He's no trouble."

"Why don't you care for him?"

Ricky shrugged, annoyed she questioned him. "I've a life to live."

She giggled. It came out light and full of joy, but its judgment hacked at his motives. "What life? You don't have one."

He tightened his thighs round the branch and shuffled to improve his balance. Parted leaves, his eyes on any sign of the Ghost Boys. "I have all this. What's all this if not life?"

"Don't you ever want out of here?"

"Why?" He didn't know how, but he'd given her the wrong answer. Why'd she want to leave all this? It's an escape from Town, with nobody snooping around their lives. The wide open. Adventure. They could see the City from here. That place held nothing special as far as he could tell. It glowed beneath the sun with its big glass buildings and important brick offices, but so what? Freedom nestled this side of the river. Over there – commitment to others, who'd chain you to boring tasks so that all life drained from your bones. That'd make anyone a limp-wristed shell. It tangled his insides that her mind had wandered from him, to the bozo on the motorbike.

"Does your pa ever knock Carrie about?"

"He should."

Ricky didn't believe Mr Panowich ever beat his wife. Couldn't imagine his own pa hit ma. Angry noises Ricky'd heard in the night over many years, before he headed for San Francisco ... just tricks his mind played.

"That man I told you about – the one who stinks and wears a cap low over his eyes – he saved my ass yesterday."

"What d'yer mean?" She leaned forward.

"Ma ran out of gas, went to fetch some from the station,

and some man attacked us - me and Brett."

"'Brett and me'. What did he do that for?"

"Crazy, I guess. Hit at the door with a metal bar. Tried to crowbar it open. Spouted some shit. Then ..."

She nodded, engaged. "Yeah?"

"This man – his name is Floyd –" and he told her the story.

"I knew it. He's your Guardian Angel. He has to be. We should find him. Thank him."

"We?"

"Well ... you should."

"You can come with me."

"I don't know, Ricky. I don't reckon I have time."

He shrugged at her non-committal drawl. Whatever. But the whatever corroded his stomach. He pretended to concentrate on the house those bastards had taken over. Hoped Bixby hadn't used up all the water he gave him. Didn't want him to wander the neighborhood dazed, his tongue a flap of skin dangling out of his mouth. Whatever the Ghost Boys wanted last night seemed to have been worked out. He saw no other activity since they climbed this tree an hour ago.

Ricky climbed down as if he didn't care what Liz said. Marched towards the houses to shake guilt about not hosting Bixby at his home. He'd snuck him into the shed instead.

There, that tingle of satisfaction from the noise behind him – she ran to catch him. The ass on the bike couldn't compete with years of friendship. He spun around at the bee. Liz flapped hands, too, though they couldn't see the insect. The thing hovered high above.

"That's huge." Liz squinted and shielded her eyes from the sun. The black dot dropped a little and buzzed off.

"That the thing sent Tanais tumbling into the river?"

"God, yeah. No wonder she panicked."

"I reckon they're breeding in the Dragon Lands."

She laughed and put an arm through his. "Jesus, I hope not."

He released himself and asked her to wait outside. The house Bixby settled in, from which the gang chased them the night before, didn't twist sinister in the golden sunshine. Its ground floor showed no signs of activity other than the blood streaks and squirrel heads from Bixby's feasts. The little peepers and half-opened mouths of the critters held his attention for a minute until the creak in the floorboards shifted his morbid fascination. Liz curled hair behind her ears and swiveled here and there. Her eyes popped at the severed skulls.

"What else does he have to eat?" Ricky shrugged. "He can't rely on us bringing him sandwiches all the time. It's only same as cutting off a fish head."

She shaped an *ewww*. "I know – but you don't see fish climb trees every day. Looking all cute."

Ricky rolled his eyes and looked down the basement stairs. Pulled the door open bit-by-bit to avoid creaks and moans. The hinges sounded like a duck being strangled anyway, so he went full hog. The screech picked at his nerves. Liz crossed her arms and stood by him. The stairs dropped into their ancient fears as they peered into the basement's black secrets.

"What is it? What do you think is down there?"

He scratched his arm red. "Dunno. But you can pass me the flashlight Bixby uses."

She took her time, spooked at his behavior. He hissed at her to hurry. She threw her hands towards the ceiling in frustration at his tone. He clicked on the light and down they headed. Almost tumbled down the stairs over each other at the "hello?"

Tanais' voice fluted downstairs and made the shadows a little less eerie. She hummed. A few words materialized and dissipated into an instrumental thrum. Ricky half-expected birds to settle on her shoulders and a deer to muzzle her palm.

"We're down here." Liz rapped the stairwell wall.

Ricky snorted at the joy in Liz' voice. What, she wanted a third wheel to keep her balanced in his presence?

"Ooohh, it's dark down here."

Ricky checked behind him. Tanais' features glowed in the flashlight's reflected beam.

"What's going on with you? We haven't seen you around for days?" Liz soft-punched her upper-arm and ignored Ricky's side-eye.

"Daddy kept me in." Tanais' face wobbled in confusion at Ricky's explosive laughter. "He had a freak out when I told him about my new friends. He thought I'd been hanging out in the development."

"You told him about us?" He overlooked Liz' screwed eyes at his tone.

"Of course – don't you tell your mom about us?"

He nodded, as non-committal as Liz' earlier drawl.

Tanais bobbed her head as if to comfort herself. "Where's Bixby? He's got the hump with me, though I don't know why. I'm always nice to him." She shrugged, all sad, as if that's how her world worked and she'd accepted it. She can't have looked at the squirrel heads.

"He's in the shed at the bottom of my back yard."

"What's he doing there?"

She discovered why when the door clicked. Ricky's flashlight illuminated a bunch of containers he'd never seen before, all plastic with fitted lids. Who they belonged to now stood at the top of the stairs. The man stared at them, beneath his hood, like a problem in need of a fix. Ricky, Liz, and Tanais clattered into each other, each reaching for the other's body to morph into one protective shield. This man, this monster unchained, took a step which dug animal grunts from the children. Hands found other hands, nails burrowed into skin.

The man's next foot forward triggered a domino effect until he reached the bottom. He rendered Ricky's flashlight ineffective with a flick of a switch. They blinked at the glare from the painter's light filling every shadow. Glinted off the knife in the man's right hand.

20

The man stared at them from beneath his hood, face a shoe-polished blankness Ricky painted a dozen monsters across, the Ghost Boy patting the blade's flat side against a thigh. The newcomer's breath pumped loud, his movement forcing the friends back in one involuntary motion. Came close to knotting them into a shivery bundle. He herded them into a corner and grabbed a length of plastic line. Threw it at Ricky. Pointed the knife at Tanais and motioned to Ricky to tie her up. Ricky remembered a reef knot and a thief knot, but only the names from the two Boy Scout sessions he attended. A thief knot, the master told him, is easier to untie than most. He should have paid more attention. His hands shook and he doubted his ability to secure even a simple bind. He wound the line around Tanais' wrists.

The man grabbed Ricky's collar and threw him across a couple of containers. A lid scraped off one to reveal a container of little bags, dusted in a white powder. Liz mumbled a mass of panic and tears streamed down Tanais' face. Ricky sprung back to his feet, senses on fire. Lifted his heels off the hard concrete, every finger a stalactite. The man jerked Tanais' hands behind her back instead of the front, where Ricky tied them.

"Leave her alone." Ricky kicked the open container. His adrenaline overpowered logic. Told him his skinny ass could handle the hulk.

The man slapped Tanais across the face and she fell with a howl. Liz shook, unable to function. The big guy turned to Ricky, knife primed to thrust. No words escaped him, but Ricky could see details in the man's boot-polished features as the lamp hit him. Lips sat as fat as melon rind below a dagger-like nose. Those lips curled the shape of murder. Knew what he had to do. Had done it before and he'd do it again. Eyes said he should have done it last night to him and Bixby.

A buzz distracted their assailant. Someone tapped the letterbox windows high in the basement walls. The man swung an eye at the source without losing sight of the children in his web. The knock persisted, sowing doubt. His granite lips loosened into fear. He wound backwards round the maze of boxes to the window and stretched his neck to see outside. Another tap. A black dot against the blue sky. It buzzed away, hit again as fast as his eyes could focus, and flew off once more. Just a bug. A big one, but nothing more than some bee. Maybe a bird.

Curiosity deserted their captor. He gestured at Ricky to resume work on Tanais and do a better job this time. Ricky twitched as he coaxed her hands behind her back. He wrapped the plastic line loose round her wrists and tied a single knot. Did the same for Liz, who watched him over her shoulder to garner some, any, comfort. The man twirled his finger for Ricky to turn around. Ricky faced Liz and grunted as this bastard pulled his wrists back and almost tore his shoulders from their joints. Liz held those tears. Made Ricky proud of her. Hoped she felt the same about him. Tanais sniffled and made little Chihuahua noises at the smack to her cheek. She must never have known danger. Grew up in a ball of cotton wool. But her whimpers soundtracked his state of mind.

Why didn't the man talk? Why didn't the Ghost Boys speak? They haunted Town like Grim Reapers. The plastic line gnawed Ricky's wrists. He gritted his teeth to bar fear. Their captor would get no satisfaction from Ricky, no matter the pain he inflicted. He'd bear it to the end, and if he got out of this, the man would pay. A thousand times more.

The gangster nipped Ricky's neck and forced him to the ground. Ricky threw his shoulders and let out a howl at the burn. He swiveled and kicked at the man's shins, who danced out of the way. The Ghost Boy towered over Ricky, stabbed him in the stomach with a knee and leaned in. Ricky grunted. Eyes popped. They'd bounce off the walls any moment. Lungs emptied and pulsed beneath the weight. His hands and arms tingled and lost feeling under the rope's tight bind and the attacker's bulk. His head floated light and the room's glare whited out all detail. He concentrated on the red of Liz' hair and Tanais' dark skin. Avoided the man's face as much as he could. Until they locked eyes and this demon's features set in his mind. Ricky flinched at the knife's icy surface on his neck. The sharp point under his chin stamped a final warning.

The big bug rattled the window further. Hard and determined to get inside. The dumb bug might just crack the glass. It piqued the man's interest enough for him to push off and check outside again. A bang made the man jump back and almost lose his balance. "What the fuck?"

There – a voice at last.

He charged across the room. Tanais, still on the floor, scrunched herself into a protective ball. Liz cringed, submissive, and scrunched on the ground. Confused, the man kicked out at the defiant one – searing Ricky's shin in shock. The boy growled and rolled around at the shot up his leg. It could have hit worse. The man wore sneakers and the shock forced Ricky's reaction more than actual pain. Pretended it hurt sooo bad. The Ghost Boy plunged a hand beneath his hoody and drew out a gun. Ran upstairs and closed the door behind him. Clicks and knocks muffled through the floorboards.

Ricky, Liz, and Tanais eyed the ceiling where his footsteps hit, until he exited the house. Ricky jumped to his feet. Liz used the wall to push herself up and encouraged Tanais to her feet. The man never tied their legs or gagged their mouths. Not so much experience in all this, then.

"Turn your back to me." He jutted his head at Liz to encourage speed. She shuffled around until they stood back-to-back. He squeezed her fingers tight before he pulled at the line. The single-knotted bind gave up easy.

"You're a sly bastard, Ricky, I'll give you that." Her voice squeaked out reedy. "But he'll kill us." She untied him.

"He'll kill us anyway. He has no choice."

Tanais hugged him once he released her. He shrugged her off. This is business. Get organized. Organized how? They noted how his hands trembled. The thug had locked them in. Ricky half-opened his mouth to tell Liz, but she edged the door open, an eye through the crack.

"The basement doors don't have locks. None of these houses do."

All this shit in the basement and they didn't install locks on anything? Must have thought padlocks invited attention. Or they relied on their reputation to keep people away.

Liz snuck up the stairs first and scanned the area. Light

from the bare bulb above glared off the sweat on her face. She nodded them upstairs. The man paced the house's backyard, his hood down, hair spiked like a flame. His gun-hand conducted threats across the air as he spoke into a phone. The friends slunk towards the front, caterpillar-slow. Ricky trailed the other two. His jaw ached, mad at Tanais' lack of awareness. She stared at the big man through the broken back door instead of shifting her butt. It irked him so much he pushed her into escape. She stumbled into Liz who fumbled her footing and crashed into the front door. The slam frightened a gathering of birds on the porch. They twittered and cawed from danger and snapped the man's head their way. The Ghost Boy needed to adjust to the shadows from his position in the sun's bright glare, but he straightened and pointed the gun at their direction. A crack sent them into a run. A thud hit the door frame. A splinter speared Ricky's wrist and he charged out with his arm streaked red.

They zig-zagged to the next bush and the next tree until they reached the end of the development's road. Caught their breath. The factory's massive steel door invited them across the scrabble. It would leave them wide open to a turkey shoot. Ricky checked behind. The man hadn't cleared the brush yet, so Ricky ran for it and hoped the girls followed in his slipstream. He pumped those arms hard, despite his empty stomach and the pain in his wrist, and slipped inside the factory gate. Twisted his neck back. Stepped out again to urge Liz and Tanais to follow him. The sun burnt his eyes and heat made the girls wobble to-and-fro as if in torment. The Ghost Boy pounded through the last stretch of tall grass and panted to a stop, gun arm extended. If someone must die, let Tanais take the bullet. Last in, first out, and all that. He bit his lip at the thought and prayed to God both survived.

The shot rang out. Ricky ducked. The girls fell to the ground and dust plumed above and settled on their prone bodies. Ricky fisted the wall. A dull ache from the impact stretched up his arm and connected with his thoughts. Breathing came out in stumps and all his weight shifted into the door, like his roots tore from the earth. A rat ran up and down his windpipe until he gagged. He'd known Liz since they threw each other about in elementary school. They rolled and tumbled through the years as they played. Ricky never shed a tear for her. Until now. A single roll turned to a stream and the red mist took him.

He thrust himself into the open to confront the man, invincible to any bullet this bastard could fire at him. Halted as the Ghost Boy dropped to a knee, gun by his side, loose as a wind chime. Tanais swiveled her head and Liz pivoted to her haunches to watch. The man rested on both knees, and someone approached from behind him. This boy pointed an object at their attacker. The gangster dropped, one palm in the dust for balance, his hair a greasy sheen in the glare.

Ricky bolted to Liz, tightened a hand around hers. Tanais wanted a part of it and they opened up for her. They linked, Liz in the middle, as they approached the man. The Ghost Boy, now they had the leisure to examine, looked about twenty. A bit of fluff reached out of his boot-polished face like fresh shoots from scorched earth. He winced and plunged into the dust. Stared at them out of one sorry eye, gun still in hand, a finger on the trigger. Ricky stepped on the gun. The man's wrist bent awkwardly, but he did not try to move.

"You killed him." Liz trod, all tentative, around the man and wrapped Bixby in both arms. Kissed his cheek multiple times and rested her head on his shoulder. Tanais joined her. Ricky zig-zagged his foot until his heel rested on the man's hand. Pressed down hard until the fingers uncoiled from the weapon. Bent to take the gun. The man's eyes dulled as his last breath wisped away.

"I didn't kill him. I never pulled the trigger."

"It's okay – you saved us." Ricky eyed the girls on Bixby and tore off his jealousy. Only moments ago he feared Liz dead.

"But I didn't. I ran when I heard the shots. I think ... I think I would have pulled the trigger, but I didn't. Honest."

Ricky half-expected smoke to curl from the muzzle. "I counted two shots. You must have panicked and just killed him."

"I swear I never."

Liz and Tanais rubbed one of Bixby's arms each. Tanais eased the weapon from his hand. "Where'd you get the gun from?"

"I ... It ... I didn't shoot, guys, I didn't."

"We're not accusing you of anything, Bix." The squirrel heads on the kitchen counter boxed around Ricky's head. "You killed the bad guy. We'd all be dead now if it wasn't for you."

Bixby wrenched a smile. "Yeah? Yeah. You're right. You're right."

"We got to get out of here." Tanais attempted a step toward Town, her arm through Bixby's, but he had become a concrete pillar. "Come on, there might be more of them coming. We should go to the police."

Bixby threw her off and pushed her away. She kept her feet but palmed her chest in shock. "We're not telling any cops. Not a single one."

"We should tell the cops this time, Bixby. We can't ... we

killed a man for God's sake." Liz roped Ricky for help.

Ricky frowned at the gun in Tanais' hand. Sunshine prickled the back of his neck. His phone vibrated. Ma's name pulsed from the blue screen. He flipped it open. "Hi, ma."

"You okay, son? I'm just checkin' in with ya, making sure everything is good."

"Everything's fine. Everything. Yeah."

"Our boy alright?"

"Yeah. He's asleep."

"That boy's always comatose. What do you do to him?"

"It's the boredom wears him out, ma. Tires me out, too." He imagined how she would bite her lip at that one. It did her good for him to inject a little guilt. Kept her sweet. The world swirled. His friends gawped at him, stunned at the casual conversation.

Ma blew him kisses. He told her to stop it. Once she ended the call he shrugged. *What?*

"How'd you keep your cool? How'd you do it?" Liz wrapped arms around herself.

Ricky ignored her. "If we tell the police, they end all this."

"End all what? We can have fun elsewhere."

"Like we had fun in town? You loved that, right? Throwing firecrackers at crazy people and being chased down alleyways by men with guns? This is our place. Or have you forgotten?"

"There's a life out there, is all."

"I don't want a life out there." He pulled a face at the eyes she gave him. Pity elbowed her anger out the way and that fury filled him instead. "Yeah, call the police. They'll be round our houses asking all sorts of questions. Then what do we do about Bixby? We lie? Or not mention him? I can't even tell ma he's living in our shed. She'll tell people and then they'll take him. Adults, Liz - they all deceive."

Bixby stiffened. "I'm not going away. Never again."

"Take you where?" said Tanais.

"Back to the City."

"The City? You lived there?"

Bixby kicked the ground as if he wanted dust to smother this conversation. "I don't wanna talk about it. But if you call the police, you betray me."

"I'll never betray you, Bixby. I want to help."

He flattened his expression for Tanais. "You can help by leaving me alone. Nobody ever invited you here. You wormed in and –"

"That's enough, Bixby. Leave her be." Liz wrapped an arm around Tanais. "She's been nothing but good to you. Brought you sandwiches and all."

"I didn't ask for them."

"But you ate them. It's as good as asking."

Ricky flashed eyes at Bixby. *Tanais is not like us. Her parents are together. They have fancy jobs. Connections. She's already told her dad about you. Be nice to Tanais.*

Bixby's upper lip reached for his nose. He stared at the body and sighed. Shaded his face from the sun when he turned towards the stretch of soft earth that merged into the river. "We have to drag him out of sight. Bury him with the other prick."

Ricky skimmed the area. Expected Tarantula Man to arrive any moment. He knew Ciaro. He'd know this one, too. If they hid him well they could get through this holiday. They'd hit mid-August already and September threatened. Liz would head off to high school and by the time he reached ninth grade she will have dropped him from her thoughts. He'd never see her there, anyway. The school is huge. He'd wandered its long, mazy corridors before, when he tried for a travel basketball team. Every step turned his bones to iron bars until he ran from entrapment. Liz needed to make the most of this summer. She didn't take her freedom seriously enough.

Tanais handed the gun to Ricky. He put it down the back of his pants and led the way. He hooked the man's black slacks and grunted at the weight. Gestured for help, all sarcastic. Liz grabbed the other leg and they pulled him to keep Ciaro company. The cold sweat warmed at the effort and Ricky prickled at Tanais and Bixby's slack efforts behind them. Tanais snapped out of it and fetched the shovel while Bixby sat on a rock. Could act as the bastard's gravestone. Tanais sliced the ground with a hard thrust and stood on the edges as she would a pogo stick. Ricky gifted her a smile of encouragement. She pursed her lips, dislodged the solid earth and swung it over a shoulder. Made herself complicit.

21

A breeze rolled off the river and caressed their fears into manageable tremors. Liz washed Ricky's blood from the splinter. It hadn't penetrated deep. He'd gotten away with it. Ricky and Liz walked Tanais home. Convinced her to keep quiet. She nodded. She'd helped bury the man, after all.

Liz patted Tanais' back. "You're different – you don't know what it's like for us."

Tanais arched away from the condescension. "How am I different?"

"I don't mean it that way. I mean, you're normal. There's no consequences for you."

"What consequences? What are you talking about?"

Liz' forehead pinched and her eyes turned to hard stones. She hadn't expected Tanais' tone to ever rise above meek. Liz the mentor, Tanais the tutored. Tanais had sought them out, so it's she who must fit in and box her desires. That note in her voice pulled her out of the box and demanded equality. She'd seen things. Been through them as their equal.

"Just ..." Liz tripped over her expectations of Tanais and how they'd expanded. "Just, that ... you're, I mean, listen ..." The scrabble and scrag which made up much of the town smoothed over, here, as though a giant iron had descended from the sky and steamed the ground into golf course grass and pothole-free roads. These incomers walked around with notions above anything ma or Liz' pa had. "You have this to come home to."

Tanais shrugged her shoulders. So what? "What do you have to come home to?"

Liz wriggled her shoulders in return. "You wouldn't understand."

"No, I can't say I would. Because you never invited me to your home. Not once have you asked about me. Not that I crave to be the center of attention, but, come on ... do you even want me hanging around?"

"Yeah, Tanais. We do. Course we do." Ricky nudged Liz out of her silent anger.

"My dad says there's a consequence to everything." Tanais gritted her teeth, angered at the tears ready to break the banks of her eyelids. "That there for the Grace of God go we."

"What does that mean?" Ricky said. She blinked and now took pride in her emotion. That she had feelings. Ricky followed the path of her tears to dots in the dust. *Girls*.

"One thing can change everything. Like, a single mistake at his, my dad's, work could see us become ..."

"Become what?" Liz' lips had become a coal fire.

"Become like everyone else in this town."

* * *

Liz pinched her eyes until Tanais disappeared around the street's bend. "How dare she?"

"I don't know what she said that was so bad."

"Come on, Ricky. You're young and all, but – "

"I'm a grade younger than you."

"It makes a lot of difference. Anyway ... she thinks she's better than us."

"Ah, come on, I don't know about that, Liz."

She swung round on him, arms stretched by her sides. Skimmed around his eyes for a spot to punch. He pulled his neck back for a second, but *pfffed* and walked on.

Mr Panowich sat Brett ready for him on the steps of his porch.

The man stuck two thumbs in the top of his pants and rocked his heels. "That boy is good as gold. You look after him – maybe take him on one of your adventures Liz used to talk about."

Used to? Summed Liz up at the moment.

Brett bounded ahead of Ricky after a bright sunny "bye" to Liz' pa. Ricky locked onto his friend, but she avoided him. Viewed him as a mistake she didn't wish to acknowledge.

"See you tonight, then?"

She hunched her shoulders, soured her lips, and made a noise which *shhhhed* out of her nostrils. "You need to take a shower."

He threw a hand in the air to shake her off and put his back to her. *Be that way. What do I care?* But she sat in his mind all the way home. Every enthusiastic word out of Brett buzzed in one ear and flew out the other. They kept to the path ringing the fields and woods, darting into the high grass and trees when they saw anyone they didn't like the look of. The occasional time-warped car whizzed past without concern for speed limits, and an old person struggled through syrup, beaten by the sun. Ricky shushed his brother through the alleyways and shooed him away from cats and stray dogs pulling his attention. You don't stay still for long in this town. As the houses closed in on him, he longed for the fields again. He checked his shoulder for the factory. It seemed little, but from here he imagined it a palace. His. The tip skewered the sky. What a place to watch over his City of Forts.

"Ricky." Brett slid an arm through Ricky's and pulled.

"What?"

The man marched past, his eyes those in a medieval painting school showed them once, the kind that watched you from any angle you viewed it from. Until your head is almost back to front. Ricky's "Thank you" slipped down his throat, unused. The man turned his head again, dragged the peak of his cap low, and merged into the alleyway's murk. Ricky picked up speed and tried to snort the man's moldy musk from his nose and spit it out into the weeds. He sniffed his own armpits and cussed at Liz.

22

Mum watched Ricky above her morning coffee. The curious look put a ferret in his pants – he'd been so used to her eyes on the cheap clock above the oven, or out the window.

"You showered today." Ma twinkled in this early hour. "Something you want to tell me? Something you got hidden behind those circles?"

"Nah." He wolfed down the cereal to occupy his mouth and hands. Pulled long sleeves over the small splinter hole in his arm. Bounced his heels up and down, impatient for Liz to arrive. Worried Mr Michael Trent would pop up at the window. Liz never said she would come round. He just hoped she did. Had it in his head she should explain all her strange behavior. Offbeat even before any of that stuff happened yesterday.

Saturday. His day off from Brett. At least, a break from planning how to keep him off his hands. Ma squeezed Brett's cheeks, and he planted a double kiss on her forehead. Brett jumped off his chair and continued his battles between the medieval soldier and another toy. Ricky couldn't recall how he played when this age. He only remembered he had to care for the kid on ma and pa's constant nights out. Still had no idea how or what to feed him, apart from chips and yogurt.

Ma did a better job fixing lunch for his brother.

"You sat on a rattlesnake?"

"I just need to get outside, ma. Need to breathe. I'm stuck indoors with him all day, every day."

Brett watched him through his sword swings. Blasted a *ha ha* as though the soldier said it. Ricky shot him a slap-round-the-cheeks kind of look. Brett trotted to the living room neighing like a horse.

"Well ... you can play. Just ... just stay around the block. We're about the only respectable neighborhood left in Town."

Ma socialized little, so she didn't know a thing. Work and home is all she saw. Knowledge of Town emerged out of her own worries. Not that she guessed wrong, Town had turned into a land of the dead. Haggard eyes filled creased faces. Hunched shoulders showed how life's slab weighed on everybody round here. She had seen Mr Michael Trent out for the count by the side of their car ...

Ricky lifted the bowl and chugged the milk dregs, wiped his mouth, and scraped the chair back to start his day.

"Hold on Tonto, give me a hug."

Ricky scratched a line down his arm to map an escape.

"Come on, boy, you're not too old for a big kiss."

He leaned into her as she scrunched him to her breasts and pitter-pattered kisses on the top of his head.

"Now ... have you been pissing up the side of the shed?"

He pushed from her, his face a twisted ball of confusion.

"I'm just asking, is all. There's a tang of urine round there, but not strong enough for a skunk. Doesn't quite stab you in the nostrils." She stroked his hair. "Just wondering if you knew anything."

"Nah."

Once she headed upstairs with Brett, he grabbed bread, made a few ham sandwiches, and snuck out as if ma never permitted him to leave.

* * *

He bobbed like a lemming in case Trent lurked nearby. And Floyd. Ma's bedroom faced out the front of the house. Ricky gawked up at the windows round the back for a minute to make sure she and Brett remained on the other side. He double-knocked and entered the shed. Bixby lay on a few cardboard boxes, in his old sleeping bag between bicycles from Ricky's toddlerhood, hands behind his head. Stared at the ceiling. Ricky handed him the foil-wrapped sandwiches. Bixby ripped the silver and stuffed his mouth.

"Thanks, man. My belly's about to rip out of my body and look for food on its own."

"It's your favorite cheese, too."

"I can taste it. You're good, Ricky. I always tell that to Liz." Bits of ham hung from cracks in his crooked teeth when he smiled. The smile sat a little kinked since the events of recent days.

"What's Liz say to that?"

Bixby's eyebrows flapped like crow wings. "She gives shrugs, these days. No zip, anymore."

Ricky quashed the shiver distilling in his chest. "Come on, let's get out of here. It's Saturday."

* * *

Bixby heard it first – the clack of stones against a wall.

142

The dull thuds made him and Ricky sit on their haunches. Anticipated gunfire aimed their way. The factory's red brick tower watched over their fate – protected them. It wouldn't allow a bunch of whackjobs to drive them out.

They inched around the wall as the clacks hit with higher frequency. The sandy hair of the thrower sent the boys scurrying, as if the Ghost Boy who Liz whacked on the head found them to exact revenge.

No.

Ricky peeked and elbowed Bixby, who readied a stone the size of his palm. Bixby raised an arm, ready to hurl, but Ricky shot a palm out to freeze his friend's instinct.

Ricky scrunched his face. "Charlie?"

Charlie Vale's next throw landed limp in the tuft of grass hugging the wall. "Hey."

Ricky and Bixby approached as though they needed a chair and whip in hand, but dropped their guard at Charlie's lazy smile. The kid's harmless.

Ricky squinted up at the tower. "What you up to?"

"There's a window up there. Still has glass in it."

"Shit." Bixby shielded his eyes to locate Charlie's target. "How'd we miss that?"

Charlie duck-billed his lips. "Takes an eagle-eye."

Bixby offered him fuck-you eyebrows, but stepped back and opened up to Ricky. Ricky's aim messed up Charlie's ambition, and the two boys' jaws dropped to their chests at the smash.

"Yeah, Charlie, but it needs a pitcher's arm to hit it." Ricky gripped a second stone, ready in case he missed with the first. He let it slip to the ground and enjoyed the congratulatory slap on the shoulder from Bixby. Charlie offered a cheesy grin, grated.

"You here by accident?" Bixby eyed Ricky and turned back to Charlie.

Charlie shrugged. "You guys are cool."

"You wanna be our friend, though? Or you stepped out your door in the City and got lost? Ended up here – somehow?"

Charlie's shoulders drooped, indifferent. "I'm here. What do you want to do?"

* * *

Ricky called ma. Begged her to let him hang out with Liz longer. Ma talked more to herself, distracted. Johnson at work and Brett in her ear. Sounded like she'd downed a vodka or two. Words slurred into next week and beyond. He took that for assent.

Liz refused to hang out in the City of Forts. They met outside her home. She contained her frustrations about whatever within folded arms. Ricky invited her to put an arm through his. She rolled her eyes, but accepted – an elbow in his ribs.

"What's he doing here?"

"He's decided he wants to hang with us."

"He decided? What, we're friends with anyone who asks these days?"

Ricky shrugged and watched Charlie and Bixby keep shoulder-to-shoulder, each communicating without the expense of words. Charlie checked his shoulder, smiled at Ricky, blushed at Liz on his arm.

Had he wormed his way in for her?

"I, you know, I found it hard to say no to him. His dad – he has something."

"What are you on about, Ricky-boy?"

He stiffened at the nickname. *Not in front of the others.* "Somethin' I never see from any adults in Town. He's together, you see what I mean?"

"You're getting soft."

She offered him a sad smile – he worried he showed her a crap night of entertainment compared to what Biker Boy offered. Had her new man stood her up? That's why she's here? The boys slowed ahead and Charlie walked backwards to engage them all face-to-face. Dragged his t-shirt off to expose his chiseled abs.

"We need to wind up this town."

Ricky nodded Charlie on. "By takin' off your shirt?" Charlie's tattoo matched the emblem on his pa's boat. Who's this Leo?

"We can blow shit up, or something."

Liz' eyes rolled over Charlie's bare torso, though she tried not to show her fascination. Ricky puffed his pigeon chest, but quit the competition for Charlie's clear head start. He surged ahead, jerked Liz' arm, and left her behind.

He eyeballed Charlie. "We're past excitement." They hadn't checked the latest dead man's identity as they had Ciaro's – to tag him with a name made it personal – Ciaro already wandered through his dreams every night.

"I'm for blowing up shit." Liz brushed by Ricky.

"Me, too." Bixby swung an arm around her shoulder.

Ricky resisted the droop in his shoulders. "Let's blow up some shit, then."

The sun splayed on the horizon and the gang claimed ownership of the streets. Their voices rose with Charlie's confidence and they strode shoulder-to-shoulder down sidewalks and dared anybody to break the chain keeping them together.

Ricky broke this stride, his walk more a dawdle as he edged to the fringes of this new, Charlie-led crew. The intruder shouted at some old man, who hurried away at the sudden noise. Ricky flashed his eyebrows at Bixby and shook his head at how Liz joined Charlie's whoops. Ricky kept his mouth shut and bristled. They followed Charlie up metal ladders and across rooftops. Bixby slipped on a loose tile and Charlie reached him before Ricky to check his status.

"A little shaky, but I'm good. I'm good."

Charlie threw the tile at a cat. It scrambled to cover, where it cast them an evil eye. Ricky nodded to the animal in sympathy as it slinked away. Ricky already wanted this night to recede to half-forgotten memory. They jumped, climbed, piled over rooftop obstacles until they reached flatter surfaces. Dropped loose stones down chimneys and ran from the cusses of residents who dared scream their anger. The troop hit street level and drifted towards Town's center in the shadow of a tower block, the building a dagger thrust into the landscape.

Even out of the sun, as it dipped from sight, the heat sat on them, the breeze an oven fan. Ricky rubbed at the tingle on his radiated skin. He longed for the fields. All this brick and gray, even beneath a glorious twilight sky, made charcoal of his insides. Shackled him.

Charlie jerked the entrance door and kicked it in frustration when he realized it locked him out. "Our apartment has a doorman, but why would you lock this place up? Who's gunna rob this dump?"

Liz stood aside as Bixby joined Charlie's exaggerated kung-fu kicks against the entrance, amused by their stupidity. Her lids drooped in contempt and Ricky caught her swivel a few sly peeks here and there for escape. Ricky inched away from

146

this bullshit. Mr Vale came across as a good man — owner of a speedboat, after all, who had made it in the world. A man who knew what he wanted and understood his place around others. What did his son need to prove?

The parking lot heaved with sedans, some rusted, some with dents, others old enough that you needed to handle-wind the windows down. Ma's Datsun would fit in here. A BMW sat in a slot marked 'Reserved' beneath a streetlight. The owner must have requested the spot to check on it from his window.

Ricky craned his neck to see up the brick building. Scattered lights made a checkerboard of the front wall. Some man parked his car and hung around. Checked his cell, sly glances their way. Thumbed his phone again. Important business – or the man stalled in hope the kids would go away, leaving his car safe. Charlie and the others didn't notice him. Liz had folded her arms, patience now as thin as her wrists. She pointed at the little tattoo just below Charlie's collarbone. What's with the Roman soldiers? Charlie didn't appear Italian – more German or Swedish – but then neither did Ricky's pa, and his name is Nardilo.

"Your dad let you have that?" Liz needed gum to complete her affectation at half-assery.

Charlie slapped the tattoo and grinned at her renewed attention. "I can have anything I want. Dad says no sometimes – but I just go to mom. Problem solved."

"Must be nice." Liz tightened her arms.

"You wouldn't believe."

Ricky *pfffed* and toed the BMW's tires. Edged around it so he didn't set off a car alarm disco. Cupped his hands to the windows, but the tint kept its secrets from him. A shadow stretched across the car's hood. Ricky spun. Expected a crowbar attack from Tarantula Man. Instead, the man who'd just parked his car and hoped they'd all disappear faced him. Must have hit his thirties by now, though he stood only a couple of inches taller than Ricky. His boiled potato face tried to connect with him, but Ricky couldn't tell the man's eyes from the pits in his features.

"Yeah?" Ricky preferred to act respectful to his elders, just as ma had drilled him – even if adults had all the qualities of a vinegar milkshake – but he found it hard to acknowledge this man as somebody worth his deference.

"You shouldn't mess around that car, kid. You don't appreciate who it belongs to."

"I know the owner. I don't give a shit."

The man twisted his face and merged some of those craters. Checked his shoulder for spies or CCTV. "You know Michael Trent? You work for him?"

"No. I'd like to kill the bastard."

The man scrutinized Ricky's friends by the entrance to the apartments. "They with you?"

Ricky shrugged. *They're with me. What the hell can I do about it?*

The man slouched towards the building. His bulk made up for his shortness. Ricky watched how he talked to them. Inspired a few laughs into palms. The man waved Ricky over, keyed a number into the door's security panel, and held it open for them all to enter.

"There're no cameras here. You do whatever you want."

* * *

They flew up and down the stairwell, cruised the lift as if

they expected to fire into space, and ended on the apartment block's flat roof. The air washed over them cooler up there. They leaned over the low wall running along the roof's perimeter. Charlie jumped up and walked with tightrope arms across the wall's narrow top.

"You don't have friends over there?" Bixby flicked a coin over the edge and eyed it until it clinked the asphalt below.

"You talking to me?"

"Yes, Charlie, you."

Ricky willed Liz to lock onto him, but she sat on the wall at a half-turn to overlook Town. He couldn't figure out what attached her interest – Town jumbled together as if a kid had sprawled a bucket of Lego across the floor.

"I have friends. Sort of. You heard my dad."

"Your pa doesn't think much of you, it sounds to me." Ricky expected a bite, but Charlie nodded.

"He doesn't. Thinks I should act his ideals out in the world – which I will, but not in the exact way he wishes."

"He wants you to hang out with us and here you are and all. But do you want it?"

"Am I invited?"

"Dunno. I mean, what do you bring to our party?"

Charlie wobbled and arced back to the roof side before he splattered the parking lot with his brains. "I bring me."

"Which is what?"

"Adventure. A laugh. Plenty of stuff."

Ricky shrugged. "We have all that already. Bixby, tell him the time we borrowed that speed boat last summer, took it for a ride, and returned it with no one knowing."

Bixby jumped up on the wall with Charlie and faced him. "Oh yeah."

The kid frowned – Ricky guessed it annoyed him they'd shown how they didn't need him, but as Bixby's story rambled on, he remembered the little Roman helmet emblems he'd seen around Mr Vale's boat. His skin tightened and his fingers grew cold.

Charlie interrupted Bixby, whose hands threw wild turns on the speedboat and his feet danced close, too close, to the wall's outer edge. "What's wrong with you, Liz?"

Liz had one of those faces his ma sometimes set, which a chisel and hammer couldn't shift. Her mind wandered over the rooftops, down to the streets, and out on the highway where Biker Boy bared his chest to the wind. He didn't doubt she wished herself on that motorbike. Charlie jumped off the wall and landed with a dramatic thud.

Ricky took no notice. "Come on."

* * *

Ricky led them through the building's hallways, down the stairway from the twentieth floor to the eighth, until a thump-ing bass drew them to the seventh and room 718. A man sat on a folding seat outside. The door bulged with every beat, ready to fall off its hinges at the next demented bassline. Ricky crept up on him, raised an eyebrow at the gang in wonder the man didn't examine them. In the dim corridor light, the man's expressionless eyes told them all to run and never come back. He wore a faded black t-shirt and jeans, despite the heat, and glared at space.

Charlie stood by Ricky's shoulder and leaned close to the guard. "He's painted his eyelids."

Ricky extended his neck forward. Awaited a booby trap.

Painted pale eyes – so the man could see even in his slumber.

"Let's go." Liz tugged at Ricky's arm. "This is weird."

He released her grip and turned the handle. Expected it locked, but the door pushed in. The music's pulse pulled him in, Charlie and Bixby behind. A deep voice droned, hypnotic, about killing society and starting again. Ricky wanted to take Liz' advice, but Charlie had riled him on the roof. Ricky would show him adventure. Into the lion's den, then. Haze hung its dirty laundry in the air. It reached up his nostrils and plucked his sense of smell. The apartment floor, wall, air, all shook. From the music. From the bodies. Men, women, black, white, they all danced in the middle of the living room. A couple French-kissed on a sofa. A dirty beast talked to a hazy-eyed woman, a hand halfway up her dress. Most of the crowd sat around, dazed. The thick air must have weighed them down. The apartment's exit called.

"Who the fuck are you, kid?" A man in his twenties, hair cropped close to his skull, and chin stubble you'd shave with an ax, delved into his intentions and yanked.

Ricky darted from this wiry man with the rat face and held steady against the stumble over some woman's outstretched leg. Charlie clamped the man's arm and told him they had invites, though Ricky couldn't make out his exact words over the thump-thump. The man eyeballed Charlie's hand, soured his face from grape to gooseberry, and from the force of displeasure removed Charlie's hand without touching him.

"Get the fuck outta here, both of you, before I rip you a new hole."

The boys nodded, but the extra step tumbled Ricky over the woman's other leg and he fell on his ass between the legs of a man. The man grunted and groaned, high as a jet trail, and opened his eyelids. Whatever substance he abused watered his chocolate brown eyes creamy. They wobbled, unfocused, and he scratched at his dreadlock hair, which bounced as he shifted from discomfort.

Ricky's heart galloped up his throat as Tarantula Man's eyes pinpointed and examined the kid in his lap. He could feel the man's gun against his leg. Ricky could pull it now and end it. Whatever *it* is. The man wrapped his arms tight around Ricky and nuzzled his cheek. "I know you." Ricky fought the crawl across his flesh and bent into the nuzzle to keep the man in his state of bliss, but ...

The wiry man who'd told them to get the fuck outta here gripped his arm – fingers meeting his palm round the other side – and jerked him to his feet as if he snatched one of Brett's toys from the floor after it stabbed his heel.

"Fuck off home and don't let me ever see you again." He thrust both Ricky and Charlie out the door back into the strip-lit corridor. Bixby snuck out from behind the man before he became trapped inside. Liz leaned against the wall further down the corridor and ray-gunned her annoyance, but fluttered when the man on the chair snorted awake at the noise caused by the boys' exit.

He reached for his weapon. Waved it in their direction as they pounded the corridor and down the steps, their hearts too stressed to risk the elevator.

23

Ricky and Bixby knifed in and out of alleyways the next day. "Floyd's always hanging around these places. He must have shot out of some alley when he flattened Trent."

Bixby swung a stick at weeds in practice for anyone who dared launch at him. "Is he safe?"

"I guess. He saved me from that maniac."

"Why?"

"Dunno. To be nice, I reckon."

"It's creepy is what it is."

"He said he wants to protect us. All of us." Nothing matched the creepiness of Trent's hug the night before.

"He should join the police, then. Weirdo."

"Like he could do any good with them."

Bixby wiped his dehydrated mouth. "Where'd you put the gun?"

"Back where you found it. Where else?"

"What if we need it now? This town, man, it ..." He dragged a lungful of stale air and blew. "It's reaching our hideaway. Our forts. It sucks ass."

"Everything is changing." Ricky scratched at his arm.

"Things change all the time, Ricky. I just want a place to

be."

"A place to be what?"

Bixby beheaded the purple head of a flower. "To be."

"What does that even mean?"

Bixby burst ahead. Climbed a chain-fence to the top of an adjacent brick wall. It flaked on his first step. Ricky followed him and they balanced across thin-edged walls, the occasional wooden fence, and the rooftops of duplexes and rows of houses. They fenced each other with sticks in the abandoned supermarket parking lot, careful not to twiste their ankles on potholes pockmarking the ruined blacktop. Promotions of goods long past their sell-by date peeled from the windows.

Ricky whipped Bixby's arm. "What's with the squirrel heads you've got all over the house?"

Bixby rubbed at the sting. "They're my enemies."

"What?"

"I spend most of my time alone, Ricky. What you want me to do?"

Bixby sliced away questions with a swing and a thrust, forcing Ricky to hop and forget his questions. They pushed at the supermarket's doors. Locked. Bixby suggested they smash the windows and explore inside. Ricky squished his face to the glass. Cupped his hands to the side of his head to shield the glare. Overturned shelves and scraps of coupons is all that littered the floor. He worried about cameras – but what would they protect? Bixby told him to grow a pair as he dislodged a loose slab of sidewalk. He lifted it high and almost dropped it on his foot when Ricky nudged him. Through the large window pane they saw, on the supermarket's other side, bare feet, toes pointing to the sky from out the car's window.

The boys snuck around the building until they stood by the car. Floyd's feet streaked black and pink, with tree bark calluses on the soles. Pants rode up to the knees, loose on wiry legs. The friends plunged their hands in pockets and stared. Concocted images of what those legs led to. Ricky extended his stick an inch short of the soles, unsure whether to poke or tickle. Bixby shouldered him. *What you doing?* Ricky shrugged, all what-you-gunna-do? Bixby bit his lip and brushed the stick up and down the ancient Honda.

"Hello, boys."

They gulped. Gripped their sticks close to a snap and side-eyed each other. *What do we do? What you want to do? Run? You run first. No — you run first.*

The man inside crossed his feet and scrunched his toes.

Ricky recognized his voice would come out thin as soup, so he cleared his throat. "I just wanna, you -"

"I don't know."

Every smell and detail hit real sharp. The sunset rust on the car. The silver scratches down the doors. The smell of dead rat in somebody's armpit.

Ricky picked his nose, coal deep. "I wanna say thank you. For what you did."

"You're welcome."

"The man's name is Michael Trent. The one you beat up."

"I told you that."

Bixby stood on the tips of his toes to cast an eye over the window's rim. Ricky wanted to step forward and make contact, but events had deepened and the bottom of this well might trap him forever. His fingers trembled. Advanced up his arm, and into his chest until his heart slow-drummed a retreat. He wrapped Bixby's wrist with a clammy hand and stepped back from this rabid stray.

"Okay. Bye, then." Blood buzzed his head at the stupid comment, but a silent withdrawal would have come off rude.

Floyd never replied. Crossed those battered feet again. Once they retreated to a safe distance, they turned and ran, the sun Floyd's fiery eye on their backs.

* * *

They dawdled down Main Street, Bixby in battle with his thoughts, Ricky sad at the CLOSED sign on McGarry's door. Not even a notice to direct customers to his new address. He side-eyed the gray car rolling slow as a hearse behind them. The windows had a slight tint so he couldn't make out who drove, but he noted big hair in profile.

"I think you should get out of here." Ricky back-handed Bixby's upper arm.

"Why? What happened?"

Bixby noticed the car. Its familiarity dripped into his consciousness until it shaped his eyes in horror. He gripped Ricky to absorb solutions from his friend. Ricky panicked.

"Walk on, as if you don't have a care in the world. Go ... down that alley. I'll stay here as if we're still hanging out. You run as soon as you get out of sight ... Move it." Ricky elbowed him anew, told him to remove his giveaway stare from the car. "Casual, Bix. Casual." He loosened Bixby's clawed hand finger-by-finger and dug into his ribs to kick-start him down the alley.

Bixby's steps swayed off-balance, but he made it. Ricky breathed again when he heard his footsteps disappear faraway. He'd follow in a few seconds.

"Hey there."

Ricky had turned away from the car, but her voice stopped him. He watched her in the empty shop window reflection. She bunched her deep red hair into a palm tree. Couldn't see why she scared Bixby so much. He opened a smile for her, a little shy at the woman's pleasant, attractive face.

"Hey." He shuffled. Would have run, but that'd mark him with some kind of guilt.

"My name is Veronica Shaw."

"Hi."

"You don't have a name?"

"Sure."

She waited, but narrowed her eyes at his reluctance. "I'm looking for a boy called Bixby Schmidt. About your height. Last time I saw him, he had cropped – a buzz-cut – dark hair. Slim. Blue eyes."

Ricky nodded, but only to show he understood her words.

"You know him?" She pushed a smile out through her teeth.

"Never heard of him."

She tapped her fingers on the steering wheel. "Your friend, the one just by your side, is he familiar with him?"

"Doubt it."

"Can I ask him?"

"Dunno where he is."

"Okay. Well, you keep an eye out, right? If you want to take this card ..."

Ricky shrugged his shoulders, reached for it as if he navigated over barbed wire.

"He's missed very much by his parents. His foster parents."

"I don't know him, Miss. But I'll call if I bump into anyone who matches your description."

"You're a polite young man, you realize that? I appreciate any help you can give. That boy needs all the help he's offered.

"You take care now."

Ricky nodded as she drove away and watched until the car turned a corner. He suspected she had an eye on him and might follow his direction if he left the spot right then. He sat on McGarry's step and crumpled the business card she'd handed him.

24

Ricky hunched down on one knee, forearm over his eyes to block the glare. He watched, through the parted grass, a couple of trucks bounce over the uneven road by the Forts. Men shook hands, checked their shoulders every so often, and unloaded boxes. Tarantula Man overlooked the bustle in his white t-shirt and fiddled with a smartphone for some expected call. Michael Trent ran the Ghost Boys.

"These bastards are here to stay."

Ricky scurried away on his hands and knees and jerked his head back to another intruder. Held his heart hard to keep it in his chest. "Jesus, Charlie, what you doing sneaking up on me?"

Charlie grinned. "Should I honk a horn for my arrival?"

"Not what I meant."

Charlie shrugged and strained his eyes at events by the Forts. "I was bored. Wanted to hang out. You want to hang out?"

Ricky cocked an eyebrow but kept his attention on Tarantula Man. "Sure."

Charlie offered him his hand and jerked him from the ground. Ricky almost flew. Charlie wore some serious muscle. They ran in zig-zags similar to soldiers dodging bullets Ricky saw in old war movies. Ricky could have hung out at home, but boredom squeezed him out the door. The pull ... led him here every time. Would this place always hold him tight enough to prevent a good life away from this damn town?

They sprinted and jogged between trees, Ricky ahead, sometimes Charlie in the lead and above on a ridge. The rich kid would twitter weird bird noises to let him know his whereabouts, and disappear. Ricky jumped out at him from a shrub Charlie hadn't expected. Expected him to jump away, startled, and laugh it all off. Charlie stared at him instead, his eyes dead – *don't do that again.* Their feet scraped the bark of one tall ash tree until they overlooked the City of Forts from a great height, through a gap in the already browning leaves. They bobbed for a better view until Charlie reckoned they should break off a branch.

Ricky shook his head. "We'd have their guns all over us."

"Fuck 'em."

"Yeah, fuck 'em, but I'd like to fuck 'em with something in my hand." The two handguns they accumulated lay in one of those abandoned houses. No use, now.

Ricky leaned over to track where some noisy, overweight squirrel came from. Liz monkeyed up the branches instead, agile as a gymnast, even with that stupid book in her grip.

"Hey." Ricky offered his hand for her last step. She ignored it and cast a curled lip at Charlie.

"I could hear both of you from back there. Pair of elephants trying to climb a tree." She blew the bangs from her eyes.

Charlie nodded. Contained his smirk, though his eyes danced electric.

"What you doing here?" Liz followed their gaze to the men by the houses. "What they doing?"

"Import/export." Charlie dropped down a branch to get near Liz. "All kinds of shit. Drugs, I reckon. Guns. All away from the view of cops."

Liz wrinkled her nose and caught how Ricky mirrored her disdain. Ricky enjoyed the blush of red coloring Charlie's face as he clocked her reaction. Charlie touched her arm. She cricked her neck and swung round the other side of the trunk to stand by Ricky. Charlie pulled at bark. Stripped a piece as big as his hand. He stood a few inches taller than Ricky, and had more bulk, but straightened to emphasize his size. Rubbed the bark against the branch above as if he wanted Liz to see how he could make fire and take care of the clan.

"They can do what they want, those people. Just like me, I suppose. I do whatever I choose."

"I know." Ricky squeezed Liz' calf, which caused her to laugh. "You told us."

"You should all come to my house. High as this tree. Better view. Mom would feed you and we could do all kinds of stuff in my room."

Ricky and Liz shared a glance. Charlie's brow rippled as if they skimmed a stone across his forehead. "If you want, that is." His confidence stuttered at their silence. "But not Bixby. Not him. He's raw. I mean, what the hell?"

"Fuck you, Charlie."

"Ricky, come on, he's as rough as a buzzard's ass. What does he contribute?" Charlie fingered the Roman helmet tattoo beneath his t-shirt.

"He's my pal. He's our pal."

Liz cricked her damn neck again — she didn't quite agree with Ricky. Charlie latched onto the gesture.

"Fuck you. Fuck you both. I've been friends with Bixby

forever. He's been through some shit your pampered ass could never dream of, Charlie. So fuck you and your fancy home."

Ricky dropped lower and threw an accusing eye at Liz. She shuffled her feet at how he'd left her behind with Charlie. He heard him ask her if she wanted to kiss. Ricky stilled, a crocodile patient for the buffalo to reach into the water. She scraped the branches on her way down until she met Ricky at the bottom. He breathed again.

Charlie called after them. "We're friends?"

"I don't need no more." Ricky cared little if the Ghost Boys heard – Charlie had to know nobody gave a damn about him.

Liz put an arm through his for half the way to her home. She pushed off him and shook her head. "I might be done, Ricky."

"What do you mean?"

"I think I'm finished." She nodded, all sad, and walked away, book clutched to her chest.

* * *

Ricky found Bixby in his shed, arms around his knees and eyes on the ceiling. Tears smudged the muck on his face.

"Miss Veronica seemed nice enough."

"What you tell her? Did you give me up?"

"No. Why say that?"

"She's the devil. She'll drag me back to those people."

"What they do to you?"

He shook his head and scowled. His lower lip trembled, and he rocked himself to his feet. "Let's get out of here."

Ricky and Bixby edged around the fields, watchful and ready to crouch behind any tree. The breeze rolled the grass in waves. What shark hid in there? They knew all this better than the

Ghost Boys, but every nook spooked them. The boys reached the back of the woods leading to the Dragon Lands. Crept to the factory's rear – one false step might wake a beast. Heaved through gaps in the boarded windows, which no longer offered the building much protection from trespassers. It still stunk of chemicals and metal, but the damp hung over it all. They landed on hard concrete and padded across rickety platforms and stairwells, careful not to alert unwanted attention. The office on the upper level overlooked the cavernous factory floor. The bosses must have seen Ricky's grandpa as nothing more than an ant from up here. He surveyed the space between thumb and index and squished. Grandpa talked of the noises blaring out of this place. The clang of metal, the fire sparks, the roar of machinery, and the shouts of men as they strained to be heard above it all. Special, he'd said. Felt a part of something magnificent. The world's workshop.

Grandpa towered over the men he knew now. Everyone in this town walked slumped and bitter, or with a swagger they'd not earned. He turned, pulled at the boards which obscured the light from outside. Bixby joined him. They each planted a foot on the wall, hands on the board's edge. Grunted and growled until they ripped it all off. The humidity pushed down on their shoulders. They rested, heads through the opening, lungs pumping for air, and sweat swamping their eyes. All worth it for the view. Their City of Forts arced below, and the City across the river glinted, a gaudy diamond compared to the Dollar Store town they endured.

"Looks nice over there."

Bixby shrugged his shoulders and fixed on the abandoned houses. Ricky could tell he watched the City from the corners of his eyes, but he never gave it a direct glance. It might turn him to stone. Bixby sucked his yellow teeth and scratched his arm with blackened fingernails. Ricky shook away thoughts chiming with Charlie's. Bixby could have a good life across the river. A working bathroom, food in a fridge, a ma and pa to care for him. If they lived in the City, they'd have money, too. Miss Veronica only wanted the best for Bixby, didn't she?

"Look." Bixby thrusted a finger at the last house in the crescent, nearest to the factory. Ricky squinted, but couldn't make out Bixby's focus. Bixby shifted into his friend so they touched shoulder-to-shoulder and pointed again so his index seemed Ricky's. Ricky scrunched his nose to cut Bixby's odor, ablaze at how he might have smelled the same to Liz. Charlie sat on the porch, a dot at the tip of Bixby's fingernail. Threw objects at some other object. At the Town-end of the row of houses a truck bounced and swayed with every bump in the ruined road. A couple of men stood in the open back, hands tight on a bar to prevent a head-over-heels throw from the vehicle as it dropped into one pothole after another.

"Oh, shit." Ricky's voice hit high as a deflating balloon.

"We have to get down there."

Ricky hesitated. "Why do we have to get down there? What's to do down there?"

Bixby punched his shoulder. "Because – that's why. You stay here if you want. I'm going."

Ricky spat out the window and followed, his face sour and mashed at Bixby and Charlie. Should have kept his mouth shut. Absolutely, they had to go down. But ... damn it. After what Charlie said about his pal?

The factory rattled with every step as the friends jumped, swung, and scurried in a blur to the entrance. The Tasmanian devils stirred dust and birds into the air. Locked their ankles as they hit the turf, as stones beneath the surface might bring them down. The truck slow-coached down the road, but its occupants made no sign they'd seen the boys ducking low behind stems and bushes.

"Hey." Charlie's lazy smile slid from his face as he saw how they ran and the urgency in their eyes. "What's happenin'?"

"We got to go. We got to go, now." Ricky gestured, urging him into the depths of the weeds and scraggy brush. Charlie gesticulated confusion, eyebrows gymnastic. "Now. Or we die."

Charlie sprung from the porch, a firecracker up his ass, and flew into their company. Ricky headed for the factory again, but Charlie hooked his sleeve and nodded to the river. "Who's chasing us?"

Ricky scowled. "The Ghost Boys."

"You mean the hoodies?"

"Yeah, the fuckin' hoodies. You know what they're doing here and you sit on the porch as if you're waiting for lemonade ... what's wrong with you?" Though none of them wore hoods. Maybe he'd got it all ass-upward, but history told him to leave.

Charlie checked him over his shoulder. They swerved thorns in the thickness by the river's edge and slunk into the water one at a time. Waded along the bank with noses just above the surface until they noticed the line, the rod it belonged to, and the man who held it. Charlie's pa stood, alarmed at how the kids approached him, then sat on his haunches as he sensed the danger tracking them. He reeled in his line, stowed it away, slid the paddle into a practical grip and made his way to the boys. Pulled each in, urged them to get low on the deck, and rowed them out of this syrup. Ricky risked a glance over the boat's rim and noticed a man, without a hood, enter the house where they'd feared for their lives recently. He planted his cheek on the surface again and clamped his breath.

They made it out past the broken bridge. Ricky worried each stroke of the oar would be the last. Expected a bullet to pierce Mr Vale any moment, followed by a hailstorm to send them all to a red river bed.

When Charlie's dad stopped, Ricky squeezed his eyes and gritted his teeth. Almost salmon-jumped out of the boat as the engine smashed the silence. He opened an eye and breathed. The boys sat upright and nodded to each other, allowed themselves a smile until Charlie's pa whipped them away with an angry growl. "What the hell was that all about?"

Ricky stared at the helmet engraved on Mr Vale's oar. It had slits for hidden eyes and a brush-like arc at the top. The man loved his Romans.

"Well?" Mr Vale bashed the oar on the boat's rim.

Ricky and Bixby glared back at the houses and shook their heads.

25

M r Vale shifted to a higher gear and the force whipped their hair to all the angles. Ricky had never felt such speed, even inside ma's car when he'd been late for school. The distance they gained from the fields made it hard for Ricky to breathe, as if some cord to Town stretched his innards to breaking point. He jerked his neck back to pour in air.

"Sir." He must have mumbled, his words muffled by the engine's blanket. "Sir."

Mr Vale checked around him, eyes crossed as though a fly hovered in his face. Ricky tried again until the man located the noise's source.

"Yeah?"

He cut the engine and let the boat coast. A tarpaulin covered much of the deck. To protect all the fishing equipment from the weather, Ricky guessed.

"Sir, I kind of have to get home now."

The man nodded. Guided them close to the bank. They all sat in silence until the boat bobbed in a single spot. Charlie's pa heaved himself onto the deck and crouched to face the kids.

"You want to tell me what happened?"

"Some men going through my damn ..." Bixby spat over the

side.

"Some men – what? Are you boys in trouble?" His hard eyes made them shrink a little. "Charlie?"

Charlie shrugged and a smile played on his lips. "I was just sat on the porch minding my business, pa."

Ricky grimaced. "Pa" didn't sound right coming out of his pie hole. *The City boy's all plastic, trying to mold himself into one of us. He's artificial and throwaway.*

Mr Vale nodded, all sympathetic. "There's some tricky people out there, boys. You must take care. Understand?"

"I understand, alright." Bixby spat again. Didn't notice the twist in Mr Vale's mouth, though Ricky agreed it seemed rude to spit in front of an adult, as useless as they all are. Mr Vale's eyes sat sharp in his face. Aware, full of purpose. Unlike Mr Panowich, this man knew life's map.

"See, maybe you ought not to play in those fields."

Ricky razzed the back of his throat to make sure his words showed their guns. "The fields, the City of Forts, Town, it's all the same."

"City of Forts?"

"A whole rabbit warren of hiding places, pa. A safe spot from the shit that goes on in Town."

"Used to be the case." Bixby spat again. At least the swim in the river dampened the reek from his skin. Mr Vale didn't twist his mouth anymore. Accepted the boy's rough habits.

"Well ... sounds fun. Sounds a lot of fun." He swept a hand to the metropolis. "But I reckon you boys should hang out in the City for a while. Until it's safe back there."

Ricky hardly left Town. Never realized if he did. Most towns melded into another, rust connecting them all. The tall buildings gleamed as much as the toys at McGarry's. Made him nervous to touch it, as if Mr McGarry still watched Ricky's dirty hands on his goods. That single gray and white cloud seemed a dead cert for the toy shop owner's beard.

"We're okay, sir. We don't care for the City, thank you."

"I like your manners, son. That'll take you far."

Bixby rolled his eyes, but rubber-stamped Ricky's decision. "We don't need the City. And I'm sure the City don't need us. Thanks for the jaunt, mister. We saved your son, but we can make our own way back now." Bixby wobbled to his feet, arms out to ride the craft's tilts and bobs, and clambered over the side. Ricky stood with him, almost dry already from the breeze's heat.

Charlie stared at the boat's bottom, his eyes holes of disappointment. Mr Vale pursed his lips, wistful. "Well, as I said, the offer stands. You boys … you're good for my kid."

Ricky didn't want to throw lines from his forehead, but they wrote his annoyance clear. "How so?"

"I grew up in a town like yours, son. Back then, you had work whenever you wanted. I could quit a job in full knowledge I'd walk down the other end of town and get another one the same afternoon. All that changed the moment our great nation discovered oceans of humanity overseas. Could do it all cheaper. Now – you have to hustle and own some brains. As much as I love my life, it's all material. The people over there, in the City, they're nice and all, but everybody's all surface. All shiny robots with glossy trinkets. Their sons and daughters spoilt brats with no taste for what's real, unless it has 'artisanal' slapped on it."

Ricky shuffled. Had no idea what the hell the man jabbered about.

"My boy, here, he was turning into one of them, despite my

care. But ..." His mouth arced wide. Perfect teeth, good skin, a little stubble but well-kept, and no tang to his breath Ricky could make out. A touch overweight, but ... "... but since he's been hanging out with all of you, and your friend, Liz, he's a different person. Now, I understand you all had a falling out, but that's what boys do. I mean, for God's sake, I fall out with my pals all the time. If I dwell on any of it I'd have no friends left. You fellas, you're real. You're real without being dumb. Man, there's some ..." He shook off his thought, but Ricky understood what he meant.

"Pa ..." Charlie made an "aww shucks" face, his head low as he focused on a spot between his feet.

"I'm outta here." Bixby gestured to Ricky to hurry the hell up as he hopped over the underbrush.

Ricky scratched a knuckle. "Charlie said you could do something for Liz."

Mr Vale glanced between the three boys. Waited for an explanation.

Charlie swung a hand between his legs to occupy himself. "I already said. Liz likes to read. She loves all that stuff. I told Ricky you know people. People who write books."

"Oh, yeah. Sure. Sure I do. Listen, inform your parents, then come and visit our home in the City. Bring Liz and I'll sort something for her."

"Why would you do that?" said Bixby.

"Because ... because I love how you guys want to help another - no strings attached. Because I owe you all. For bringing my boy back to Earth. For giving him a bit of salt. You come over and see how the other half live."

"I gotta get out of here."

Ricky scowled at Bixby. He splashed overboard into the river

170

and offered Charlie's pa a nod and an awkward, tight-lipped smile.

* * *

"Who the hell does he think he is? Fuck me." Bixby swung a thick branch at everything. Yellow and purple flowers lost their heads and unseen beasts scurried from potential execution.

"He seemed alright to me. Better than his son."

"We give Charlie a little salt? What does that even mean? I'm certain the old man wants to feed me dog food and pat me on the head."

The boys had strayed far from their usual haunts, round the bend in the river to the foot of the hills. They climbed the slopes over boulders, stuck out the Earth like a giant's hip bones, through trees and thickets which snagged at them to stay, to become part of the land.

Out of the trees, the black earth smoldered, and the ground burned beneath. Pa told him of an ancient mine underground, where fire still sparked, but old stories of dragons fired pace into their steps. Plumes of smoke drifted – the ghosts of miners long gone, killed in the mines or dead in the heart for a past that trapped them in amber. That's how ma put it. Said pa couldn't get out of his own head for years. Perhaps he escaped his mind by leaving Town. Town is all Ricky ever knew. What could Charlie's pa offer him? He pulled at the branch of a lonesome tree, already half-snapped from the trunk. Yanked until he scratched his palm, red in the face from the effort and the gall at how strength failed him. He jerked it free at last and swiped at wisps of smog. Damn the dragon. Damn Mr Vale. Damn Charlie.

He'd relish a ride on that boat again, though.

26

R icky arrived home dog-tired. He scoped the place out, ma and Brett's absence allowing him to smuggle Bixby to the shed, safe. Bixby's slumped shoulders showed he'd given in for the day.

"We're brothers, right?"

Ricky grabbed his hand tight and pulled him in. "As long as you don't decorate this place with squirrel heads."

Bixby sparkled. A tear? If so, it held behind the dam. "We should do the blood thing. Slice our palms and mingle us together."

"Nah, I'm not doing that, Bix. That's just movie stuff."

"Well, whatever, you're the brother I never got, and I've had some real bastards try on the role."

Ricky nodded. Authorities fostered Bixby around like the farting dog everybody realized too late they didn't want. Families found his blue eyes didn't make up for the shit he dove into. "No noise. And no pissing up the back of the shed. Ma can smell it. You've had it if she finds you here."

"She'd grass me up?"

"I dunno, Bix, I think we'd both be knee deep in it if she knew. She's ... she's just got it in for me right now."

He double-clicked his tongue. Squeezed Ricky's hand once

more for a good night, though the sun hadn't dunked the horizon yet.

* * *

Brett slept on the sofa, his head on ma's lap. She stroked his hair as she dug into Ricky with tired eyes. "Where've ya been?"

"Out and about. With Liz."

"That girl ..."

"Yep, that girl."

He sat beside her and she curled an arm around his waist. Wanted to lean into her, but history froze his bones, so he let her do all the emotional work. Ma watched some cop show, stocked with cheesy chat and over-egged outrage. Nobody seemed nice. Truth, he supposed. Who the hell is nice? Even Liz turned. Ma had the family photo upright again on top of the TV. There's the biggest fucker right there. Pa, with a smile full of content. Liar. He left them all a year after they snapped this picture. It took talent to fake happiness like that.

Unless ma drove him away. It's possible she did that. She's a bitch sometimes. Whatever, you don't disappear out of your kids' lives because you can't stand the woman you live with. More useless adults – but at least ma had done a better job than Bixby's parents, who left him with an aunt, who also then kicked him down the bank into crocodile waters.

People must shed skin at a certain age and become snakes. Though not Charlie's pa. An outsider, sure, but different. There's a clear-eyed man who would show him stuff. Might he take Brett on, away from Mr Panowich?

"Before you get comfortable, can you check the shed?"

"Huh?"

"Huh is no kind of response for your ma, Ricky. Go check the shed for me. There's a dead rat in there, or worse, God save us. I attempted to enter earlier, with a rag soaked in Dettol over my maw, but Jesus, the stink broke through even that. Go on, help your ma, before it gets too dark."

He moped, scratched a leg, swung his other, but she nudged him out of his procrastination. Had no choice. Couldn't allow her out there, then she'd notice he spent her work days in big bad Town and brought all its strays home. But the stink? What's she on about? Had he gotten used to Bixby that much?

"We need a babysitter, ma." Sunday arrived tomorrow, a day killed in dread of Monday. A day to think about what to do with Brett. How to get rid of him. Mr Panowich made it easier, but that Carrie woman whined about the kid's presence.

"Who's gunna babysit? Who is gunna watch over you?"

"I dunno. Can't you hire someone?"

"And pay them my stashes of gold? You climbed a beanstalk lately?"

He patted his pockets and chastised himself for the action. He hid the money he stole from Ciaro deep beneath the junk under his bed. With the few hundred dollars left, he'd employ a babysitter. "How much is it to hire one?"

"More than we have, son. About fifteen to twenty an hour."

"Dollars?"

"No, pesos. What do you think?"

"Just asking." His cash wouldn't last long, then. "Nobody from our family?"

"Nobody."

"Pa's side?"

Her hand clamped a tuft of Brett's hair tight enough to

make him stir. She relaxed her grip and huffed. "I've told you they're all in Idaho, and as useless as he is."

Ricky closed his eyes to find a solution.

"And they don't wanna relationship with you. Or your brother."

He twisted to her, hurt by people he didn't know. "They said that?"

"As good as. Your pa married white trash, apparently."

"I'm not white trash. I'm ..."

"Don't get all soiled about it, son. They ain't worth the salt of your tears." She seemed pleased by the phrase. "But you'll always have me. Always. And little Brett."

Ricky balled his fists and bent his knees in fight mode. He'd like to slap his pa's side of the family around right now, if only they showed their damn faces.

"I said – you have us. And that's enough."

* * *

Not enough at all. He pounded the concrete slabs leading to the shed, the Dettol-soaked rag ma made him use in his hand. He double-knocked so Bixby recognized his visitor. The place did stink, and he squeezed his nostrils with the cloth. Bixby snored, light, content he'd managed a day killing nobody, and remained out of the red-haired woman's hands.

The smell watered his eyes, but it didn't come from his friend. Ricky risked a rag-free sniff and gagged as he followed its source. There. Round the back of the shed, where the backyard met the woods, smoldered a pile of Bixby's shit. His pal must go.

* * *

Ricky tip-toed into the shed early Sunday morning, as the sun already bullied the day. Place stunk of shit and sweat and mold. He lifted a shovel from its hook on the wall and tapped Bixby's sole with the flat side.

His friend pig-snorted and sat up, ready to fight. He focused, gifted Ricky a smile, and rested on his palms. "What's the story?" Frowned at Ricky's serious jaw.

"Got you a shovel. For your shit. You need to fling that stuff into the woods. Deep. And next time ... just do it right in there."

Bixby scratched his scalp and smirked. "Sorry. It was the middle of the night. Back there looks scary in the dark. Who knows what's in there. Bears, or big cats, or a damn crocodile for all I know. Definitely ticks."

"You live in the City of Forts, so what you talking about? You shit by the shed again and it'll be my ma who eats you up and throws you to the red-haired woman."

"She wouldn't ..."

"Ma doesn't know you. She'd do it in a heartbeat."

"You'd tell her I'm your friend, she'd back off ... yeah?"

Ricky shook his head. "I doubt it."

"Damn, that's cold."

Ricky flinched a little. "You wouldn't shoot her though, right?"

"Jesus, what you take me for? I didn't shoot that man, I swear. At least, I feel I didn't." He ran a nail up his bare forearm in concentration. "Maybe I did, I can't really tell. I just can't remember firing the gun. No recoil up my arm at all."

"I'm pulling your leg." Ricky toed Bixby, playful. "You saved us. A proper hero."

Bixby grinned, but hugged himself tight, too. "It hit me last night. I hardly slept. I know I'm wild and all, but to kill a man. Think about it, Ricky. To end a life? My stomach is all over the place. And you're so cool. What the fuck is wrong with you?"

Ricky shrugged. "He deserved to die. And you slaughter squirrels all the time."

"They're only rodents. And I need to eat."

"I'll grab you something, but don't munch in here. I feel sick just opening my mouth to your fumes."

"Any chance of a shower?"

"I'll unlock the back door. We've got to go to damn church." Ricky mumbled about some stain on his only white shirt and thought better about high-fiving Bixby. He doubted his friend washed those hands after doing his business.

* * *

Ricky sat in the makeshift pews of their Baptist church, the congregation lost in the center of a strip mall on the outskirts of Town. He hoped Bixby left no traces of his musk in the house after he'd done showering. Prayed he tidied after himself to show not a single trace of his presence.

The preacher babbled on about honesty. Spent about twenty minutes-or-so exasperated by people who didn't believe in Jesus Christ. They must place their faith in the Lord. Seemed a useless speech to Ricky, because none of those folk would bother to come here to listen to a call for their conversion. The priest should head for the streets and tell them – see if they'd pay any more attention there than Ricky did here. Ricky wished he preached this sermon on the streets – at least he'd have the freedom and space to escape the drone of his voice.

The church should use the abandoned factory. Ricky would lose himself in the place's history. What they made, how they made it, and how they sent it all out into the world.

Scratch that. He'd allow nobody to sully their haven, not even a man of God.

* * *

Ma smacked her mouth and held the scream. Not too well, because it came out a shriek coyotes make deep in the scary hours. She slammed the brake and jerked them all forwards, backwards, up and down. They settled and stared at the cop cars outside their house. Ma feared flames until Ricky reassured her that no fire truck sat in their cul-de-sac.

"Oh, God, thank the Lord for that." She crawled into her driveway and nodded at the police officer by the front door. Brett bounced on his booster seat and waved, excited by the uniform and the gun in his holster.

Ma took her sweet time. Dreaded to find what happened to her home. Cusses and accusations spun in her mouth and Ricky winced at what would happen if the lid came off in full-spin. She shouldered open the door and glared at the man.

"Ma'am." The cop removed his hat.

Someone had died? "Officer Ray ... What the hell is going on?"

He recalled Officer Ray. One of pa's old friends. Hadn't seen him in years. Ricky opened his door, but ma shooed him back inside. He turned the car engine on and twisted the air-con high. It worked today. Wound down his window to listen. The two adults stared at him, worried he might drive off. Carried on once they realized he just needed cool air.

"A neighbor called, ma'am. They noticed unusual activity, knew you went to church, and so called us out. Your back door's unlocked. Did you lock it before you left?"

"I check every door and shut every window, officer, before I leave the house, even when I'm in a rush. Come on, you patrol the town we live in."

A rueful smile shone. "If only everybody were as vigilant as you, ma'am."

She folded her arms and scuffed the ground with a heel. "Well, if only all officers were as considerate as you." His forehead slatted. Suspicious thoughts peaked out the blinds. "I'm sorry, officer, that was uncalled for. I'm sure they're all as good as you." Ma touched his sleeve to caress her apology home. The cop didn't recoil, but let that human touch iron his features clear.

Another policeman appeared from round the side of the house and nodded at his ma. "Mrs Nardilo …"

"Officer Gretzky."

"How are you?"

"What do you think? I'm standing here, all shaky that my few goods have scampered from my home. You?"

Ricky stared at the shed for signs of life. If Bixby made it back there, great. Even better if he ran clear of the area. But if he's still in the house …

"Sir, did the neighbor get it wrong?" Ricky's belly flinched, but he flattened the ripple ready to roll over his skin.

The Gretzky cop watched Ricky over ma's shoulder. Turned to his colleague and back to Ricky. "I can't say, son. Your ma, more than anyone, would know best."

180

He invited her into her own home and followed her inside. Ma told Ricky to stay in the car. He heard Gretzky ask about pa.

The other officer, Ray, chewed his mouth's interior it seemed, threw an accusation at the sun with a squinty eye, and dawdled toward them. Brett clapped his hands and shouted "policeman" a few times until the wax in Ricky's ears shredded. The officer waved and leaned on his thighs, the smile of champions on his lips. It pulled Ricky in for a moment. Such a smile demanded trust, but Ricky fought it. Adults don't kindle faith. Policemen even less.

"Young man." Twinkle in his eye. You can tell me anything. I'm an officer of the law, here to serve you. I'm acquainted with your pop. "Why'd you ask if the neighbor got it wrong? Has he a history of mistakes?"

"Not that I know of, sir. Never talked to him."

"Okay." He tilted his head. Smiled at Brett again. Little brother guffawed and kicked his legs. The cop pointed at him and goofed his teeth. Settled serious eyes back on Ricky. "So what would make you say that?"

Ricky shrugged. The pilot light lit beneath his ass and burned him right up. "Just ... our home looks normal to me."

"Can you think of anyone who might have been inside?"

"Why would I?"

"Just asking, young man. Just asking. You'd tell me if you knew anything, though, yeah?"

"Sure." Ricky worked and worked to keep his eyes on the cop's. He concentrated on the officer's pupils and imagined them a deep well, curious about what lurked at the bottom. Nothing much, it seemed. The officer straightened like a flick knife, stuck up a thumb for Brett, and swung round. Took his position by the front door again. Ma accompanied the Gretzky cop outside. They peeked around the shed, ma telling him of funny smells. The officer scanned the interior and behind the structure, said he saw nothing to worry about, "though a tang does sit in the air." Ricky stepped out and unbuckled his brother as ma waved the cops goodbye.

Her lips slid to the side. "Did you unlock the back door?"

A niggle deep inside urged him to tell the truth. Ma's the adult. She can help Bixby. Even adopt him into the family. Horseshit, of course. She'd muck it up like she had her life. It'd end messy, and he'd lose a friend. Another rock in his world.

"I didn't touch the back door, ma. Why don't you ask numb nuts, here?"

Brett froze from his bounces around the drive, a *what did you call me?* look on his face. He shrugged and jumped about more.

"Ricky, cut out that language. He can't turn the lock. He doesn't understand how."

"You're so busy working, you don't see half of what he can do."

She resented the comment, but she sagged, defeated. For now, at least. "Let's go eat."

He snaked past her through the door so she wouldn't spot his grin.

27

It took Ricky the journey to Liz' home to shake off the cop, Bixby, church, and how he hurt ma. He carved a place at the back of his head to store them away, and gave Mr Panowich a respectful, familiar nod. Liz' pa saluted him as he sat on his scraggy white porch chair. The man's eyes shone brighter each day.

"How's that boy of yours?"

Ricky planted a foot up a couple of steps and swayed to-and-fro. "He's good, sir. Real good."

"He's a great kid. Makes me youthful again." Mr Panowich rocked on the chair's back legs and studied him. Ricky plunged hands deep in his own pockets. "You here for Liz?"

"Sure."

"Sure is sure, you young buck. She's mooching around like a wronged cat right now - I don't know what her problem is. Maybe you got something to do with it? Eh, boy?"

"Doubt it, sir. She's got rats biting her ass about everything."

Mr Panowich laughed. "You have a mouth on you, son. Such as what? What's got her goat?"

Ricky frowned at the stained, cracked lower step and shrugged. "Damned if I know. She ... she just ... she's just mad about all kinds of stuff. Confusing is all I can say."

He blew through his teeth. "You got that right."

The man's woman shouldered the front door open. A cigarette drooped over her bottom lip and a beer bottle hung like a pendulum between her middle fingers. Mr Panowich asked if she brought a beverage for him. She pursed those thin lips. "I see your feet."

"Jeez." He slammed those feet to the deck and slouched inside.

Carrie surveyed Ricky toes-to-eyes as though she might exchange him for cash. "She's fourteen."

Ricky tilted his head. She made him fidget and scratch. Wanted to pull her spider-leg hair from her face and yank it into a ponytail.

"She's fourteen, and that's all you need to know."

"I've no idea what you're talkin' about."

"She's in heat, boy. If you want to play your cards right ... though, looking at you, I doubt you'll ..." She rubbed an eye and snorted. "Never mind."

Mr Panowich bounded outside, happy with the beer, and clinked his bottle against Carrie's. Raised it to Ricky. Ricky smiled, expanded it as Liz poked her head out the door. She eyed him as she would a childhood toy she'd long left behind.

"Hey, Liz." His wave stood limp as a defeated battle flag.

"Hey, Ricky." She slipped back inside. Like she avoided him.

Carrie snorted, took a drag, and scowled at an approaching car, glittering beneath the sun. A ramped-up pickup truck, red as fire, high as a bus shelter. The man inside thrust his head out the window and waved an exasperated hand. "Get a fucking job, you lazy bastards."

Mr Panowich almost knocked Ricky over his heels as he charged across the scrabble by the bottom of the porch steps. "Fuck you, asshole. Go sit on your mother's dick."

The driver sped off with a hoot from his mouth and one from the car's horn.

"Dick. What a goose-fucking dick. It's Sunday, goddamn it."

"Ignore him, baby. You have more balls than his entire family put together." Carrie winked at Ricky. "And he has three sons."

Mr Panowich stiffened his whole body for her inspection and saluted her with the bottle. "Ricky, boy … you get your brother round here in the morning and I'll make a man of him. He's got to learn to survive this cruel world." Mr Panowich spotted Liz, who'd stuck her head out, and charged indoors. They must have gone to the kitchen at the back of the house because their voices reached him muffled, though sharp.

Mr Panowich, despite the beer, seemed as clear-headed as Ricky'd ever seen, but he didn't have a patch on Charlie's pa. Mr Panowich's beard harbored previous meals, plenty of germs – he'd bet. Wouldn't surprise him to find a hawk if he dug around in there. Ricky sighed and turned. Spun again at the hard hand on his upper arm. Carrie attempted to grip him tighter, but he pushed her away with both palms.

"What ya doin'?"

She flicked the soggy cigarette stub into the gravel and jabbed him with that glare. "You need to keep your boy from here. My man doesn't need another fucking brat in his life. One's enough. Don't you be multiplying his trouble, d'yer hear?"

Her yellow tobacco teeth didn't dull her tone. Ricky's nose

screwed tight, and he ground his molars at the woman's gall.

"Seems to me my brother is doing great things for Mr Panowich. Got a bounce in his step."

"No, you're bringing the world to the man. Reality. Opening him to pain. God, you selfish little fucker, don't you know what the poor man's been through? You give him hope and he'll sink all the more when the real world hits him anew – who knows, even harder than before."

"You got me all wrong, miss. I just want to see Liz."

"And I'll make sure you never hear from her again if you continue being a selfish little cunt. You understand?"

Liz burst out the door. She grabbed Ricky's arm as rough as Carrie had, but this one sent a thrill up his spine. He studied Carrie's sly smile as Liz led him to the brownfield over the road, where trees and bushes battled junk and garbage for space.

* * *

"Who loves you?" Ricky ran a finger through the grooves of her name carved into the tree. A love heart framed "Elizabeth."

"Everybody loves me, Ricky-boy."

"Don't call me that."

She poked at the carving as if she could turf it from the bark. "You wanna head down Main Street?"

"Nah. It leads to nothing I wanna see."

"Where should we go, then?"

"You want to go somewhere with me?"

"I don't want to stay here with you. Let's eat, or do something."

"We can –"

"No." She flattened her palm against his chest. "We cannot go to the fields. Ever again."

She pushed off him and headed to Main Street. Across the road, Carrie watched him, ready for any bullshit he might throw at her.

"Wait up, Liz." He caught her pace, checked his shoulder for any magic Carrie cast at him. "Why's your old man with her?"

"If you could just find me the answer, then I'm yours forever. That bitch needs to get washed up in a storm and carried down the nearest drain."

"That's powerful stuff. What she do to you, Liz?"

"There's something real cold about her. I don't know where dad found the skank, but she's latched onto him and won't let go. She eats his insides, keeping her all nourished, as she weakens him. She's just ... just so wrong."

"She hurt you?"

"Every fucking day."

Carrie rested her chin on the back of interlocked hands and leaned against a neighbor's fence. She turned away when a black car pulled up by the house. Ricky's forehead hurt as he squinted at the vehicle, but the book under Liz' arm distracted him. "You reading that, or is it a damn ornament?"

"I'm reading."

"Yeah, but what?"

She lifted the book, waved the cover in his face, all sarcastic, and flipped a few pages. Tested his question's sincerity.

"I'm serious. What is it?"

"You care?"

Did he? She buzzed awkward these days and conversation didn't flow like it had. He didn't much care, but if she told him, it would at least ward off her skin-prick silence. "Yeah, lay it all out." He grated his teeth at how that came out sarcastic and whiny.

She held it steady this time, so the words didn't blur with movement.

He studied the cover, then read the title. "*Great Expectations.*"

"You can read."

"Who'd have thought, right?"

Her lips curled – a cut cherry. Radiated limited warmth. "You read it?"

"No."

"You ever gunna?"

"No."

She huffed. "Figures. Why not? You against words?"

"I couldn't think without them."

"You don't think in pictures and images?"

He backhanded her arm, playful. "Words *and* pictures. Words even come out of my mouth. When I want."

"So you should give it a chance."

"Don't need to. You'll have told me the whole story by the time we get to Main Street."

She summarized the novel as they kept to the shadows, past houses as scraggy as Liz', through lonely spots humming in the stillness, and past factories as old as America. Or so it seemed by the weeds clasping them back to nature.

"I've not read it all yet, obviously. But that's where I am."

"So, this Pip doesn't have much ambition, then?"

"Yeah, he does. He wants to be a gentleman. I think, anyway."

"A gentleman? What's that?"

"Someone who's not poor."

Ricky laughed. "What?"

Her eyes set hard as marbles. Ricky barked louder at how he made her mad.

"I'm just sayin', he sounds like an idiot. That's all he wants, to be a gentleman? We all chase riches, but what's the gentleman stuff?"

"It's in different times, when people thought different. But …"

"But what?" He leaned into her. Hoped she'd slip an arm through his.

"You should just read it. There's so much to it."

"I'll pass, thanks."

"Just like that? You have nothing, do you Ricky? Nothing up here." She hammered a finger against her forehead. Left a dot to match her hair. Liz' attention darted to a couple in the Bagel Bistro. Dust motes plastered the window and obscured both man and woman. The sun reflected more of Liz and Ricky than it revealed the lovers. They sat opposite each other, both their chins on a cupped hand, eyes locked on each other's. Ricky squirmed at the sight. Seemed out of place, flowers in a coal yard. The buildings squatted round here, hunched and small-windowed to avoid the gaze of passers-by. Even the neon signs at night glowed dull, as if embarrassed at the regard they didn't quite draw to themselves. He didn't see a history of romance in any of the bricks and flaky wooden sidings.

Liz lost herself in the woman's eyes, much as the man had. That novel infected her. Pulled her head-first into a life not hers. The lady in the window caught the ache in Liz. Her face wobbled from surprise to anger at the intrusion, to some recognition of a past feeling. The woman settled into some sympathetic smile and forced Ricky to snatch the book from Liz' hand. He ran down the street, waving it in the air.

"Hey."

Ricky hooted as she hurtled after him, soured by how she chased the text and not him. He let her catch his arm. Fenced the book behind his back. She reached around him to get it, hissing as he twisted, turned, snorted, shook off her anger. Until she kneed him in the balls. He hit the ground with both hands on his nuts and the novel on the sidewalk. She grabbed it and threw some harsh words down his ears. He didn't hear a thing for the sound of blood.

"Lizzzzz."

"You're an ass, Ricky. It took me long enough to see it, but I realize it now."

He staggered off his knees and planted a hand on a wall for balance. "Then why don't you go and see your biker friend?"

Her face twitched between shock at his knowledge, and anger. "That bitch told you?"

"How old is he?"

"He's – none of your business, Ricky Nardilo."

"He's old enough, though, right? Old enough to get in your pants."

Her nose scrunched. Built some steam, he was sure. "He's never been in my pants."

"Only a matter of time?"

"You're a fucking prick, aren't you?"

That verbal whip hit him as much as if he crossed Town's threshold. "Ah come on, Liz. Don't you think it's weird? He's got a beard and tattoos. You're fourteen."

She flung the book at him. He could have dodged, but he

needed it to strike him.

"You consider me a slut?" Voice as level as a dagger's flat side, eyes as sharp as its tip. "His name is Steve. He's twenty-five. He's just finished college –"

"College?"

"Yeah, college." She said it like getting into such a place required magic wands and broomsticks. "He's going to help me."

"To do what?"

"I don't know. But whatever it is, it'll get me out of this place."

Ricky hugged his arm. "You'll never leave –"

"Just because you'll be stuck here forever, another wart on the landscape –"

"What?"

"You'll never quit here – you'll just turn into the type already stinking this joint up."

"Like your pa?"

She snatched *Great Expectations* from the sidewalk and held it tight to her chest. "Just like my dad. Don't be the same as them, Ricky. Come and meet Steve. He's teaching me all sorts of things. Aims for a life in California. He's so exciting. Has really opened my eyes."

Ricky shrugged. "We'll see. You should spend the day with us and Charlie's pa."

"You intend hanging round with Charlie? Still? He's an asshole."

"Likes hanging with us. His pa is a good man."

A man in his twenties exited the Mexican deli and leaned against the entrance wall to bite into his wrap. Ricky nodded down the street and they shuffled from the man's ears.

"I don't want to be chased by men with guns anymore."

"Bit of excitement. Not the same as piggybacking with your new squeeze, I'm sure."

"Grow up, Ricky."

He glanced over at the man, who stared at nothing in particular, but Ricky could tell his ear cocked from how he feigned disinterest. Ricky moved tight to Liz and grabbed her arm. She wriggled, hit him with a *what you doing?* face. He clamped his teeth shut, in case the intruder could lip-read from behind, and whispered. "That man. In the doorway. He's listening to us. Let's go." He jerked her, subtle, so she didn't check on the listener. Once they gained distance, Ricky removed his hand. "Why do I have to grow up?"

"To keep up with me. I've changed. You're still the same. We see things different, more and more."

"Come and spend the day with Charlie's pa."

"Where's he want to take us? And why?"

"To the City. Because we're good for Charlie, apparently."

"The City?"

"That's got you, hasn't it?"

She shouldered him and smirked.

"He said he knows people who write books."

"He doesn't look the type to know anyone who reads, never mind writes. What's his dad do for a living?"

"I'm in the dark about that. He's a bit of a pudge, but has more glamour than everybody we know."

They turned their necks to giggle at each other. Caught sight of the man right behind them.

28

The stalker showed his teeth as if he intended to sell a banged-up Honda Civic as a brand new Porsche. Ricky backed away, snatched at Liz as an afterthought, and dragged her with him. The man flashed the gun in his waistband as a warning and re-covered it beneath his Pantera t-shirt. Glanced around to make sure nobody saw. Could have waved it in the air and this ghost town would pretend it never happened. Ricky recognized the man wouldn't show his lack of brains and use it out in the open, so he catapulted down a path of weeds and deformed asphalt between buildings. Some, if not most, sat empty. Ricky didn't doubt any witness to the chase would turn the cheek. Nobody wanted a gun-toting psychopath's attention. Shut the blinds, raise the TV volume, wash the sight from the mind.

Liz twisted free from Ricky's grip but kept by his shoulder. They didn't need to check behind. The man's steps slapped the air. Ricky eyeballed every nook they might squeeze through. Expected a shot at any moment, and he'd make certain of their end if he chose the wrong escape route.

Liz's squeal made an abattoir of the closed-in strip they raced down. She stumbled, arms out for balance, toppling and rolling until momentum lost its power and she spun to meet the expected assault. Ricky put the brakes on and swiveled with her.

"What? What? What?" Why did strangers chip his world away? Why couldn't he just enjoy the rest of his summer like anyone else, without all the drama?

"Quiet down, kid, you'll have all kinds of curtains twitching."

"Fuck you."

The man laughed. Eyed Liz up and down. "You're Panowich's girl. I should have recognized you."

"I don't know you."

"You wouldn't. I'm always boot-polished and in a hoodie."

"Not now." She bit her lip.

He slid the gun from his waistband. Ricky's heart punched his ribs. His hands drained slab-cold. The man clutched Liz's ponytail and yanked. She gritted her teeth but held the scream. The man pulled her head back. Exposed that milky neck she'd offered to Ricky's lips not so long ago. The bastard jerked her into his groin and laughed. His head wandered to the gutter and let his gun hand dangle. Ricky leapt and kicked at the pistol. Hoped it wouldn't puncture anybody but their attacker if it fired. The man yelped and shook the sting from his fingers as the gun clattered to the floor. Liz broke free and dove for the handgun. He booted her sideways. Her face scraped the blacktop, but she jumped to her feet. The attacker's shoulders jigged, pleased with himself. He reached for the gun, lazy as he stooped. Ricky plowed into him from the side. His skinny frame made dust spirals as he bounced off and sprawled the ground. Their assailant winced. Ricky must have hit a bone, somehow. The Ghost Boy snatched the weapon this time. Jerked Liz's defensive arm like a one-armed bandit and thrust her on top of Ricky.

"Stay put, both of you. Important phone call." He keyed in a number and pointed the weapon at them. Connection. "Hey, chief. Aha. I have a couple of prizes right here. Boy and a girl. The girl is Panowich's daughter. She's the one who whacked me on the fields ... That time we saw them near the factory, where we have our little base ... Yeah, we chased him and she came to the pussy's rescue ... Hit me across the head with a stick. The boy matches your description. Should I just plug them, let them go, or bring them in? ... Aha ... aha ... okay, chief. I'm off Main Street, by Robert Fulton Drive. Okay ... okay ... See ya."

He slipped the phone into his knee-length shorts and grinned at them. "Looks like we have to wait round here awhile for a pick up. You guys have questions to answer."

He jackhammered Ricky's thigh and kicked him into the bushes to dampen his cries. Liz blurred through his tears – a hand over her mouth. The man's words muffled under the pain shooting through Ricky's bones, but he guessed the man threatened Liz with the same treatment. The bastard grabbed him by an ear, dragged him from the bush and pushed him forward, amused by Ricky's cusses. Waved his gun at Liz to keep ahead. Ricky limped with no hope of bursting to safety. Before this ass chased them across the City of Forts, this was a game. Even Ciaro's corpse didn't tell him of their seriousness. Well, they didn't account for the fury in his chest. That'd get him out of this, and the Ghost Boys out of his sanctuary. That confidence rose and dipped in quick succession as they swam through humidity. Liz sniffled away her angst, determined to remain defiant. That's the Liz he knew, not some sop to a tattooed prick on a motorbike. Ricky slowed from his snail's pace and the man slammed him in the back to speed up. He landed on his hands. Twisted his neck to glare and received another kick, this time in the ass. He sprawled. Burned his cheek on the stove top surface. Wanted to launch to his feet, but pain made any attempt equal to the man's beatings. A squirrel, a rat, some animal, scurried through the bushes.

"You doing this because we hit you over the head?"

"That hurt, you know. You little bastards gave me concussion. But we have people missing. You hang around those abandoned houses. You witness all kinds of shit."

Liz faced him. "We've not seen a thing."

"Shut your pretty fucking mouth, girl, or I'll put something in it to make sure you never open it again. Place one foot ahead of the other and repeat until I tell you to stop."

"Where you taking us?"

"You're off to see the wizard. The man – our lord and master."

Their captor's grin sprung wide as a trap and invited a length of wood nobody saw coming. The bat smashed his front teeth and made his mouth a white picket fence a truck crashed through. The man collapsed to the ground, blood between his fingers as he pushed against the agony. Another strike, this time to the knees. He rolled and grunted harder than a pig in its end moments. His other hand stretched for the gun he'd dropped, but his digits crawled in the wrong direction. His assailant shattered an elbow next, and the man's groans slid up and down his windpipe. Their savior stepped on the handgun as he surveyed the dour back trail. Any windows overlooking them offered only a milky eye. Ricky pressed his thigh, nodded at wide-eyed Liz, and smiled at the newcomer all awkward.

"You fucker." The bastard on the floor found his voice, a cocktail of whine and revenge. "You're fucked. You die, man. You die."

His tormentor reached down for the gun. Examined it. Made his prey heel the ground to push away. The Ghost Boy's marble eyes rolled across the one now in control – at the heavy boots, the torn jeans, the bulky coat which must make it at least a hundred and ten degrees within. At the lank hair hanging beyond the greasy cap. Ricky searched for a better view of his face beneath the low peak of his hat. Shadows. The man lived in them. Floyd focused on the gangster down the barrel of the pistol.

"No, please ... please, I meant no offense. I can get you out of this, I can. I promise."

"Get me out of what?"

"This situation. This shit you're now in. I'll help you."

Liz stood over the cripple. "What do you know about my dad?"

Desperation twisted his grin. Sweat made tire marks in his dirt-crusted eyebrows. Saw a lifeline in Liz. A girl. He could appeal to sentiment. "He's a good man. A real good man. I love that man."

She shielded her eyes to examine Floyd.

Ricky hobbled until all three stood over the Ghost Boy. He brushed Liz' shoulder with his. "I told you about this one."

This groveler darted between them and the gun. Liz nodded a thank you to Floyd and turned her attention back to the sandy-haired man on the ground.

"How do you know my dad?"

"I deal a bit. Your dad does some blow. Nothing much. Just to take the pressure off, right? And your mom, she's real good, too."

"She's dead."

"No. No way? Oh my God, my ... what was I thinking? Carrie cannot – "

She shook her head at his insincerity. "She's not my mom. My mom is dead."

"Riiight." He bit his lip. Concentrated on Floyd, who still directed the gun at his forehead. His voice hit all the scales. "Look, I ... Why don't we just get on with our day? You go your way, I go mine. Yeah?"

"You were gunna kill us."

"Is that right?" Floyd cracked his neck. Finger twitched.

"No. No, I wasn't. That's not true. I intended to take you to my boss, who— "

"And who is that?"

"He's powerful, man. He's the shit round these parts. You don't wanna get on his wrong side."

"Can I have it?" Ricky wrapped a hand around the gun's muzzle. He glanced at Liz's reaction. She had got lost in how this filth associated with her pa. Floyd relented, amused. The man on the ground squeaked out a laugh. Ricky squinted down the gun. "I want you out of my life, sir. That's all I want. I just want my summer back, with no drama."

"Yeah, sure. I mean, that's not too much to ask, right? You can have it back. I'll give it you back."

"Don't you need permission from your boss – to give me back my summer?"

"I ... I have influence."

The man licked sweat from his upper lip. He burned red. Floyd plunged a hand into the man's pockets and emerged with his wallet. Slid out cards one by one until he had his driver's license.

"Darren Grealey." Floyd grunted at the picture. "Don't understand why you look so smug. I'll wipe that clean for you."

"Is my dad one of you?"

"Sweetie, he could never be one of us. Doesn't have the temperament. Now, please, come on, let's ... let bygones be bygones."

Floyd reinserted the license into the wallet, removed the tens and twenties, dug for Grealey's phone, which he dropped, and shoved everything but the cash back into the man's pockets. He cracked the phone with a heel, and stamped it useless.

Ricky held the gun firm. Tempted to pull the trigger. Just a squeeze. Relax all joints to roll with the recoil. See the blood spill and soil the ground, fascinated how life would leak from the body. Would the feeling differ from the time Bixby shot that other Ghost Boy?

Floyd dragged Grealey upright by the hair and locked his arms behind him. Ricky turned his nose from Floyd's stench – maybe Grealey had soiled himself. The captive guided them toward his car, a beat-up Chrysler with a busted front grill similar to its owner's teeth. Floyd released him when they reached the end of the alleyway and eased the gun from Ricky. Offered a rag to Grealey so he could wipe the blood from his chin. Grealey's eyes matched his red face.

Floyd stabbed the weapon into the man's back from within his long coat's pocket and encouraged him forward. Grabbed his shirt to halt him again, and told the teenagers to leave. Ricky protested. Wanted to see how this played out.

"Go home, kid. I have it from here."

"What you gunna do?"

"Make you safe, is what I'm gunna do. Now get the hell outta here before I bust your chops." He jabbed Grealey. "Can you walk, you son of a bitch?"

"You might have to carry me, but I don't think your skinny ass can handle it."

Floyd kicked the back of his legs and he fell like a doll. Filled his mouth with cusses, he worked hard to bar behind his teeth. "I can drag you, if I need to. Now get up. Walk me to your car."

Liz pulled Ricky's wrist, but he stood firm and examined Floyd. The photo on top of the TV - a thin man, a frown a permanent scar on his face, about Floyd's height.

"Are you my pa?"

Floyd owled his head and burrowed into Ricky with those factory-forged eyes. "I'm not your daddy, son."

Ricky watched after him as he pushed the man from the alley's shadows into the day's white glare all the way to his car. Floyd pinned him with careful study as Grealey grimaced into the driver's seat. Glanced back at them. A black car drove by, squealed its tires, and did a U-turn. Ricky backed up the alley. Liz bit at her nails. The black car rolled slow beside Floyd and stopped. Two men stared at him. Floyd made the gun prominent in his pocket, pointed at the driver's head. Possible he could take both out with one bullet. Floyd's the man.

One look at Ricky and Liz would put them both in danger. Floyd didn't flinch at all. Set his sights on the skinheads and never lost his target — the men Grealey had called in to transport his captives to God-knows-what. The passenger made a gun from his fingers and pow-powed Floyd, who absorbed it with a grin. They drove away with a squeal. Ricky and Liz didn't move until the growl dipped into the distance. The couple from the bagel place walked by on the road's opposite side, oblivious. Floyd slid into the passenger seat, agile for a homeless man, and Grealey followed his direction.

Ricky sped past Liz, skidded round the bend, bent down, and burst back to her. Tongue hung out like a hot and bothered dog's. Handed *Great Expectations* over. Her eyes showed appreciation, even if her mouth didn't.

"That's the least you could do, Ricky Nardilo."

29

Ricky found Bixby kicking a can two streets from his cul-de-sac. A couple of old men sat on their porches drinking from a bottle. Watched Bixby as if he represented a past version of themselves. Ricky told Bixby about what happened on Main Street.

"We gotta take it back. We gotta get 'em outta there, Ricky. Floyd ... man, what a star."

Ricky patted his friend's arm, excited by events. He had walked with Liz half-way to her house. She wore a steely stare he enjoyed, though she hadn't explained where the point of her thoughts directed.

"We'll sort it all out, like we always do, right?"

Ricky nodded. Promised him he'd bring back food. He walked home hard and fast to still the shakes. Ma read a book with the TV on as background noise. Brett bashed at the air with the toy soldier he'd broken. She asked where he'd been and he told her lies – which thrilled him.

"I need you to stay here, sweetie, and look after Brett."

Ricky froze. His brow spelled annoyance.

"Ricky, I know it's your weekend, and you're such a darling as to care for your brother all week, but we're family, and we do things for each other."

"How long?"

"Could be an hour or two – could be until evening."

"Ma –"

"Please, sweetheart, no maaaa. You're not a dyslexic sheep. I work all day, every day, for the both of you. To feed, clothe, and shelter you both. Cut me some slack."

"You need to break your back today?"

"No, it's … yes, it's work-related."

Ricky danced in the doorway, on the verge of a tantrum, hands on the frame. He huffed, blew hot air, scratched his torso.

"Don't give me that, Ricky. I'm your ma. Do as you're told – for once in your life."

"Can I take Brett out?"

"In the yard."

"No. Out."

"No, son. He's six. I have palpitations when you edge beyond the end of the road, never mind him."

"But –"

"For me, Ricky. For me."

She sprung off the sofa, pulled him to her breast and pitter-pattered kisses on his forehead. She couldn't do that much longer. He'd do it to her, if the want burst past his stony heart. He watched Brett through slit-eyes. The kid heard it all. Pretended he hadn't. When ma hurried on her shoes by the doorway, his brother mouthed Mr Panowich. Ricky shook his head and scrunched his nose to warn him.

"Mr Panowich," Brett said aloud.

"Who's Mr Pavlovich?" Ma grunted, second shoe almost on.

"His made-up friend." He balled a fist and planted it in the palm of his other hand. Brett smirked. Rebellious. "Seriously, ma, how long you gunna be?"

"You got somewhere to go?"

He shrugged, his face melted sullen.

"You've all the hot season for that. Relax."

He scowled at her until the Datsun disappeared from view. Its trail of smoke dissipated in the air just like his damn summer. He weighed the picture frame from the top of the TV. Pictured how the man in the photograph would look in a cap pulled low over his eyes.

* * *

Carrie's voice scraped his ears all the way from Liz' backyard. Ricky hunched in sympathy for Mr Panowich. Ah, he'd made his bed. Must have his shoulders stuck in a permanent shrug by now. Carrie's tone caused Ricky to tip-toe to the house. He didn't announce his arrival, just stretched his neck to see the lay of the land. Mr Panowich and that woman reclined on sun chairs, her belly folding over the bikini. Mr Panowich wore long pants and sandals, but no shirt, his hairy chest a burned forest of tree stumps.

Liz sat in the neighbor's shade on a ruined wall at the garden's end. Poked dirt with a stick for some lost memory of her pa, the ground she scratched mirroring her forehead. That paperback she'd showed him rested by her side. Ricky half turned to leave her alone, but held himself at that woman's tone. She affected a baby voice.

"Come on, Liz, darling, why don't you join us for a drag?"

Liz pretended she didn't hear a thing. Carrie called again. Liz opened the book and read a line. Ricky reckoned she read the same sentence over and over. Could tell her temperature rose. That woman flicked her smoke. It hit Liz's shoe. Liz turned a page, and with a shuffle of a heel, smushed the joint into the earth.

"You little fucking bitch."

That woman shot from her lounger and aimed a blow at Liz' head. Ricky shifted to see Mr Panowich, who loafed there with his attention on the blank blue sky. Balanced a joint in his mouth like the tip of an airplane on take-off. Liz swayed to avoid the strike and the next, pounced to her feet and smacked the stick across that woman's upper arm. Carrie yelped.

"You ungrateful little bitch. Full of waste."

She pointed a finger at Liz. Liz whipped her stick at it and struck. That woman stood dumbstruck, her digit ablaze. She thrust it beneath her armpit and howled.

"You little whore. You fucking slut bag."

Liz dangled the book open by her side. She wouldn't use that as a weapon. That woman swung her good hand toward Mr Panowich. "You gunna let that happen, you useless piece of shit?"

"Huh?" Mr Panowich lifted his head, surprised at the disruption to his thoughts. "What happened?"

"She hit me."

"Liz? You hit her?"

"Aha."

"What you hit her for?"

"She tried to punch me."

"You try to smack her?"

"Uh, yeah. She wasted a fucking joint. Which cost money."

"You were smoking a joint?"

"No, dad. She threw it at me."

"What you doing offering my girl some blow?"

That woman shook her head. Curled her upper lip. Spat at Mr Panowich, who jumped from his lounger.

"Carrie? What you spitting at me for?"

"Because ... you should control your fucking offspring. Jesus, man, will you grow some balls?"

"Jeez, give me a chance to handle her before you go ballistic. Man, what is wrong with you?"

"I'd like some respect round here, is all. I know I can't be her ma, but please, come on ... if I'm pleasing you, she should be pleased with me."

Mr Panowich planted both hands on his hips. "She's right, Liz. She pleases me. That should be enough. You treat her right, right?"

"I don't want none of that shit you smoke, dad. Leave me out of it."

"Sure. We're all friends now. Right?"

Liz glared at that woman. Carrie folded her arms and inhaled deep from a new spliff. "Suppose." Carrie settled on the lounge chair.

"Liz?"

She nodded, which gave him permission to sprawl on his lounger again.

Liz perched on the wall. Ricky smiled at her determination to enjoy the evening outside. She read the back of the book, ran a finger up and down its spine.

"You know, that boy you're seeing – Ricky – he's welcome anytime."

Ricky scowled at how his name spilled out of her mouth like sewage. Why the attempt at nice?

Liz knotted her brows, but didn't engage her eyes.

"I'm serious. I might have gotten him all wrong. Guess who I had round here, earlier. Michael. He knows your boy. Said he's a great kid. Could do with that kind of kid. Bit of summer work. Would do him some good instead of wasting his earning months away."

Ricky wound his neck back in and dug his nails into the house's vinyl slats. His hands vibrated – from their words, from his heart, from the razz of the motorbike heading his way. The biker pulled up, his fly-eyed sunglasses trained on him. Arms thick as tree branches and tattoos circling his neck and popping off his chest – guns, knives, skulls. He switched off the bike, which had drowned the hostile voices in the backyard. Liz zipped by, grabbed the spare helmet, and pierced Ricky once she saw him, a squashed bug against the wall. She shook her head, shoved on the helmet, and wrapped her skinny arms round the bulk of the man. Ricky stared at the gym sticker on the bike's butt to avoid her eyes. They sped off, and Ricky rushed home with a belly full of bile.

30

The morning heat sucked Ricky's juices dry. Ma came home late the previous night and hurried to work in the early hours. Ricky rifled through her CDs to overwhelm the old kitchen clock's tick-tock. She didn't play them often. Preferred the sound of an open door and the company of TV nowadays. She'd throw one on when dad still lived with them and force him to dance along. Like drunken chickens. Swung Brett around in her arms when he didn't resist. Done it with Ricky once, too.

Ricky didn't open his ears to much music. Only what came out of Liz. He'd listen to her all day. Otherwise, the breeze in the grass and trees, even the winter howl through the back alleys of Town, is all the music he wanted.

The man who blared out the speakers now sang about getting it on. Ricky turned up his nose because ma listened to it, but once it filled the space, he hummed as it burrowed down his ear hole. Brett sat listless, eyes on the popcorn ceiling as if he counted every bubble.

"You gotta stay here on your own, Brett."

"No. Last night scared me."

Ricky burned. Brett didn't whine that "no." Stated it as a matter of fact. Ignored his older brother. His boss. Brett's lips moved. Ricky couldn't tell if he tallied, sang along to the song, or complained about his proposal.

"Yes, Brett. Yes."

"Don't wanna be on my own. Take me out with you. I'll go with Mr Panowich. Shoot a gun."

"Do you really fire a gun?"

"Yeah. It's so cool. You ever shoot one?"

Brett's a brat. A real pain in the ass, but that Carrie spooked him. Who's the Michael she talked about? *The* Michael? Tarantula Man? He wouldn't hand Brett over to Mr Panowich today. Or the next week. Until he understood what the hell she meant. Shit, Grealey knew Liz as Mr Panowich's daughter. He recalled the black car which parked outside Liz' home. Looked like Trent's BMW.

He called ma's cell. She didn't answer, so he tried again and again. She answered all puffed. That godawful job wore her out. "Ricky, what is it?"

"When you back?"

"Damn, you got ants in your pants or somethin'?"

"I can't relax, ma. The not knowin' – I need to know when you're done."

He heard a crumple, somebody grunt. A man asked, "Who is it?"

"Just my boy."

Just my boy?

"Ricky, maybe about eight or nine tonight. It's a long shift."

"Shit, ma, that's forever."

"Watch your language, Ricky."

"Shit, shit, shit."

He cut the call and dragged Brett off the sofa. The kid yanked free. Ricky darted for him and missed. Brett shot for the stairs, but Ricky caught this piglet's leg and hauled him down.

* * *

Ricky flicked his tongue through his teeth. Floyd stood a dozen yards from the riverbank's edge, his feet roots deep in the soil. Watched them float away, a sentinel over their safety. Floyd's stance said Darren Grealey would no longer cause problems. Ricky rubbed the dull ache in his leg and held the boat and his brother's shoulder tight as the breeze rolled wave after wave. Brett lapped it all up and licked the spray from his lips. Bixby scowled at every shadow, ready to dodge a sudden hand dragging him back into the system. Charlie grinned and rested his elbows on the boat's side.

"Where's the girl?" Mr Vale checked both shoulders to see if he'd lost her over the edge.

"Reading *Great Expectations.*" Ricky shrugged.

The man stared at the horizon as if that shone light on her reasons. "Ah, that flowery ass." He shifted some lever on the boat and they sped faster. He swerved, spun, slowed them down, and jerked the craft back to full speed. It's fast. Ricky knew that. What's Mr Vale out to prove? Ricky toed at the canvas keeping the man's fishing gear out of the weather. Charlie's pa veered left and Ricky almost tumbled right into the river. The City sparkled under the sun, a place set in the future. Ricky glanced back at the mess of his Town. It pulled at him, as if upset by his wandering eyes. He pushed the guilt down until its sharpness dulled beneath waves of acid in his stomach.

Charlie's pa moored the boat to a post and helped them all out. Made Charlie get out by himself. A young woman handed

Mr Vale a blazer, which went with his chocolate brown pants.

"Well, little man, this is the City. You ever been here?"

Brett shook his head, that goofy grin still plastered strong. Where's Mr Panowich, now, eh? Which drew him back to how Liz' pa knew Grealey, and through him, Tarantula Man. It didn't seem credible the big dope swam in those waters.

"You good?" Ricky nudged Bixby. The effect of Bixby's shower had worn away and his regular scent regained its rightful spot. Bixby's cudgel lips told him to not ask again.

Charlie planted an arm around Ricky's shoulder, which stiffened his frame. Not that Charlie recognized. "I like Town better. The City rots your mind."

"How'd you mean?"

Bixby lifted his knuckles from their drag along the ground. "You look under the skirt and there's nothing."

Ricky duck-billed his lips and wondered at how that's so bad. Charlie laughed and patted Ricky as if they had grown up together and forged a bond not even an ax could sever. Charlie had forgotten how that conversation up the tree ended – or he shrugged it off.

Charlie crinkled his nose. "It smothers your face, crams its thing down your throat, and hollows you right out. Until you're useless."

"Why's your pa live here, then?"

Charlie's words sounded like his old man's mantra.

Ricky scratched his arm. Wanted to punch Charlie off his body. The heat already simmered the blood.

"Business. But his heart lives in Town."

"He can drive over."

"You've seen the bridge. Pain to get there on the back roads. And in winter, forget it. We're stuck here. Godddd, I wish I lived your life, Ricky."

Ricky side-eyed Bixby, whose eyebrows stapled his hairline. Charlie's pa one-arm hugged the woman, slithered into his blazer and invited them all into his car. Ricky wished he told ma about his plan. Nobody knew this man, though he'd showed his care for them many times over. *I'm ungrateful.* Still, Mr Vale, like his son, had invaded his summer. *Ah, stop it. He's just showing us a good time.* Liz would leave a scar on the day in her current mood – it shouldn't ruin his time in the City.

That man she rode with, Jesus, what did she do with him?

The frigid blast from the air-conditioner evaporated his imagination and dragged him inside. The air-conditioning in ma's car worked when it wanted, and never blasted as fresh as this. Mr Vale's ride blazed metallic blue, its seats facing the rear window, a table to play all kinds of games across. The sweat on his neck frosted at the drop in temperature and Ricky hugged warmth into his bones. Rubbed at his bruised legs and imagined Darren Grealey lifeless as the other two buried in their City of Forts. Brett uttered variations of *wow* every other moment until Ricky back-handed his chest. The kid screwed his eyes at him. Ricky didn't like this new rebel. He sensed words locked tight in his brother's throat had loosened, carefree. Loaded on the tip of his tongue.

"That's the City Hall. That's the Museum of Art. That's ..."

Charlie's ramble merged with the hum of the car's air-conditioner. Brett shuffled into Ricky's body for warmth. Mr Vale broke into song. His cheeks wobbled with the strain of some tune, about somebody who told his ma that he'd just killed a man and didn't want to die for it.

"The City, boys, the City. Crown jewel of our glorious State.

A beacon for all those who aspire. Where many fall into complacency and degradation." He laughed. "I'm scaring you fellas. This place is a shithole, pardon my French, filled with robots. The robot revolution is right here. Automatons everywhere you go. Yes, sir – no, sir – three bags full, sir. You want anything here, you get it, as long as your credit card is valid and you have the ..." He chuckled to himself and nudged his glasses back up his nose. "Charlie?"

"Dad."

"How many people do you know here?"

"In this car?"

"Nooo, in the City."

"Lots."

"Give me a number."

"Puh, I don't count. A Hundred-or-so."

"What number would you say are your friends?"

Charlie scratched inside a nostril. Shuffled his ass in embarrassment. "Dad ..."

"None. Not one of them. They all sit in their expensively decorated bedrooms with their hands like this ... it's embarrassing. They're breeding monsters."

Mr Vale swiveled his head toward them all and offered an embarrassed smile at his rant. "Sorry, boys, I'm killing the party." He pressed some button on his steering wheel and the music volume pulled and pushed his blood as if it controlled its tide.

The City pulsed with life. White people, black people, brown people – all kinds of folk. Ricky and Brett stared at the black kids on a basketball court, about twenty of them, mesmerized by a sight he saw on TV.

"Ya don't see many of those in Town, do ya?"

Ricky snapped out of it, annoyed that he caught his lack of experience in the world. "I've seen 'em, though. Around." He didn't like how the man shortened 'you' to 'ya.' Made him feel insignificant, that Mr Vale thought he only understood small words.

"I'm just playin' with ya, kid." He burst into song again, this time about girls with fat bottoms.

Ricky turned to the world outside. A removal truck sat outside a new store where a ma and her two kids peered in the window. A kite perched high in the display, in imaginary flight, above a line of bears and old-style cars as long as his forearm. Mr Vale stopped at the traffic light and Mr McGarry locked Ricky's eyes. The toy store had moved here, surrounded by glitz and free from iron bars in the glass panes. Mr McGarry's outlet yanked at him across the years. Ma always changed speed as they walked by in the hope he couldn't read the sign or see the toys from the blur of movement. Mr Vale pulled away at the green and the toy shop owner nodded in recognition at the sad snap of a tendon to Ricky's past.

People strode with purpose around here, every step impatient to reach its target. People in suits, some on pedal bikes, some with fancy bags over a shoulder. Tons of stores, all open. Brett pawed at the window, a cat at the closed entrance to a bird cage. A blink in Ricky's eye set off a flutter, and he turned from the sensory overload. Bixby slouched low in the seat, his chin close to his folded arms.

Charlie's home crowned the top of an apartment block. A man greeted them at the building's entry. Wore white gloves and a hat, which he tipped to Charlie's pa. Knew Mr Vale's name and held the door open. Once up there, Ricky ran a pinkie along the penthouse wall to make sure his imagination played no tricks. He plunged both hands into his pockets when Mr Vale arrowed an eyebrow. The man smiled, but of the sort which equaled the wag of a finger.

Ricky leaned into Bixby. "My house would fit twice into this."

Bixby shrugged. The man asked them to remove their shoes. Brett ran to the window. Charlie's pa laughed and slid the door open to a balcony. He flicked his head to invite them all out.

"Is that you, Harry?"

Mr Vale sang his "yes" and bent over his wife. She idled on a lounger with a fancy glass in her hand. Stretched her neck to reach his kiss. Ricky pulled a face. Brett, Bixby, and Charlie mirrored him.

The balcony arced out of the building, a discus wedged into the upper floors. It overlooked the bustle of the street below, the river in the distance, and Town far away. A haze hid much of Town behind its curtain, which is what people of the City wanted, Ricky guessed. Ricky would have spat over the shoulder-high railing, but he didn't want one of those smiles from Mr Vale to crawl up his spine again.

"Hello, boys." Charlie's ma raised her glass to the new-comers. Three of them smiled and played with their fingers. Charlie, on his home turf, lost the cocky air which annoyed them all. His pa put a clamp on that tongue of his.

"We're so glad you made a friend of Charlie. You really have brought out the best in him." She swiveled to a seated position. Slim woman, a hard stomach exposed by her bikini. Ma had a little flab. Enough to hide a grape in the folds. Not this lady. She worked out.

Charlie stood by him at the railing and eyed the street like a monkey in a cage. "Pa, Santi just pulled up."

Mr Vale checked his watch. "A day early. What the heck? Let me go down. See what he's up to."

Ricky followed Charlie's gaze and ignored his question about basketball. You can't play basketball up here. You'd lose the ball too easy. It'd kill someone down there. A stocky man got out of the big white pickup truck. Another pulled up behind. A third squeezed into the last gap. Those trucks in the City of Forts, which hounded them to the river. That's not Santi, whoever the hell Santi is – they're with Tarantula Man.

"Shit, Charlie, they're the men who chased us outta the fields. They tracked us."

Charlie pulled a face like he just exited his ma. "What? What you talking about?"

"Three white trucks. Some Spanish guys. They were on the hunt when we ran to your dad's boat."

Bixby joined him and bobbed about for a better view. "Fuck, he's right."

"Boys?" His ma's lips bent and quivered in disapproval. She heard a cuss or two, but restrained from accusations. Left the suggestion in the air. Bixby nudged Ricky to answer. Ricky made circles of his eyes in mock-confusion. She cocked her head, suspicious, but as she didn't want to believe her ears, or confront her boy's new and only friends, she lay back again and sipped her drink.

"What we gunna do?" Ricky grabbed Charlie's arm. He seemed relaxed about it all. "Come on, Charlie, what we gunna do? Your pa's heading down there. Does he think them maintenance men? They'll kill him. Shit, Charlie, why you looking at me like that? They'll murder your pa. They're after us all, now."

Charlie sighed, as though reluctant to save his old man, but he'd do it, anyway. "I'll tell him."

"Too late." Bixby pointed to the street.

Three men stood around Charlie's pa, arms folded. Mr Vale rested a hand on a hip. From here, looked like all the talk came from him. Unaware of danger. Ricky didn't want to tear his eyes away despite how tension twisted his gut. He gripped the railing, scared he'd splat on the sidewalk below if he let go.

The Latinos nodded. One laughed. They shook hands. Mr Vale patted the chief man on the shoulder. Arched his back at some hilarious comment. Bixby turned to Ricky in disbelief. Ricky hunched his shoulders as he searched for meaning. The men drove away and Charlie's pa came back up a conquering hero.

"Dad told them to get out of here." Charlie put an arm round both Ricky and Bixby, and Mr Vale nodded in satisfaction. Bixby wowed. Ricky's heart beat a tune of admiration for the big man. No wonder the man's rich. He could talk his way out of a prisoner-of-war camp.

"You boys want to tear the place up?" Mr Vale grinned.

"Can we?" Brett didn't even glance at Ricky for permission.

"Within reason, boys." Charlie's ma raised her glass, beamed a smile to compete with the sun, and opened her book. Ricky thought of Liz. This is the life she wanted.

Charlie boasted a game room full of stuff Ricky didn't comprehend. He had a lined mini-basketball court with baskets, a soccer net up against a wall, a couple of video game machines – one had a motorbike to make the race real - and a corner dedicated to a game console, fitted to a massive TV, and a bunch of chairs for friends Charlie's dad said he didn't have. Unless he'd bought them just for their visit today. They still had a just-unwrapped sheen.

Weird.

They played basketball and shoved Brett out of the way. He whined for the first time, but consoled himself by riding the video game bike. Tired his fingers and thumbs on video games for a while. A thrill for about ten minutes before the great outdoors pulled at Ricky and Bixby. Ricky snuck away to the balcony. Mr and Mrs Vale reclined on loungers and surveyed what Ricky guessed their kingdom. Neither said a word to each other the full minute Ricky stood, awkward, in the doorway. Charlie's ma placed the book on the side table. Didn't have an important-looking cover. Liz would disapprove.

Ricky coughed and plunged into their realm. Held the railings which barred him from the world. Smiled at both and surveyed the view.

"Thank you, Ricky. Thank you so much." His own ma's smile never buttered him up like this.

"What for?"

"Oh, come now, kid, you know why." Mr Vale smacked a thigh. "Enjoying the view out there?"

"It's amazing."

"Isn't it?"

"What do you do, sir?"

He laughed, planted a hand on Ricky's shoulder. "Sir?" He gestured to his wife. "Don't you love his manners? There's plenty back in Town would laugh at what I do."

"Which is what?"

"I manage my wealth."

Ricky shook his head. "What do you mean?"

"I have money in stocks. I check it all out daily. Sell here, buy there. I manage my money."

"To make more?"

"Yes. Lots of it." Mr Vale swung a hand around his home. "For all this, you need a lot, son."

Ricky gaped at Mr Vale. Had this man landed from the stars? The sun glowed a golden sheen across him. "Money makes money?"

"You see, this is what's wrong with the education system. They teach you nothing about cash. They'll happily instruct you the ins-and-outs of Charles *bleedin'* Dickens, but not the tools we really need to survive." He sniffed the air and sighed. "I should meet your mother."

"Ma? Why?"

"To get you started."

"On what?"

Mr Vale sat on the lounger's edge, legs wide open, hands on each knee. "Charlie gets embarrassed about his lack of friends. He used to think it was his fault, but now realizes he hadn't met the right kind. You're from over there." He waved in Town's direction. "You come from a place like that and got out of it – that makes you a true winner. Many don't make it. Become bitter and twisted. Losers, every one. And people born into all this ..." He swept a hand across the balcony and his wife. "None are true winners. They've never struggled for a minute of their pampered lives. All - bigger losers than the mob over there. Ah, they have money and comfort, but up here ..." He tapped his head twice. "They're as dead as a brontosaurus.

"You are life, Ricky. You bring my boy into existence."

Ricky glanced between them, at the floor, and out to the City. They made him sound like Jesus, for God's sake. His heart jumped for joy at Charlie, who threw a basketball at him to gain a firmer grasp of another object. Ricky overhand-cupped the ball so it didn't fly over the railing and crush somebody's skull, though he reckoned Mr Vale would buy his way out of such trouble.

"You don't like video games?" Charlie placed a small, bug-type thing on the ground and shaped his hands around a controller as if he still played his console. Shifted his thumbs and the toy lifted into the air with a buzz. "It's a drone, Ricky. You never seen one?"

Ricky shrugged, annoyed at the implied ignorance. Mr Vale had it right — Charlie needed normal people around him. But Ricky didn't want to act as his guide.

Charlie flew the drone so it hovered over a decorative pebble and caused the thing to pick it up. Bixby and Brett laughed at the novelty. Ricky eyed Mr Vale, who smiled, content with the attention aimed at his boy. He raised it higher, its buzz a strain against the weight. Swerved and twisted it, with a few *whoas* from his audience, over the side of the building, where he made the machine drop the stone.

"Jeez." Bixby triggered a stampede to the railing. The kids squeezed their faces into the gaps and Mr and Mrs Vale leaned over to see the mess. Some man sprawled on the sidewalk, his cane a foot-or-so by him.

Charlie's dad grabbed his boy by the front of his shirt and marched him back to his bedroom.

31

C harlie's pa dropped them back at the river bank upwind from the City of Forts. He'd left Charlie at home with words to ring his ears all night.

"What I read in the papers about Town worries me. This is a safe spot to pick you up in future."

He gave the boys a warm smile and apologized for his son's behavior. They waved to Mr Vale until he became a speck in the gap between Ricky's thumb and index.

"I thought Charlie killed that old man. Jeez, what a lucky bastard." Ricky's head swayed in amazement at Charlie's pebble-drop and how his victim found his feet.

"Charlie's a damn nuisance."

Ricky gave his friend an elevated eyebrow. "I like Mr Vale."

"Charlie'll get us in trouble. He'll bring us trouble. Mr Vale'll let the system sneak in through his stupid son."

Ricky guided Brett forward and put an arm around Bixby's shoulder. "How's he gunna do that?"

They kicked at loose stones and swung sticks at the under-growth.

"He'll attract cops, who'll involve a whole bunch of bastards, and that woman will lay her red eyes on me."

"Bastards." Brett parroted the word again and again as he

ran off.

"Hey, watch that mouth, you little ass."

"Bastard."

Bixby laughed. "Bastards, Brett. They're all bastards. Don't trust anyone."

"Bastards, bastards, bastards."

Ricky burned at his brother. Brett could cuss all he pleased as far as he cared, but if he repeated it in front of ma, then she'd have it in for her eldest son. "The Veronica woman has red hair, not red eyes. Those are green. Like Liz'."

"You liked the look of them?" Bixby shook Ricky off his shoulder.

"You can't miss them. Pull you right in."

"What, into snitching?"

"Piss off, Bix."

Bixby punched his arm, playful. "You saw the Latinos, yeah?"

"I've seen Latinos before. They're not aliens."

"Not what I'm saying. Did you notice how Charlie's pa handled them? I shit my pants when they chased us, but he just dealt with them as if he did it all day."

"Maybe they fear him –"

"Or work for him?"

"As in actually do his yard – balcony – what do you mean?"

"His muscle. They do bad stuff for him."

Ricky laughed. "He's a ... he ... he manages his wealth."

"What the fuck's that?"

Ricky shrugged. "Did you hear how he sings? Dangerous as Tanais."

"Or Liz. Ha."

Ricky scowled. He'd gone to the City with Mr Vale to do

something for Liz, and he forgot. Yeah, he thought of her, but only in relation to that tattooed ass on the bike. If he hadn't become so distracted by the damn wealth the man managed – that balcony, that massive game room, that wife – then he'd bring news to excite Liz.

"You sleeping in the shed tonight?"

"No way, friend, no way. Not after the cops tried to grab me. Not a chance."

"So where you going?"

"My home. Our City of Forts."

Ricky checked his shoulder, jumpy that a Ghost Boy snuck behind to stab him in the ribs. "Are you crazy?"

"I'm good. I've been watching them. They stick to the one house. Shift stuff in and out at different times of day. Use the river to transport it all. I should steal some of it. People in Town pay solid money to shove that shit in their system."

"Jesus, Bix, you can't sleep right next to the assholes who want—"

"Best to keep them in view, don't you think? If I snooze in your shed, then I'm worried about cops turning up out of the blue again. There, I know exactly where these Ghost Boys are. And ... our guardian angel watches over us."

"Floyd?"

"He's the man. He said he'd protect you, and he has."

"Yeah – me. Protected me."

"I'm telling you, I've been thinking about it. He's the one who shot that man who chased you guys to the factory. I did not pull the trigger. I swear."

Ricky nodded. Bixby held the gun, but Floyd seemed to always be where they needed him. Made sense.

"I'm heading there now, Ricky-boy."

Ricky shook his hand, told him to take care.

Bixby squeezed it hard. "You talk like this is the end. We're gunna win this. It's our place. Forever. No invaders."

"See ya, man."

Brett walked backwards and shouted, "Bastard, bastard, fuck, fuck."

"Come here, you little fuck."

Brett scampered off, his laughter louder than the birds he scared away.

32

icky and Brett made it home just before ma. Ricky instructed Brett to roll around the sofa like a playful dog to get rid of that fresh air smell before she returned. Ricky mirrored him on the carpet. Rested against the armchair once he reckoned the house aroma settled into his clothes. Ma offered them a smile thick with guilt as she entered and Ricky breathed free.

"How was work?" He kept his attention on the TV and shot Brett a warning.

Ma slipped off her sneakers and cleared embarrassment from her throat. "Same as ever, son – work is work. Has to be done. Got to feed you boys, an' all."

Ricky nodded. Brett giggled.

"What you giggling at, monkey?"

Her question made magnets of the brothers' eyes. Ricky's sat dark as a well. Brett shuffled to the edge of the sofa, far from his sibling.

"Just happy you're home, ma."

She rested by her youngest, ruffled his hair, planted a kiss on his willing head. She tried it on Ricky, but he pulled aside.

"Ah, I wish you were still my baby boy, too. There's no lovin' in those teenage bones."

"Come on, ma, you don't need to talk like that."

He slid out of bed that night once he heard the rise and fall of ma's snore, and leaned out the window. Batted away a few bugs, but didn't shut the bug screen. The stars reached inside him for reasons he couldn't work out. Tugged. That's some apartment Charlie lives in. Hardwood floors you could skate on. Massive bedroom. Could fit four or five of Ricky's room in his one. And all that stuff. Tons of stuff, most of it ignored by Charlie. Too much junk. How would you choose what to mess around with? And that balcony. What a view.

All that from managing wealth. How do you manage it? You need wealth to begin with, right? Ma should have a ton of cash. She has three jobs. But they only just get by, because dad sends nothing back. He thought of Floyd ...

That apartment is a cage. Mr Vale isn't wrong. His money turned Charlie into some strange thing. Aggressive, but clingy. Turned Ricky off. He stared at the largest star as he shifted excuses like a Rubik's Cube.

I'm sorry, Mr Vale, thanks for the day out. Your apartment is cool, an' all, but we can't let Charlie hang out with us.

Why not?

Well, he's just a little weird.

He tries to dominate, but gets sulky if we pay him no attention.

We're not good for him. We lead him astray to bad things.

It's not Charlie, it's us.

Ricky pulled the world's air into his lungs and flopped backwards onto the bed. Fell asleep almost as he hit the pillow.

* * *

"Oh, God, Ricky – really?"

He opened an eye. Blue sky. Silhouette of ma against the window. The open window.

"Bugs everywhere. Dammit, kid, will you take some responsibility? What would your pa think?"

"He wouldn't."

"Excuse me?"

"Pa doesn't think. He just does."

She slid the bug screen shut and whipped the comforter off his bed. He grunted as he snatched, and missed, for his cover.

"You overslept. I'm off to work. Brett is eating breakfast and watching TV. Make sure you keep that boy occupied. I don't want him turning …"

"Into me?"

"I was thinking of your pa, but yes – you, too."

He waited for her departure before he hopped out of bed. It would amaze her to think of how he organized things around here. He jumped two steps at a time downstairs. Brett watched some cheap cartoon, milk on his upper lip. Didn't say "morning" or anything. Ricky slapped a few ham sandwiches together, shoved them in a paper bag, and dragged Brett out without him brushing his teeth.

* * *

A man sat on a step outside the house where his kind had held them hostage. Smoked a cigarette, fascinated with some object by his feet. Brett wanted to make noise until the Chinese burn Ricky inflicted on him shut that mouth of his.

"Why'm I here with you?"

Ricky stayed alert as a gazelle near a pride of lions. "Because

Mr Panowich is no good."

"What yer mean?" Brett swiveled to protest.

"He's ... ill. Very ill."

"He looked alright the other day."

"He did, didn't he? But it's amazing what can happen in twenty-four hours."

Ricky stopped still and raised a hand to quieten Brett. Bixby couldn't hang around any of the houses. Too close to the dodgy men who ruined their summer. Ricky spun, slow, to see if he sat in a tree somewhere to monitor things. He saw no sign of him, so he led Brett towards the factory, their heads down, tongues clamped to the backs of their teeth.

The regular entrance in the big blue gate spent him a few grunts to get it open. Brett pulled and slipped in to push out so Ricky could squirm inside. Didn't need to work so hard. Ricky's bony frame slithered in like a rat beneath a door.

Whispers like a murmur of ghosts flitted around the cavernous expanse. Brett reached for Ricky's wrist. The older sibling wriggled him off and led the way to target the source. Bixby's sharp tone crystallized, Tanais' came out of the haze, but the adult he couldn't identify. Adult, yes ... The man's voice rumbled across space. Ricky froze and planted a palm on his brother's chest. Shushed his lips with a finger. Ricky couldn't form a plan. His brain worked, but fear clogged the cogs. If he inched closer, he'd put his brother at risk. As big of a pain in the ass as Brett is, the shared blood pushed Ricky's steps backwards almost down every creaky and rusted step to the factory floor and out the gate.

Tanais sounded tortured. Bixby, cool as a cucumber, remained level as if he negotiated with gangsters each day. That made Ricky head closer again. He crouched low and swung to

Brett. "You gotta stay here, pal." Brett nodded a dozen times, his mouth open. Ricky pinched his lips shut. "Don't make a sound."

Ricky took the next few steps with his neck craned to his brother. The light thinned to smudged black this far up, with the door above closed. Their words formed as his distance shortened and he reached the top of the stairs.

"Look, kid, all I know is that my daughter has been in terrible shape for the last few days. Full of the shakes. Waking up in the middle of the night in a sweat, screaming. I hear your name all the time. She comes out here to play. What the hell did you do to her?"

"And I keep telling you, mister, I did nothing at all."

A kind of relief hit Ricky, but why did Tanais bring her pa into this? Did she doubt them all?

The dad's exasperation burst through the door's seams. "Who are you?"

"You know my name. Clearly."

"And where do you live? Who are your parents?"

This factory might have forged this man's voice, even if it came out gentle. He pictured the man with a clipboard, a concerned smile on his face. Tempted Ricky to barge in and tell the man some lies.

"That's none of your business, mister. None at all. You can't come bargin' in here layin' down the law."

"You say 'barging in here' as if this is your house, Bixby. Is this your house?"

Ricky raised his voice and opened the door to make out he'd arrived home from a hard day's work. "Bixby, Bixby, you here?"

Bixby sat on the floor with his back against a pillar for

support in his entrapment. Light flooded through the un-boarded windows. Tanais' face twisted in panic at how she had ruined their friendship. The man examined Ricky over his glasses. Made Ricky itch under the lab conditions.

"And who are you? Let me guess ... Ricky?"

Ricky blasted a glare at Tanais. She shook her head and grasped at her pa's arm. She might as well have pulled at the arm of a statue for all the result she gained.

"I'm Bixby's brother. Who are you, sir?"

"Tanais' father, as you no doubt presume by now. Where do you boys live?"

"In Town, sir."

"Where in Town?"

Ricky controlled his breath and directed his eyes for Bixby's benefit. *Come on, move it.* "Our ma told us never to talk to strangers, sir. So, we'll be out of here. If you don't mind."

Amusement and anger fought for control of the man. He pushed his glasses up his nose and swung his arm to the doorway, an invitation for Bixby to get out of there. Bixby edged past, wary the man would make a grab at him.

Tanais palm-squeezed her cheeks. "I'm so sorry, Bixby. It wasn't my fault, I swear."

Bixby shrugged his shoulders at her and kept his attention on the exit. It changed her dad's acceptance of his own powerlessness to an aggressive snatch of Bixby's shirt. He swung him by the neck of his cloth and pushed him to the pillar. "You don't treat my girl like that."

"Dadddd."

"No. No, Tanais. Have some self-respect." The spittle hit Bixby's eyeballs. He blinked it away and tried to smash the man's grip off him. Her pa held firm and drove him again into the concrete. "I'm not sure who you think you are –"

"My name's Bixby, and this is gunna get you fired."

"I know your name, son."

Bixby squirmed free and ran for the exit door. "Fuck you, old man. Fuck you." He jumped two and three steps at a time. Startled Brett down there. Ricky glanced between Tanais and her pa. She folded in on herself, terrified and angry. The man rested a hand on his hip, sad for his kid. He'd been powerful once. Broad shoulders and a wide frame didn't hide the slight paunch or the social studies-style beard and glasses.

Bixby stormed out of the building. Hit the great blue gate with an old iron bar so it rang out across the fields and sent a score of beasts deeper into the bushes. Sweat dropped off his lobster-red face as he beat a rhythm. The beat captured scrutiny. A man by one house got to his feet. Another joined him. Cocked ears to the air – a pair of wolves sniffing potential meat.

Ricky grabbed his arm and pulled. Bixby raised the rod to him. Ricky stepped back and yanked Brett behind him. "Settle down, Bix. You're getting us some attention."

Bixby glared over his shoulder and nodded. "Let's get the fuck outta here."

They semi-circled around the far side of the factory and ran with their heads down below the growth. Ricky dragged Brett, who knew better than to protest at the forced pace. Through the bushes they watched the two, three men, head to the factory. One had long strands which fell to his shoulders. Ricky jerked at Bixby's arm.

"They're going inside."

"Good. We fooled them."

"Tanais' in there. And her pa."

Bixby clamped his teeth shut and bared them as if someone tied him to a fence all week without food. "Good."

"What do you mean *good*? They might … you know."

"Suits me fine. Then they won't stick their noses into my business and I can carry on free of the bastards."

"What bastards?"

"The ones who want me back in care. Who do you think?"

"Tanais doesn't want you in care."

"She brought her dad to see me. To help me."

Ricky ignored the sarcasm. "To support you, yeah. She's not about sending you to wherever it is you're scared of."

"Her pa works for them."

"For who?"

"For the government. They'll send me to more of those families who treated me like a dog. I just wanna live here, Ricky. I won't be anyone's pet. Ever."

"What did they do to you?"

"It's not what any of them did, it's how they were."

"I don't get it, Bixby. You had people who wanted you. What's the problem?"

Bixby pointed the metal rod at his friend. Touched his belly with the tip as a warning. "Don't turn into Tanais."

Ricky stuck his hands in the air. Wanted to stroke away the trembling from his brother who wrapped an arm round his waist. Feared the touch would infect him. "Tanais is terrified up there. You're her main pal out of all of us. She brought you all them sandwiches with no wish for reward. You treat her shittier than any of those families did to you."

Ricky fidgeted for a view of the men. They planted themselves still in the bare ground before the gate. Swirls of dust licked their legs. Tanais and her pa blinked into the harsh

232

light as they emerged from the safety of the factory's bowel. Her old man nodded at the men in surprise at their presence. Tarantula Man shuffled his feet apart and rested both hands on his hips. The other two lifted their shirts a little to reveal weapons.

"Bix, let's move. The gun. Let's fetch that gun. Now."

Bixby checked the scene and shrugged. "Do what you need to do. She's not part of our gang. You recognize it. She's an intruder. She's brought us trouble."

Ricky pushed the rod's point away and broke for the house. Brett's lower lip trembled, but Ricky could have ruffled his hair and hugged him for how he held that whimper down deep. He tensed, expecting a thud, or bang, a sign the gangsters shot father and daughter. He skidded to a stop once he got outside the dwelling next door to the one occupied. What if they had men inside that, too?

The door creaked loud in the heightened silence. He peeked down the hallway into the living room, the kitchen, and up the stairs. He made his first step, afraid it would trigger a giant rat trap. Safe. He pulled Brett with him, more worried about him alone on the outside than in the potential quagmire of the house. Ricky leaned over the large hole in the floor and circled it. Squinted into the shadows. "Okay."

They padded down the stairs, and Ricky shoved Brett into a corner. "Stay here, pal. Okay?"

"I'm scared."

"I realize."

"You should have left me with Mr Panowich."

"I shouldn't. Really, I shouldn't."

"I don't want to stay in the dark."

"It's just a game. Don't move until I come back."

"It's not just a game – is it?"

Ricky grimaced and shook his head. "No. So remain still and don't make a peep."

He grabbed the handgun from the unused tire and left, satisfied at Brett's nod. "I'll return and get you. Promise."

Ricky fast-walked out of the house and crouched low beyond the gang's base, the gun stretched out ahead of him in both hands. As far as he could see, five people on ten legs remained upright. Ricky had to stop and breathe in the air, hot enough to suffocate, relieved they lived.

Sweat built silt in his eyes. Every step cracked thunder, but the men didn't hear a thing. How would he fire three shots before retaliation? How would Tanais' pa react to any of this if he escaped? Would it mean them all in social care? Even Liz? Is Bixby right? Tanais' dad ran his life through the book. Straight ruler of a man. A robot who followed the rules and thought them more important than people's needs.

Still. No reason to let him die. Ricky swerved to the left to have the river behind him. It shook him that he might hit Tanais and her old man. Her pa waved his hands and ran his palms deep into his beard and hair to rub reality into the moment.

Ricky kneeled. Changed target again and again, judging where the most danger lay. This would end okay. Floyd would stick an oar in and paddle them all away from this horror. Tarantula Man grabbed Tanais by her ponytail and made her kneel by his feet. One of his men pulled a gun and smashed it into her pa's temple. He crumpled, held his head, but stayed with the living. Tanais' voice scorched the earth. The same man kicked her pa in his ribs. The third watched, amused. Checked his shoulder to see if he'd have to deal with outside trouble. Ricky's finger tightened around the trigger, but he trembled so bad he knew he'd hit tree bark in the distance, or blow Tanais' head clean off her neck.

He edged closer. The thinning grass would give him away soon and force him into action. What would happen to Brett if this turned against him?

'Tarantula Man smashed a boot into the social worker's ribs again. Must have pulled some roots from Tanais' scalp with his kick-motion. She flapped hands at her captor. He slapped her down, but she flipped to her feet again as a cat would at danger. Trent blazed at the challenge to his authority. All three focused on her. This is the time. The grass covered him now as much as the heat's haze.

"Shit."

The man who'd done no more than observe pointed at something in the distance. Ricky almost plugged him, but the man's finger arrowed to the City of Forts. Ricky blinked away sweat, dreaded to see Brett all sad, lonely, and on his way to this horror. He followed the trail of smoke rising into the sky, bent to the breeze above the HQ the bastards set up for themselves.

Brett? The little shit must have started a fire. Should have stayed in his dark corner and waited for events to play out. Jesus, now Ricky needed to save three people. Nah – Brett didn't understand the deal, here. Floyd. Floyd again. The man wants to protect us. He must be pa. Why else would he watch his back like this?

The trio of goons stared at the house, mouths full of cusses, forgetful of Tanais and her pa for the moment. Ricky held his breath. The tall stalks swayed in the breeze and exposed him with each gust. Tanais' pa gained his feet, a wince on his lips from every movement. He latched Tanais' forearm and guided her a foot or so until she transformed into the leader and helped him from their hell, an eye on the men with their backs to them. Ricky let out air as they merged into the scrub and trees.

Tarantula Man hit one of his men on the upper arm with the side of his gun. "Kill these two fuckers."

He turned, as did the associate he'd ordered, and bristled at Tanais and her pa's disappearance. "Go fucking find them. Now."

Ricky scrambled backwards to take the back route to the houses. Rode bumps and tangles which would trip him at a moment's lapse in concentration. These shacks offered little resistance to a spark. The drug den shimmered and danced as flames curled out the interior and up the outside wall. F-bombs emerged from an enraged white noise. Ricky would have laughed, but a snap in the weeds behind shut down his mechanics in an instant.

33

Ricky held his bowel tight. He half-expected a click, a bang, and his brains splattered before him.

"Are you gunna move or what?"

Ricky spun. "Bixby?" He followed a line between his pal and the smoke.

"Yeah, now let's get the hell outta here."

They took advantage of the shouting and the fire's crackle to rush by on the river side, dragging Brett from his shadowy prison, and running until they made it to the wood trail. Jackknifed off the road once they realized it exposed them and picked their way through tangled underbrush and thorns. Dared to scan back once, sweating they'd tempt fate if they did so too often. They brushed themselves down as they returned to the streets. Town's mess never appeared as warm as that moment. A car gave them a wide berth. The woman who drove craned her neck to check the danger in them. Another approached, slow. Ready to shoot? Ready to bundle them all in the trunk? No. It edged past, cautious about their careless plunge into his path. The man sped off once satisfied he couldn't hit either by accident.

They melted into alleyways and blended with the dust as best they could. Some kid with a baseball cap pulled low over his eyes lifted his chin high to eye them in his tunnel vision. Worked his leg to speed up his silver scooter as he sensed an edge. A jogger slowed her stride at the sight of them, but bit her lip and charged past, earbuds in her hand, on alert for any move from the boys.

"Where am I gunna sleep, now?" Bixby straightened.

Ricky followed suit, tired of the low monkey-gait he'd carried for a couple of miles. "The shed. Just don't shit in your own nest, okay?"

"I shit behind the shed, amigo."

"The stink reaches ma's nostrils."

Brett covered his mouth. "You're the shed monster?"

Bixby grinned at that one. Growled at the boy. "Yeah, I'm the shed monster."

Brett's lower lip quivered, a sound wave ready to hit high volume. He grabbed Ricky's wrist and Ricky planted a hand over his for comfort and to dampen the kid's urge to make noise.

The night smelled of pizza and their sweat. It trickled down his back to the rim of his pants and the cold handle of the gun in his waistband. "Damn it, the gun." Had the kid on the scooter and the jogger seen it stick out?

"Hide it in the shed."

"I ... shit, Bix, this is out of control. I squeeze my eyes shut every night as if that'll push it all out of my mind, but I just see Benny Ciaro in my head. And now you've gone and burned all their stuff. I think that crap is worth an absolute fortune."

"We burned it, Ricky – we."

"What?"

"You said I burned it – I." Bixby prodded his chest, all aggressive.

238

33

"You did."

"Nah, we burned it. I did it for you. If I'd not made ashes of that place, they'd have killed all four of you. So we all burned it, right?"

"Jesus, Bixby, yeah, we all fuckin' burned it. I got it. And I appreciate it. Alright?"

Blxby clicked his tongue and grinned banana-wide. "Sure, buddy. Let's go."

* * *

They entered Ricky's house the back way to avoid Mr Walters' restless eyes. Bixby stared, wordless, at the TV for an hour, even when Ricky prepared sandwiches for everybody. Ricky kept the rear door unlocked for Bixby's escape once ma crackled the driveway gravel.

The boys Jack-in-the-boxed to the window as she pulled in. Bixby just avoided a trip over the coffee table as he scrambled out the back. Ma stood in the doorway, lamplight warm on her face as the sun sank behind her. Her eyes wore a tired satisfaction. Planted a kiss on her sons' heads. Ricky looked over his shoulder to make sure Bixby remained out of sight as she returned the family photograph to its normal upright position. She hesitated, her attention still on the old picture. She turned, noted the third dinner plate, and tutted.

"Rickyyyy, come on, just wash the plate once you've used it. Don't waste a new one."

* * *

Ricky burned in the night. Stuck his feet out of the covers,

239

but the air-conditioner in the window had seen better times and only fanned the flame in his blood. He sat up and almost screamed the house to its foundations at the spirit before him until Brett's shape formed in the murk. The boy bore his cheap Captain America shield over an arm, certain that would save him from Tarantula Man. The kid draped the superhero across every wall in his room. Ricky's bare walls said nothing about his own interests. Had no time for any of that. He'd move his feet from their regular pattern when ma spun a record or CD, but otherwise his passions called for him from outdoors.

"Brett, pal, go back to bed."

"I can't sleep."

Ricky pulled his comforter open. "You wanna jump in?"

Brett nodded, head a woodpecker's at unbroken wood.

"Come on, then."

The kid jumped in, bashed his big brother's chin with the shield, and almost got himself kicked out. Once Ricky berated him enough, he felt the tremors from his brother and hoped they hadn't all gone beyond a point of no return.

* * *

He clocked ma's mood from the hallway the next morning. At the table with arms folded across her chest to prevent whatever boiled within her from exploding. Froze him mid-step. It would take effort to open those hard-set lips, but her eyes told him she gained knowledge he'd kept from her. He scratched the back of his head and shuffled in. Across from her sat the officer who'd been around the other day when Mr Walters called in the cops.

"Hello, Ricky." Officer Ray nodded once and his eyebrow

pointed, as if at evidence.

"Hello, sir."

"Would you like to take a seat?"

"I need some breakfast."

"Sit down, Ricky."

That tone from ma made something of a comeback, a reminder of her first days without pa. Ricky, another male, disappointed her. He sat, careful not to let what they didn't need to know tumble from his sleeves, the bottom of his pants, off the end of his dry tongue.

"Yesterday, about six-thirty pm, you were seen at the old factory by a Mr Rogers and his daughter. You were with your younger brother, Brett, and a boy, Bixby Schmidt, who's on the missing persons list. The man had been upset about Bixby and how he treated his girl, Tanais. Said you told him Bixby's your brother."

The cop impregnated a pause and crossed his hands on the table. Drilled his eyes into Ricky, who tried hard to draw strings across his forehead – the best confused frown he'd created yet. Officer Ray had honed that crease in his temple, forged those pinpoint pupils in fire. It must work with criminals. Turned them into blabber-mouthed wrecks and sent them straight to a cell, no doubt. Ricky sensed if the cop played another note, the quiver on the edge of his lips would spill enough information to send him somewhere Bixby once traveled.

"No, sir. I was here all day. With my brother, Brett. You can ask the neighbor, Mr Walters."

"He'll vouch you were here all day?"

"I can't tell if he saw me, but he's always at his window. He would have seen me leave."

The cop offered ma his concern, a smoldering look that didn't sit right to the situation. She shoved a smoke in her mouth and concurred. Shouted to Brett to come down. Called again until Ricky heard his brother's tired steps. Ricky's quiver verged on a full twang until he dampened it with little nibbles behind his lower lip.

Brett's eyes widened at the sight of their visitor. His fingers spiked out and he couldn't escape the pull of the cop's attention. Ricky shuffled so his chair scraped on the linoleum. Brett shot a glance at his brother, which poured a bucket of concrete into the kid's nerves.

The cop repeated his story, but Brett could only retreat into ma, who stubbed her cigarette in a hurry to wrap her little sweetheart into her arms.

The cop tapped the table. "If you were in the factory, neither of you are in trouble. Okay? That place is out of bounds, but I'm not worried about that too much. We were all kids, right?"

Ma avoided the officer's gaze and stroked Brett's hair.

"I'm just curious, is all, if you know anything about the fire in one of the abandoned houses? We found a lab and a whole lot of contraband burned to ash. We've made a few arrests."

Ricky almost shot rod-backed straight, but he maintained a slouch and blinked away the wonder-roll from his eyes. The cop leaned forward to him and landed a meaty paw on his shoulder.

"These men are not to be messed with. Absolutely not to be trifled with at all. Do you understand?"

"Sure." He pulled a *why are you telling me?* face. Why had Tanais' pa not mentioned the assault he suffered? The goons must have intimidated him. Shopped Bixby and the rest of them to feel like he'd done something for his daughter.

"Now, you sure you haven't seen Bixby Schmidt around?"

"Not since they dragged him from his pa."

* * *

Ma leaned against the doorframe and targeted Officer Ray at the end of her cigarette as he headed for the neighbor. Ricky circled the spoon around his full breakfast bowl, his stomach too unsettled for food. Brett swung his legs beneath the table and demolished his cereal. Ricky slid to the window, hands clamped to the counter's edge. The cop held his hat in a hand, conversed with Mr Walters, who shook his head and shrugged. After a while the officer walked back to his patrol car, nodded at ma, and chewed the inside of his cheek as if he'd remembered something new.

"He saw nothing. He said he was near his window all day. Didn't notice if Ricky left or came home." After a stony silence from ma, Officer Ray turned, and turned again. "Caitlin, if you ever need anything, you know where I am."

"I do. See you around, Officer Ray."

The cop slouched back to the car, a dog who'd had his nose beaten with a newspaper. As he sulked round the bend of the cul-de-sac, Ricky snuck to his seat and the untouched cereal. The scratch of her new smoke as she stubbed it on the outside wall made him jump. She flicked it to the drive's end and came in to face him. Squeezed her upper arms.

"I notice a lot of food has flown out the fridge."

Ricky pretended he saw patterns on the table top, and they had important things to tell him.

"A significant amount of food. Ham, lettuce, cheese, relish, fruit snacks – like you developed an appetite all of a sudden."

"You've been tellin' me to eat since I can remember, ma."

"I'm glad you're takin' my advice."

"Well, I gotta feed."

"And yet ..." She grabbed at his upper arm. "... you're still a dish rag. You've put on as much weight as if you ate air sandwiches."

He pulled himself free of her grip and stood. "Ma, what's your problem?"

"Don't you lie to me, Ricky-boy. I see little weight gain from your brother, neither. So, you're either eating and going out and about without my permission, or you're feeding a third person, from my hard-earned money."

"Ma –"

"You say *ma* in every sentence when you spout untruths. Look at me. I said look at me." She gripped his shoulders, harder than he could believe. "I love you, son. Adore you. But I notice your tan, and my boy's. I'm unsure what you got up to yesterday, or any other time you've defied me, but you're heading for a fall. And I'll tell you this - I don't want to lose my sons. You're all I have. But if I must lose one to save the other, then I will send you to the authorities quick-smart. You're old enough to know better, and it'll be you that suffers the downfall, not my baby."

Ricky's chest heaved. The yack-yack from Brett's busy mouth dissipated. Ricky built a wall behind his eyelids to dam those tears. His words would wobble if he set them free. He backed away from the clamp of her hands and slow-walked upstairs to his room. Shut the door and slid down it, hard to the sobs of his mother.

34

Ricky stayed in his room for two days. He listened to Brett potter about the house and feed himself, ignoring his brother's plaintive appeals to play. Made lunch and dinner for Bixby, but demanded he stay in the shed. Brought his own food back to his bedroom when hungry. Bristled any time Officer Ray drove by to check on him. Same when ma came home. She knocked on his door, popped her head in, asked about his welfare, and headed down the stairs again at his noncommittal grunt. He sensed guilt in her every step. Understood he should feel bad about his deceptions, but, come on – she tortured him with her demands to look after Brett and remain locked up all day long. The kid could care for himself. He'd proved it many times over. Ricky just felt unable to tell her he'd left him alone so much.

Had the cops arrested Tarantula Man? He hugged himself as he recalled how the man dragged Tanais by her hair and knocked her pa to the ground. Ricky peeked out the window, suspicious Michael Trent stood outside in wait for him.

On the third day like this, ma called from work and requested Brett. He bristled at how she cooed at her youngest. When Ricky held the cell again, she said, "We can't go on this way, son. You can't stew forever."

He shrugged and demanded she sense it, because he didn't want to say a thing.

"Are you home?"

"You know I am."

"You have no right to that tone. Turn the TV on."

"Why?"

"So I can tell you're home."

"Maybe I'm at someone else's house."

"Just switch it on."

He thrust the remote towards the TV and jabbed the button. It buzzed like only their old piece of crap did. "Satisfied?"

"Satisfied, son. Very."

Ricky shrugged again at her attempt at cheerfulness.

He called Liz on her cell. When she didn't answer, he tried the house phone and hoped she picked up. That Carrie woman answered, her voice a bitter crust. He listened without saying a word, embarrassed for her at how she got mad at what she imagined a crank call. His embarrassment settled into enjoyment until she said she knew him and he'd be sorry. He ended the one-way conversation and stared at the phone as though she eyed him through the receiver. Of course, she bluffed, but he threw down the old piece of junk and covered it with a pillow.

Stupid. He snatched it back, ran upstairs to his bedroom, and tried Liz again. She answered this time.

"What do you want?"

"For you to come over."

"Why?"

"Because, that's why."

"I can't."

"You with lover-boy?"

"You're a dick, sometimes. Bye."

The *burr* as she ended the call hit as hard as an f-bomb. He kicked the mattress and danced as his toe caught the metal frame. "Damn, damn, goddamn."

He limped downstairs and ignored ma's little cupcake, who amputated the toy soldier's other arm. Ricky exited through the back door. The neighbors had no view into the yard because pa planted conifers years ago. Ricky checked around the shed. Good, Bixby had learned his lesson. He knocked on the door and whispered his greeting. Stuck his head inside at the lack of response. A moment passed before he realized the dark had not hidden his pal. He turned to scan deep into the woods for Bixby's trail and yelped at his sibling stood behind him.

"Jesus, Brett."

Brett blinked at the blasphemy. What would the minister say?

"Don't sneak up on me."

"He's still here?"

"You know he is. Don't act the little fuckin' angel."

"It's not my fault ma likes me better. You're still my favorite brother."

Ricky laughed and ruffled his hair. "You're mine, too. But I have to leave you here."

"Why?"

"I have to go see someone."

"Who?"

"Don't you worry about it."

"Are we telling ma? I feel real bad we don't tell ma about stuff."

"Ah, man, I don't know, Brett. I love her. As much as you

do, but ... I gotta live."

Brett grasped his wrist. "I can come with you. I won't mention it."

Ricky pulled the kid into a headlock. Scrubbed his scalp until the boy's laughter infected him. He kneeled in front of him. "I can't let you join me. If something happened ..."

"Will you get hurt? I don't want you to get hurt, Ricky."

"Nah, not that, just, it might be a shock."

"What?"

"Shit ... you should know."

"What?"

"Come on."

They climbed over the chain-link fence and entered the woods for cover. The cool beneath the green canopy made them reluctant to step back out into the sun, but they emerged at the opposite end from their home. A lush grass carpet threaded bare onto candy wrappers, crushed soda cans, and distorted asphalt. Ricky expected men in hoods around each corner. Shuddered that someone might jump from the doorway of the Schultz millinery store. The name remained above the door despite a dozen other owners. Now stood a shadow of its former glories. Ricky always glued his eyes to the sidewalk – counted cracks to counteract boredom – in order to avoid adult attention, in case one offered to sell him goods he didn't want. With his brother in tow, he clocked every movement – a gazelle on a plain of lions. Liz noticed some of these folks. She talked to them. Said hello to them. But then, she enjoyed people. Trusted some adults. Such as Biker Boy. She'd get bitten. Then she'd run back and tell Ricky her sorrows.

They charged through back streets, where heat tattooed the

248

stains deep, and across busy roads. Cars honked, most drivers bulls in bids to assert alpha status. Harassed Ricky. He longed for the fields, the ruined houses, the silent factory.

Ricky relaxed once the noise hummed in the distance behind. The abandoned supermarket sat like a dirty old box, surrounded by flaky wooden pallets and orange-brown shopping carts turned over on their sides and backs.

Floyd hunched with his back to the brothers, poking a stick at something, the air above him waving and flickering. Cooked some animal over a fire, its fur stretched out over a rock.

"Boys? What brings you here?"

Ricky stood opposite Floyd, the fire between them, and straightened his spine. Brett rushed to his side, behind a leg. "I just wanted to thank you, is all."

"Again? For what?"

Ricky shook his head at the man's determined mysteriousness. "For rescuing us from that man. You know what. Jesus, why do you act like this?"

Floyd lifted the animal, a squirrel, for inspection. He twisted it this way, and that, sniffed, twisted his nose, and lowered it to the flame to finish the roast. "I'm homeless, Ricky. No home, no job, no wife –"

"No kids?"

"I'm a bum. But even a bum needs a role." He raised his chin to engage Ricky, though the man revealed little beneath the stained cap's beak.

"I'm your role? I reckoned that's so." He nudged Brett, but the kid's smile aimed only to please.

"Come on – let's meet the one who would have slit your throat." He stood, bit a chunk from the animal, and led the way. Ricky's heart drilled him into the ground, and Brett used him as a barricade. Floyd halted at the cracked glass door and turned his head. "You comin'?"

A single, hesitant step morphed into a rush to avoid his pa badging him a coward. He ducked beneath the man's arm and into the expansive interior.

"The little one stays here."

Ricky scanned the area, inside and out.

"He's safe – I get no visitors round here – except for these bad boys." He waved the impaled carcass. "You wanna bite?"

"Nah. Thanks."

Floyd shrugged and nodded him forward.

Ricky patted Brett's shoulder. "Just stay here, pal, okay? I won't be long."

"Rickyyy."

"Brother, I won't be long. And don't ass around with that fire. Alright? Alright?"

Brett folded his arms and turned. Kicked a stone so it pinged off the car the homeless man, their pa, used as a bed. He pursed his lips and skulked off to stare at the flame.

Ricky and Floyd's steps echoed in the emptiness. Empty of shelves, only the chessboard floor remained, plenty of gaps to trip up. Floyd hunched. More than loneliness weighed on his shoulders. They picked their way through a corridor lit by shards of sunshine from above until they entered the storage area. The drop in temperature pinched his neck and crawled down.

The dim gray light revealed a mass slumped on a chair. Ricky halted, hooked Floyd's eyes, and waited for an explanation. Floyd encouraged him forward. Ricky followed the trail of ancient sweat and cooked meat. The Ghost Boy, who had who-knows-what intentions towards him and Liz, rested blue and black on a metal armchair, glued there by his own blood. Puffed flesh folded over his eyes and dried crimson trickles stretched from his ears to his t-shirt collar and down his chest. Ricky thought Floyd lowered the squirrel for the man to bite on, but the red hole in the center of the man's forehead told him different.

"You killed him ..."

"Look at me, Ricky. I'm a lost soul. God has given me a role. To protect the people of this town. Especially you boys. You're its only hope."

Reminded him of that sci-fi movie pa always watched. Floyd had to ... he had to ...

"But I'm not sure anymore. I no longer understand this God like I used to."

He removed his cap and a bushel of blond shone in the minimal light. Pa never had blond hair, and Floyd couldn't afford bleach to have such fanciful colors. Is Floyd his real name, after all? Ricky backed away, his breath short in his chest. Shadows ran along the walls and a creak set off a ripple across his skin.

"Who are you, Floyd?"

Floyd bit into the squirrel. Bared his meat-flecked teeth. "I'm unsure. I don't know a damn thing anymore."

Ricky barreled down the corridor and into the main area through the double doors. He slipped on the checkered floor, a pawn in the shadow of kings and queens who never showed their hands. He scrambled to his feet and barged the exit door open. Grabbed Brett by the arm and force-marched him back to civilization.

"I asked you to stay outdoors and not follow us. What did you see?"

"I didn't move. I just poked the fire."

Ricky squinted back into the supermarket's darkness, sure the shadows crept along the walls and followed him outside.

He scuffed the back of his brother's head. "I told you not to play with flames."

35

Ricky stood his brother in a spot and wagged a finger. "Don't move. And look that way. At all times."

"What you gunna do?"

"Just do what I say, yeah?"

Ricky walked backwards several yards to make sure of Brett. Satisfied, he grabbed the iron pole he'd spotted and headed to the row houses, empty as the City of Forts. He cast his eyes about, but his only witnesses flew above. A sea of rubble from demolished factories smothered by weeds would stay dumb. He swung the pole and smashed the first window. Enjoyed the glitter sound as glass sprinkled to hard ground. His breath heaved, though the action hardly ranked the highest dare in this wild summer. He gritted his teeth and growled until he sprung primeval. Swung at the next pane and the next, and stopped only when a series of windows stared blank at him. He threw the iron bar like a javelin at the eleventh and snorted as it crashed through. Floyd's a nobody. Not his pa at all. Nothing more than a God-botherer and just a few degrees more mental than his minister.

He whistled for his brother to run over when he spotted a white car in the distance. They raced round the back of the brick houses to avoid the cop, through a heavily signed factory yard warning against trespassers and dangerous toxins. They smashed the few remaining windows that still reflected the sun, Ricky careless about what Brett thought. Trekked to a busy part of Town, tongues parched. The gym stood between a pharmacist and a carpet store, as squat as the meatheads inside. Iron bars crossed the windows. Ricky ran a finger across the motorbike's mudguard. Rubbed the muck away with his thumb. Sat on the wall by the entrance.

Waited.

Bit nicer round here, though it couldn't hold a candle against Mr Vale's residence. Brett leaned against him, shy at the side-eyes he received from men and women who passed by. White skin, brown skin. A mix he'd seen at Liz' future high school and over in the City. Made him blink, unsure what to think. Everyone in Ricky's life looked similar to him. He knew how to act around them. How do you carry yourself around these guys? Adapt or die, pa always said.

He nudged Brett. "Sit on the bike."

"You kiddin'? It ... It doesn't belong to us."

Ricky pushed Brett off his leg and circled the machine. Poked the plate, the skull sticker, the electric guitar magnet. The gym sticker had not spewed out of his imagination like toxic fumes – it clung to the motorbike with the help of grease and dust. No marks showed any love of books. This joker led Liz on a merry-go-round.

"Go on, get on. Grab the handles. Nobody minds around here."

He helped Brett onto the seat. Encouraged him with a nod and a smile. Brett jumped up and down and twisted the accelerator. Told a tale about how he'd ride it into hell and destroy the monsters under his bed. He struggled with the high, wide handles, but he growled and brrrred as if he motored across a highway to Satan's paradise.

Ricky faced the gym to observe both the entrance and his brother. And out he came. Took his time. Ricky shifted from foot-to-foot at the sight of him. Arms meatier than Ricky's torso. His tight-fit t-shirt defined his carved-from-a-quarry pecs. Bug-eye sunglasses hid any expression and his buzz-cut screamed how he didn't truck with nonsense. But the beard sat lame on his chin. Ricky's tongue fattened and blocked his throat.

"Hey, what the fuck?"

Liz' boy, Steve, charged down the ramp, a flesh GI Joe and as stiff. Ricky slid his brother backwards off the seat. The boy's frame collapsed, limp and putty-like. Ricky guided him behind his back, where the boy eyed the man-mountain.

"What you doin', kid?"

Ricky shook his head. "Cool bike, is all."

"Don't play with my fuckin' machine. Who do you think you are?"

"Liz' friend."

Biker boy made scalpels of his eyebrows. Inserted them beneath Ricky's surface. "Liz Panowich?"

"How many Liz' do you know?"

He laughed. "Smart ass. You're the kid stuck to the wall of her house the other day? Jesus Christ, you a stalker?"

"Nah. Her friend. Her true friend."

"Huh. And what do you think I am?"

"Dunno. But you definitely look like a pedo."

"What? What, you little fucker?"

"You heard. She's fourteen. How old are you? You dirty bastard."

Biker Boy laughed, but Ricky's needle hit a zone. The man scanned for listeners. "You little shit, you know nothing. I help her."

"Help her take her clothes off, yeah. I got ya."

Hand on hip, a disappointed glare at the sidewalk. "I broaden her horizons, kid. You need to shut that dirty mouth of yours."

"Pedo."

The man glanced, embarrassed, at the interested faces passing by. He darted at Ricky, who flashed around the vehicle to keep it between them. Shielded his brother and maneuvered him as he dodged Biker Boy's hands. Liz' lover leapt across, lost balance and tumbled over the bike, bringing the machine on top of him. Ricky kicked stones in his face.

"Leave her alone, you dirty pedo."

He dragged Brett into step with his run, only halting at the growl of a motor behind. They plunged into an alleyway.

36

Ricky and Brett stopped at the bagel place and lapped up coffee and a sausage, egg, and cheese sandwich each. The lady who served rolled her eyes at the penny he didn't own to make the full payment, but did it with a smile. Ricky returned a grin, happy a stranger didn't want something from him. They ate at a window table and stared out at the road. A steel gray car idled on the opposite side of the street. A woman with sunglasses, red hair long and over her shoulder, smoked a cigarette, attention on him. He swore she offered him a little finger wave. The bagel lodged in his throat. He coughed and drank his pipes clear, shrugged off Brett's back-smacks.

"Come on, let's go." Ricky growled away the hoarse from his voice.

"I've not finished."

"Walk and eat, pal. Multi-task."

Brett groaned, but followed him out the rear exit. They reached home on time. Ricky sprinkled bread crumbs over two plates and left them on the kitchen counter. Poured water into a couple of glasses and made Brett drink half.

When ma came through the door, irritable and worn out at just past eight, she found them slouched on the sofa watching wolves chase a caribou on TV.

"My boys. How was your day?"

Brett wrapped his arms around her neck and smothered her in kisses. Ricky concentrated on the caribou's death and nature's cruelty. He hurt for the prey, but it made him nervous for the wolf, which would die if he didn't kill. Is it what drove Tarantula Man?

"Ricky?"

"Ma."

"Your day?"

"As always." The man with the hole in his head. Floyd on about God and his role. The woman in the car who wanted Bixby in her maw, as her job demanded. "All good."

He pushed off the sofa and stared at his pa in the photo. Ignored ma's query about dinner. Pa fitted Floyd's frame – slim, agile, similar height, angled face. Dad's hair is brown, however.

"You certain pa headed out west, ma?" Could he have drifted off the road into the river, like Liz's ma? He contained the shiver, waiting for a trigger.

"That's what he said. Where he's at now - no idea."

She once had a tremor in her voice when she talked of him. She'd dumped that in the river for sure. A *couldn't care less* tone took its place.

They all jumped at the loud rap on the door and the incoherent, enraged tone. They eyed each other. Ricky grabbed Brett and ran him upstairs. He slid ma's bedroom window open and leaned on the windowsill.

Brett followed suit. "Mr Panowich ..."

The man raised his head, eyes bright in hope, but too late to catch Brett as Ricky dragged him from view. Shushed him with a finger to the boy's lips. "No words. He doesn't look right. Let's listen."

They snuck back to the windowsill and frowned at each other at the repeated, aggressive knocks.

"I know you're in there, Ricky Nardilo. I can see movement. Yeah, you get out here and talk to me."

He'd parked further down the road, headlights on full beam for all the light he needed for his lazy eyes. Ricky bit his lip as ma approached the doorstep. She switched on the outside lamp and it sprayed a sick yellow on the wasted figure swaying before her.

"What do you want with my boy?"

The tone stunted Mr Panowich. He veered as if a tidal wave of booze in his stomach tilted him this way and that.

"You come knockin' on my door like this, you better have an answer, otherwise I'm gunna send you over my fence head first. Who are you and what's the deal with my kid?"

Ricky smiled and balled his fist at how ma stood up for him, though against what, he didn't know.

Mr Panowich dropped an anchor and made his stance firm. How had he driven here? "I'm Liz's dad, Mr P'nowich."

"Who the hell is Liz?"

"My daughter. Liz is my girl."

"Ah, that girl. The one who hangs out with my boy ..." Her tone changed from dismissive to panic-stricken. "Is she pregnant?"

The man see-sawed as he absorbed her question. Ricky shuddered. Did that freak of a meathead impregnate his pal, ruining her life? *God, no.*

"My boy would ... he would never."

Oh, man, she suspected him, and the yuck of his ma's

imagination almost tumbled him out the window.

"Noooo. No, Mrs Nardilo, no. Nothing like that." He scowled at the thought. "No. I ... I just wanna know where the boy is."

"Well, now you're here, it seems you know exactly where my child is. But why you want Ricky, I have no idea. In fact, you're freaking me out."

"Don't freak out, Mrs Nardilo. Please don't do that. And it's not Ricky I want. I wish to check on his brother."

"Brett?"

"Yeah. Brett."

Brett stuck his nails in Ricky's wrist. Ricky didn't notice because of the baseball bat ma pointed at Mr Panowich's face. She walked him backwards to the edge of the drive. "And what the fuck is your game with my baby?"

Ricky rubbed his temple. Trouble clawed him into ma's fury. Here goes. He jumped down the stairs, slipped as he missed a step, and joined her confrontation.

"Yeah, what do you want with my brother?"

Mr Panowich's lazy eyes turned to saucers along with his mouth as he stared between mother and son, his tongue a hooked bass on the river bank. Tears streamed into his patchy beard.

"I had a son, Mrs Nardilo. Sweet, sweet kid. Died in a car crash."

"I'm sorry to hear that, but what are you saying?"

He glared at Ricky in horror. His steps backward landed weak. His legs would crumble soon. "Just. Just ... we had a bond. Something special. Like my son returned to me."

Ma swung wild eyes at her eldest, back to Mr Panowich, again at her son. Ricky glued his to the man, afraid to meet hers.

"I'm sorry. Sorry to bother you. I'm so sorry." He staggered away, confused, shaking his head at Ricky's attitude.

"What the hell was he talking about?"

Ma bored into his mind, on the lookout for holes in his story.

"Dunno, but that's the freakiest thing I ever heard." Mr Walters' silhouette filled his window. "What's he looking at?"

"Come inside. The bugs are biting."

Ricky relaxed his aggressive stance and crumpled into worry. Stopped short as he saw the woman slouching out the car to help Mr Panowich into the passenger seat. Carrie shoved her lover into the vehicle, like a cop guiding a crook's head so he wouldn't bang it. She turned to survey Ricky. Ricky flinched first and scurried inside to the welcome of his ma's folded arms and flustered face.

"Well, Ricky?"

An internal winter hit Ricky. He didn't wish to budge and admit to all he'd done this long summer. Ma harangued him in front of Brett, demanding the youngest explain himself. But though his face melted at conflicted loyalties, he held firm for Ricky, bawling his eyes out until ma sent him to bed with kisses, cuddles, and reassurance.

"You told me that Brett had invented this Mr Panowich. I don't know if I'll believe a word you say ever again."

Ricky made sly steps backward until he got to his room and closed the door behind him – but she swung it wide open and attacked his retreat. His teeth set so hard they'd become immovable. He wanted to collapse onto the bed, his energy flashing red lights. He stared at the carpet and drowned her words beneath a wash of thoughts. Her arms darted here and there to conduct the truth from him, but he'd switched off, and before he knew it he sat alone with the hot ceiling light in his face, his eyes in puddles.

Adrenaline shot him back to life and forced him to pace the bedroom floor. He eyed the drainpipe. Would it hold his weight? In this state, he would slip and break his neck. He'd not reached that point yet.

* * *

Ma usually left around 7.30 in the morning. He idled in bed and listened to each little move she made. Waited for the door to click, announcing her exit. The hand tick-tocking the seconds on his wall-clock must have turned into the minute hand, because it shifted every blue moon it seemed. 7.35 arrived and ma slammed the cupboard. At 7.45 she scraped a chair. By 8am her voice became nails down a blackboard as she instructed Brett to do some task. A tentative tap on his door signaled ma had gone to work at last. Brett came to see what adventures they would have today.

He popped his head inside, his hair a toilet brush. "Ma wants you, Ricky."

"What? She's not left yet?"

"Took the day off."

"Took the day off? Is she mad?"

"She's real mad."

The kid retreated from the battle ahead. Ricky didn't hear him go downstairs and guessed he'd bunked up in his room to avoid the tension. He sat upright and pulled the comforter over his head. So many fears trembled through his bones that he wanted to seek ma's comfort, but the idea hit his ideal of independence and he couldn't bring himself to ask for her help.

He made it down the stairs, upper teeth nipping his lower lip, skinny body a hunched sack of skin ready for a beating. He straightened, narrowed his eyes, and marched into the kitchen. Ma sat at the table, back to him. Officer Ray nodded to him as he entered the room.

"Here he is. Hello, Ricky."

Ricky's stomach lurched for a sick bag. He kneeled on that nausea, but the effort sent ripples up his wind-pipe and made a mess of his voice. "Sir?" He glanced at ma, but she stared at some point to balance her temper, hands round a mug of coffee, back straight as Ricky's road to hell.

"Caitlin ... your ma ... has asked me here. Last night, you had a visit from Mr Panowich."

"Yeah."

"He talked of Brett as though he knew him. Intimately. As a son."

Ricky made for the kitchen counter and leaned against it. Folded his arms. "He did that, yeah."

"And?"

"And, what? The man's a nut."

"Why would he say such a thing?"

"He's seen Brett before, when I've been with Liz. That's all."

"That's all?"

"What else? Has he committed a crime?"

"I've no doubt he has. Is there anything you ought to tell me?"

"Nope. Except, after last night, can you keep him from coming here, acting so weird?"

Ma stared out the window. "When you were with Liz?"

"Yeah, when I was with Liz."

"Where, with Liz?"

"Just round here. And he'd come and pick her up some-times."

"So more than once?"

Ricky blinked.

The officer cleared his throat. "Caitlin, there's no law that

264

says he can't be at home alone. No age limit. He has to show responsibility, is all. I think there's no doubt about it."

Her scowl must have stabbed him because his flinch, for so burly a cop, would have knocked a vase to the floor if one rested nearby.

"We live in a dangerous neighborhood. You warned us about the drug den down by the old factory."

Officer Ray so wanted to help, it made Ricky cringe at his helplessness. "I can pop round every day to make sure he's okay."

"And keep him in the house?"

Officer Ray pinched his eyes and lips, shifted his ass, and cleared his throat again. "What age is he? Thirteen? Caitlin, I … we … spent our summers outdoors. Only came home once we heard our ma or pa shout us inside."

"It was safer round here back then. And we had both parents. My ma was always home for me. I don't have that luxury."

"He's a boy." The cop said it beneath his breath in a failed attempt not to reach Ricky's ears. "You can't expect him to be cooped up like a chicken all day long."

Ricky stood straight, excited by the cop's words. No adult stuck up for him anymore. Not his ma – apart from last night – not his teachers, not his useless pa. Ma squeezed the tip of her nose. It seemed Officer Ray outlived his usefulness. "Thank you, Officer. I'll deal with this on my own. I appreciate your time."

Officer Ray slid a hand across the table in a move to reassure her, but she'd locked herself up behind those arms, so he planted his cap back in place. Straightened the peak. He radiated a sorry-ass, but she didn't budge.

"I'll take time off work. I should look after my kids."

Ricky pushed off the counter. The idea of ma home all day equaled a plastic bag over his head. "You can't afford that. How would we eat?"

"My offer stands." Officer Ray stared at her until ma's lack of reaction signaled her rejection. "Okay, but if you change your mind." He nodded to Ricky. "Don't think everybody round here is as bad as your ma thinks. There's good people in this town. They're just not loud and visible as the bad ones."

Ma's lips twitched at an idea. "My boss will give me a break."

"All three of them?" Officer Ray shook his head and glanced at Ricky. "And they'll pay?"

"Johnson, at the supermarket, won't think twice, and he'll pay me, yes."

Officer Ray snorted. "What, you seeing him or something?"

Ma rubbed at the table's edge and turned a shade of beetroot.

"Right, then. Okay, I'll take my leave. Call if you need me."

He'd made it halfway through the door when her guilt thrust a shout of thanks at him. He nodded, but didn't search her face until he stepped back to make way for a fresh visitor.

"Mr Vale? You know Caitlin?"

"Not yet, Officer ..." His deep voice didn't match the man-boobs, but it shoved Ricky into a defensive stance. His fingers flick-knifed straight. He raced for coherent thought. The man stepped past Officer Ray after their awkward greeting and offered ma an apologetic smile. How'd he find out where he lived? Officer Ray snuck away as if he needed to escape his boss.

Mr Vale tilted his head to Ricky. "Hello, kid. How you doing?"

Ricky could only nod as his eyeballs ping-ponged.

"Can I help you?" Ma swung her attention between them.

What new madness had her boy brought her?

"Sure. Alright if I sit?"

"I don't reckon so. I don't know you from Adam."

He laughed – hearty, a hug of a smile. "I do apologize for the intrusion into your life. I'm Mr Vale, Charlie's dad."

Ma's lips curled at the confusion buffeting her. "And who is Charlie?"

Mr Vale softened that hurt with a disappointed beam at Ricky. "Well, he's your son's friend, Mrs Nardilo. They've been hanging out this summer – right, kid?"

Ricky made tent poles of his eyebrows and left it at that. Ma's breath came out the same as a bull's, ready to spear her tormentor.

"Mrs Nardilo, I'm not sure what's going on here. I would have thought Ricky here had told you about me. After all, he spent a half-day at my apartment across the river, along with Brett, my son, and my wife, just last weekend. I'd like to inform you, now, that I asked him to inform you. But, my bad. My bad, I should have demanded to talk to you first. Please forgive my faux pas."

He guffawed, and the rumble rolled over the linoleum and up Ricky's stone frame.

"Well." She slammed her palms on the table top, the aftershock to Mr Vale's earthquake. "All your chickens are coming home to roost, my boy."

Ricky glanced between them. Wanted to chew his nails to bloody stumps.

"Mrs Nardilo, don't be mad. Your boy has done me a magnificent service. Please, please, let me finish. My boy, Charlie, he's a funny child, I can tell you. Stays in his room most nights and plays his video games. I thought it harmless at first — my wife, Stacey, said it's better than him being out on the streets where he'd get up to God-knows-what. And ... I'm a busy man.

"But, one night at dinner, after I watched him shift pixels for a solid two hours, I asked him what he saw in them. He told me, get this, that it was his escape from reality. He's fourteen, Mrs Nardilo. Fourteen, and he's already scared of reality. I tell you, that's a reality that scares the bejeezus out of me."

He took a breath which could have vacuumed all the house's dust. Invited himself to sit at the table opposite her.

"Earlier this summer, against my wife's fervent protestations, I sent Charlie across the river on our boat, untethered from his mom and pop." He rapped the wooden surface and laughed. "Believe me, it made me nervous. As soon as he became a pin on the opposite bank, I almost reeled him right back in ... but I reckoned that would have kept my boy in aspic. The boat - by God's will, by some cosmic connection, by pure chance - floated to your boy, Mrs Nardilo, and he's making a man of mine.

"What I'm saying is this — I love your kid's self-reliance. His drive. His spontaneity. I love how he wants to please you, but also do as he pleases. You should be proud."

Ma's eyebrows knitted themselves into a sound wave of fury, though she muted the volume for now.

"The kid has potential. I want you to give permission for him to come and work for me. Nothing major. Don't worry, I'll not send him down a coal shaft with just a canary for company. I mean real work."

She puffed stray hair from her face. "What kind of *real work*?"

"I manage my wealth, Mrs Nardilo. Shift it here and there

to get the best returns. Now I'm ready to invest in some actual brick and mortar. A warehouse. Ricky would do some tasks around the place. Nothing exploitative. I won't run him into the dust. And I'll pay him decent, without turning him into an entitled brat. But it's time I showed interest in others, again. He's done wonders for my boy. I want to repay him, and, in turn, you. Show him the world of employment. Give him the taste. And help him help his family, too."

Ricky would have jumped at the chance if it didn't mean he had to spend hours with Charlie. He blanched as Mr Vale turned to him and beamed.

"What do you say, Ricky? You interested?"

Ma folded her hands and leaned into the table towards him. "Mr Vale, I have to admit, this is all a little overwhelming, and all. I just met you and you want to take my boy across the river to work in a warehouse. My son has been to your apartment without my knowin' a damn thing about it. You tell me, what should I think of such a fancy proposition?"

"Now's not the time to give me a decision. You need to brew your ideas until they've fermented into something concrete. I came to plant a seed in you and your boy's head. Nothing more. It's a take-it-or-leave-it proposal, but ... single mom – finances are difficult, I'm sure."

He deflected her glower with his good humor. She stood, scraped the chair on purpose, and planted herself by the door. He took the hint and nodded to me as headed for the exit. He slid a business card from his wallet and offered it to her in the doorway. Her thin-lined lips told him what she thought of his offer. Ricky watched him crunch the gravel in the driveway and slip the card into the post box. He extended one last hand in the air and beamed a bashful grin, more at the intrusion into their home than the proposal he'd made. He rode out of the cul-de-sac like a stag who'd won his breeding rights.

* * *

"Well, you are a little shit-pea, ain't ya?"

Ricky stared at his feet and shrugged. Ma stepped into his space and slapped him hard across his cheek. Ricky pawed the sting, wincing, to check its reality.

"Don't you shrug at me. You have gone against my wishes and done all kinds of crazy shit. I see it all in your red face, your slumped shoulders, and your darting eyes – you can't even look at me. You understand you're in the wrong and you're embarrassed." She gripped his upper arms. "Your damn pa, I hope he's in the gutter somewhere, because that's all he deserves. He's turned you into him. Another sorry betrayal. I oughta put you into care. See how you like that."

Miss Veronica streaked through his head.

"I'm only upset that I have to go against your wishes, ma. I'm not embarrassed by anything else."

"You oughta be."

"Why?"

"Because ... because I was clear you must stay home and look after the boy. And yourself."

"I don't need looking after, ma. No way. I'm ... I'm invincible out there."

She snorted and held her mouth – mocked the offense she caused him. Ricky slithered from her hands and headed for the door.

"You walk out and I'll have you in care at the drop of a hat."

"You won't, though, will you? What'll you do with Brett?"

"He can come to work with me. Johnson's a good boss."

"All day at the supermarket, then all night at your ware-house? You need me. I'm your son, too. You can't police me, ma. You can't."

Her stance turned from rock to jelly. She scuffed the floor with a foot, threw her eyes around the room for inspiration, but squirmed in the end, after all. "I'll arrange for our friendly neighbor to watch you."

He shuddered and glanced toward Mr Walters' house. He could see the glow of his TV from here. "No way."

"You watch me."

All day with Charlie seemed better. "Allow me to work for Mr Vale. Earn some money. Then we can drop Brett in daycare or somethin'."

She tapped her teeth together. He'd never seen her want to beat him so bad, but the idea latched and shifted her mood a little.

"Let me try it out, at least. I can't stay home all day, ma. It'll kill me."

She jabbed his arm as she pushed past him. He rubbed at the ache but watched her kick stones into the chain-link on her approach to the post box. She turned the business card this way and that, as if it might change in the light to trick her. She squinted back at him beneath the sun's scorch and nodded enough, without a shred of enthusiasm, to show her assent.

38

Ma took the rest of her day off. They'd take a hit in the belly, but she assured the boys they'd manage. Ricky knew she'd eat less so they could have her share. She allowed Ricky out, alone. He saw the conflict in her decision and how it troubled her. Any danger to him would have come from her assent. He squeezed her arm, a token for her trust. Her eyes flashed in surprise, but she held the emotion tight. Good. He hated how it piled guilt on his shoulders. He stepped out of the house without resentment's cramp in his stomach. Smiled at Mr Walters, who watched him from his window. The neighbor's jowls wobbled in response.

Once Ricky escaped the cul-de-sac, a different sort of cramp settled on him. He walked in the shadows, eyes those of a mouse as it darts between cracks to dodge a hawk in the sky. Whoever the cops arrested, they hadn't touched Tarantula Man. If they had, he'd not clutched jail bars for long. The hairy man gesticulated at Mr Panowich in Liz' backyard. Ricky didn't get close enough to hear. His heartbeat filled his ears, but he could see the fear in Mr Panowich. That Carrie woman watched them both, perched on the edge of a lounge chair. Scratched her cheek – but the itch seemed elsewhere. She spotted Ricky and lifted a hand to Tarantula Man. The itch to snitch. She lowered it, unsure whether to interrupt the man in his rage. Might result in a purple patch across her face. She stared at Ricky, fish-cold, a curl in her lips.

* * *

On Monday, Mr Vale arrived at Ricky's house. Ricky turned to ma, a terse smile hurting his face, and climbed into the SUV's belly. The inside gleamed and lights blinked. He held tight to the handle above the door. Charlie grinned and showed him the game he played on his phone as his pa sped down the streets. Ricky watched, goggle-eyed for a while at what they could do with those things, but boredom soon averted his eyes. Charlie sensed it and huddled to the door to play in private. Ricky shrugged. Seemed Mr Vale didn't try too hard to pull his kid from these games.

The drive to the City took forever and Mr Vale cursed the bridge with its lip in the estuary.

"Why won't they fix it, Mr Vale?"

"What's the point?"

First bit of pessimism Ricky witnessed from Mr Vale. "But you have to travel so far to pick me up."

"You can make it to the river bank next time, where I dropped you off."

The outside world looked like a silent movie, the car cocooning them. Ricky heard only the purr of the engine and the air-conditioner's whoosh.

Mr Vale treated them to a big breakfast in a fancy diner. The check landed much bigger than ma's weekly shopping bill and Ricky protested, embarrassed at the man's generosity.

"You need to eat, kid. How can you work if you don't eat?"

Charlie grinned above his phone.

"Charlie, put that thing away, will you? Talk to Ricky."

Mr Vale sat back, folded his arms, and waited for some conversation to flow between both kids. Ricky's scalp prickled. The boys made awkward eyes at each other and hoped the other would trigger something. Ricky managed only a frown, so Charlie withdrew his head into his shoulders and blasted some dumb alien to bits. The pressure got to Ricky.

"What's the game, Charlie?"

Charlie cocked an eye over the phone. Searched him for sarcasm. Shifted to a straighter position at Ricky's open expression. "So, you play one of the few survivors of an apocalypse –"

"A what?"

"An apocalypse."

"What's that?"

Charlie tilted his head, eyed his pa for a moment, and almost slunk back into the booth's corner, but he recognized Ricky had no idea about apocalypses.

"It's when the world has died. Or all the people are dead, or most of the people."

"Ah. So you're trying to ... do what?" Tedium curled a finger into his lower lip and pulled at a yawn. Ricky glanced at Mr Vale. Resented the man's desire to be impressed.

"Well ..." Charlie shuffled his ass close to Ricky, so their shoulders touched. He shared the screen and pressed at the surface. "... these aliens caused the apocalypse and they want to take all Earth's resources. My job is to destroy them. Look ..."

His fingers danced all over the phone. Shot an alien here, another over there. He turned up the volume and growls mingled with screams and gunfire. The action should have interested Ricky. He loved a good action movie, but his eyes glazed over and his nods of fake appreciation slowed.

"Would love to do it for real." Ricky scratched his arm and slid the dessert menu over. Charlie put his game away and folded his arms. Mr Vale laughed.

"You want dessert, Ricky?"

"No, sir, I just like to see what they got in this sort of joint."

"You can have all the dessert you choose, kid."

Mr Vale bounded out of the diner, kids in tow, and they drove along the water's edge. Ricky glanced between the City and home across the river. Town's dowdy comfort had its pull, but the City dug a little optimism out of his cynical coals. They pulled up at the small wooden pier where Mr Vale docked his boat the last time. Charlie unmoored the craft, and they all jumped in. Ricky tilted his head to nose beneath the tarpaulin, but Mr Vale patted the air down and encouraged his patience. Ricky enjoyed the cool wind in his hair, but he'd waited long enough for Mr Vale to explain. "Sir, I thought I was gunna work in a warehouse?"

"There's time for all that. First things first. An education is broad and holistic."

What the hell is holistic?

"I can't just stick you in a warehouse. You need many skills if you're to work for me. This is day one."

Ricky could live with a speedboat ride down the river as part of his learning. He leaned back and rested his elbows on the side. They slowed opposite the City of Forts, maybe a hundred yards out. The still air attacked his cool. He wiped sweat from his face and levered himself forward in surprise at the destination. Mr Vale and Charlie grinned at his confusion, scanning the fields and houses with binoculars. The boat bobbed in a steady position.

Mr Vale noticed how Ricky fidgeted. "One thing at a time, son." Son? "Everything in life is a test. A test of character. You need to show what you're made of - every day."

"Won't I just pack boxes in your warehouse?"

That smile again, which is not a smile.

A family of deer padded into view and rested at the top of the bank. They gazed over for a second, decided the distance kept them safe, and concentrated on stuffing their bellies.

"Why don't you lift the tarpaulin, Ricky?"

"Sure."

It seemed a big thing now he had permission. What did Mr Vale conceal beneath? A body? His fingers shook at the stupid idea. The sun glinted off the blue material and made it seem water rushed into the boat. He crouched and lifted a corner, ready to jump over the side. Three cases. A box. Mr Vale nodded his approval to open them. Ricky shuffled over on his knees and opened the nearest. A rifle.

"Wow. What's this have to do with your warehouse, Mr Vale?"

"Nothing at all to do with the technical aspects of the job, young man, but everything to do with who you are as a person. Do you like guns, Ricky?"

Charlie's examination crawled all over Ricky. The gun Bixby used to shoot the Ghost Boy fascinated him, sure. The weapon now hidden in the shed. God, what if ma found it? Brett had fired a few of Mr Panowich's rounds. Now he worried about Mr Panowich's gun. Had he shoved it in his waistband when he visited the other night?

"I like guns, sir."

The man patted him on the back. "You ever shoot one?"

The sun glinted off the metallic surface of another object in the box. Ricky squeezed his fingers together, taken aback at the giant beetle. As his eyes followed its contours, he realized it was the drone Charlie flew from the balcony of their apartment.

Ricky turned to study Mr Vale. The man remained amused, but his judgment bore down on Ricky and threatened to smother his summer same as those bastards in the hoods. He just wanted to rest on the river bank with Liz right now. She could talk about Charlie Dickens all day if she chose, and he'd be okay with it all.

"No, sir, I never shot one."

Charlie's eyes widened at his dad, and Mr Vale's face fell. Disappointment scrawled his forehead. Ricky set his jaw at the first failure in this test of character. *Whatever.*

"Well, take it."

Ricky lifted the rifle and Charlie showed him how to prepare it. Ricky fixed the scope after a little confusion and switched from one blurred image to another. Figured how to focus the lens. Eyed the deer, their ears twitching as much as Ricky's stomach.

"Okay, Ricky, place the stand on the edge of the boat. Yep, good boy. Rest the butt tight against your shoulder for the recoil. Yep, that's it. Before you shoot, take a deep breath – and as you pull the trigger, let it out real slow. Reeeal slowww."

As Ricky made himself comfortable, man and son set up their rifles and aimed. Ricky watched the deer above his scope. Two females and three fawns, with a stag at the back, suspicious at the tension in the air. Didn't sit right. He could kill an animal, he had no doubt, but to take out a family went against the spirit.

"Will you eat all of them?"

Charlie said *sure,* but his tone suggested *pussy.* Ricky avoided Mr Vale's scrutiny and scoped between the females, the offspring, and the stag. He settled on the stag – the fawns would need their mother more than him.

"Hey, Ricky, you focus on the younger ones. You're the novice. I'll have the big fella."

Mr Vale's cheerful voice triggered rebellion and Ricky fired at the bigger animal. He hit its body, maybe the rib cage. The whole family bolted, even the stag. Ricky scrambled back to his position from the recoil. The beast ran for several yards until it came to a standstill. It panted hard for life. On a chilly day, its breath would launch great clouds of steam. Ricky's chest thumped in sympathy for the beast. It stumbled a step, then two, until it dropped to the ground as if it needed rest. Its family twitched, set their feet, ready to flee again.

"Ricky ... boy ... I told you I would take the stag."

"Sorry, sir, but I got it, yeah?" He wound the pain away by making a windmill out of his right arm.

Mr Vale squinted towards the animal. "You got it, but that thing will be suffering. You didn't hit it true. Let's put it out of its misery."

Ricky shivered with guilt and excitement and jumped at the next shot.

"Charlie ... God damn, the moment has passed."

"But I didn't get to shoot."

His pa pursed his lips, shook his head, and reached over to back-hand his son's upper arm. Charlie sulked and weaved to see what he'd hit. Raised the binoculars for a better view.

"One, two, three ... four. You missed, son."

Ricky thrilled at the pride and one-upmanship, but wanted to reach the stag. Charlie leaned into him and whispered. "I should have shot you."

Ricky side-eyed him. His pa fought for a lost cause with this one. Mr Vale placed a hand on the motor, gliding towards the bank, but movement in the field stilled him. The boys followed his gaze to a man – slight build and gangly as a teenager, but tall – whose face they couldn't see for the hood over his head and the painted features they examined through their scopes.

"A Ghost Boy."

"Is that what you call them? I call him a waste of space and taxpayer money. And he has a damn cheek hanging around here after the police scoured the area."

"You know about that?"

"I know just about everything, Ricky. I'm an active member of the community, so it's my business to see it all."

"But you live in the City."

"Sure, but I grew up in these parts, and the rot kills me. Root it out or the body dies. Your ma is one of the good ones. I could tell straight away. She brooks no crap from anyone, not even you, I guess. Then there's your dad, who takes flight at the slightest bit of pressure and leaves you all – his dependents – to fend for yourselves. That's bullshit right there."

Ricky flushed and cursed Charlie under his breath. Damn tattler. He glanced between the pa, the son, and the Ghost Boy. They observed the intruder through their fancy binoculars. Ricky watched through and above the scope. The man crept along, wary he might wake some monster from the Dragon Lands if he produced too much noise. Checked his shoulder and searched the woods for the gunshot's source until he noticed the boat and the three of them with their sights set on him. He froze, same as the deer. Pondered his position. Wanted to flee. His doubt blossomed to fear. A crow cawed in the distance and turkey vultures circled above, impatient to peck at the stag. The hot air mixed with tension and thick fabric must drench the man wet as the river. Mr Vale scanned the bank for any of the intruder's compadres. A jetliner trailed a white streak in the clear blue sky. Seemed a perfect day to enjoy freedom. But not now.

The shot tumbled Ricky backwards into the side of the boat. Banged his head so hard he had to blink to refocus. He pushed himself to his knees and peeked over the boat's edge. The man disappeared in a puff of smoke. Mr Vale sat straight and bloodless, his rifle's butt resting on the boat's deck, the muzzle over his shoulder. He invited comment from Ricky. Charlie had the rifle ready to fire, gaze intent through the scope. The Ghost Boy must have crouched low and dove from sight. That's what Ricky reckoned until he stood and saw, through weaves of grass, that the man had crumpled into the earth.

Bugs tick-tocked the seconds away. Mr Vale's eyes clamped tight, almost shut, as he pinpointed every abandoned window within view until satisfied nobody witnessed any of this. He motored to the bank and stepped out. Encouraged the boys to hurry and check the stag. Ricky sat still, his belly a spinning washing machine.

"Ricky, son, come on. Let's go."

Ricky stared in wonder at the man's strong, tender voice. He floated out of the boat, his bones and muscles numbed. Charlie's pa led them as if he knew the City of Forts better than anyone. The Ghost Boy's face smushed into the dirt, his legs crooked. Charlie dragged the hood back. A gash in his temple showed where the bullet landed.

"Good shot, son."

Charlie beamed, a little shy at the compliment. He lifted his shirt to tug the pistol from its holster and marched to the stag. His pa followed. Ricky hesitated, but staggered after them after a questioning look from Mr Vale. The animal had fallen on its side, eyes wide at the shock, breath short, breathing like a motorbike in the distance. Charlie glanced at Ricky to make sure he watched – and executed the deer.

Ricky fought the shivers loading every muscle.

"Well done, son. No animal should suffer. No criticism of you, Ricky, my boy. You haven't fired a shot before, right? That man over there, he's waste. Clogs up the drains and makes a stink of society. We gotta use Draino sometimes." He planted a hefty hand on Ricky's slender shoulder. "I know you think on similar lines as me. Prospects for a kid like you are slim around here."

"Sir ... what is this warehouse job?"

"You're looking at it."

"Killing deer? Or ...?"

"Continue the *or* thought, Ricky. We're in dangerous times. We've got people flooding into the country who don't respect a damn thing about us, and our own kind have become a bunch of sloths. Losers. Time we created Spartans of ourselves. I'll need fine, solid, go-getting boys like you to tame the helots."

Spartans and helots? What's all that? "I'm just a kid, sir."

"Yes, you are. Young enough to absorb. I know a good 'un when I see one."

Ricky made his way, all stiff, back to the human corpse. Glared at the gash in his head. The fuckers had hooked and reeled him in.

He latched onto Mr Vale's eyes. "I have a place we can bury him."

39

Ma leaned in his doorway as he readied for bed. She gave the air-conditioning more of a rest these days and Ricky walked about the house shirtless.

"He worked you hard?"

Ricky shrugged her conversation away, but she persisted.

"That's one hell of a bruise on your shoulder. You got into an accident?"

"Just not used to it, is all."

She watched him in a way he didn't recognize. Not since he was Brett's age, anyway. The pins prickling his shoulders and down his back told him she fostered some pride in him. It made him switch off, because ... what would she make of the truth? The truth scared him, thought it might put her and Brett in danger. He rubbed a tender finger over the purple patch on his shoulder and leaned in to ma's kiss.

"My firstborn. Love ya."

Ricky smiled but didn't say he loved her, too, until he heard her footsteps' patter on the kitchen linoleum. He switched off the light and scanned the street outside. Saw Tarantula Man behind that bush, in the neighbor's window, up that tree. Heard him in the breeze and the flutter of leaves. Mr Vale had lost Trent another man. He wouldn't take any more.

* * *

Ma took Brett to her workplace the next morning. Ricky watched them leave and locked up that empty pang for his brother. The kid annoyed him for his neediness, so he recoiled from rose-tinting their adventures together.

Mr Vale made him trek the alleys and skirt the City of Forts, and wade into the river to reach the boat. Charlie waited for him, alone. He offered Ricky a hand, but Ricky clambered in by his own efforts and pretended he didn't notice the outstretched limb.

Charlie whooped at the speed and spins, and pouted at Ricky's neutral expression.

"Where we going?" Ricky skimmed the water with his fingertips. "The warehouse?"

"Yeah, the warehouse."

"Am I packing boxes?"

"Sure."

"You want me to drive the boat?"

"No way." He whooped again, but Ricky locked his enthusiasm away.

"Go on, let me. You can play your video game."

Charlie checked his shoulder to read potential mockery. Ricky conjured as much innocence as he could muster.

"Fine. You know what to do?"

"I've seen your dad do it a few times. And I watched you, didn't I?" He'd done it before, too, with Bixby.

That pleased Charlie. He slowed the boat to a crawl so Ricky could take over. Ricky needed a thrill before the day with Mr Vale began. What would today bring? Another death? He couldn't handle another, and the thought made him lose the wheel and retch over the side. His empty stomach gave up nothing but a burn in his throat. The boat lurched left, Charlie yelled, and something heavy hit the deck. Charlie steadied the boat before they flipped.

"Get my phone back, will you? Goddamn it, if that had gone in the water, I'd have thrown you in to fetch it."

Ricky yukked his tongue at the aftertaste and swayed in search of the cell. Didn't doubt Charlie would kick him overboard if the urge took him. He snatched the phone and lobbed it at the young Vale.

Charlie scowled at him. "Why don't you like me?"

"I never said that."

"No, you never did." Charlie spat into the river.

* * *

Mr Vale drove them at a polite speed, past crisp, polite people with important strides. They stopped outside a warehouse and Mr Vale pulled the handbrake with a satisfied smile. Turned to Ricky, excited.

"You should read Dickens."

Ricky laughed. "*Great Expectations*."

"Ha, you do read him."

"No, sir, but Liz does." Mr Vale called him a 'flowery ass' not so long back.

"Liz. Mythical Liz. She still trying to write?"

Ricky jutted his chin as if he didn't give a shit. "She just reads."

"Come on, in we go."

Mr Vale unlocked the door. Nodded Ricky inside and growled at Charlie to stop dragging his feet. Made Ricky sorry for him in the moment. The warehouse had enough strip lights to tan your skin green and make you thirst for the sun. Thousands, millions, billions of cardboard boxes piled against the walls and on top of others, compressed in pillars. Dozens of conveyor belts snaked the floor space, silent. Once it all started it'd buzz like a wasp's nest.

Ricky only had question marks in his eyes. "Am I packing?"

"You'll be packing, son."

"Packing what?"

"I'm an active member of my community. Go to church. Sponsor local events. And I have gathered most of the local artisans and artists together to help distribute their wares. It's good for them, good for me – as long as they're actively pushing themselves."

Ricky shrugged – *as long as he earns money.*

"And then, there are the ones who just don't cut it." Mr Vale pulled a small lever concealed in the wall. It opened a gray door he hadn't seen. Mr Vale flicked a switch and marched down the metal steps. The floodlights from the high ceiling shone dim, so Ricky had to squeeze his eyes to see. At full glow they revealed cages, gun targets, locked racks of rifles and handguns, and towards the back of the room, a cardboard cutout of a street with sharp corners and windows.

"You need to learn some stuff, kid."

Charlie opened a locker and thrust a handgun at him. Ricky gawped at him, swiveled to Mr Vale.

"I want you to shoot straight. You hit the deer. Not bad for your first rifle effort, but the recoil almost sent you, and my gun, into the river. You must know how to handle all of it."

"I can handle it."

"You can get better."

"I think I'm pretty good."

"For someone who never fired a gun, right?"

Charlie feigned disinterest, but he enjoyed his pa's comment. Ricky held the gun out to him. "Help me shoot properly, Charlie."

Charlie melted, eyes popping between Ricky and daddy. His soft hands positioned Ricky's and Ricky let him show the way. Charlie stood behind him, close. Made him wince inside. Charlie's breath stunk of stale cornflakes. He gripped Ricky's forearm and whispered encouragement. Mr Vale set the targets in motion, and Ricky fired as each one pinged into view. He hit them all with Charlie's help and missed a few without. In the street section, Ricky rested his outstretched arm on a plastic mock-wall and shot at objectives appearing at the windows. He found a rhythm and enjoyed the ache pouring over his shoulder. Reloaded and blasted away, gained confidence from Mr Vale's cheering and the silent smile from Charlie. Ghost Boys rushed through his head. Tarantula Man leaped out from an upper-floor window and retreated with a hole in his chest.

His last shot hit the target in the forehead, just off-center. He laughed. A little too hard. Brett's panicked face, when Tarantula Man tried to crowbar his way into the car, regurgitated . Their imprisonment in the City of Forts basement pulled him back to reality. He dropped the gun.

"Mr Vale, I don't get what you want from me. You told ma I'll work for you by packing boxes."

"Ricky, boy, I like you."

"I know you do. You keep telling me, but what's this all about?"

* * *

Mr Vale bought them ice-creams, and they sat on a wall to watch the City go by. Ricky could have laughed. He'd gone from blasting mock-humans to licking ice-cream like a five-year-old.

"Look at everyone around here as they walk by." Mr Vale nodded at a man with a ponytail, shorts and an open shirt exposing a Nirvana t-shirt beneath. "Him. Good or bad?"

"Bad." Charlie almost jumped off the wall in triumph.

"Shut up, Charlie, I'm asking Ricky."

Charlie slumped and stuck the remaining ice-cream cone in his mouth.

"Bad?" Ricky hunched, nervous Mr Vale would bark at him, too.

"Decent effort, but no, he's good. I know him. Some of his paintings have merit. Another ten years and he might find his talent … What about her?"

Ricky didn't want to judge, but the man prodded him. "Good."

He shook his head, all dramatic, and swished a finger in the air. "She's bad."

"You know her, too?"

"No. I can tell by the way she walks. By the way she carries her handbag. By the way her blonde hair invites a man, any man, in. Not good at all."

Ricky couldn't see how he made such a judgment, but Mr Vale had more years on him, so he must have learned a trick or two. He nodded, complacent, and jerked his head to the big man on the opposite side of the road. "Bad. He has a tattoo which peeks below his sleeve. That crisp white shirt beams all upright, but the man wears it like a crown of thorns. Shifts his briefcase from hand to hand as if he doesn't want any association with the thing."

Mr Vale slapped his thigh and roared. Calmed himself as passers-by picked up their pace to get by his over-the-top gestures. "No. He's as respectable as they come, but hates his job, and yes, that tattoo wraps up his arm and strangles his neck. Horrible. But an honest man, nonetheless."

"I feel uncomfortable, sir. I don't know any of these people. Makes me itch to be makin' comments on them."

"Which marks you as a good person, Ricky, no matter what anyone says."

Ricky glanced at Charlie and blinked. Now the boy had slammed the ice-cream down his neck, he returned to his fancy phone. Ricky might have his own nice, shiny phone from Mr Vale, but he worried it would turn him into Charlie, or even Mr Panowich.

"And I'm looking for good people. Always searching for talented people. And it's often best to grab them young, before they're tainted by adult worries. Because adulthood, if you let it, turns some folks from something pure. Makes them rot from the inside and become leeches on society." He slapped his thighs again and smiled at the thoughts in his head rather than the bustle of life in front of him. "Like the man we shot yesterday."

40

Mr Vale dropped Ricky off at the river bank. Handed him a couple hundred dollars and told him to take Wednesday off. He'd pick him up again Thursday to learn how to pack the goods.

"You can't hunt helots every day. You need to keep up your discipline in the quiet times."

"I'll boat over tomorrow." Charlie's mood had lifted as high as the jet streams after teaching Ricky. "We can hang out."

Ricky curled his lips in acknowledgment, but he couldn't light the candle in his eyes. "Yeah. Definitely." He didn't shift an inch as he watched them speed off. Once they became a speck, he shot away, a rabbit from a distracted fox. He asked again, what is a helot?

He arrived home, relieved. "It's me."

"Okay." His ma sounded cheerful. Another voice made his muscles tighten, but he relaxed at Officer Ray's deep tones. He popped his head into the dining area and nodded a hello at the policeman.

"How are you, Ricky?"

"Good, sir. Good."

"Nice to hear."

They tilted their heads to each other, pursed their lips,

and Ricky disconnected from the conversation. Ricky threw himself on the sofa and clicked on the TV. The family photo remained face down. He looked out the window every minute, expecting anything these days. Voices emerged from the screen as its buzz dissipated . Local news. *Switch*. Some old comedy show where everyone wore big hair and white socks beneath too short pants. *Switch*. Bunch of older men, one wacky, cigars, machine guns, terrible aim. *Switch*.

Ma's voice dropped to the thrum of the freezer. "Ray, you don't need to come and see how I am. I'm in a better place. And ... you were, you know, Tom's friend."

"I'm still Tom's friend, though he doesn't like to get in touch anymore. And I'm not here for that. I always cared for you both. I just, I can't hack either of you ending up in stupid situations."

She laughed. "You never came to my home when we had kids. And *stupid*? You're here to correct my judgment? What have I done that's so dumb?"

Ricky pretended to concentrate on the nature show, but his ears pricked like this squirrel at the approach of a wolverine.

"This Mr Vale you've cozied up with –"

"What are you talking about, Ray? He's got my boy working for him, is all. He had no other intention. I'd never met him before to even offer a wink and a smile. My, you are a worrier, aren't ya?"

"No. I'm not. Vale's a big shot over in the City. I checked him out more. He seems legit, but ..." He flashed an eye out the window as if saying his name brought bad luck.

"But what?"

"He ... I don't know – whispers, rumors, urban legends."

"He the devil? Ready to impregnate me with his child?"

"No ... but even my superiors seem a little shifty when I mention him. Tell me to keep my mind on the geeks and freaks around these parts and not worry myself about what goes on over the river."

"There you go."

"The men I work with are hardened and long in the tooth, so when they flinch ... No matter that it was the subtlest flinch you ever saw."

"He's married, if that's what you're worried about."

"Jeez, Caitlin, will you get over yourself?"

"Ha, what am I meant to think? Come on, now, you're like a dog in heat. You need to get laid, is what you need."

"I get laid."

"Paid laid?"

"God, Caitlin ... No. What you take me for?"

"How is it I never see you with anyone?"

"Because I'm in my patrol car, in uniform – working."

"There is that."

Mention of the devil made Ricky push into the sofa. Still, he clung to the tag because what had Mr Vale done but ruin his summer with his batshit ideas about cleansing the streets of dirt. He'd listened, gone along with it, but the gash in the Ghost Boy's head stared at him like an accusing third eye. The little bloody trail told Ricky where all this led.

* * *

Tanais' house sat behind well-tended earth banks that hid the rest of Town from the development. They'd built this place two years ago. Ma said it would attract money, but apart from the development itself, Ricky didn't see evidence. Its sheen mocked the rust surrounding it. Ricky cringed at the stains on the sides of his home now he inspected the fresh white walls of Tanais'. You could play golf in her backyard. No patches in the grass. No fade in the green. He almost wanted to roll in it.

Ricky ran down the bank to the back fence, making himself look casual to anyone watching. Neighbors' upper windows overlooked him and guilt settled at the base of his spine. He trapped it there. He'd done nothing bad except come from the wrong part of Town.

Nobody lounged outside. The heat would roast you to pork rinds if they stayed too long on the fancy wooden lounge chairs in Tanais' backyard. Ricky pushed into the fence to dodge the sun's laser focus. That guilty conscience skipped a ridge in his spine as he realized how suspicious he must look to anyone walking by. An elderly man on the other side of the bank croaked at his dog to get a move on. Ricky recoiled, checked his shoulder, but the man sounded old enough to find this mound as tall as Mount Everest.

"Damn it, Charlie, come back here."

Ricky shot round. Charlie? Here? He followed him? A dog topped the slope and wagged his tail. The small, shaggy thing puffed at the heat. It let out a friendly bark and waited to see if Ricky would pat him. Ricky shooed his hand to send the hound on its way, but the stupid mutt took that for an invitation and risked his arthritic legs on the decline. They gave up, and he tumbled and rolled near to Ricky, who leaned into the fence hard enough to become one of its planks. The lead wrapped the animal's neck and the plastic handle beat its chest as it shuffled around Ricky's ankles. Expectant eyes. Tongue a wet autumn leaf hanging out its mouth.

"You need to piss off, doggie."

"Charlie." The man mirrored the dog. Hand on his side from exertion. Baseball cap patched with sweat. Bony arms like lightning strikes out of his t-shirt. "I'm sorry, young man. He's friendly, old, and about as threatening as a dodo's feather."

Ricky nodded, still hunched into the fence. The man's smile faltered. "You live here, do you?"

"No, sir. I'm here to see a friend. Just waiting for her to come out."

The 'sir' helped the man's lips curl back up, but his eyes balanced it out with skepticism. He scanned the fence, which didn't have a gate. "She going to climb over? It's pretty high, there."

Ricky nodded, his mouth open and crooked. "She likes to climb. She's into parkour."

The man's head tilted and his mouth straightened to a thin line. The conversation died. His mind, Ricky could tell, wandered to his phone and the number 911.

"Ricky?"

He jumped, recognized Tanais through the gap, and laughed in relief. "Tanais."

The man huffed, whistled at his un-petted mutt, and with all the pace of a drugged turtle, they dropped out of sight.

"What are you doing here?"

Tanais disrupted their previous unity. He spent his summers, every year, with his trusted triangle of Bixby and Liz. He'd only regained Bixby this summer after two years in the system. What did Ricky care for Tanais? Her face in the factory, when her pa cornered Bixby, showed how she cared for them.

"Tanais, why'd you tell your pa about Bixby?"

"He works in social care – I thought he could help. I ended

up telling him how he hurt me, at how he treated me, that's all. I was upset. Dad took it on himself to get involved."

"He told the cops about what happened?"

"Yeah. Wouldn't you?"

"Not sure. I don't know many cops. And the way ma talks about them ... I can't say I would." He hadn't revealed a thing to Officer Ray.

"Well, that man ... Dad's kept me indoors since. He's even nervous about me out in the garden. Damn it, Ricky, I'm like Rapunzel."

"What?"

"I'm on a Disney binge."

"You need to get out of there."

"Yes. I miss you guys."

"Including Bixby?"

She sucked on her bottom lip and nodded. She wouldn't miss him so much if she heard what he said before Tarantula Man cornered her.

"Can you sneak out?"

"I reckon we'll not stay here long. Dad talks about nothing else but moving out. Maybe even from the state."

"Jesus." It made his stomach hurt to hear it. Surprised him how she'd needled into his life. "Your pa home?"

"Working. Mom's in the living room, asleep."

"Then?"

"Now?"

"Couple of hours."

"I don't know." She swung a glance at the house. "Mom's always sleepy. She loves to hit the pillow."

"Then?"

"Will Bixby want to talk to me?"

"All you have to say is sorry, and he'll be putty in your warm hands."

"I do have warm hands, don't I? Yeah, sure, but I have to get home before dad returns."

Her laugh tinkled in his ear. He bounded away and scratched at his peeling skin. Needed sunscreen, but ma never bought any as she always expected him to stay indoors.

Tanais' house gleamed. Straight lines, trimmed bushes, flower beds clear of weeds. Order. Liz' looked like its owner. Once sure Tarantula Man didn't lurk in his BMW around some corner or in her backyard, he knocked. When no-one answered, he knuckled harder until it seemed the door might swing from its hinges.

Carrie opened and squinted as if she stared at a hundred-watt bulb. The slit she managed couldn't let much light in, but she stuck a scabby finger at him and said, "You."

"Yeah, me. Is Liz home?"

"I've seen where you live. All I have to do is give the word."

Mr Vale. Floyd. Ricky could do the same, and the score would read Ricky 4, Tarantula Man 0. The momentum lay with him. Still, he had to clamp that stutter to the floor of his mouth.

"Is Liz home?"

"In her room. What you want with her? You ruined her life enough already."

"Who is it?" Mr Panowich shouted out, startled by some-body at his door.

"That stupid-ass boy your stupid-ass daughter likes so much – or not so much anymore."

"She's not a stupid-ass, ma'am, she's my friend."

"You can forget about that, now, you idiot. You threw that one under the bus – hey, mind yerself, young lady."

Liz barged past the woman and out of the house, gripping Ricky by the wrist and leading him across the road down to the gritty patch of grass where the tree declared its love for her.

"Well, Ricky-boy, you're a son of a bitch, aren't you?"

He shrugged and kicked at a stone.

"First, you make my dad look like a bastard –"

"Hang on, he came round my house and made trouble for me."

"How?"

"He was asking about Brett."

"So? ... You ... you never told your ma, did you?"

"How could I tell her? She thinks I should never leave the house, never mind drop off my brother with a man she's never met."

"You're an asshole. A real asshole."

"All I want –"

"What *you* want? You want to scare away my friend by calling him a pedophile? Nice job – real nice."

"Isn't he?"

"I told you, he never laid a hand on me. Apart from a pat on the shoulder for good work."

"What good work?"

"He's educating me."

"Is he now?"

"Get your filthy mind out the gutter. We read literature. He helps me with science and math."

"You read literature? Like, you read it aloud together?"

She nodded.

"You read that Dickens out loud, sat together? Where?"

"Under a tree. In a café. Wherever the fancy takes us."

Ricky laughed. Ridiculous. "The man has tattoos. Rides that stupid motorbike. He doesn't read Dickens, or anything else."

"He does it all, but you only see the zit on the end of your snout."

Ricky rubbed his nose. "But why? What's in it for him?"

"His dad burned his books when he was young. Told him to stop fairying about and do stuff. Man stuff."

"That's why he rides a bike and has tattoos?"

"He likes manly things, too. But he loves to read. Into odd music, too. Some weird British shit. Hurts your ears at first, but you get into it."

"And you met him where?"

"At a diner. I was with dad. Dad is always out of his head and about as conversational as a box of matches. I had my eyes on a dumb novel – loved it at the time, but my tastes are open now – and he steps up to our table. Asks what I'm reading. Tells me how fresh it is to see someone with a book in their hands – in public. You don't get that round here. I asked him if he'd read it. I could tell he turned his nose up, but he didn't want to discourage me. He sat with us and told me what he had on his plate."

"He brought his breakfast with him? Freak."

"Idiot, no. What he had his head in. Come on, Ricky, keep up — the book he was reading."

"Oh."

"Some novel called *The Crow Road*."

He hadn't asked. "I'll get round to it someday. What did your pa say?"

"He didn't. I don't think he even realized he'd joined us."

He nodded, searched for a word which might hit. Gave up.

"And it went from there."

"But what is *it*?"

She clambered up the tree with a grunt and squeezed her eyes at her home up the road. "Why you here?"

"You told your pa where I live."

"So?"

"Michael Trent is looking for me. He's the one who tried to get into our car the other week."

She glanced down at him. "He is not …"

"With a crowbar. With Brett in the back."

"He's just one of my dad's drug dealers."

"More than that. He hit Tanais' pa with a gun. Would have done more if Bixby hadn't set the fort on fire."

Liz dug a nail into the branch. Swung her leg. Cast a reluctant eye on him. "You really hurt my dad. I've never seen him so happy than with Brett. Like my brother returned to him."

He lifted himself to sit beside her. Shouldered her in sympathy. Half-expected tears in her eyes, but they remained Arizona dry. "You not good enough for the old man?"

"It's different. I'm independent. I wanna do what I wanna do, not what dad suggests. He gave up on all that when I hit eight or nine. I can't park my ass in a boat for three, four hours and wait for a fish to bite. Not my nature. I could read a book, but dad would huff and puff until he had my attention, and then say nothing I wanted to hear."

"Ma loves Brett more than me. Said she'd send me where they sent Bixby if I put him in any danger."

"She did not."

"Did."

"But, she's right – if you put him in danger …"

"S'ppose."

"You're a selfish bastard, Ricky."

"No more than you. I'm sorry for what I said about your boyfriend."

She rabbit-punched his shoulder. "He's not my boyfriend."

"Lover, then. Fuck-buddy."

She jabbed him again until the numb pain made him wince.

He rubbed where she hit him. "Come and help me tell Charlie no."

"What's he want?"

"To be my pal. I just want you and Bixby. And Tanais. And that's it. Just for this summer, Liz, before I lose you forever."

"Shit ..."

He folded his arms and dropped his head into his shoulders at that response. Made him regret what he did to her boyfriend.

"We gotta get outta here." He slipped down the tree. Tarantula Man pulled up outside Liz' house. He gesticulated some anger. Carrie hung out her door like an exhausted dog's tongue.

Liz hit an ankle, banged a knee, scraped her cheek as she hurried to the ground. Carrie pointed a finger their way. The man held a hand over his eyes to frame them from the sun's glare. He threw a package at that woman and slipped back into his car, coiled to strike.

Liz locked her fingers in Ricky's and led him from his stupor. He only picked up her pace once Tarantula Man screeched his BMW from its spot. Trent hadn't taken care to check his mirrors – another car hit his BMW. In the chaos, Ricky and Liz shimmered away into the heat's haze.

41

The factory made dolls of Ricky and Liz, little details against its vast entrance gate. Tanais arrived ten minutes later, tight and hunched in the expansive space. They waited so long for Bixby they gave up and entered the building. The humidity inside settled without the warm breeze outside disturbing it. It cooked a musty smell, the ghost sweat of men from days gone by.

"Hey."

Ricky did well not to grip Liz' arm. Charlie, in a red t-shirt with Jay Z splashed across it, sat on an old roller in the middle of the factory floor. They had to focus to see him through a jumble of scattered gray, orange, and green debris.

"Hey, Charlie." Liz tried to sound cheery, but it came out droll. What else, nowadays?

Charlie kicked his heels against the metal and smiled, defensive, hopeful, a little shy, a little defiant. "You brought the gang."

"I did." Ricky tilted his head for a phone attached to Charlie's hand. Expected the bleeps of some alien invasion. He guessed he reserved all that for his pa's company.

"Cool, though I think I said just yourself, Ricky."

"That's fine by me." Liz headed for the door, but Ricky

jerked her to stay. He threw her question marks back at her.

Charlie rubbed his hands and swung his legs again. "I thought we were gunna do stuff, then head to my place."

Ricky grinned, but no words escaped his gritted teeth. He shouted, a little too loud, his greeting for the new entrant, Bixby, who slouched inside, careless, as if in search of a sofa to loaf on. Nodded at Ricky and Liz, glared at Tanais and walked by her. Tanais, unlike the other day – when her face melted – shook her head and studied him. Saw him for the first time?

"Hey, Bixby, how are yer?"

"Charlie." Charlie cocked an ear to hear him better. "Hey, Charlie."

"Hey." Charlie smiled. Two-faced asshole.

Ricky stepped forward towards the younger Vale. Didn't want to hide behind Liz, even if he wanted her moral support. "You've been great these last few days."

Charlie inclined his head. His mouth fell open, ready to deflect Ricky's words with his own.

"Really great. Your pa, he's ... he's somethin'. I really like him."

Charlie offered vague agreement, though he seemed offended at the same time. "Are you just saying stuff? Is that a question?"

"Nah ..." Ricky pulled at his t-shirt. The casual execution of the stag. The Ghost Boy's assassination. There's a swamp to drain out here, according to his pa. It all made Ricky's words stick on his flypaper tongue. He conjured saliva and coated his throat. "Just, I'm so grateful, so ya know, but ... I ... I don't wanna be your friend. I ... just don't."

A frog sat in Charlie's craw. He glanced at Bixby, who shuffled his feet. At Liz, who stared, indifferent at obvious facts. At Tanais, who squirmed at yet more confrontation. He settled back on Ricky and gulped that amphibian down. Light hit the water in his eyes and he fought to prevent any spilling down his cheek.

"That's a little ungracious, don't you think?"

Ricky shrugged his shoulders. What else could he say?

"I mean, my dad plucks you from this shitty town and gives you an opportunity, and this is how you repay him?"

"What opportunity?" Bixby threw his hands in the air at how Ricky ignored him.

"I'm not ungrateful. I like your pa. He's interesting and all, but I don't see how ... Look, I ... you know how we feel. We've been through this before. You're not part of the gang. You're ... you're just not."

Charlie sniffed. Nodded. "We were there for you. Who rescued you when that thug locked you in that basement with Liz and Tanais?"

Bixby shook his head, realization's eye over the horizon. "You? You shot that man?"

"Daddy and I, we see it all, out on that boat."

"You spy on us?" Liz jutted her chin.

Charlie grinned, growing out of his awkward skin. "With drones."

Ricky nodded. Of course they had.

"It got you out of the shit you put yourselves in, right? I flew one this close to the basement window and saw what kind of trouble you had. I rescued you. Including her."

Tanais jumped. What? *Her*? *Including* her? What did that mean?

Charlie lifted his t-shirt. Revealed two handguns, both holstered. "I thought we could both shoot shit up."

Ricky fiddled with the phone in his pocket. Asshole guilt bubbled his blood and made him itch. But ... "Man, I'm all grateful, an' all, but ... it just doesn't change things. I – we – don't enjoy hanging out with you. It's not personal. We hardly match up together, that's all."

The boy's expression turned ice cream in the sun. Despite how he tried to iron out his face, it scrunched all bitter. "I don't have any friends. None. I thought you guys could ... I thought ... Why? Why do none of you want to be my friend?"

Bixby laughed. "Because you're a prick and nobody likes you."

Liz elbowed air as if Bixby stood by her side. "It's not that we dislike you. As Ricky said, you're not the right fit. But ..." She glanced at the guns still on display. "You can work on it, right?" She glanced around for moral support, but everybody stayed transfixed on the outsider.

Ricky stiffened. The kid stocked up on firepower. Bixby should shut his trap. Ricky kept his tight. Charlie stepped on a tightrope between New York skyscrapers and didn't care if he fell. He slid a gun from its holster and held it out, handle first, to Ricky.

"What should I do with that?"

Charlie, shoulders slumped, pulled the other free, too. He stabbed the air, impatient for Ricky to handle the one he offered. "Take it."

"Why?"

"Take the gun."

Ricky eyed his friends, shaken he'd invited them here for moral support. Should have had the backbone to do it alone. He reached out, hands hot, sweaty, and infected by shakes. The handle stuck to his palm as if it had come home. Held it tight. Charlie aimed his weapon at Ricky's chest and hurled an eye towards Liz and Tanais.

"She's not part of the gang, either."

"Liz?"

"No, the dark one."

Ricky's laugh gurgled with nerves. Tanais' wide eyes shone their panicked spotlight on him. He turned the gun in his hand. "And?"

"You can shoot her. If you like."

"I don't like."

"Shoot her anyway."

"Charlie –"

Liz unglued her voice. "What is wrong with you?"

"With me? I'm not the one playing favorites."

"Favorites? What are you talking about, you fucking crybaby?"

Ricky guessed Charlie never had such words rocketed at him. His ma coddled him in cotton. The children of his pa's friends must avoid Charlie until no doubt remained that they didn't want to hang with him. All that shit he had in his bedroom won't bite back. Master of his own little kingdom, it emptied him so much he could fly away with the breeze.

"I'm not shooting Tanais. No way, Charlie. No way."

"Then, I shoot her. And after, I kill you."

Ricky backed up a step. Liz gripped Tanais' wrist. Tanais turned into a statue. Sweat pocked her forehead, ready to roll.

"I'll shoot the pain-in-the-ass bitch."

"Bixby?" Liz would have thrown *Great Expectations* at him, if she possessed it, to knock his teeth out of that filthy mouth.

Charlie grinned and waved his weapon at Bixby. "Take the gun and do it."

Bixby, as cold as the river, pulled at the handgun. He prised one of Ricky's dumb fingers away, then another, and almost had it when Ricky regained his grip and pushed him into a backpedal. Almost sent him over the barrel behind.

"Give me the gun. Let's get this done."

"Bixby ... what the hell is wrong with you?"

"Bixby, what you doing? Ricky, what's wrong with him?"

"Give me the fuckin' gun. He'll kill us all otherwise."

Silence settled on them. Tanais stepped to Ricky and insisted he give her the pistol.

"Whoa, you move away from that thing." Charlie slid off the roller and pointed the muzzle at Tanais' head.

Tanais offered the handle to Bixby, who took it. "I'm not sure what I ever did to you apart from try to be your friend. Every sandwich – I made with love. You got me laughing, at first, but now – it's all bitterness. I don't know what I did, but go on, end it."

"You brought your damned old man into my life, that's what you did."

"I didn't. You imagined I would, maybe, but ..."

"So what was he doing at the factory? You're a parasite. Get your claws into me, make me like you, then have the system drag me off to those fuckers across the river."

Tanais' shake of the head wouldn't have disturbed a butterfly. "He wanted to see what upset me. You brought him here, with your weird attitude. Why did I ever have feelings for you, Bixby? I seem to have wasted it all on such a selfish little dick."

Charlie grinned, tennis eyes on both. His smirk pulled Ricky from the pair's argument. Charlie, engrossed and amused by the fracture he'd caused, let the gun rest on his lap. Ricky lunged, and the pair tumbled over and behind the roller. Charlie bore the brunt of the fall and his yelp echoed off the factory walls, bringing back a crowd's roar for the gladiatorial contest. They struggled for the gun in rolls and jerks. A shot rang out. And another, until Bixby jabbed the end of the other gun to the side of Charlie's head. Charlie glanced sideways at them all as they bobbed around him.

"Let go of it or I pull the trigger. I don't give a shit."

"I reckon you don't."

Charlie released his grip and Ricky snatched it. Wiped his sweaty hands over his t-shirt and prised Charlie's teeth open with the muzzle. Inserted until he gagged. "What's wrong with you? What is wrong with you, you fuck?"

Mr Vale invaded his mind, and he pulled away. Kicked the ground and shot a couple of bullets into the far wall. Charlie hauled himself to his feet, careful not to set off Bixby's trigger finger. Liz rubbed a hand up and down Tanais' arm, who shrugged her off and marched to the exit, no glance back as the sun swallowed her up.

Charlie brushed himself off. "I was playin'. That's all. Nothing serious."

The Ghost Boy's blank stare from the other day told Ricky something different. He so wanted to put a hole in the boy, but he forced his trigger finger from danger and wrapped it tight around the handle. "It's this kind of shit we don't want to deal with, Charlie. We're done."

"We're not. You forget my dad."

Ricky snorted. "If I tell him —"

Charlie's laugh ended that thought.

"I'll have my guns back. Please."

Bixby shook his head at the request. "You go —"

"My property. Can I have them?"

Ricky fired the gun until he spent its bullets and Bixby followed suit. Threw the weapons at Charlie's feet and told him they didn't expect to see him again. Charlie narrowed his eyes, his chest a piston. Ricky swept past to the big blue gate, Liz and Bixby shoulder-to-shoulder with him. Hardened his mind for Mr Vale's expected visit.

42

They launched out of there before the Ghost Boys craned their curious necks towards the gunfire. Together, Ricky and Liz broke from Bixby. She hacked gunk out of her throat like she worked the coal mines forty hours a week. The effort to control himself made Ricky's skin tremble in sync with the hundred degree air.

Liz smacked Ricky's arm. "This is not how I envisaged my summer."

He frowned to the horizon. *Envisaged* is a word Biker Boy must have taught her.

She swung her arms, determined to battle what lay ahead. "What do we do about Bixby? I don't know him anymore. I mean, he says he had no intention of shooting Tanais, and all he meant was to confuse Charlie, but ..."

Ricky had done with bars around his thoughts. "He's been a bastard with her. And the squirrel heads ..." He told Liz about the day Tanais' dad visited the factory and how he didn't care what Tarantula Man did to either of them.

Liz' already white face became transparent. Her freckles swam in the clear hue.

"Yeah, Michael Trent." He needled her until a spasm forced her to clamp herself tight.

"Dad's ..."

"He's looking for me and that Carrie woman knows it. She's dying to tell him where I live."

"Ricky ... I ... she wouldn't dare. Dad wouldn't let her."

"Forget it. Let's see what we can do with Tanais."

A black cloud floated across the sun and put a little sting into the breeze's tip. The weather blew hot and cold for a while until other dark clouds rolled and stitched together. Liz had one hand in her jeans pocket, shoulders hunched. She glanced up at the sound of a motorbike's un-muffled razz and watched it fly by as they exited the fields. The odd spot of rain cooled their foreheads.

"Good job you don't have that damn book with you." He warmed at her smile and laughed at the sad nudge she gave him.

"Why we going round the back, Ricky-boy? These fences don't have any gates."

Ricky shrugged and changed course. Her dad won't have arrived home from work yet. Tanais answered her door after the third knock and an urgent press on the doorbell. She'd buried that open smile she once had. Her flat eyes viewed them behind slits. Her round face now sharpened, shovel-shaped.

"Why you here?"

Ricky stood straight as a soldier. "Wanted to see that you're okay."

"Done, is what I am."

"Tanais –"

"I don't need your patronizing pat on the arm, Liz. You all treat me as an outsider."

"No –"

"Not in so many words, no – but it was always clear. I

interrupted your cozy little lives. But you're all death. You kill everything around you."

Ricky fought the urge to shrink at her accusations and the noise from inside the house. Girded himself for Mr Rogers to sweep them the hell off his property. A weak voice called out Tanais' name. Ended in a whine which made Ricky look for a child in need of attention.

"Your mum? She alright?"

"Fine. Even better when you leave. More so when we do the same."

Ricky splayed his fingers. "It's happening?"

"Dad got himself a job elsewhere. Out of state."

"Then he's a pussy." Ricky couldn't stop himself. "You said he came here to help people, but he's gone in a puff of smoke – at the first hurdle. That's bullshit."

"You might be used to all this, but dad doesn't like being whipped by a gun-wielding maniac, and I'm not into being held captive in some abandoned basement. We're leaving – and I can't wait."

Shame reddened him, but he kept his eyes on hers and dug. Tanais fired hers back at him until her defiance twitched and softened. She reached for the connection and nodded.

"Dad always moves around. I never make friends. For long, anyway. You guys ..." A gulp smothered whatever sentiment wanted to escape, and she closed the door.

Ricky and Liz, feet set hard to the ground, stared at nothing. Ricky twined his fingers through Liz'. She let him. They turned to the steel gray car that pulled up to the curb. The woman, sunglasses on top of her red head, watched them beneath amused eyebrows.

At the summer's birth his little gang had been cast in stone.

He didn't want change. He dreaded Liz' entry into high school – even as he stood hand-in-hand with his life's love. He squinted at the black clouds like the sun had trained him to narrow his eyes, and squeezed Liz' fingers. The car's door handle held the day's heat, but Ricky held firm and pulled.

"Hi, kids." The woman greeted them with a quick smile, all business in her acknowledgment of how the decision pained them both. Once they settled on the back seat and shut the door, Miss Veronica glided out of the development.

43

Miss Veronica checked Ricky and Liz in the rearview every so often for a good mile before she spoke again. The rain's pitter-patter softened the silence's edge until she smiled, all bright and expansive, and said, "You kids like ice-cream?"

"We're fourteen." Liz side-eyed Ricky. "Not toddlers."

"I'm thirteen."

Liz mouthed her "sorree" and rolled her eyes.

"Ah." The woman winked at them in the mirror, which Ricky hoped she'd use on traffic a little more. "Then waffles and maple syrup?"

Ricky nodded. His belly jumped at that. Liz shrugged. She knew what she must do, but she didn't have to like it.

* * *

The woman – she said her last name several times, but Ricky let it slip out of his ears – bought them appetizers, and a hefty lunch of pancakes and syrup, with bacon, and key-lime pie for dessert. With betrayal at hand, they might as well use the lady.

She drove them back to the City of Forts at their suggestion and pulled a card from her purse. Pressed it into Ricky's palm.

"I gave you one of these already, but just in case, take another. Let me know if anything changes."

He skimmed her mint green eyes and tilted his head. She smiled and drifted away as soon as they shut the door. Liz leaned into him. She felt soft and inviting. He wrapped an arm around her and scrunched the lady's card. What need did he have of it now?

* * *

"You alright?"

"Fine. So is Tanais."

Bixby's nose wrinkled. He wiped it clear. "Good."

"Yeah."

"Hey, Ricky, you believe me, right? I just wanted to distract him. We did it. I don't think he'll fuck about with us no more."

Ricky blew his cheeks out and wished it so.

"We good and all that?"

Ricky's small smile hurt. "You should stay here a while. I'll bring you food."

"And toilet paper. Goddammit, my ass is sore from all the dry leaves."

Ricky clicked the shed door shut, quiet, and snuck to bed before ma awoke and set the house alight with panic.

* * *

"You not going to work today?" Ma's eyes needled, all forensic.

She leaned on his doorframe. He should install a lock. He

---

blinked the eye floaters away and 9.15am wobbled into focus.

"No. You?" He sat up as if that confirmed sincerity.

"Late start. You okay?"

"Hm."

She pushed off the woodwork and paused at the top of the stairs. "If you say so." She hopped down the stairs as though her years equaled his.

9.15 clicked to 9.16 and 9.17. He stared until he realized 9.30 arrived.

He entered Brett's room, ruffled the kid's hair, and stood by his window. The bedroom looked out the front of the house, like ma's. He patted his pocket for the card Miss Veronica handed him, but he had thrown it away. He mulled over Bixby's actions. His explanation would make sense if not for his talk during Mr Rogers' pistol whipping.

Ricky cracked the guilt out of his knuckles and stopped. He leaned into the window, squishing his nose against it. Condensation spread to hide his face from the outside world. He rubbed it away and made pinholes of his eyes. A figure across the road, beneath the drooped branches of a tree, set his feet apart, hands in pockets of a thigh-length coat, hood up against the rain. Wind blew at him so his coat pressed tight against his body, and worked at his hood, billowing and deflating it again and again. Inflated enough to expose dirty straggles of matted hair. Ricky stumbled backwards and trod on a hard plastic dinosaur Brett had planted to terrorize little toy soldiers. Ricky slammed into the wall and sprang back up. Brett's protests remained smothered under Ricky's rush of panic. He dared another glance, but the man left only his memory. Checked all angles to see if he approached the front door. Rushed back to his room and scanned the backyard. He

315

snatched his phone. Missed calls. Liz.

He pounded her name, once, twice. Third time lucky with his useless fingers.

"Ricky." Sharp. Urgent.

"You called."

She sensed his panic. "Pa kicked Carrie out the house."

"Yeah."

"You know?"

"No, but I can see the result. She told Michael Trent where I live."

"Oh, God. Is he there?"

"Lost sight of him."

"Call the cops."

Even now, he hesitated, but events loomed so large they stood skyscraper high and overwhelmed him.

"Ricky. Get rid of your issues, and call the damn cops – or I'll do it for you."

"Yeah."

"Yeah, what? Do it now."

"Errr, Ricky?" Ma. Voice a violin string.

He shot out of his room, insides aflame. Flexed his fists. "Ma?"

Liz called out, tinny now he had the phone against his thigh.

"You know what's goin' on?" Ma targeted him from the bottom of the stairs.

Where to go? Out the front? Out the back? Where'd Trent gone? His tongue locked. He reached out to close Brett's door and padded down the stairs. Turned the phone off and pocketed it.

Two cop cars parked outside, one belonging to Officer Ray. Ricky shook his head and twisted his face in confusion, until he saw the steel gray car and Miss Veronica stood with the cops.

"The kid that Officer Ray was on about. Bixby ... he's in our shed. I called the services."

The burn of guilt from his betrayal cooled compared to the panic of Tarantula Man's appearance.

"You did what?"

"Was I wrong?"

She released her arms and took him in, a kiss on his forehead for ...

"No. No. No, you showed initiative. Responsibility. My boy." She held his cheeks with both hands and led him to the door. He stayed back. She understood and he watched from the kitchen window as policemen exited from all three cars.

Officer Ray whispered something to ma. The red-haired lady joined in the conference, and the other cops rested against their vehicles with all the urgency of a donut break. He heard "shed." Soon after, they trod, careful, down the walkway to Bixby's hideaway. Ricky crouched to follow the action and see how this played out. Something, someone, cracked fallen twigs underfoot in the trees behind their home. Ma followed Officer Ray and the woman. They stopped for a moment to catch the noise's source, but these woods are jungle dense and can hide Bigfoot at this time of year. Officer Ray shrugged and marched on. Miss Veronica placed a hand on the cop's sleeve and took the lead. She rapped on the shed door and called, soft and sweet. "Bixby."

Gusts whistled a substitute for Bixby's lack of response – he must have heard their arrival and snuck out of there. The woman knocked again, raised an eyebrow at the cop, and tried once more. Ma, in a t-shirt and shorts, shivered at the squalls.

Hugged herself tight as she edged towards them. Ricky wiped shame-sweat from his forehead. His armpits hummed at the swamp. A tingle hit him and a needle turfed his memory.

Shit.

He sprang out the door and reached for ma as a bang shot over the weather. The cops by the other cars jumped off their hoods, hands on weapons. Ma turned to Ricky. What freshly laid turd had he brought home now? Did they hear right? The woman, her face creased with intent, shrugged off Officer Ray's hand – which suggested he should lead.

"Don't go in." Wind grabbed Ricky's voice and tossed it away as his teachers would. He pulled at ma's arm and dragged her backwards as the two other cops made careful steps toward their colleague.

Another shot. The gun he'd stored in the shed. Where ma never stepped foot. Miss Veronica, who defined control – with an amused smile never far off – collapsed to the floor, a hand on her shoulder and screams out of her mouth. Red leaked between her fingers and Officer Ray pulled at her arm to take her from danger, which only increased her volume. The other policemen fired at the shed. Splinters. Holes dotted high, low, and across. The three cops stared down the end of their guns and edged forward to better see their work. Ricky shook. Infected ma until she had eyes only for him, as if he lay dead inside instead of Bixby. He released himself from her life-rung grip and ran for the shed's entrance.

"Don't shoot, Mr Ray. Please."

"Ricky, get out the damn way, you idiot."

Ricky spread his arms across the entry, unable to meet his fraught ma's gaze. A groan made him turn to one of the black bullet holes. Shafts of light sliced stripes and dots in the murk.

Brett's voice, ma's, Officer Ray's, the other cops, the outrage from Miss Veronica who groaned on the ground – all merged into white noise beneath the growl from the shed. Bixby's accusations shot out in rage and spit.

"Fucking traitor. You fucking traitor."

Ricky hung onto the doorframe for support. The door swung in the gale and hammered at his shoulder. He didn't feel it compared to what came out of Bixby. He wanted to lie to Bixby – that this woman found him from her own detective work. But he prioritized Tanais.

Bixby shuffled and winced. Why move if it hurts so much? Snot bubbles exploded and ran over Bixby's lips. His red eyes focused on the gun by his feet. Ricky stepped inside, unsure. Wind slammed the door behind him. Officer Ray dragged it open again. Ricky toed the firearm away from reach and knelt beside his old friend.

If Bixby's look could burn, Ricky would burst into flame. "They'll send me back there."

"To what?"

"To them."

"What did they do to you?"

Officer Ray pulled at Ricky. Ricky resisted, but the two other cops shunted him from danger.

Ricky twisted and deadened his weight. "Let me talk to him."

They didn't listen and their grip on him tightened. Forced him, with little thought for his feelings, back to the arms of his ma.

An ambulance arrived and he, ma, and Brett watched as they took care of Miss Veronica first. She stared at the violent sky and twitched at the branches of trees throwing shapes above her. She didn't see Ricky. No longer knew anything except the pain in her shoulder.

Another ambulance carried Bixby away. His lips mumbled as the paramedics carted him past. The words never rose above a whisper.

Ma loosened her grip until she left him alone in the elements. He craned his neck to see through the doorway, watching her sat at the table, head in her hands. Brett kicked his legs beside her in support. Ricky scratched his scalp to relieve the summer itch. Undergrowth snapped loud enough to beat the wind. The hooded man shifted and blurred in the foliage until he became nothing but a smudge. Ricky back-stepped into the house and shut out the world. Half-expected the glass in the storm door to shatter from a shotgun blast any moment. No – the neighbors watched from their windows. Mr Walters stood at his gate.

He rubbed at the beast in his chest and winced as he entered the kitchen.

44

The cops fussed around them for an hour or so. Ricky wanted to run upstairs, shut the door, plunge himself under the comforter, and hide from the world until it forgot him. Especially once the policemen departed. Instead, he clamped his teeth and sat opposite ma. Locked onto her until she raised her red eyes to him. Her dull-eyed examination pierced sharper than any previous fire she lit beneath his ass.

"I just wish your pa was here to deal with you."

Ricky's contempt showed in the shake of his head. "What did he ever do except abandon us all?"

She slid the chair back and Ricky prepared for her to slap him. Brett almost tumbled from his seat.

"Put your sneakers on, Brett, you're coming to work with me."

"Maaaa."

"Zip your lips and get your sneakers on. Now."

Brett dawdled to the front door. Ma's words dammed in her throat, scared to unleash them in case they caused irreparable damage. She pushed off the table, tired, alone. Her skin had dulled over the year. Bird feet stamped the corners of her eyes.

"I don't wanna go to work with you, ma."

She grabbed one of Brett's arms as she shuffled into her sandals. He whined and twisted, but ma's strength forced him out of the door. Ricky scratched the table's surface as he listened to his resistance, the gravel's crunch, the slam of doors, and the engine's cough.

Bixby had to go. It would do him good. But to get shot? *Jesus, why did I leave the gun in there with someone who cut the heads off squirrels?*

Out back, the hooded man leaned against a tree and watched. Ricky ducked and pressed to the wall. Crawled beneath the living room window. Shuffled along the floor to drag a chair and angle it to the front door and another to the rear. Locked both entrances. Crouched as he checked every window.

Ma said she'd sold all pa's guns, but the way she worried, she must have some weapon. He searched her drawers, embarrassed at the invasion. Beneath the bed, loft, linen closet – no firearm. The cops had taken the one Bixby used on Miss Veronica.

The man disappeared again. Ricky pressed his head against the bedroom wall and thought the door handle rattled. He crept downstairs. Avoided the step which creaked. A dark blotch stood silhouetted behind the frosted glass in the back door. He could make out the hood.

Some car screeched at the end of the road and Michael Trent froze as if he'd met Medusa's gaze. The wind howled and Ricky shivered at this wolf pack. With Trent behind, Ricky planned to escape out the front. He crawled, though he doubted Trent saw him through the frosted glass. He reached for the front door and shot backwards at the figure outside. Trent couldn't get to the front with such speed.

He worked his breath into a slower rhythm and peeked

around the wall to the back door. Two of them, each at both ends.

"Shit."

The man at the front pressed his face against the glass to search for his prey. Round the back a slab scraped concrete. Trent readied to smash the window. Ricky scratched at the carpet, grabbing for comfort. He fumbled his phone for Liz. Voicemail. He stabbed Mr Vale's name. Voicemail.

A dog barked. Both men cocked an ear. The man at the front offered a strangled "hello" to someone outside. Ricky darted across the floor and dared to raise his head. Mr Walters, whose voice he'd never heard all his life, nodded at the intruder and bared his suspicion with a glare to straighten any criminal. The neighbor put roots into the sidewalk and let his mutt piss. His animal must have flowed a river because his owner didn't budge for what seemed like forever.

The hunter by the door shuffled. "Guess nobody's home, eh?"

"I guess not."

There. Mr Walter's voice came out as shots of gravel. Ricky offered him the occasional nod over the years, but stern, judgmental stares are all he ever had in return from Mr Walters. The man's tone could drill through the earth's core, a growl which must have accumulated from all the disappointments in his life. Trent's goon abandoned his post. Ricky backed into the shadows and watched him head down the street. The man pulled his pants up his ass for want of something to do with his hands. Checked his shoulder, quick, and drifted away into the gray at the cul-de-sac's end.

Trent remained at the back door, a fox's ear for both chicken and hunter. Ricky scanned between him and his neighbor, who stood taller and far more solid than he'd ever realized. The old man decided he'd check round the other side. Trent heard and slithered over the chain-link fence and into the woods. Ricky dropped to his knees and heaved in air until dizziness almost pulled him to the floor's hard embrace.

He willed the neighbor to stand guard all night and every day forevermore. He'd supply him with milk, cookies, and anything stronger until they didn't need him anymore. Ricky thumbed 911 into his phone and stared at the number. Ma forever drilled into him how useless they are, and how nobody trusted them. A boy's club. They sought their roles for personal power, to lord it over the peasants.

What if Trent held them in his pocket? They shot Bixby, didn't they? Officer Ray - yeah, he seemed reasonable, but he also fired, all indiscriminate, into the shed, too. And he's his hopeless pa's supposed friend. Fucking adults. All useless. Even the red-haired lady, who'd come off full of confidence. She didn't see those bullets coming, did she?

The sky, already as black as the abyss, grew darker with the lateness of the day. Ma and Brett would not return for hours. He studied the 911 on his phone, covered it when he realized it shone a Vegas spotlight on his whereabouts.

"Not yet."

Let's not bring more chaos home. Not fair to ma, as much as he wanted to rebel against her control. He slipped out the front door while a sliver of light still lit the day. Locked it behind him. Pounded the street as if nobody dared touch him. Mr Walters had checked the back and headed for his couch. Ricky scanned for Trent and his friend. Expected they watched him from the bushes and trees. Licked their lips at the prey on the prairie. Daylight would keep him safe. Mr Walters eyeballed him from his window, stern as always. Ricky thought this a fine moment to introduce himself, but the man pinched his eyes, shook his head, and retreated into his castle. The cul-de-sac threaded into a scruff of streets where owners used their porch as storage for old shit they no longer needed. Some enjoyed a little table-set for pleasant evenings and some added color with a variety of plants hung from baskets. Most porches stood bare and unused by those who, Ricky imagined, didn't dare pop their heads out of the door. Ricky noted details he'd never seen before, his attention on everything.

Including footsteps behind. He dropped his phone to the ground and kneeled to scan. It had slipped from his hand so many times, without damage other than a scratch to its black case. The man who'd stood by the front door marched toward him, thirty yards away, his stride confident of the inevitable.

Mr Walters should have come out again. Why did he check round the back of their house if he didn't want to play his part to the full? Done his damn duty, Ricky supposed, and now retreated into minding his own stupid business.

The dented BMW cruised alongside at Ricky's pace, and the driver slid his window all the way down.

45

Trent smiled at him as he leaned over the passenger seat. Last time he'd been this close, Ricky smelled weed on his stained teeth. They had a sunshine glare under these black clouds.

"Ricky Nardilo, why don't ya get in?"

"What for? I don't know you."

"You know me. Come, let's go for a ride."

The other man slowed down as if he had completed the job. A man across the street spied on them from behind a curtain, and a woman with a kid in her arms rocked while she watched the scene from her window. Everybody stayed indoors, out of the cold and wet and trouble.

"I've nothin' to tell you." Except Mr Vale kills people, and no doubt killed Benny Ciaro.

The man's grip on his steering wheel tightened. Used to getting his own way. He pulled at his hood and licked his teeth. The other man broke into a run. Ricky side-stepped, ducked, swiveled and launched down an alleyway over rusted strollers, worn tires, buck-wheeled bicycles, and slimy concrete. The man lurched in after him, his strides longer. Heard his already exhausted breath behind him. Ricky hoped the chaser's lack of stamina would save him. He almost relaxed, but recharged as the man's demands shot near. Ricky feinted left and right, over all kinds of shit people dumped without care. The man grunted and cursed as he bashed his shin on a busted tricycle between two broken wood pallets. Ricky mapped his next turn. The wind fanned through the alleys and blew the man's hood down. Rat face, shaved head, and a couple of front teeth which could open beer. Muscle. The beast in the apartment – who'd smacked them out of the weird party.

Ricky's lungs burned. His phone weighed like a brick in his pocket. He fumbled for it and pressed from memory so he didn't need to take his eyes from his target – an overgrown bush spanning the alley. His pursuer fell a few feet further behind, but had not given up. Ricky glanced at the screen. Blank. Held it to his ear. Not even the *sshhhh* of a seashell. He shook it and checked again.

"Damn it."

The bush looked thick and firm. Drooped a little beneath the weight of rainwater, but appeared impenetrable. As he rushed towards it, he expected to see gaps where kids or animals climbed through. Kids round here can't have much adventure in them – the shrub would eat and shred him.

He had no choice. He couldn't clamber up the high walls, and the man behind picked up his pace again as he anticipated a result in his favor. Ricky arrowed his hands ahead of him and dove into the bush. Branches punched his ribs, whipped his face, tore red streaks along his bare arms. He wrestled to open up the bush's other side. Snapped and rustled, and squirmed at the hand reaching in.

"Got you, you little fuck."

The neck of his t-shirt ripped, but his skinny frame – which ma always complained about – got him through. He staggered out of the opposite end and spun to see the man through the leaves. Rat-face fumed, a devil whose reach failed to drag Ricky to hell. Pulled a weapon. Aimed. Ricky zig-zagged, crouched, and sprung into a sprint. Almost pissed his pants at the thud of bullets as they whistled and ricocheted around him.

Ricky left and righted through a maze of side and back streets, past alarmed cats, excitable stray dogs, and some beasts of the night that roamed out early. If the man made it through the bush, he'd still lose his opportunity. Ricky leaned against a wall. Didn't know if it belonged to a house or a place of business. Lost his bearings. The ground squelched beneath him where moss had taken hold. His breath rolled in great billows of steam, as agitated as the clouds above threatening a heavier downpour. If he stayed here much longer, these alleyways would digest him. Every step sucked at his sneakers. These nowhere places nibbled and chewed at his reason, conjuring monsters in wait around every corner.

He jabbed his phone. The drop on the blacktop had busted it. All those times it hit the floor and came out of it safe and sound – and now it breaks. He snorted and shook his head. Swung his arms to control the shakes.

Mr Vale is right. You have to clean up this town. Some people don't deserve life. If he could only call him to his rescue. Ricky lost his mystery to Trent. The man knew where he lived and would dish to ma what he'd served Tanais' pa.

He rested a hand against a wall for balance and cried. Gulps the size of ping-pong balls blocked his windpipe. Rain, tears, snot, all mingled.

Floyd.

He sprung from the Town's rotten intestines and tested

the main streets. Once he found his bearings, he made his exhausted way to the abandoned supermarket.

46

The broken car behind the supermarket contained a tattered blanket and one-half of a pair of holey Converse sneakers. Ricky called for Floyd in a hushed voice, hoping he reached the homeless man's ears and nobody else. He wound the old vehicle's windows up so the rain didn't make his protector too uncomfortable in the sleeping hours. Poked his head inside the building. Screwed his eyes into the dark corners. Crossed the chessboard floor fearing the tiles would collapse into some dungeon if he stepped too hard.

He pushed through the flap-doors into the corridor's murk and the bowels where Grealey met his end. The supermarket seemed to hold its breath, listening, its still air sitting on him colder than the breeze outside. He peered through the little glass window that led into the loading area. Peeled the wet t-shirt from his skin.

A skylight provided thin light. The chair remained, but the body had gone – to some shallow ditch, maybe, just like Benny Ciaro and his pals. He pushed through the door and held it open in case he needed to escape. He loaded a call, but kept his tongue cocked. The silence expanded.

He burst it. "Floyd."

He picked his way over debris. Some noise he couldn't

identify came from the far corner, the creak like that of Mr Vale's moored boat. The tremble in Ricky's lower lip dipped and ran through his ribs. He tensed his stomach so tight it ached.

"Floyd?"

He prayed Floyd hadn't turned on him. Creepy as he is, he'd held his word to look out for him. Ricky offered his sad life the purpose he craved.

He crunched broken glass, bumped into crates and boxes. Adjusted to the dark and jolted stiff as if pliers pinched a nerve. Two feet, one in a sock and another in one-half a pair of Converse, dangled by his face. He stumbled backward. The sneaker had stained red. Dark patches quilted down the legs' pants. The murderer had ripped Floyd's long coat open and a thick crimson line streaked down his bare chest. His blond hair matted over his features, but not so it covered the gouged eyes staring down at Ricky. The killer cut off his nose, leaving a gaping hole. Ricky kneeled at the object on the floor – Floyd's greasy baseball cap, now his cleanest garment. He followed the rope from the man's neck to the steel beam.

A gasp, a whine, a grunt escaped him. A scream might have exploded but for the hand which smothered his mouth. His attacker prevented him from spinning, grasping him so hard his windpipe shut tight. Ricky wriggled and caught a flash of shaved scalp. Rat Face. He thrust Ricky's right arm so far up his back he could almost scratch the rear of his own neck. His calls died in the man's palm. His captor paused a moment to check on his handiwork with Floyd, and frog-marched him out the building to the parking lot. Tarantula Man smoked a cigarette. Leaned against an old Lexus. The tail lights lit bright against the dusk.

Ricky expected an explanation, but Trent propelled off the car, popped the trunk, and stood aside. Rat Face dove into Ricky's pockets and emerged with the cell. Pressed its keys and shrugged at its lack of response. He shoved Ricky into the trunk. Ricky banged his elbow and yelped, shuffled round to plead, and cowered into the depths as the lid slammed down.

"Please."

He cringed at the crack of his phone beneath the man's foot.

Their footsteps dimmed beneath highway traffic from beyond the woods. Ricky kicked and punched at his cage until the hurt overruled his fear. Another car's engine purred into life and drove away.

He curled into a ball and cried at what they might do to Brett and his ma.

47

Ricky lay crooked in the trunk all night with a crick in his neck, a hardware store of knick-knacks in his back. He could have argued that time stood still, but his tears had dried and the agony in his knuckles from the punches to the lid dulled – so the hours must have passed.

He scraped dehydration goo from his lips and rasped away the blockage in his throat. Called out, but his head hurt so bad he wanted to open it and scoop out the pain. He walked his hands around the limited space for bottles of water. Punched the underside again and winced at the surge of punishment through his skull and fist. He worked some spit to wet his pipes, but the effect didn't last long.

He ran a finger along curves and crevices to identify shapes and a way of escape. All to dampen images of Brett and his ma in the same state as Floyd. It didn't work. He curled tight into himself until exhaustion took him deeper into his nightmares.

* * *

Morning light bleached Ricky's vision. The blurred figure he saw through the open trunk prodded him with some object. Shouted, "The kid's okay," and slammed it shut again.

The car jerked from its slumber and groaned for a stretch. Ricky knocked and heard a muffled, "Shut the fuck up" for his efforts. He slid about around corners, up and down hills, and over potholes. Cringed at the headache tearing a hole in his thinking. Could sand a table with his tongue.

The journey didn't last all day, but it wouldn't have surprised him. Hopes rose and fell at every traffic light. He needed a destination. An end. What would pa do? If he's even alive.

What would ma do?

The engine stopped, the car relieved. Ricky swiveled from the glare burning his retinas. A hand grabbed his wrist, rough, and dragged him out. He lifted an arm for shade and blinked away the dryness. The man let go and Ricky tumbled to his ass. Rat Face thrust a plastic bottle of water into his hands. Could have been piss for all he knew. His senses deserted him. Smelled only dust and his own BO. He unscrewed the top, anyway, and gulped.

Ricky made a stab hole of his eyes and took in the view. Warmth circulated the air again and mist hovered over the ground – the ghosts of however many bodies Michael bastard Trent buried around here. He finished the water and shuddered that he'd soon join them. Rat Face grabbed the neck of his torn t-shirt and dragged him through the fog. It swirled and snatched until they reached an opening in the ground as black as night. Smoke bellowed from its mouth - the anger of a long abandoned mineshaft. He wouldn't mind some creature snatching him from these men.

Trent's nest-of-snakes hair swayed in the wind. He had the air of a geek in the knee-length coat, with his hood a bulk behind his head. Two dents bent his right cheek as though pegs had hammered through, and a rough line scarred the back of his hand. Trent understood pain. Had come through it. Hardened to it. Ricky fought his bowels. He wanted to release, but a gear kicked in.

"I need a piss."

Trent spat. "Piss in your pants. It won't matter soon."

The bald one's fingers trembled. Ricky's tongue filled his mouth.

Trent flexed his fists. "Where's Benny Ciaro?"

"I've seen nobody."

Trent eyed Rat Face, who jerked Ricky closer to the hole in the ground.

"You fucking kids hang round the old factory all the time. Don't tell me you know nothing. The man I'm looking for is this tall, brown eyes, scruff on his face. A square face. You know him. I can see from your eyes you cocky little fuck. Where is he?"

"Why'd you kill Floyd?" Ricky knew he must have found out about the other Ghost Boy Floyd had killed - murdered.

"Who the fuck is Floyd?"

Rat Face released Ricky's t-shirt to gesticulate. "The man in the supermarket back there. Strung up on a beam. Eyes and nose missing. Fuck, that's a bit much, Mike."

Trent screwed his face, raised an eyebrow quick, and nodded. "Well, that's what you get. Now tell me where Ciaro is."

Neither of the men had drawn their weapons, and Rat Face removed his hands from him. Ricky could make a run for it. Get lost in the mist and smoke of the Dragon Lands – or even jump down this void. Would he burn down there? How would he find his way back?

He had this moment, but his first step landed flat with indecision and Rat Face read it. Grabbed his arm tight and jerked him to the ground. "Don't think of it, kid. Hey, if we're gunna do this, I should just shove him down the hole. I don't wanna do what you did to the man in there."

Ricky relaxed so his captor would loosen his grip. He'd bolt at his next opportunity. Stupid damn idiot for not taking advantage before. Trent's shuffle showed Floyd's route to his maker affected him as much as his jittery partner. Taken him to where he had nothing left to lose.

"I can show you where Ciaro is."

Trent pumped his arms, and would have barged aside any obstacle in his path if it barred him. Gripped Ricky's hair tight enough to pull the scalp from his skull. Thrust his head close to the hole until the boy coughed from the smoke. "You tell me where he is – no tricks."

Ricky spluttered for breath. Tears ran, nose burned, lungs suffocated. The death-noise hacking his throat made Trent drag him back to cleaner air. He threw him to the ground and glared at the sky, his dreadlocks dangling. Through Ricky's red eyes, they spun a web to tangle him up for later use.

"Tell me."

Ricky tightened his lips so his heart wouldn't spill out. Shook his head. Trent would kill him if he let it slip right then.

* * *

The breeze departed along with the chill, and groundwater lifted its misty fingers for its last stretch. Ricky scratched at fear. His bones ached after the bumpy ride over the City of Forts' dirt track. He walked the men around the crescent of abandoned homes, eyeing the burnt shells they used as shelters from this adult world. Guilt snipped his innards at what he'd done to Bixby, but he'd trade places with him now. Ricky stopped at the burial ground. Even after the downpour, the ant hill of a mound remained, and the old shovel still stood in the dirt. The corpse's stubborn toes pointed at the sky, its sickly stench attaching to the mist and clinging like bats inside their nostrils.

"You dig." Trent pushed him in the back. Ricky tumbled, slipped, attempted to find a foot-grip, but tripped over the shovel and onto the mound. The rain turned the dirt to slime. His palms slid through the mud and layered between his fingers. He hopped off the grave as if hands of the dead would pull him into death's company. Stared at his feet so he didn't give away the other graves.

"Where'd you go last night?"

Rat Face laughed. "Just dig, kid. Just fuckin' dig."

Ricky sniffled. Brett and ma, with their eyes spooned out, hit him again and again. The buzz of flies irritated the men. Both of them beat about their ears to ward them off. A dominant buzz mingled in there somewhere.

"Jesus Christ, dig." Trent pulled his gun and tapped it against his thigh, one eye for the big bug.

If she's alive, ma would have called Officer Ray to tell him Ricky had gone missing. Officer Ray would put two and two together and he'd come charging down here. The cop sniffed around ma enough for Ricky to recognize he'd want to please her. Ricky cut through the songbird and the lapping river to listen for police sirens or the crunch of loose stones beneath a patrol car's tires.

The shot jumped him from his reverie. Trent pointed the gun at Ricky's chest and nodded. Ricky dug around the edge and judged how much impatience he could build in his captor before he blew. He exposed the body's feet and knees until Trent slapped Ricky across the cheek and snatched the shovel from him. Ricky, floored, heeled himself away as the man sliced into the mud until he could use his hands to shift the rest from the man's face. The stink strung innards up his throat and Trent retched to the side. He recovered and scooped until he revealed Benny Ciaro. The two men had thrown their entire attention onto the body. Ricky had a chance to leg it, but he craned his neck to see how nature affected Ciaro's face. Slick with sludge. Cheeks sunk, his hair like hay trampled by horses.

Trent recognized the corpse and hid his head in his forearm. Convulsed. Not from the burn in his throat, but at some kind of twisted emotion. His eyes watered. "This guy, man ... I ... I just loved this man."

Rat Face consoled him with a hand on his shoulder as the tarantula-haired psycho kneeled by his dead friend. Trent shrugged off the sentiment and bit his fist, careless of the mud. Rat Face flashed a look at Trent, but transferred the anger to Ricky.

"Did you kill him?" Rat Face shook his head at Ricky, unsure he could have done any of this.

"No."

"What? Speak up, you little shit."

"No. I found him."

"Found him buried like this?"

Ants, slugs, spiders, centipedes all crawled across Ricky's skin. Seemed so, anyway. His flesh rippled and stretched and shrunk all at once.

Trent emerged from his crouch as a mountain from the Earth's crust. "Found him, how?"

"In the basement. In a house over there."

"And then what?"

"We ... I ... buried him."

"We?"

"No ... Me."

"You dragged him from a basement over there to here? On your own?"

"Yeah. Took me ages. But I did it."

"Why? Why didn't you call the cops?"

"Because this is my place. My place. Not his. Not yours. Not the cops'. I wanted nobody invading my damn place. It's my escape. Mine."

"Who the fuck do you think you are?"

Ricky couldn't hide his fear any longer. He expected to fill the hole with, or in place of Ciaro, any moment, and he'd never wanted to live more than now.

Trent jabbed the point of his weapon at Ricky's forehead. "Who the fuck are you to do such a thing?"

Ricky squeezed one eye shut. The other peeked out of a thin-slit. "I didn't know what he was doing here except to spoil my summer. I just found him dead. With a hole in his back. I didn't call the police, didn't tell my ma, didn't tell a single damn person – because I don't want people swarming all round my property as if they own it. This is my place."

"This is your property? You own it?"

"Might as well. I'm the one who makes most use of it."

Trent stabbed the point of his gun further into Ricky's flesh. "I think you killed him. You and your little friends. Then –"

"Mike ..."

"Then –"

"Mike ..."

"Jesus, what?"

Trent and Ricky followed Rat Face's gaze to the second mound. Rat Face shifted earth, checked the buzz in the air and swatted at flies. A minute's dig revealed the other man they buried. The one Charlie admitted he'd shot.

"Finn? This is where you'd got to?" Trent turned to Ricky, a funny gleam in his eye, and a hint of admiration – what to do with this kid: kill him or use him?

The bug, a giant, swooped low and made the men duck. Ricky bit at his lip and watched. The gangsters latched on to his gaze's direction. Whispered a grave full of cusses at the teenager who lolled through the bushes with what looked like a game console's control pad in his hands.

48

C harlie rambled towards them like a Sunday stroller walking his dog. Trent shifted to a half-crouch but recognized the kid had seen them all. He ran a hand through his tangled knots and roared with confused laughter. Didn't attempt to hide his weapon, just let it dangle by his side. He exchanged some telepathic thought with Rat Face before cocking an eyebrow at Ricky.

"One of yours?"

"Don't know him."

"Hey, Ricky, what you doing here?"

Ricky scowled, but was glad to see Charlie. Trent grunted and under his breath Ricky heard, "Lot of grave diggin' today."

Charlie smiled like he had practiced this moment, without the cruel twist in his mouth Ricky, Liz, Bixby and Tanais had become used to. Charlie twiddled with the controller. It had a little screen between the thumb sticks. He concentrated on the image and ignored Trent's "What the fuck?"

Charlie offered Trent a quick glance. "Hold on. Hold on. Here it comes."

The buzz vibrated the air above. Trent waved, aimless, but kept his eyes on the boy. He only glimpsed away because of Rat Face's gasp. The drone smacked Trent in the face and must have spun a propeller into his eye because he stumbled backwards with a hand to his socket. Trent's gun slipped from his fingers. Ricky, determined to take his chance this time, threw himself to it. Rat Face patted himself for his weapon and scurried away on his ass, then onto his back from the shot. Birds flew at the bang and Ricky rolled to avoid bullets. Rat Face screamed and Trent's breath came out scattergun through clenched teeth.

"Who the fuck are you?"

Charlie swooped for Rat Face's gun, which had fallen from the waistband of his jeans, and examined it as he covered Trent with his shadow. He threw the controller at Ricky to look after. Pointed Rat Face's weapon at Trent. "I'm Charlie Vale. The son of Harry Vale."

Trent lowered his hand. Bloodshot eyes widened at this news. "But ... but ... he's the one ..." Trent swung his attention on Ricky. Before he could say another word, his head jolted backwards and squelched into the wet ground. His chest deflated and the red hole in his forehead glinted in the sun.

"Jesus." Ricky fumbled Trent's gun. Trent deserved everything he got, but how casual Charlie had ended him.

Charlie's cruel mouth returned. "You're a believer? Good for you."

Trent's execution acted as morphine to Rat Face, who stared, silent at the two boys. Charlie settled himself above the man, just out of reach from any possible kick. Red blossomed from the man's thigh and between his fingers where he pressed the wound. Ricky wanted to run, but morbid fascination held him still. He studied Rat Face from behind Charlie's shoulder. Charlie smirked back at him.

"This is what buddies do for each other."

Ricky didn't dare contradict him. The sun nipped his neck. Skin peeled from the back of Charlie's and exposed raw flesh beneath.

"You need to finish this." Charlie stepped aside so Rat Face became an obvious target for Ricky.

"You want me to kill him?"

Charlie nodded and waved his gun at Rat Face.

"Hey, hey, hey, no. No, no, no. I just wanted to warn you, kid. I just wanted to warn you. I don't like what Mike did to the man in the old supermarket. Not my way. Not my way at all. Come on, you must see that."

"Shut your mouth, dickhead. Michael Trent didn't kill him ... I did."

Ricky faced Charlie. "What?"

Charlie grinned. "Waster. A drain on the county, the state, the country."

"Wha ...?" Charlie's confession punched the wind from Ricky. He hardly had strength to hold the gun.

"Don't waste your sentiment on him, Ricky. Floyd worked for dad. Helped him in so many ways. Dad paid him to keep an eye on you."

"Paid?"

"You know – in food, drugs, drink, whatever he needed. But, like many from this town, he had no gratitude. Just wanted to take, take, take, and not set himself straight. Dad gave him his chance and he didn't take it. Continued to be a burden. So I killed him. On dad's orders."

Ricky scanned the river. Listened for the thrum of his old man's motorboat. "Why'd he use you? Why not do it himself?"

Charlie spat at Rat Face's feet. Shook his head. "Jesus, I've tried with you, Ricky. Dad saw something in you – an asset in his life's work. But I don't get it. I've tried, but I don't see it. I guess it's what public school does. You've been round my home, you'll have noticed the literature, the ornaments, the pictures."

"Of what?"

"Sparta. Sparta. No? Nothing? Holy shit, you're a know-nothing. The Spartans would send out their sons into the country to hunt helots."

Rat Face laughed at Ricky's confusion. "They're not animals, kid. They were the underclass. Beneath the Spartan jackboot. Worthless to the Spartans. A drain." He spat at Charlie's feet. "You sick little motherfucker."

"Shoot him."

Ricky's grip on the firearm tightened. The stag he'd shot wandered into his thoughts as it had that morning. Like Ricky, it had not run away from the danger it sensed. Wanted to know how it all played out. But curiosity got him.

I'm that damn stag.

He raised the weapon and slugged Rat Face in the chest. The man gasped and dug his fingers into the mud, a glug the sound of drowning in his throat. A shit shot, same as the bullet Ricky fired into the animal. Ricky panicked at the man's pain. His insides turned over each other until he thought he'd drown in his own vomit. He shot again and again – and again, until reason stilled his finger. He dropped the firearm, wheeled, and fell to his hands and knees. Gagged. Spat the remnants out and wished he could go home and forget about all this. His stomach ached and rolled. He sat on his ass, without care for how the wet ground seeped through his pants. Closed his eyes at the distant roar of the motorboat.

The bastards had sucked him into their world for good.

49

The rasp exploded, too aggressive for a motorboat engine. Charlie threw Rat Face's gun at its owner's body and urged Ricky to do the same with Trent's weapon. Ricky toe-flipped the handgun. It smacked the side of Trent's head. The motorbike growled across the fields, Biker Boy's arms out wide and high on the handlebars. A kite-tail of red hair flowed behind him and Liz yelled at him to stop. Charlie had ducked, but Ricky stood as upright as a lamppost.

She jumped off the bike, all concerned, and ran to Ricky for a relieved embrace. Stiffened when she noticed Charlie low in the long grass and the bodies with their ragdoll stare into the blue heavens.

"Ricky?"

Charlie transferred all his weight to one foot, a hand in a pocket. His own gun in the back of his pants. Liz turned to Ricky. Searched for his sunken eyes. Followed the marks on his face, the purple on his arms – she picked her way through the gore to stand by him. Her man, all cautious, slipped from his bike and called to her.

"I'm okay, just … what the hell happened here?"

Charlie kicked at the floor, proud of his work, but still awkward around the girl. "These men had us both under their

346

control. They argued about what to do with us and all, and shot each other. Look, their guns are by their sides."

Liz shifted her attention from the bodies to the firearms – to Ricky's defeated eyes. Why had she come here? Why had that prick on a bike brought her?

"My God, Ricky, Carrie did tell him where you lived. We've been all across town, even to Ciaro's house, to search for you. Your ma is worried sick. She's got the police out for you and all. What was he gunna do to you?"

Ricky shrugged. "You should go. Get out of here. None of your business, all this."

Her man drew a sharp breath. A squeak escaped him at the shock. "What the fuck is all this? You guys alright?"

Charlie waved a hand. "We're good. Thanks."

Charlie's tone created shapes of doubt in Liz' face, which transferred to Biker Boy.

"You should leave, get the cops or somethin'." Charlie set himself ready to fight.

The man nodded, but didn't move, reluctant to leave her here. The way Liz shifted an eyebrow, or moved her stiff hands and arms, made Charlie point his weapon at them all.

Steve *whoa'd*, his palms out to Charlie. Ricky raised his heels, bent his knees. Liz stroked a strand from her eye and screwed her lips at him. "I knew you were a bullshitter, Charlie. But I don't know what you're hiding. Did you rescue Ricky or not? If you did, well done – why the bullshit story?"

Charlie reddened and narrowed his eyes.

Steve made little steps backwards and urged Liz to follow him.

"I ain't leaving without Ricky."

"You should leave." Ricky stroked her forearm with the

back of his hand.

"This is not a time to prove how you've matured, Ricky. You need to jump on that bike with us and get the hell out of here. You've done well, Charlie, real good. Now let us get out of this damn place."

Ricky flinched and surveyed the City of Forts. It had brought nothing but one shit storm after another, but it pulled and tethered him even now.

Her man lost patience. He swung his leg over the bike and ignited its engine. Charlie fired and hit him. He fell head over heels.

Liz sucked air. "Steve."

"Don't fucking move." Charlie's tone stopped Liz mid-run.

"I have to see. I have to fucking see, Charlie. What monster are you? What is wrong with you?"

Charlie's lip trembled. He fought back those tears. "You're not meant to be here."

"Charlie, please, let me go to him. Or are we all for it?"

"I just wanted to hang out. That's all. It's all I needed. You smug bastards, all superior, and for what reason? You live in this shithole. What you got? You'll all turn into ... same as every asshole who lives in this town."

Ricky had made it to Trent's side and maneuvered the gun into position for the swoop. "You're just parroting words your pa blurts out." He bent, swiped the firearm, and pointed it at Charlie, who aimed his weapon at the bike as if he expected an undead rising from Steve. The shots Ricky fired at Rat Face still ricocheted up his aching arm, but his finger retained memory of the action. Charlie would shoot him if given the chance. Ricky burned – from the sun, the moment, the likelihood Charlie's pa targeted a crosshair on the back of his head.

The word on Charlie's lip triggered Ricky's index. He missed. Charlie blew a whistle. Ricky fired again and hit. The older boy slumped, a hole in his chest, a ragged sound in his throat. Ricky ducked, sped to Liz, and tackled her into the dirt. A splash in the water, too big for a native fish, shifted Ricky and Liz's gears.

"What now?" Her tone bore a scalpel's edge.

A storm of cusses from the river bent them close to the ground as they brushed through the undergrowth, unsure of their direction. A howl of sorrow and revenge pierced their ears, but the thud of Mr Vale's footsteps behind made sure they didn't slow until the grass shortened and died at the cracked asphalt by the factory.

The massive blue gate loomed over the pair. They shook at the giant man heading for them, Mr Vale, his rifle in the air, a mountain of rage intent on ripping holes in their bodies.

50

Ricky and Liz weaved around broken machinery, fallen joists, and pipes snaking between floors. All rough to the touch. Mr Vale clanged old metal, reverberations driving through Ricky as if the man beat his bones with a steel rod. Ricky pulled Liz below a conveyor belt.

"There's a way out the back. Can't remember which turn to make, though. One corridor's a dead end."

She held a finger to her lips. His voice carried. They pushed tight into each other at the shot. Their predator aimed at the ceiling, the action to clear these birds from their hiding place. She wiped away tears, Steve in her thoughts. Ricky pressed his jealousy down deep. A stupid time to let such pangs affect him.

They shuffled to the shadowy side of a wide pipe on the factory floor. Another shot. This one whistled low and pitched off some machine with dusty dials. The bullet's direction cut off their path to the corridor. He slipped out of his sneakers and held them tight. Led the way up metal steps. Liz, sneakers also in her grip, followed, but she tugged his t-shirt. Her face said "why are we going up?"

He jerked his head upward. *Because.* He padded up the steps, two at a time, checked his shoulder to make sure she remained behind. Had her eyes on the damn phone.

"Dammit, Liz."

She mouthed, "The cops."

He frowned, embarrassed, and turned the corner. They'd circle around, and get out the front again. Pillars helped them keep out of sight and more machinery littered the ground. Shards of glass daggered from window frames overlooking the factory floor. Boards dimmed light from outside. Easier to hide.

They crept through side rooms and corridors that smelled of metal and rat shit. They paused to listen and shuddered at the metallic clangs from their hunter. He'd found their staircase. Ricky never explored the second floor. His gang either ran riot around the factory's bottom, pounded the metal walkways above, or rushed straight to the top. They pitter-pattered from one pillar to abandoned machinery to another pillar in search of the next staircase to escape.

Ricky extended his neck to see Liz' phone. "Why aren't the cops answering?"

Its blue light exposed her gaunt worry. "No signal. Ricky, I hope you know your way round."

"I'm worried about being out there. We'll be easy targets in the fields."

"We can't stay here – move."

Another bang whipped their ears and scurried them from their rabbit hole. Mr Vale must have heard their panic because he burst into a run. The whole factory seemed to shake beneath the giant's weight.

A staircase. They crept down and their hearts sank into their bowels at machinery on top of machinery, blocking their exit. Light filtered through the tightest gap. Liz arrowed her hands, but she'd need a rat's spine to negotiate the hole.

"Ricky." The man's voice, raw, roared as if the steel plant kicked back into action. "Ricky. I just want to talk."

A glimmer of hope burst bright. Frittered away again at the bullshit. Ricky killed Mr Vale's son. He either escaped, or he died. The man called louder. Made Ricky nostalgic for Trent. This nook made a fine place to hide as the light turned the friends into dull gray blobs. You'd need to squint to spot them. Unless Mr Vale wielded a flashlight.

Ricky still had the gun. He didn't know how many bullets remained and did not know how to check. He could wait here and take the risk his aim was true – or …

They slipped back to the upper floor and continued all the way to the top – to the room where Tanais' pa cornered Bixby.

"Shit."

Town must have boarded the windows again, with fresh nails and sturdy wood.

"He funneled us here." Liz shook her phone, pounded it against her thigh, knuckled it. It offered no response.

Ricky slipped into his sneakers after another screw stabbed the sole of his foot and danced him into giving them away. He charged to a window, remembering that it overlooked a slope jutting from the building. Pulled at the board. Liz did her part. It cracked and complained until they jerked it free and crashed it to the floor, splintering their nerves. Overcooked air strengthened the stink. They leaned out the opening, Liz negotiating the splinters jutting from the frame. She pulled herself up, bolted through, twisted, and held tight to the window frame, wincing at the shard in her palm. Ricky planted a foot on the sill. Should have jumped and followed Liz round the perimeter of the sloped tile awning, but he craned his neck and stared wild eyes at Mr Vale. The man emerged from the dark like a ghost through a wall. Raised his rifle. Jolted Ricky back to action.

Mr Vale fired and hit Ricky in the leg as he lunged through the opening. Ricky missed his handle and landed on a lung, a kidney, he couldn't-tell-what. Breath deserted him. He rolled a yard and steadied. One more roll would have snowballed into an unstoppable tumble, splashing him across the asphalt below. The sky glared orange as the sun bloated and filled the horizon. Ricky fought for air, his breath small grunts, as if Mr Vale pressed a heel on his throat, pedaling up and down to control his intake. A thud hit further up the slope and the man's feet clacked the tiles. Ricky's lungs recovered enough to bellow a scream. The ache in his thigh blossomed into a streak of red hot pain. His scream jerked into sobbing. How could he die at thirteen? Would Liz miss him? Would ma and Brett?

"Come on, now, kid, cut that blubbering shit out."

Ricky banged a fist against the tile and bit his other knuckle. Didn't dare to glance at the hole in his leg.

"I hit flesh. I doubt the bullet even tickled a single bone."

He raised his rifle and followed a target. Ricky worked to focus and spotted Liz as she zig-zagged through the fields. "No." His voice croaked. Her red hair seemed to set the grass on fire and he cried hard at the idea he'd never see her again.

The crack of his gun shook Ricky. He fired again, again, and again. *Run, Liz. Duck, feint, get the fuck out of this damn hole and never come back.*

"Well, she's a fast one. I suppose I'll have to let her go."

"Don't you touch her, you bastard."

"You killed my son."

"You sent him to do ... to do God knows what."

Ricky couldn't tell if tears sat pregnant on the man's lids, or he just saw him through his own. The man settled beside him, legs over the roof's edge.

"I own all this land. All of it. This factory, those houses, these fields. I would like to own the river one day, but I doubt my new town, or the old, would allow that. Still, my plans will raise Town from its decay, back to the times when everybody was a god. Won't happen overnight. Outsiders – those with money – will flock and set a standard. Then all in this shithole can either emulate them or continue to lose at life. You know what happens to them, right?"

They leave or they die. Ricky could only shake in response. He hoped Liz'd reached a phone signal by now so she could call the cops. By the time they arrived, Mr Vale would have kicked him over the edge. Or maybe not. The man surveyed his kingdom with a content eye and enjoyed the breeze calming the day's burn. A minute passed without a word and Ricky shuffled to a seated position. Checked the drop for a soft landing.

"You killed these people to protect your land?"

Mr Vale snorted. "I did it to toughen up my kid. Make him a man of the world. Show him the difference between winning and losing. The shitheads he attends school with – entitled little pricks, all of them. He needed to escape his bubble – work, take charge of his destiny. To forge a path above and beyond the herd."

Charlie's ma popped into Ricky's head, and how she wrapped her boy in cotton wool.

That tuft of grass down there might cushion his fall, then he could skirt tight to the factory wall to avoid a bullet. His ragdoll leg rebelled against the idea, but what choice did he have?

"I like history, Ricky. Ancient Greece, in particular. I sent my boy out to prove himself worthy. To put his foot on the heads of those beneath him. The little fucker did well, up to a point. Don't misunderstand me – I love him. Always will. He'll live long in here." He beat his chest with a single punch. "But he failed. You stepped above him. You see, I know all about Michael Trent and his activities. How they had the damn nerve to set up a drug den on my property. I've used them to harass you – not directly – but as a means to involve Charlie with you and your merry band. To test my boy with you, and against them.

"But you – you're reluctant to join my meager Spartan unit. I wanted you and Charlie to wipe out these sons of bitches and prove yourselves worthy. Charlie told me you wanted nothing to do with him. He cried like a bitch. It was time to set Michael Trent on you and see how my boy would reel you back in – if you survived.

"And how you survived. You did great, Ricky-boy. A true Spartan."

Ricky's attention transferred from the tuft of grass to the man beside him, his eyes wide. "Sir, I killed your boy."

"And you win. You're the boy who should be my son. My Charlie, my Charlie — he proved himself weak. The kind of kid ancient Spartans would have thrown over a cliff." He laughed like a chubby uncle at a joke nobody else understood. "Don't get me wrong, I'm not that heartless. His end had to come from his own actions, if he couldn't push past his deficiencies. Nature has taken its course, and it has chosen you.

"I sense reluctance, still, in your bones, boy. I'm not asking you to decide now, but it's in your interests to join me for the long term. You'll grow into a fine Leonidas. It just takes training and acculturation."

Ricky squeezed his eyes shut at the casual attitude of this man. The pain in his leg surrendered to the horror spewing from Mr Vale's mouth. He swayed from dizziness and reclined on the hot surface to avoid a fall. Drifted to unconsciousness, the last sounds he heard those of sirens and the clatter of boots across tiles.

51

Ricky let the rhythm of the school bus knock his head against its window. He'd carried the letter in his backpack all day, buried beneath books to crush whatever words it contained. He recognized the handwriting and didn't want ma's eyes all over it. It reached for him so he couldn't concentrate on any of the math and none of the English.

A pothole banged his head harder than expected and ripped him from melancholy. He dug the letter out and tore it from the envelope. Couldn't wait for his room's privacy any longer.

Patrick Baschi sat next to him, who craned his neck for a peek. All through the journey, he'd wittered on about how Superman and Batman should never share story space, and Ricky should come round his place so he could prove his theory. Ricky turned his shoulder and scanned the words from Bixby's angry hand – his handwriting a pitter-patter of ant feet. Bixby cussed in every sentence about betrayal and reckoning.

Ricky scrunched the paper tight, but held it fast. It carried no danger if he kept it close. His heart pumped guilt and he ached from it all. What had Bixby really done? He had it in for Tanais and squirrels, and Tanais' gone. Ricky sighed. Should hang out with Patrick Baschi to avoid that lurch in his belly.

The bus ran by the City of Forts. Yellow diggers and trucks flashed through the trees as they dug foundations for luxury apartments and single-family homes. The plans looked real nice and all until he'd checked the prices. Ma worked herself to the bone just to maintain the mortgage on the scraggy house of cards where they lived. He squinted to glimpse Mr Vale on the site, but all the men wore yellow helmets and looked like they came out of the same toy box. It hurt to see the place plowed into a sea of brown. The Dragon Lands spooked him, and nobody showed much interest in hanging out in the fields and woods anymore. Kids at school either thought of themselves as gym rats or the types who lounged about in coffee shops.

"What you doin' tonight?" Patrick shoulder-nudged him as if they'd been pals all their lives.

"Dunno. I might stay home."

"And do what?"

"Dunno."

"You can come round my house. If you want."

Ricky pursed his lips and offered a non-committal nod. "I'll definitely think about it."

"Well, I have some brilliant comic books and ... stuff. If you like that kind of thing."

Ricky laughed and shoulder-nudged him back. "Maybe."

A silver Chevrolet with Arizona plates sat outside his home. Glittered all glamorous in the sunshine. Ricky made fists of his hands and squinted to penetrate the tinted windows. No shapes materialized, so he tip-toed the best his limp allowed to the house's front door, his mouth dry at Mr Vale in his kitchen. Who else drove such a car? He wrapped a hand over his other wrist and rubbed the shakes away. Expected a jolly laugh from the man toward ma, steel jaw for himself. He hobbled round to the back. Months had dulled the pain in his leg, but it sometimes sharpened, reminding him of the big man.

"Son."

Ricky edged in, a cat past a kennel. Took a moment to recognize his old man through the manicured stubble and bronze tan. "Pa?"

Pa nodded, smiled a California – no, Arizona – grin at his son. Held out his arms for a hug. Ricky slipped the bag off his shoulder so it hit the ground with a thud. Ma rested against the counter, half inside herself, lower lip between teeth. Ricky skirted his pa and curved an arm around her. She could have bitten through her lip at the action, but she recovered and mirrored him, still shaken from the summer's trauma.

"You've grown, son." Pa's grin drooped, uncertain.

"Aha."

"I've come bearing gifts."

"Are you moving back in?"

Pa's smile stabbed out of his face. "Well, no, not exactly."

"Then why you here?"

"What kind of question is that?"

"A reasonable one, pa. Don't you think?"

"I've rushed all the way from Arizona to see you –"

"I'm honored."

"Ricky." Ma squeezed his waist in mild criticism.

"Nah, I don't give a shit. You've been gone for too long. Without a word. Ma has worked her butt off doing all sorts of jobs to keep us fed and happy. You show up back here and reckon you can save a relationship with gifts?"

"I've been slack – I admit it, but I'm your pa. When I heard about the crap you've been through – well, here I am. You could show some damn gratitude, kid."

"We share blood. That's all. I just need ma and Brett. No-one else."

The doorbell rang. Ma let him go, all reluctant. Ricky shook his head at pa's whispered complaints behind him. Made him happy how ma defended her son, despite it all. His skin crawled for a moment. For the last few months, he'd expected Mr Vale at his door. Mr Respected. The man who caused people to avert their eyes, pretending they never heard his name. The man who made Officer Ray change the subject so he didn't have to compromise his profession. The man who informed the authorities he'd saved Ricky from the low-life, Michael Trent.

Liz greeted him with an embarrassed, hopeful smile. He laughed in relief that Mr Vale did not tower above him. At the bun in her hair, the glasses perching on the end of her nose, and how she stood with her hands behind her back.

"You shouldn't laugh, Ricky, what with your hop-along leg."

He stuck out his tongue and noticed her dipshit boyfriend-not-her-boyfriend, Steve, in his car, his face carved from some dark mood he'd lived in since Charlie shot him. The motor provided more anonymity than the empty growl of his motorbike.

"We're off to a literature meet."

"A what?"

She laughed at how she sounded. "We're reading Dickens' *The Old Curiosity Shop*. You wanna come?"

She displayed the book from behind her back. He saw more work than pleasure. He glanced over his shoulder at his impotent pa as he rattled ma's ear. She'd done with him, too. Ricky heard Officer Ray's name pop up amongst angered utterances.

He returned to Liz. "Maybe next time. I'm gunna hang out with Patrick Baschi."

"Who the hell is he?"

"A pal I made in school. He likes comics."

She nodded, but he enjoyed her disappointment.

"Well," she said. "We should hang out, too."

"Definitely."

He waved her off and turned to back up his ma.

* * *

Ricky slouched on the sofa. Ma sat between him and Brett. They watched shoals of fish on TV shimmering their way out of a multi-pronged attack from sharks, whales, and dive-bombing birds. Ricky wowed with the rest of them, but his thoughts wandered away to the City of Forts and the ruined fields.

A slam made him jump to the kitchen window. Pa must have arrived for round two, but at the drive's end, Mr Vale stood behind the open door of his SUV and watched. Offered him a good old nod designed to induce him outside to rekindle the chat they'd had on the factory's slate roof. Another car pulled up at the entrance to the cul-de-sac.

Ricky slipped into his sneakers and told ma that pa wanted to slither into the house. She rolled her eyes and struggled to her feet for the chore ahead. Ricky blinked into the glare outdoors.

"Son ..."

Ricky swerved past pa as he would a stray dog and ignored the frustrated quips at his back. Mr Vale tapped the roof of his car, a thin smile on his lips. Town had become a cesspool. Become? It's all he'd ever known. Michael Trent's dead, but Officer Ray said another Trent would jimmy into the vacuum he left behind. That one would get whacked and yet more would replace him. Could be that Mr Vale's the man to mop it all up?

"Ricky-boy …"

Mr Vale's appreciation dissolved as Ricky trooped on without acknowledging him. Offered a smile to Mr Walters, who strangled and pulled weeds from his soil. The man nodded, open-mouthed from exertion. Ricky exaggerated the limp for Mr Vale's benefit, biting down the old niggles still afflicting him. Let out all the breath he'd held as he approached the road's end.

"Ricky, you alright?"

"I'm good, Officer Ray. I'm really good." Ricky climbed into the passenger seat.

"Shall we?"

Ricky tilted his head and Officer Ray drove all Sunday-driver past Mr Vale, curved around the cul-de-sac and beeped for Ricky's ma. She emerged blinking in the sun, hand tight around Brett's, and smiled at her eldest. She left pa in the doorway, frustrated at her sunny disregard for him. Ma and Brett climbed in the back and Officer Ray set off. They cruised down the main road, Mr Vale's grim face a warning that would push and pull at their thoughts all the way to the station.

About the Author

Born and raised in England, Jason now lives in New Jersey, the first state he ever visited. From there, he travelled across the country, working in Pennsylvania, Illinois, Ohio, Indiana, Kentucky, Wisconsin, Georgia, Florida, and North Carolina. He writes noir, crime fiction, and the occasional haunted or fantastical tale.

He's an optimist, but suspects there's a body in every shed. That suspicion in no way projects any guilt about his past.

You can buy Jason's work from Amazon and read his work at *Spelk Fiction*, *Shotgun Honey*, *Close to the Bone*, *The Flash Fiction Offensive*, *Punk Noir Magazine*, *Punk Noir,* and *Pulp Metal Magazine.*

You can connect with me on:
🌐 https://wordpress.com/view/jdbeech.wordpress.com
📘 https://www.facebook.com/MessyBusiness

Subscribe to my newsletter:
✉ https://substack.com/@jasonbeechauthor

Also by Jason Beech

American Spartan (City of Forts #2)
An officer of the law. A brother on the slide. A personal war threatening to tear his family apart.

"Reads like it should be on the big screen."
- Stephen J. Golds

Where It Hurts (City of Forts #3)
He returned to save his brother. But is it
himself he must rescue?

"Worth the wait." - Murder in Common review site.

Keep the Motor Running
A murderous ex. A stolen bag. A chase across New Jersey. This is one screw-up she must escape.

"Beech doesn't sacrifice momentum as he develops the players on the page into high resolution characters. Well recommended read." - Murder in Common

Never Go Back
Jealousy made him plunge a knife into a man's chest. Now he's on the run back to his hometown. He's about to find that home comforts are rare.

"I f***ing love this book." - David Nemeth, Crime Fiction reviewer

Moorlands
A valuable ring. A missing sister. A debt that will kill him.

"This book has some serious grip." – Amazon Reviewer

Bullets, Teeth, & Fists
One murder is a coincidence. Two is confirmation. He saw both before they happened. Is he losing his mind, or is somebody beyond the grave telling him something?

"Great anthology of shorts." – Amazon Reviewer

Bullets, Teeth, & Fists 2
It's not easy working as a gangster's punching bag.

"Keeps you turning the pages." – Amazon Reviewer

Bullets, Teeth, & Fists 3

She's heavily pregnant and handcuffed to a pipe. Her kidnappers want money and the clock is ticking.

"Good characterisation throughout and clever storylines, each with a satisfying twist and an unexpected ending, make for a highly entertaining read." - Isobel Blackthorn, Noir Fan

Breaking Point

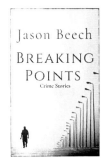

Hiding from himself only brings his enemies closer.

"There are edges in every sentence. They keep the reader attentive and slightly off balance, alarmed maybe by what could jump out from the next page." - Martine E. Poels, Noir Fan